BERSERKER KILL

Tor books by Fred Saberhagen

THE BERSERKER SERIES

The Berserker Wars
Berserker Base (with Poul Anderson, Ed Bryant, Stephen Donaldson, Larry Niven, Connie Willis, and Roger Zelazny)
Berserker: Blue Death
The Berserker Throne
Berserker's Planet

THE DRACULA SERIES

The Dracula Tapes
The Holmes-Dracula Files
An Old Friend of the Family
Thorn
Dominion
A Matter of Taste
A Question of Time
*Seance for a Vampire**

THE SWORDS SERIES

The First Book of Swords
The Second Book of Swords
The Third Book of Swords
The First Book of Lost Swords: Woundhealer's Story
The Second Book of Lost Swords: Sightblinder's Story
The Third Book of Lost Swords: Stonecutter's Story
The Fourth Book of Lost Swords: Farslayer's Story
The Fifth Book of Lost Swords: Coinspinner's Story
The Sixth Book of Lost Swords: Mindsword's Story
The Seventh Book of Lost Swords: Wayfinder's Story
*The Last Book of Swords: Shieldbreaker's Story**

OTHER BOOKS

A Century of Progress
Coils (with Roger Zelazny)
Earth Descended
The Mask of the Sun
The Veils of Azlaroc
The Water of Thought

[*Forthcoming]

FRED SABERHAGEN

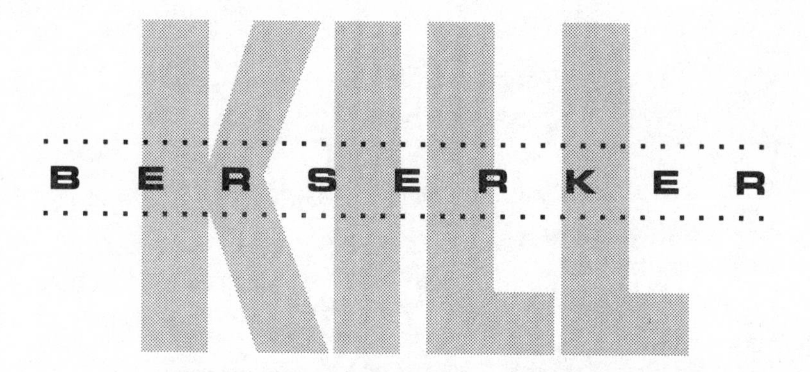

KILL BERSERKER

A TOM DOHERTY ASSOCIATES BOOK

NEW YORK

This is a work of fiction. All the characters and events portrayed in this book are fictitious, and any resemblance to real people or events is purely coincidental.

BERSERKER KILL

This book is printed on acid-free paper.

A Tor Book
Published by Tom Doherty Associates, Inc.
175 Fifth Avenue
New York, N.Y. 10010

Tor® is a registered trademark of Tom Doherty Associates, Inc.

ISBN: 0-312-85266-5

First edition: October 1993

Printed in the United States of America

0 9 8 7 6 5 4 3 2 1

PROLOGUE

The ship was more intelligent in several ways than either of the people it was carrying. One task at which the optel brain of the ship excelled was computing the most efficient search pattern to be traced across and around the indistinct, hard-to-determine edges of the deep, dark nebula. Most of the time during the mission the ship drove itself without direct human guidance along this self-selected course, back and forth, in and out among the broad serrations, the yawning, million-kilometer chasms in the clouds of interstellar gas and dust that made up the Mavronari.

The only reason that such ships weren't sent out crewless to conduct surveys without direct supervision was that their intelligence was inferior to that of organic humanity when it came to dealing with the unforeseen. Only breathing humans could be expected to pay close attention to everything about the nebula that other breathing humans might find of interest.

. . . .

A man and a woman, Scurlock and Carol, crewed the survey ship. The couple had known for months that they were very right for each other, and that was good, because being on the best of terms with your partner was requisite when you were spending several months in the isolation of deep space, confined to a couple of small rooms, continually alone together.

Carol and Scurlock had been married shortly before embarking on this voyage, though they had not been acquainted for very long before that. By far the greater proportion of their married life, now totaling approximately a standard month, had been spent out here nosing around the Mavronari Nebula.

The ship was not their property, of course. Very, very few individuals were wealthy enough to possess their own interstellar transportation. It was a smallish but highly maneuverable and reasonably speedy spacecraft, bearing no name but only a number, and it was the property of the Sardou Foundation, wealthy people who had their reasons for being willing to spend millions collecting details about some astronomical features, certain aspects of the Galaxy, which most Galactic citizens found highly unexciting.

At the moment the young couple and their employers' ship were many days away from the nearest inhabited planet, even at the optimum pattern of superluminal jumps and journeying in normal space at sublight velocity that the survey craft could have managed. Not that such remoteness from the rest of humanity had particularly concerned either Carol or Scurlock, up to now.

Scurlock was rather tall and loosely muscled, with pale eyes and long lashes that made him look even younger than he really was. Carol was of middle height, inclined to thinness, and had several physical features suggesting that some of her ancestors had called old Earth's Middle East their home.

Both young people tended to be intense and ambitious. But just now both were in a light mood, singing and joking as they made the observations of nebular features comprising today's work. Some of the jokes were at the expense of their shipboard optel brain, the very clever unit that was cradling their two lives at the moment, assuming responsibility for piloting and astrogation during most of the voyage. But no offense was taken; like other ships, this one never knew or cared what its human masters and passengers might be making jokes about.

One of the secondary objectives of this mission, politely but firmly impressed upon the couple by their employers, was to discover, if possible, some practical new means of ingress to the nebula, an astrogable channel or channels, as yet uncharted, leading into the Mavronari. The existence of such a passage would greatly facilitate interstellar travel between the inhabited worlds existing on one side of this great mass of gas and dust, and other worlds, now largely unknown but possibly habitable, that might lie somewhere within the nebula or on its other side. Any such discovery would be of great interest to the Sardou Foundation, and not to it alone.

As matters now stood, most of the worlds known to exist on the other side of the Mavronari had never even been thoroughly explored by Solarians, largely because of the difficulty of getting at them by going all the way around.

But the discovery of a new passage was only a secondary purpose, no more than an intriguing possibility. The fundamental objective of this mission was the gathering of astronomical data, radiation patterns, particle types and velocities, from the deep folds and convolutions between nebular lobes, regions not susceptible to ready observation from the outside.

Since departing on this mission, Carol and Scurlock had frequently expressed to each other their hope that a successful performance would lead them upward and onward, financially and socially, ultimately to one of the several goals they had established for themselves.

The Galactic Core, eerily bright though thousands of light-years distant, a ball of dull though multicolored incandescence all mottled and muted by clouds and streaks of intervening dark matter, appeared through the cleared ports first on one side of the little ship, then on the other, as the small craft proceeded about its work with—as usual—only minimal human supervision. Now and then one of the human couple on board took note of how the Core cast their ship's shadow visibly upon some dark fold of the great Mavronari, clouds silvered on this side as if by moonlight.

Gazing at that tiny moving shadow and that immensely greater darkness just beyond the silvering, Carol was drawn away from near-poetic musings by a sudden shudder that ran through her slight frame.

It was a momentary, subtle event. But Scurlock, being close to his partner in more ways than one, took notice. "What's the matter?"

She ran brown fingers through her straight dark hair, cut short. "Nothing. Really nothing. Just that sometimes, looking out, I get a momentary feeling that I can really sense how far away everything is."

Her companion became soberly thoughtful. "I know what you mean. How far away and how old."

After a shared moment of silence, of the ship's controlled drifting, it was time to turn quickly to matters of light and life. Once more, as they often did, the couple discussed their own wish for a child in the light of Premier Dirac Sardou's colonization scheme, in which the Sardou Foundation, largely a creation of the Premier himself, was heavily involved.

"I don't know how people can do that. I wouldn't want to doom any kid of mine to any scheme like that."

"No, I agree," Scurlock immediately concurred. Not that he particularly wanted to have a child under any circumstances, any more than Carol did.

Carol would have been surprised if he had not agreed. They had had this conversation before, but there seemed to be purpose, and there was certainly reassurance, in repeating it. Talk drifted to other subjects. Meanwhile, with a watchful steadiness born of habit, the couple kept an alert eye on the course adjustments made now and then by their autopilot, and also made a point of directly taking some instrument readings for themselves. They were making sure—although the autopilot was really better at this than they were—that their ship did not stray too deeply into the outlying tendrils of the nebula. The region they were currently exploring was still hard vacuum by the standards of planetary atmosphere, but matter, in the form of microscopic and near-microscopic particles, was seeded through it thickly enough to dangerously impede ship movement. It would be damned inconvenient, and perhaps much worse than inconvenient, to find themselves enclosed by dust arms anywhere near their present position, enfolded by some slow-looking swirl of thin gas half the size of a solar system, trapped so that their little craft would lose all chance of dropping back into flightspace and returning them briskly to their homeworld in a mere matter of days.

Further talk, optimistic daydreaming of prosperity to come, was interrupted by the optelectronic brain of their ship breaking in to inform its masters in its usual indifferent voice that it had just detected the presence of several unidentified swift-moving objects, the size of very small ships, materializing out of the dusty nebular background. Whatever these objects were, they had appeared in rapid succession—in nearby space, at a range of only a few hundred kilometers.

The ship was already presenting its live crew with the appropriate displays, showing the unidentified things as small, dark, mysterious dots upon a false-color background of mottled silver.

Scurlock, staring without comprehension at the moving dots, demanded: "Whatever in all the worlds—"

"I've no idea," Carol breathed.

Nor had their ship offered an opinion. No wonder both organic and inhuman brains were puzzled: on instruments the unidentified objects certainly looked like small ships, but the chance of encountering any traffic at all in space was nowhere very large, and here on the flank of the Mavronari it was astronomically small.

In only a few seconds the young couple's puzzlement had begun to turn to alarm. A certain word had popped up unbidden in the back of each of their minds and was refusing to go away. Neither of them wanted to frighten the other, and so neither spoke the word. They moved in silent, mutual consent to clothe themselves rather more formally, until they were fully dressed, with the vague unspoken idea of possibly receiving visitors. Then Scurlock, without giving any reason, suggested getting into space suits. Carol said she didn't think that was necessary. As a compromise, they checked to make sure that suits and other emergency devices were in the proper lockers, ready for use.

After that, both human partners sat in their command chairs squinting at a holostage, which had been adjusted to display in its unreal image-space, against an imaged background of black dust, the steadily growing likeness of the nearest unidentified object.

Carol said, with an air of calm determination, "All right, Scurly, we have to make sense out of this. Is that some military thing?"

Her companion nodded. "They must be military. That must be it. Maybe an Imatran squadron. That's about the closest system to where we are now. Or maybe it's Templar. Or Space Force. One of those."

The loosely spread formation of shiplike objects—seven of them now—moving methodically toward the explorer ship was certainly no manifestation of ordinary civilian traffic. So they had to be someone's military. Had to be . . . because the only other alternative was too frightful to contemplate.

Neither Scurlock nor Carol had spoken of that alternative as yet, though it had settled tenaciously in the backs of both their minds, where it was still growing ominously. Instead of talking about it, the couple looked at each other, each seeking reassurance and at the same time trying to give it. Trying with less and less success.

It was left to the heartless ship to finally say the words, in its finely tuned ship's voice that sounded only mildly concerned, and would have sounded perturbed to an equally slight degree about anything else that happened to pose a problem. "The seven objects now approaching are identifiable as berserker machines," the ship remarked.

There was no immediate reply. Scurlock's first conscious reaction was an immediate surge of anger at the ship, that its voice in making this announcement should be so calm. Because what the hell did the ship care? It had been designed and built by Solarian humans, Earth-descended folk of the same human species as Scurlock and Carol. And Solarian designers, convinced they had good reason for doing so, saw to it as a rule that their machines never gave the impression of caring much about anything.

And Scurlock persisted in his quite irrational feeling of what the hell did a ship, any ship, have to worry about anyway? Those berserker machines out there—if indeed that was what they were—did not have as the goal of their basic programming the obliteration of *ships* from the cosmos.

No. It was something very different from ships that berserkers were programmed to wipe out. Their object was to expunge life itself from the Galaxy. Human life was a priority, because humans tended to give them a hard time, to interfere with the completion of their task. And the Solarian variety of human life was the killing machines' favorite target above all others—because Solarian, Earth-descended humanity in particular was as a rule damned obstinately, and even violently, opposed to dying.

Carol, who of the two human partners was slightly the better pilot, had already got herself into the acceleration couch offering the best access to both the manual and the alpha-wave ship's controls, and she was now sliding her head into the alphawave coronet. Scurlock, with fingers that seemed to have gone numb with fright, was now fastening himself into the acceleration chair, or couch, next to the pilot's—getting into a couch, the manuals affirmed, was in these situations more important than trying to put on a space suit.

Not that either suits or couches were likely to help much in an unarmed ship when berserkers were coming after you. In that respect, Scurlock was sure, whatever counsel the manuals offered was hopelessly optimistic.

In a moment he could hear himself suggesting in a weak voice that they might try to make their little craft as inconspicuous as possible, to slide and hide behind the nearest fold of nebula and wait, in hopes that they would not be noticed.

Both human and optelectronic pilots ignored his proposal. This was probably just as well, because neither Scurlock's nerves nor Carol's could have endured trying to make such a tactic work. And it seemed a futile suggestion anyway, coming considerably too late, because the oncoming objects were not just approaching but were closing in directly on their ship, proving that they had already been irrevocably noticed.

Carol murmured something incoherent from the pilot's couch and melded her mind with that of the ship, trying hard acceleration at right angles to the onrushing formation of killers. The drive responded smoothly, and the cabin's artificial gravity dealt efficiently with the imposed forces; the polyphase matter webs on the acceleration couches still hung slack, their occupants spared the least physical discomfort.

But the maneuver was worse than useless. The oncoming objects only changed course accordingly, demonstrating once more that whatever they were, their approach to Scurlock's and Carol's ship was not in the least accidental.

Frantically, again muttering almost inaudibly to herself, the human pilot tried again, with no better result—she and her partner, lover, lay huddled amid the straps and webbing, the latest in polyphase matter but of no more use now than so much spaghetti, of their separate acceleration couches—as if mere straps and webbing of any kind were going to do them any good.

Still both human partners seemed determined not to utter the dread word. Neither had done so yet, as if the threat could not be real until the name of it was spoken. The fact that their own machine had already named the terror to them somehow did not seem to count.

For almost a full minute the two terrified people tried to outrun the oncoming objects, getting the best they could out of their own ship, alternating between pure autopilot and a melding control. Carol was a good enough pilot to render the meld of organic and artificial intelligence superior in performance to either mode alone. But perhaps no pilot in this ship in this situation would have been good enough to get away.

In whichever mode they flew, the enemy followed each change of course, and easily, methodically gained ground. But the unliving enemy still held their fire, as if this time the berserkers were, for some unguessable reason, more interested in bringing about close contact, confrontation, than in dealing sudden death.

The survey ship was unarmed. But even a fighting Space

Force scout, which would have been twice as large and a thousand times as capable in self-protection, would have had small chance indeed against so many machines of the type now closing in. All seven of their pursuers were now clearly visible, each as big as or slightly bigger than the survey vessel, all steadily drawing near. Still no weapons had been fired.

And now Scurlock groaned aloud. His last hopes vanished. An object that could only be the berserker mothership, a drifting continent of metal as black and horrible as death itself, had come into view out of clouds a hundred kilometers in the background, at that range clearly visible to the unaided eye. Simultaneously, on holostage the thing's magnified image came groping its careful way forward, emerging from heavy dust with the dignity of an evil mountain, and at a speed that somehow seemed unnatural for anything so large and ugly. It slid forward out of the darkness of the Mavronari like the king of demons emerging from some antique vision of hell.

Long seconds crept by, during which neither person in the doomed cabin spoke. Then the couple turned toward each other, and each read despair in the other's face.

"Scurly." Carol seemed almost choking on her own voice.

"Yah?"

"Promise me something?"

"What?" Though already he knew what. He knew all too well.

Carol hesitated. For some reason she began to whisper. "If it is berserkers and they kill us quickly, I'm glad we're together."

"So am I."

"But if they don't . . . do that . . . I mean, there are stories that if they don't just kill on sight, it's because they want something . . . then I don't think I can face it . . . I don't want to—"

Carol could not, dared not, put into words just what it was she wanted her husband to do. And if she couldn't find the words, he wasn't about to help her do so. Not on this one.

Once more turning away from her partner, Carol made

a last, frenzied attempt to maneuver, to get away; but moments later they were overtaken, their small craft smothered and immobilized in powerful force fields. The autopilot reported with mad, mocking calm that it was no longer able to maneuver.

The seven attackers, all within a hundred meters now, had the little survey ship englobed, in what had at last become a tight formation.

She and Scurlock stared at each other. Time seemed to have come to a complete stop.

Their ship in its unflappable voice relayed to them the news of the next step in the catastrophe: its drive had now been rendered totally dead.

Nothing more happened until, only moments later, the same voice informed them that an attempt was now being made to open the outer hatch of the main airlock, from outside. There was really no need to tell the two human occupants that, because their unaided hearing now brought them news of the attempt in progress. The whole ship quivered under a titanic hammering, vibrated with a shrieking drill.

Scurlock, his fingers fumbling even more desperately than before, after several attempts got himself out of his acceleration couch. A moment later Carol had joined him, the two of them standing together in the middle of the cabin's tiny open deck.

"If the drive wasn't dead," Scurlock said suddenly, in a surprisingly strong voice, "we could switch over to manual and use it to—"

"But the drive is dead," Carol whimpered. Evidently the enemy had for some reason not wanted any cowardly or heroic suicides. Maybe it was the unnecessary waste of a perfectly good machine to which the berserkers' controlling computers made objection. "And we don't have a weapon of any kind aboard."

"I know."

"Scurly . . . even if we had a gun, I don't think I could do it. Not to you, not to myself."

"Neither could I." That seemed to him the best thing to say now, although he wasn't sure. "And—and I wouldn't leave you alone with—berserkers."

Suddenly louder sounds coming from only a few meters away made it obvious that the small enemy units—machines, whatever the proper term for them might be—were in the main airlock now. And now abruptly they were visible, if only indirectly. The relentless approach of death was being displayed for the humans with merciless clarity, by their own ship's brain, upon the little holostage in the middle of the control room. Scurlock had one moment to see clearly an enormous enlargement of a pair of waving grippers, and then the video pickup in the airlock was destroyed.

"Carol, I love you."

"And I love you."

Those were words they had seldom said to each other.

"They don't have any interest in making people suffer, Carol. It's going to be quick, whatever they . . ."

Scurlock was trying to make it true by saying it. True, the death machines' fundamental commandment, the goal of their basic programming, was the obliteration of all life wherever they encountered it. There was no requirement that living things be made to suffer; because quick killing was generally more efficient, quick killing was the rule. But exceptions to that rule came up from time to time, situations where the unliving enemy in pursuit of its larger aims required something more from some individual life unit than that unit's death. Neither person in the small ship wanted to think about those rare exceptions now. But they were going to have no choice, because the noises of intrusion had moved a large step closer. Metal arms and tools were very purposefully scratching, scraping, then pounding at the inner door of their main airlock.

"Carol—"

"Yes. Scurly, I love you too." Her voice sounded abstracted; almost bored.

There was no more time to talk. The inner door of the airlock was sliding open now. There followed a slight momentary drop in cabin pressure, but no fatal escape of atmosphere; that had already been taken care of, somehow, because the occupants of this ship were going to be kept alive, for the time being.

And now berserkers were entering their cabin.

* * *

Constructions of dull-surfaced metal came filing in, one, two, three, four of them, walking rapidly one after the other into the control room. They were very little bigger than Solarian human beings, though their shapes were frightfully different from those of humanity as descended upon any planet. And these machines were quite obviously of alien strength and purpose. They came into the control moving more quickly and decisively than any bodies merely human could have moved, or any organic creature of any species. Some of the intruders walked on six metallic legs, and some on only four.

What was momentarily astonishing was that the invaders appeared at first to take no particular notice of their two new prisoners. The prisoners on their part remained standing as if paralyzed, their four hands clutched together, in the middle of the chamber.

Like practically every other Solarian in the Galaxy, Carol and Scurlock had all their lives heard stories about berserkers. Some of the stories were true, some fiction, some the wildest legend. There were human worlds whose population had never seen a beserker, but no human world where such stories were never told. The berserkers in the stories always seemed to come equipped with the capability of human speech. And on the very rare occasions when people in the stories and histories came close enough to listen to berserkers and yet somehow survived, they always described the enemy as communicating quickly with human captives, spelling out for the abhorred badlife precisely what was expected of them, what they must do to earn a quick and merciful death, giving at least by implication some indication why their lives were being temporarily spared.

But these machines, having taken possession of Scurlock and Carol along with their ship, said nothing at all—unless a few peculiar clicks and whistles, issuing from one of the invaders, were intended as communication. If this noise indeed was language, the Solarians could neither recognize it nor respond.

One facet of the humans' intense terror, a dread that they were going to be immediately separated, was not realized. But any unreasoning hope that the machines would continue to ignore them quickly vanished. After only a few seconds' delay, both prisoners were gently seized and searched by deft metallic fingers and grippers that probed and patted impersonally at skin and clothing. Then the two humans were let go, not bound or otherwise physically molested. In another moment all but one of the boarding machines had left the control room, spreading out through the various accessible bays and compartments of the little ship, obviously intent on search and examination.

Their bodies temporarily free, yet helpless, the two prisoners gazed at each other in anguish. They exchanged a few hopelessly banal words, phatic utterances empty of hope. No doubt their metallic guardian was listening, but it neither punished them for speaking nor commanded them to silence.

Eventually all of the machines that had spread out to search the ship returned to the control room, where they stopped, standing motionless like so many serving robots.

"What happens now?" Scurlock abruptly demanded of the world at large. For a moment, only a moment, Carol saw him as a brave and challenging figure, fists clenched, looking at his unliving captors with the courage of despair.

The machines ignored him. One of them was at a control panel, probing with thin auxiliary limbs, probably tapping into the ship's data banks.

Carol sat down again in the pilot's couch and began to weep.

The minutes stretched on, and nothing happened. After a time Scurly sat down too, in the couch next to Carol's.

Looking out through cleared ports, the captives presently were able to get a better view than before of the berserker mothership. Scurlock commented now on the fact that in the light of the distant Core that hideous bulk showed signs of extensive damage, in the form of cratering and scorching, but it conveyed the impression of being still extremely formidable. Certain projections, he thought, indicated immense firepower. The great hull was generally ovoid, almost spherical, in shape. Sizes and distances were hard to judge in space without instrumentation, and the voice of the survey ship had fallen silent, but from the faint drift of intervening dust he estimated the monster as at least several kilometers in diameter.

Before the first hour of their captivity had passed, most of it in a terrible silence, Carol had already started to crack under the strain. She was withdrawing into a staring silence, letting remarks by her companion go unanswered.

"Carol?"

No answer. Slowly the young woman, staring at nothing in a corner of the cabin, raised a white knuckle to her mouth. Slowly she bit on it until blood started to appear.

"Carol!" Scurly lurched unsteadily to his feet and grabbed her hand, pulling it away from her teeth.

She raised wild eyes, a stranger's eyes, to stare at him.

"Carol, stop it!"

Suddenly she burst into tears; Scurlock crouched beside her, awkwardly trying to give comfort, while the berserkers looked on impassively.

For the next few hours the machines continued to watch their captives—you could see a lens turn now and then on one of the metal bodies—and no doubt they listened, but for the time being they did nothing more. The prisoners were allowed to move about unhindered in the control room and the sleeping cabin next to it. To sit, to stand, to lie down, to use the plumbing.

Eventually, one at a time and by degrees, they fell asleep.

A time arrived when Scurlock found himself in the control room, looking at the ship's chronometer, wondering why the numbers displayed seemed to convey nothing. He tried to remember, but for the life of him could not, just what day and hour the clock had shown him the last time he had looked; that had been at some unguessable interval before the berserkers came.

Carol was sleeping now. He had just left her sleeping—unconscious might be a better word for her condition—in the other room.

Slowly Scurlock went about getting himself a cup of

water from the service robot. He had to walk directly past one of the berserkers to do so, and he actually brushed the machine—their metal legs crowded the little room. He knew it could flick out a limb at any moment and kill him, and slow human sight would never see the impact coming, any more than he would see a bullet. Let it come, then, let death come.

But it did not.

Slowly he went about getting another cup of water, carrying it into the sleeping cabin, offering his human companion—who was sitting up again—a drink.

The idea of food, in either of their minds, was going to have to wait for a little while yet.

As was the idea of hope.

Eventually in Scurlock's mind—which was never going to be quite the same mind that it once had been—the numbers on the chronometer started to make sense again. With dull shock he remembered certain things and noticed that the hours since the invasion seemed to have added up to a standard day.

He noticed too that Carol was intermittently biting her knuckles again. Blood was drying on her fingers. But he didn't think he was going to stop her anymore.

With the passage of time, the first shock of terror had begun to relax its grip. The sentence of death had already been passed, and yet it seemed that life somehow went on.

Scurlock and Carol passed long periods sitting together, clinging together, on one of the beds or ordinary couches. From time to time Carol would suddenly give vent to a burst of peculiar laughter. Whenever this happened, Scurlock stared at her dully, not knowing whether she had gone completely out of her mind or not. Now and then he saw her doze or caught himself awakening with a shock from a deathlike sleep.

An hour came when she leaped up from an almost-catatonic pose, shrieking at the top of her voice in a sudden fit. "What does it want from us? What does it want?" Then, hurling herself at one of the machines, she hysterically attacked it with her bare hands, knuckles already bleeding. "What do you want? Why don't you kill us? *Kill us!*"

The machine moved one leg, adjusting its balance

slightly. That was all. A moment later Carol had collapsed, sobbing, on the dull deck, at the metal feet of the impassive thing.

Still there were intervals in which the couple talked to each other, sometimes fairly rationally, often feverishly, between long stretches of helpless silence.

During one of their more rational exchanges, Scurlock said, "I've got an idea about why it doesn't talk. Suppose that this is one very old berserker. Suppose that maybe, for some reason—I don't know why—it's been stuck in the Mavronari for a long time. That could happen, you know, to a ship or a machine. Maybe it's been a very long time in there, struggling to get out of the nebula again. Or it went in on the other side, and it's been struggling to make it all the way through."

After a long pause, in which she might have been thinking, Carol responded: "That's possible." What sent a chill down Scurlock's neck was that at the moment she didn't even seem to be frightened anymore.

When she said nothing further, he went on: "In that case, if it's really been in there for thousands of years, it might never have learned any Earth-descended languages. Those sounds it was chirping at us earlier could have been Builder talk."

"What?" She really didn't seem to know what he was talking about; the terribly bad part was that she didn't seem to care.

"You remember Galactic history, love. Long ago there was a race we Solarians now call the Builders, because we don't know any better name for them. The people who built the first berserkers, created them as ultimate weapons to win some crazy interspecies war, around the time we were going through our Neolithic Age on Earth—maybe even before that.

"And then something went wrong with the plan, the way plans do go wrong, and the berserkers wiped out the Builders too, along with their nameless organic enemies, whoever they were. I remember learning somewhere that their speech, the Builders' speech, was all clicks and whistles."

Carol had had nothing to say to that. Only a few minutes had passed since Scurlock had last spoken, and both prisoners were dozing—in Scurlock's case, trying to doze—in adjoining couches when suddenly one of their guardians spoke, for virtually the first time since coming aboard.

And what the machine uttered—in a clear machine voice, not all that different from the voice of the now-silent survey ship—were distinct Solarian words. Scurlock was snapped out of his somnolent state by hearing: *" 'I've got an idea about why it doesn't talk.' "*

"What?" He jumped to his feet, glaring wildly at the machines, at Carol, who appeared to be really sleeping on the next couch.

The same machine said, in the same accurate enunciation, but slightly louder: *" 'All clicks and whistles.' "*

That phrase brought Carol, whimpering, starting up from sleep. Scurlock grabbed her by the arm and said, "That's what it wants from us! To listen to us, to learn our language."

And at once the mimicking tones came back: *" 'That's what it wants from us. To learn our language.' "*

Carol, as if she had been shocked at least momentarily out of her withdrawal, reacted with rational horror: "We don't want to help it, for God's sake!"

"Love, I don't think we're going to have much choice. It may be offering us our only chance to stay alive!"

For a long moment the two humans were silent, staring into each other's faces, trying to read each other's eyes.

"Love," essayed the machine, tentatively.

But at the moment no one was listening. Suddenly Scurlock burst out: "Carol, I don't want to die!"

"No. No, I don't want to die either. Scurly, how did we . . . how could we ever get into this?"

"Easy, easy, love. We didn't ask to get into this. But now we're in it, we've got to do what we've got to do, that's all."

"Easy, easy, love," said a berserker's voice. *"That's all."*

There were hours and days in which the machines encouraged speech by separating the two humans, holding them in different rooms so that the only way they could keep contact with each other was by calling back and forth.

Somehow refusing to play along never seemed like a real option. In the data banks of the captured ship, as Scurlock pointed out to Carol, the berserkers had available a tremendous amount of recorded material, radio communications of a variety of kinds, from several worlds and several ships, in all the languages with which the captured couple were familiar, and some more besides.

And now their lifeless captor was beginning to play various recordings it had taken with their ship, and to mimic the sounds of human speech existing on those recordings. This, Scurlock argued, proved that resistance on their part would be futile.

"So the point is, love, it doesn't really depend on us to learn. Even if we don't talk to it, it can analyze the language mathematically, use the video material as a guide. It can find out whatever it wants to know without our help."

And again he said, "No one's going to come looking for us, you know. Not for a long time, months. And if they do, and find us—tough luck for them."

Carol never argued. Mostly she just stared. Sometimes she chewed her favorite hand.

And now the machines that held them prisoner began to prod them relentlessly to talk and keep on talking. Whenever a period of silence lasted longer than about a minute, the berserker used some of its newly learned speech to command them to keep on speaking. When that failed, it administered moderate electric shocks to keep them going, a machine gripping both of a human's hands at the same time. Thus it kept at least one of them awake at all times, shocking them and talking to them in its monotonous, monstrously patient voice.

A pattern emerged and was maintained of one prisoner sleeping while the other talked—or more precisely, was interrogated. Physical and mental exhaustion mounted in both prisoners, despite the intervals of deathlike sleep.

Time passed in this mode of existence; just how much time, Scurlock could not have guessed. Once more he had forgotten the chronometer, never thought to look at it when he was in the cabin talking to berserkers; sometimes the thought of time briefly crossed his mind in the brief interval after he had been released, but before he sank onto his bunk in the darkened sleeping cabin, and unconsciousness descended. He thought that perhaps the ship's clock, like its drive, had been turned off.

The survey ship itself had somehow been lobotomized, but its serving devices provided food and drink as before, life support saw to it that the atmosphere was fresh, and the artificial gravity held steady as it ever had. Carol and Scurlock took note of each other briefly and frequently, exchanging a few meaningless words as they passed each other shuffling between control room and sleeping cabin, to and from the endless, tireless interrogation.

Ultimate horror had a way, it appeared, of becoming bearable. The deadliness of the familiar.

But change was constant. The education of their enemy progressed. Over the course of time, exactly when Scurlock could not have said, a new note, a new emphasis, at first subtle but soon definite, crept into the current of their questioning. Presently it was obvious that their captor had strong interests beyond simple learning one or more Solarian languages. And the nature of the new objectives was ominous, to say the least.

Scurlock, the more consistently alert of the two prisoners, became aware of this state of affairs at a definite moment. He was alone in the control room with the machines, and one of them was calling his attention, by pointing, to the small central holostage.

In that small virtual space his captor, which had long since established thorough control of the ship's own optelectronic brains, was now calling up a pattern of sparkling dots representing several nearby solar systems. Stars and some planets were labeled with correct names, in the common Solarian language. Now the machine was after information on continents and cities, the factories and yards where spaceships were constructed.

In a matter of days, or perhaps a standard month, Scurlock realized, the vast unliving intellect that held them prisoner had learned to talk to them with some facility.

This realization was reinforced the next time he awoke, alone, in the sleeping chamber. An arm of one of the seemingly interchangeable boarding machines had just opened the door, and he could hear that machine's voice, or another's, coming from the next room, where one of them must be pointing to a succession of images on the stage: "This is a man. This is a tree. This is a woman."

"I am a woman," Carol responded, and her voice now sounded no less mechanical than the berserker's.

"What am I?" it asked her suddenly.

Scurlock, opening his eyes with weary dread, avoided thinking. He moved his stiff limbs to join her in the dayroom.

Standing in the doorway, he experienced a relatively lucid moment. Suddenly he was aware how much his companion, his lover, his wife, had changed since they'd been taken. Always thin, she now looked almost skeletal. Her fingers were scarred, dirty with dried blood from being bitten. Had he been passing her on the street, he would not have recognized her face. And she was not the only one, of course, who'd been evilly transformed. He knew he'd lost weight too, his beard and hair had grown untamed, his unchanged clothing stank, no longer fit him very well. He shambled when he moved.

In fact, he suddenly realized, they hadn't touched each other as lovers since the machine took them. Not even a kiss, as far as Scurlock could remember. And now there was hardly ever a moment when they were even in the same room together.

"Answer me," prodded the metallic voice. "What am I?"

Guiltily Carol, who had been staring into space, looked back at the thing from which the voice proceeded. "You are a . . ."

Her eyes turned slowly toward the cleared port through which, at the moment, the drifting mountain of the mother-ship happened to be visible. ". . . a machine," she concluded.

"I am a machine. I am not alive. You are alive. The tree is alive."

Carol, for the moment looking insanely like some strict classroom teacher, shook her head violently. Scurlock in his doorway froze to hear the dreadful cunning certainty of madness in her voice. "No. I'm not alive. I won't be alive. Not I. Not if you don't want me to be. Not anymore."

"Do not lie to me. You are alive."

"No, no!" the strict teacher insisted. "Not really. Live things should be killed. Right? I am"—she glanced quickly at Scurlock—"we are goodlife."

Goodlife was a word coined by the berserkers themselves, and it showed up throughout all their history, appearing in many of the stories. It denoted people who sided with the death machines, who served and sometimes even worshiped them.

Scurlock in the doorway could only grip the metal frame and stare. Maybe Carol in her near craziness had hit on the only way to save their lives. Maybe, he had never thought about it before, but maybe the berserkers never asked you to join them willingly. Maybe they only accepted volunteers.

"Goodlife, not badlife," Carol was going on, the hideously false animation in her voice giving way to a real sincerity, even as her partner listened. "We are goodlife! Remember that. We love berserkers—what the badlife call berserkers. You can trust us."

Scurlock clutched the doorway. "We are goodlife!" he croaked fervently.

The machine gave no evidence of any excitement or satisfaction at the prospect of its prisoners' conversion. It said only, "Later I will trust you. Now you must trust me."

"We trust you. What do you mean to do with us?" Scurlock, still clinging to the doorway, heard himself blurt out the question before he could stop to consider whether he really wanted to hear the answer.

The machine responded without bothering to turn a lens in his direction. "To make use of you."

"We can be useful. Yes, very useful, as long as you don't kill us."

To that the machine made no reply. Carol, slumped on her couch before the holostage, did not look at her human partner again. All her attention was fixed on the robot as it resumed its questioning.

Before another hour of conversation had gone by, the machine once more abruptly altered and narrowed its range of interest. Now it concentrated its questioning, at endless length and in considerable depth, upon the six or eight Solarian-occupied star systems that lay within a few days' travel of this side of the Mavronari.

Name and describe each habitable planet in this system. What kind of defenses does each world, each system, mount? What armed vessels does each put into space? What kind of scientific and industrial installations does each planet have? What kind of interstellar traffic flows among them?

The interminable interrogation veered back and forth across the subject, sometimes picking, digging, after fine details, sometimes giving the impression of being satisfied with imperfect memories, with generalities.

Carol had obviously abandoned herself completely to the one goal of pleasing her interrogator. Scurlock now, even in his most uncertain intervals tormented by the thought of what his fear had made him say to the machine, could think of no productive way to try to lie to it. He knew very little about the defenses of any of the planets in question—but some heroic remnant of his conscience whispered to him that he might try to say they were all formidable.

But if he were to dare anything like that, the machine would pursue him relentlessly. He could imagine the length and the ferocity of the interrogation. There was no reason to believe it would stop short of direct torture. *How did he know about the defenses? What did his regular employment have to do with such matters?* He would die under questioning like that, and he didn't want to die. No, he realized clearly that he still wanted to go on breathing, no matter what. Maybe someday, somehow, he would be able to help some fellow human being again. But lying now, trying to lie to the machine, was definitely not the way to go.

A man—and a woman—had to play the cards that they were dealt.

The questioning continued. Then suddenly, at a time when Carol was taking her turn at unconsciousness in the next room, it refined its focus once again.

They were an hour into his latest session, dealing with the Imatran system, when Scurlock, reciting on demand what he could happen to recall of objects in orbit round the inhabited planetoid of that sun, mentioned something that until now had genuinely slipped his mind—the visiting biological laboratory he had heard was scheduled for a stay of some duration in the Imatran system. Actually the laboratory was built into an interstellar vessel of some kind, connected with Premier Dirac Sardou's colonization project—

And the moment Scurlock introduced the subject of the laboratory, a bell must have rung, somewhere down one of the vast labyrinthine circuits of the berserker's electronic intellect. Not that Scurlock actually heard anything like the ringing of a bell, but still that image seemed to the man an apt comparison, a neat symbol for a sudden and profound reaction. Because it was soon apparent that once more the berserker's interest had been narrowed.

"Tell me more about the laboratory," it demanded.

"I've already told you practically everything I know. I understand it's a kind of traveling facility that has to do with biological research and some kind of projected colonization effort. Really, I don't know any more about it than that. I—"

"Tell me more about the laboratory."

PART ONE

ONE

Deep down among the tangled roots of human life, amid the seeds of individuality, a billion atoms, give or take a million or so, shifted under the delicate forceprobe's pressure, rearranging their patterns of interaction across the span of several of a Solarian human reproductive cell's enormous, interactive molecules. Quantum mechanics and optelectronics were hard at work, enlisted as faithful tools under the direction of a human mind, digging into yet another layer of secrets underlying the most distinctive qualities of life and matter.

But interruption came in the form of distracting noise, jarring the probing human mind out of profound concentration. Life on a macroscopic level was intruding.

Dr. Daniel Hoveler, who was nothing if not an earnest researcher, raised strained eyes from the eyepiece of his microstage, then got up from his chair to stand beside his workbench. His irritation was transformed quickly to surprise as a woman he had never seen in the flesh before, but whom he recognized at once as the celebrated Lady Genevieve Sardou, came sweeping in through the central entrance of the main laboratory deck of the orbiting bioresearch station.

The Lady Genevieve, young and small and garbed in

frilly white, was accompanied by a small but energetic entourage of aides and media people. This little band of visitors, perhaps a dozen strong, paused as soon as they were inside the huge, faintly echoing room, as big as an athletic field and high-ceilinged for a deck on a space vessel. The scene that met them was one of unwonted confusion. The human laboratory staff had been given no more than ten minutes' notice of the lady's impending arrival. Hoveler, who had heard the news and then had promptly forgotten it again under the press of work, belatedly realized that his co-workers must have been bustling about without any help from him during the interval, doing their best to prepare for the event.

For just an instant now, as the celebrated visitor paused, looking about her uncertainly, the whole lab confronting her was almost still. If the notice of Lady Genevieve's imminent arrival had evoked excitement and confusion (and it evidently had), her actual presence had the effect of momentarily stunning most of the dozen or so human workers present, Hoveler included. For the time of three or four deep human breaths almost the only sound in the cavernous space was a background hum compounded from several kinds of machinery engaged in the various tasks and experiments in progress.

In the next moment, one or two of the workers quietly slipped away from their positions or unobtrusively began to use the intercom in an effort to locate and alert the supervisor.

The Lady Genevieve Sardou, with the announcement of her marriage to Premier Dirac less than a standard month ago, had leaped out of obscurity to become one of the most important political celebrities in a domain comprising several dozen solar systems. A month ago, thought Hoveler, few of the people in this room would have recognized her face, and she would have received no more attention than any other random visitor. Now most of the lab workers stood frozen by her presence.

In another moment the lady, evidently coping with the slightly awkward situation as best she could, had begun speaking informally to some of the openmouthed faces in her immediate vicinity, turning from one person to another, pronouncing a few words of greeting in a well-coached but unpracticed style. The eminent visitor smiled and spoke politely, but she was clearly inexperienced in celebrity, her voice so soft that some people only a few meters away could not hear her at all.

Hoveler returned his attention briefly to his microstage, checking to make sure that a few minutes' inattention in real-time was going to have no seriously deleterious effect upon his project. Then he turned away from his bench and moved a few steps closer to the Lady Genevieve, wanting to see and hear her better; he realized that in the few moments she had been present, he had already begun to develop protective feelings toward her.

One of the lady's aides, whom Hoveler thought he could recognize from certain media images as her chief publicist, a woman much taller and louder than her employer, had preceded her illustrious client through the hatch by a second or two, and was now standing alertly at her side, mouth set in a professional smile, eyes glittering with the look of a predator ready to protect its young. Other determined-looking intruders, women and men carrying media devices, were busy making every trivial word and gesture a matter of public record. Whatever the Premier's new bride did or said here today was going to be news, and that news was about to be transmitted more or less faithfully to a score of relatively nearby worlds, much of whose population could be presumed to be strongly interested.

The news stories generated today would also be rushed on via superluminal courier, carried in a matter of days well beyond the few hundred cubic light-years of space encompassing those nearby worlds. The stories would go as far across the Solarian portion of the Galaxy as the publicists could push them. Premier Dirac did not plan to accept indefinitely the limitation of his power and influence to only a few dozen planets.

By now Acting Laboratory Superior Anyuta Zador had been located, and she emerged, tall and black-haired and somewhat diffident, from behind a tall rack of equipment to greet her politically important guest. Dr. Zador was dressed so casually, in lab smock and worn and shuffling shoes, that it was obvious she had been given inadequate time to prepare for this visit.

Zador was really as young as the girlish visitor, though she looked a few years older, being larger physically and dressed without frills. African ancestry showed in her full lips and dark hair, that of northern Europe in her startlingly blue eyes. The real supervisor, Zador's boss, Dr. Narbonensis, was currently attending a conference out of the system—sure indication that the Lady Genevieve's visit was really a surprise.

While Hoveler watched, feeling a touch of anxiety, the acting supervisor stepped bravely forward in her worn shoes, extending her capable hand in official greeting, welcoming the lady and her entourage on behalf of the laboratory's entire staff.

The important caller responded appropriately; inexperience showed only in her soft voice. Lady Genevieve added that she and her husband were simultaneously humbled and proud to be able to make a personal contribution to the great work of this facility.

Hoveler thought that over while he continued listening, at least with half an ear, to routine remarks of greeting and welcome. A further exchange between the two women—prompted now and then by a whispered word from the chief publicist—brought out, largely for the benefit of media targets on other worlds, the fact that this orbital facility was one of the important sites where long-term preparations were being made for the eventual establishment—at a time and place still to be decided—of an enormous colony, or several colonies, intended to further the spread and guarantee the future of Earth-descended humanity.

Hoveler, paying more attention to tones and undertones than to words during this part of the conversation, got the impression that the important visitor was now speaking rather mechanically. The Lady Genevieve definitely showed signs of having been coached in what to say, even to the use of certain phrases, calculated to convey certain political messages.

Supervisor Zador took advantage of a pause to return to an earlier point, as if she were really uncertain of what she had actually heard. "Did I understand you to say, Lady Genevieve, that you were here today to make a, uh, personal contribution?"

The small head of coppery-brown curls nodded energetically. "Indeed I am. My husband, Premier Dirac, and I have decided to donate our first-conceived child to swell the ranks of the future colonists. I am here today to do so."

There was the news item. It created a genuine stir of surprise among the listeners. The eminent visitor added to the surprise by going on to announce that the Premier himself, his demanding schedule permitting, was going to join her here in the Imatran system in a few days, certainly within a standard month.

Surrounding and underlying the small sounds of human conversation, the lab machinery continued its undemanding, polyphonic whispering. Hoveler and anyone else who cared to make the effort could look out through the viewpoints of the satellite station as it whirled through the hundreds of kilometers of its small orbit, and get a good view of the terraformed planetoid Imatra not far below, a thoroughly landscaped green surface dotted with small lakes, canals, and ponds. This map of land, alternating with black starry sky, swung in a stately rhythm from a position apparently above the viewports to one apparently below, while "down," an artifact of the orbiting station's dependable artificial gravity, stayed oriented with rocklike steadiness toward the deck.

Now Lady Genevieve, prompted by another murmured reminder from her chief publicist, was asking Acting Supervisor Zador politely how long she and her fellow workers, and their most impressive laboratory, had been in this system, and what they found especially striking or intriguing about the Imatran worlds. These particular planets and planetoids were, she implied with unskilled insincerity, among the spots best liked in all the universe by the Premier himself.

Acting Supervisor Zador, a young woman rallying well from what must have been her considerable surprise at today's dramatic intrusion, responded with a few facts clothed in some polite inanity. The lab's visit here in the Imatran system had been scheduled for at least several standard months, perhaps a year or more.

After confirming yet again that she had heard Lady Genevieve correctly, that she really planned to make a donation today, Dr. Zador hurriedly conferred with a couple of her more experienced human aides. Hoveler, being a bioengineer rather than a medic, was not among them. Then workers began moving purposefully about. The necessary technical arrangements were hurriedly begun offstage so that the distinguished visitor would not be subject to any avoidable inconveniences or delays.

Meanwhile, a pair of junior lab workers standing not far behind Hoveler had begun to murmur to each other. They were not really including Hoveler in their conversation, but they spoke without caring whether he could hear them.

One worker said, "Evidently their wedding went off as scheduled." There had been some speculation among cynical observers of politics that the premier's recent nuptials might not.

"Yes! A considerable political event, if nothing else."

In contrast to the widespread doubts as to whether the abruptly arranged wedding would actually take place, there had been little or no question that its purpose was primarily political. The union of two dissimilar families, or perhaps more accurately, dynasties, had been a high-priority goal of certain factions, and anathema to others. Thus the haste with which the alliance had been concluded.

One of the murmuring workers within Hoveler's hearing now remarked that the dynastic couple had met each other for the first time only a few days before the ceremony.

The colonizing project in which the research station played a substantial role had long been favored by Premier Dirac and by a majority of the factions upon which the Premier depended for political support. In fact there were many who called him the chief architect of the plan.

Though this visit on a high political level had obviously taken Acting Supervisor Zador by surprise, she still managed to express her satisfaction with commendable coherence. Lady Genevieve's donation would certainly increase the support offered in certain quarters for the workers here in the biolab—indeed, for the whole colonization project—even if, as Dr. Zador thoughtfully refrained from mentioning, the same act guaranteed opposition in other quarters.

While the hasty preparations continued offstage for the actual donation, Lady Genevieve and the acting supervisor went on with their public chat. The visitor's schedule in the Imatran system over the next few days—a schedule the publicist was even now making available to all, in the form of elegant printouts—was going to be a crowded one, and Lady Genevieve regretted that she would not be able to spend as much time as she would like aboard the station. Or at least that was the interpretation Hoveler put on her tired murmur, words now gradually fading toward inaudibility.

Some of the lady's aides were now trying unobtrusively to hurry the medics and the technicians along. Someone said that the small ship in which her party had arrived was standing by at the hatch where it had docked, and that the next stop on her itinerary was probably no more than an hour away.

The lady herself did indeed look tired, thought Hoveler with growing sympathy; his considerable height allowed him to see her over the heads of most of the other people now crowding around. Still, she was maintaining her composure bravely, even when some delay in the technical arrangements prolonged the awkward pause which ensued after everything that needed saying had been said.

Hoveler could understand why making the arrangements required a little time. Among the practical questions that had to be quickly answered was in which treatment room the donation was going to be accomplished, and which human surgeon was going to oversee the operation—the actual removal of the zygote from the uterus and its preservation undamaged were almost always accomplished by machine. Medirobot specialists, hardware vivified by expert and more-than-expert systems operating almost independently of direct human control, possessed a delicacy and sureness of touch superior to that of even the finest fleshly surgeon.

Presently Hoveler noted that at least the treatment room, one of a row over at one side of the lab, had now been selected. When the door to the cubicle-sized chamber was briefly open, the saddle-like device, part of the medirobot specialist inside, was briefly visible.

At last one of Dr. Zador's aides timidly informed the lady that they were ready. The Premier's young bride smiled a tired smile and announced that she was going to have to disappear briefly from public view. For a few minutes she would be accorded privacy with the machines, probably under the supervision of one carefully chosen human operator—very likely another task that would have to be assumed by the acting supervisor, for Dr. Zador appeared to be accompanying her.

The distinguished visitor, being gently ushered along in the proper direction, which took her farther from the large door by which she had come into the lab, looked at the moment rather appealingly lost and bewildered. Hoveler, on hearing a faint murmur from some of his co-workers, knew that she was evoking feelings of protective pity in others besides himself.

As Lady Genevieve disappeared inside the doorway, the PR people established themselves a few meters in front of that aperture and began to furnish commentary, explaining the need for future colonists. Their message of course was being recorded on the spot.

Hoveler, shaking his head, once more seated himself at his workbench. But he could not free his mind of the outer world's distractions and soon gave up any attempt at work until the lab should be cleared of visitors again.

Leaning back in his chair, he smiled vaguely in the direction of the treatment room. He would have liked to assure this latest donor that the medical technicalities involved in the safe evolution of an early pregnancy were brief, and with the best people and equipment available, ought to be no worse than momentarily uncomfortable. But then she must already have been made well aware of those facts.

In a very few minutes the technicalities had in fact been completed, evidently without incident, and Genevieve Sardou, the Premier's no-doubt-beloved bride, emerged smiling, looking tired but well, from the private room.

Dr. Zador had remained behind in the treatment room; Hoveler understood that she would still be communing with the machinery there to make sure that no last-moment glitches had developed.

Meanwhile the eminent visitor herself, still smiling, wearing her neat white dress as if she had never taken it off, showed no signs that anything disagreeable had happened to her during the last few minutes. Already she was once more graciously discussing with some of the workers and the media people her reasons for being here. Much of what she now said, mostly in answer to questions, was a repetition of what she had said earlier.

It seemed that the lady's rather domineering publicist now decided to do a greater share of the talking, while Genevieve limited herself to trying to make the right sounds, trying to be agreeable. In that the Premier's bride succeeded well enough, Hoveler thought. But, at least in the eyes of some observers, she could not help giving the impression of being lost.

Then Hoveler the bioengineer, still watching, gradually changed his mind. Lost was probably the wrong word. Almost certainly out of her depth, perhaps out of her place. But far from helpless. And certainly attractive; yes, definitely that. Grace, femininity, were integral parts of Lady Genevieve. She was a young, physically small woman, with something elfin about her, her face and coloring showing a mixture of the races of old Earth, with Indonesian, if anything, predominant.

And was she really pleased to be here? Really as delighted as she somewhat wearily claimed to be, at visiting what she could call without flattery the finest prenatal facility in this part of the Galaxy? Was the lady really as overjoyed as she said she was to be making this very human contribution on behalf of her husband and herself?

Well, perhaps. She was obviously intelligent, and Hoveler had somehow got the impression that she would not easily be bullied into doing anything she didn't want to do. Perhaps the donation really resulted at least partly from a wish to be free of the responsibility of raising her own child.

Now a murmur came drifting through the laboratory, a raising and swiveling of media devices, a general shifting of the immediate onlookers to gain a better point of view. Dr. Zador, still wearing her surgeon's mask—that article was now chiefly symbolic; maybe one of the media people had asked her to put it on—was emerging from the treatment cubicle, smiling as she held up the hand-sized blue statglass tile that now presumably contained the latest colonist—or protocolonist, rather—encapsulated for viable long-term storage. The tile was basically a flat blue rectangle the size of a man's palm, bearing narrow color-coded identification stripes. At the urging of the media people, Acting Supervisor Zador once more held the encapsulated specimen aloft—higher, this time—to be admired and recorded.

And now, in seeming anticlimax, the station's central communications facility was signaling discreetly for someone's, anyone's, attention. The signal was not attracting much notice, but it got Hoveler's by means of a mellow audio pulsing through the nearest holostage, a device jutting up out of the deck like a flat-topped electronic tree stump. The bioengineer, looking around, found himself at the moment nearer than anyone else to the holostage. And no one else seemed exactly in a hurry to respond to the call.

As soon as Hoveler answered, the electronic voice of Communications, one facet of the laboratory vessel's own computerized intelligence, informed him politely that their most distinguished visitor, Lady Genevieve, had a personal message waiting.

"Can it wait a little longer?"

"I believe the call will be considered a very important one," said the electronic voice. That modest stubbornness on the part of Communications somehow conveyed, to Hoveler at least, the suggestion that someone closely associated with the Premier Dirac, if not Dirac himself, was trying to get through.

"Just a moment, then." Putting on such authoritative bearing as he was able to summon up, and using his above-average size in as gentle a manner as was consistent with effectiveness, Hoveler worked his way through the jealously constricted little crowd to almost within reach of the lady; at this range he could convey the information without shouting it boorishly.

The lady's bright eyes turned directly, searchingly, on him for the first time as he spoke to her. Seen at close range, she was somehow more attractive. She murmured something soft to the effect that any direct message from her husband seemed unlikely; to her best knowledge the Premier was still light-years away.

After making hasty excuses to the people in her immediate vicinity, she quickly moved the few steps to the nearest holostage.

Hoveler watched as the machine suddenly displayed the head and shoulders, as real and solid in appearance as if the body itself were there, of a youngish, rather portly man dressed in space-crew togs, pilot's insignia on his loose collar. The man's eyes focused at once on the lady, and his head awarded her a jaunty nod. It was a gesture on the verge of arrogance.

His voice rasped: "Nicholas Hawksmoor, architect and pilot, at your service, my lady."

The name was vaguely familiar to Hoveler. He had heard some passing mention of Hawksmoor and had the impression the man was some kind of special personal agent of Dirac's, but Hoveler had never seen him before. His image on the holostage was rather handsome.

From the look on Lady Genevieve's face, it seemed that she too had little if any acquaintance with this fellow. And as if she too recognized only the name, she answered tentatively.

Hoveler watched and listened, but no one else—except the lady herself, of course—was paying much attention to the conversation at the moment. Hawksmoor now conveyed in a few elegant phrases the fact that he had talked directly with her husband only a few days ago, more recently than she herself had seen the Premier, and that he was bringing her personal greetings from Dirac.

"Well then, Nicholas Hawksmoor, I thank you. Was there anything else?"

"Oh, from my point of view, my lady, a great deal else." His tone was calm, impertinent. "Are you interested in architecture, by any chance?"

Lady Genevieve blinked. "Only moderately, I suppose. Why?"

"Only that I have come here to this system, at the Premier's orders naturally, to study its existing architecture and ekistics. I hope to play a major role in the final design of the colonial vehicles when the great project really gets under way at last."

"How very important."

"Yes." After chewing his lip thoughtfully for a moment, the pilot asked in a quieter voice, "You've heard the Premier speak of me?"

"Yes," Lady Genevieve answered vaguely. "Where are you now, Nick? I may call you Nick, may I not, as he does?"

"Indeed you may, my lady." Brashness had now entirely left his manner; it was as if an innate arrogance had now given way to some deeper feeling.

Nick reported to the Lady Genevieve that he was even now at the controls of the small ship in which he customarily drove himself about and which he used in his work.

* * *

Hoveler's interest had been caught, naturally enough, by the lady when she first appeared, and now a more personal curiosity had been aroused as well. He was still watching. It did not occur to him—it seldom did—that it might be rude to stare. How interesting it was, the way this upstart Nicholas—whoever he was—and young Lady Genevieve were still looking into each other's imaged eyes—as if both were aware that something had been born between the two of them.

It was at this very moment that the sound of the first alarm reached the laboratory.

Hoveler, with his natural gift or burden of intense concentration, was not really immediately aware of that distant clamor. The Lady Genevieve was scarcely conscious, either, of the new remote signal. For her it could have been only one more muted sound, blending into the almost alien but gentle audio background of this unfamiliar place. And the whole Imatran solar system was deemed secure, as people sometimes remarked, to the point of dullness. The first stage of an alert, at last in this part of the large station, had been tuned down to be really dangerously discreet.

For the next minute it was possible for everyone else in the laboratory to disregard the warning entirely. Then, when people did begin to take notice, almost everyone considered the noise nothing more than a particularly ill-timed practice alert.

In fact, as Hawksmoor realized well before almost anyone else, the signal they were hearing was a quite genuine warning of an oncoming attack. Even he did not realize at once that the signal was so tragically delayed that those hearing it would be able to do very little before the attacker arrived.

"Excuse me," said Nick to Lady Genevieve, not more than one second after the first bell sounded in the lab; before another second had passed, his image had flickered away.

Heartbeats passed. The lady waited, wondering gently, and for the moment dully, what kind of problem had arisen on the young pilot's ship to provoke such an abrupt exit on his part. For a moment or two her eyes, silently questioning, came back to Hoveler's. He could see her visibly wondering whether to turn away from the holostage and get back to her duties of diplomacy.

But very soon, not more than ten seconds after the first disregarded signal, a notably louder alarm kicked in, shattering the illusory peace and quiet.

This was a sound that could not well be ignored. People were irritated, and at the same time were beginning to wake up.

"*Is* this a practice alert? What a time to choose for—"

Hoveler heard someone else answer, someone who sounded quietly lost: "No. It's not practice."

And a moment later, as if in affirmation, some kind of explosion in nearby space smote the solid outer hull of the station with a wave front of radiation hard enough to ring the metal like a gong. Even the artificial gravity generators in the interior convulsed for a millisecond or two, making the laboratory deck lurch underfoot.

Acting Supervisor Zador had turned to an intercom installation and was in communication with the station's optoelectronic intelligence. Turning to her eminent visitor, eyes widened whitely around their irises of startling blue, she said, "That was a ship nearby being blown up. I'm afraid it was your ship. Your pilot must have undocked and pulled out when he saw . . ."

Zador's voice trailed off. The lady was only staring back at her, still smiling faintly, obviously not yet able to understand.

Indeed, it seemed that no one in the lab could understand. The hideous truth could not instantly be accommodated by people who had such a press of other business in their lives to think about. Long seconds were needed for it to burrow into everyone's awareness. When truth at last struck home, it provoked a collective frozen instant, the intake of deep breaths, then panic. A genuine attack, unheard of here in the Imatran system, was nevertheless roaring in, threatening the existence of everything that breathed.

"*Berserkers!*" A lone voice screamed out the terrible word.

No, only one berserker. Moments later, the first official announcement, coming over loudspeakers in the artificially controlled tones of the station's own unshakable Communications voice, made this distinction, as if in some strange electronic attempt to be reassuring.

But to the listeners aboard the station, the number of times, the number of shapes in which death might be coming for them was only a very academic distinction indeed; the lab roiled in screaming panic.

Before the Lady Genevieve could move from the spot where she had been standing, Nick's image was abruptly back upon the holostage. Steadily confronting the lady, who now stood frozen in fear, Hawksmoor now elaborated, succinctly and steadily and quite accurately, on his claim to be a pilot.

"My lady, I fear your ship is gone. But mine is nearby, it will be docking in a minute, and, I repeat, I am a very good pilot."

"My ship is gone?"

"The ship that brought you here has already been destroyed. But mine is coming for you."

"Already destroyed—"

The cool image on the holostage, projecting a sense of competence, strongly urged—in fact, it sounded like he was ordering—the Lady Genevieve to run for a certain numbered airlock, and gave her concise directions as to which way to move from where she was.

"You are standing near the middle of the main laboratory deck, are you not?"

The lady glanced around in search of aid, then looked helplessly at Hoveler, who—wondering at his own composure—nodded confirmation.

Turning back to the holostage, she answered meekly: "Yes, I am."

Nick's image on the holostage issued calm instructions. He would have his ship docked at that lock before she reached it. She had better start moving without delay.

He concluded: "Bring all those people with you, I have room for them aboard. Bring everyone on the station; there can't be that many at the moment."

Meanwhile Hoveler, though dazed by the fact that a real attack was taking place, was remembering the all-too-infrequent practice alerts aboard the station, recalling the duties he was supposed to perform in such an emergency. His tasks during an alert or an attack consisted largely of supervising the quasi-intelligent machines that really did most of the lab work anyway. It was up to him to oversee the temporary shutdown of experiments and the proper storage of tools and materials.

Reacting to his training, the bioengineer got started on the job. It was not very demanding, not at this stage anyway, and it kept him in a location where he could still watch most of what was going on between the Premier's bride and one of his best pilots.

Hoveler used whatever spare moments he had to keep an anxious eye on Acting Supervisor Zador, who the moment the alert had sounded had found herself suddenly in command of local defenses. Obviously Anyuta was not used to such pressure, and Hoveler was afraid that she was somewhat panicked by it. Because just about the first thing she did was to reject Hawksmoor, who at least sounded like he knew what he was doing, in the role of rescuer.

Another message was now coming in on holostage for whoever was in charge aboard the station, and Hoveler could hear it in the background as he dealt with his own job. It was a communication from another craft, a regular manned courier that happened to be just approaching the station. Its human pilot was volunteering to help evacuate people from the facility, which was almost incapable of maneuvering under its own power. He could be on the scene in a matter of seconds.

"We accept," said the acting supervisor decisively. "Dock your ship at Airlock Three." A moment later, having put the latest and soon-to-be-most-famous protocolonist down on the flat top of the console near Hoveler and darting him a meaningful look as if to say *You deal with this,* she was running after the Lady Genevieve. Hoveler saw Anyuta grab the smaller woman by the arm and then firmly direct her down a different corridor than the one recommended by Nick, but in the correct direction to Airlock Three. At the moment, confusion dominated, with people running back and forth across the lab, and in both directions through the adjoining corridor. Some of the visitors were running in circles.

In the next moment the acting supervisor was standing beside Hoveler again, her attention once more directed to the central holostage. "Hawksmoor!"

"Dr. Zador?" the handsome image acknowledged.

"I am now in charge of the defenses here."

"Yes ma'am, I understand that."

"You are not to approach this station. We have another vessel available, already docked"—a quick glance at an indicator confirmed that—"and can evacuate safely without you. Take your ship out instead and engage the enemy—"

"My ship's not armed." Nick sounded as calm and firm as ever.

"Don't interrupt! If your ship is not armed, you will still engage the enemy, by ramming!"

"Yes ma'am!" Nick acknowledged the order crisply, with no perceptible hesitation. Once more his image vanished abruptly from the stage.

Annie, what the hell are you doing? Hoveler marveled at the order and response he had just heard, what had sounded like the calm assignment and equally calm acceptance of certain death. Certainly something was going on here which he did not understand—but he had no time to puzzle over it now.

Right now he had no need to understand or even think about what might be happening outside the station's hull. Dr. Hoveler and Dr. Zador, who were both required by duty as well as inclination to stand by their posts, exchanged a few words about the progress of the general evacuation. Then he felt the need to venture a personal remark.

"Anyuta."

Her attention locked in some technical contemplation, she didn't seem to hear him.

He tried again, more formally. "Dr. Zador?"

Now she did look over at him. "Yes?"

"You should get off this station with the others. You're going to get married in a month. Not that I think there's much chance we're really going to be . . . but I can do what little can be done here perfectly well by myself."

"This is my job," she said with what sounded like irritation, and turned back to her displays. Old friend and colleague or not, the acting supervisor wasn't going to call him by name. Not just now.

Hoveler, his own workbench already neatly cleared and now abandoned, stayed at his assigned battle station, which was near the center of the main laboratory deck, not far from Dr. Zador's post. Regulations called for acceleration couches to be available here for the two of them, but, as Hoveler recalled, those devices had been taken away months ago in some routine program of modification, and had never been brought back. The lack did not appear to pose a practical problem because the station would be able to do nothing at all in the way of effective maneuvering.

In terms of life support, the biostation possessed a full, indeed redundant, capability for interstellar flight, and had visited a number of planetary systems during the several years since its construction. But it had never mounted more than the simplest of space drives, relying on special c-plus tugs and boosters to accomplish its passages across interstellar distances.

Not that the lack appeared to be critical in this emergency. Even had an interstellar drive been installed and ready for use, any attempt to escape by that mode of travel now would have been practically suicidal for a vessel as big as the station starting this deep inside the gravitational well created by a full-sized star surrounded by the space-dimpling masses of its planets.

Still, with a berserker approaching at high speed, only a few minutes away at the most, some panicked person calling in from the surface of the planetoid was now evidently suggesting to the acting supervisor that even virtually certain suicide was preferable to the alternative, and ought to be attempted.

To this suggestion Dr. Zador replied, with what Hoveler applauded as admirable calm under the circumstances, that even had the drive capability been available, she was not about to suicidally destroy herself or anyone else. There wasn't even a regular flight crew aboard the station at the moment.

Besides, it was impossible for anyone on the station to determine absolutely, with the rudimentary instruments available on board, whether or not the berserker (which according to the displays was still thousands of kilometers distant) was really coming directly for the station, though its course strongly suggested that it was. The Imatran system contained two or three worlds much larger and vastly more populous than the planetoid, collectively holding a potential harvest of billions of human lives. These planets lay in approximately the same direction as the station along the berserker's path, but scores of millions of kilometers farther sunward.

The two people whose voluntarily chosen duties decreed that they should remain aboard the research station were able to look into the berserker's image on a stage—Hoveler, in sick fascination, had increasing difficulty looking anywhere else—and to see the monstrous shape growing, defining itself more clearly moment by moment, coming dead-on against the almost starless background of the middle of the Mavronari Nebula.

Amid the ever-burgeoning clamor of alarms, there was no chance of putting into effective use such feeble subliminal drive as the station did possess. The propulsion system was basically intended only for gentle orbital maneuvers. Slow and relatively unmaneuverable, the mobile laboratory, even if it could have been got into steady motion, would have no chance of escaping the thing now rushing upon it from the deep.

The chances were vastly better that a courier like the one now loading, or presumably Nicholas Hawksmoor's craft, both small and swift, would be able to dodge out of harm's way.

Now, at the acting supervisor's remarkably calm urging, several dozen people, including visitors and most of the station's workers, were scrambling through the station's various decks and bays to board the courier vessel that had just docked.

The voice of the human pilot of that little ship could also be heard throughout the station, announcing tersely that he was ready to get away, to flee at full speed toward the system's inner planets and the protection of their formidable defenses.

Beneath the two competing sets of announcements, running and shouting echoed in the corridors. People who had become confused and found themselves going in the wrong direction were one by one turned around and headed in the proper way.

Acting Supervisor Zador, speaking directly to the courier pilot, repeatedly ordered him not to undock until everyone—everyone who wanted to go—had got aboard.

"I acknowledge. Are you two coming? This is an emergency."

The acting supervisor glanced briefly at her companion. "I know it's an emergency, damn it," she replied. "That's why we two are staying." Hoveler on hearing this experienced a thrill of pride, as if she had just bestowed on him some signal honor. At the moment he felt no particular fear. For one thing—though no one had yet brought up the point—there was no guarantee that fleeing in the launch was going to prove any safer than staying where they were.

That was why Hoveler had not pushed harder to get Anyuta Zador to leave.

Nor had Dr. Zador pressed the bioengineer to flee to safety. Obviously she welcomed his assistance.

Now, outside the lab doors, in the adjoining corridor, the last footsteps had fallen silent. In a few moments the last courier would be gone, and the two Solarian humans were going to be alone—except for whatever feelings of companionship they might be able to derive from metric tons of blue tiles, those myriad sparks of preconscious human life that constituted the station's cargo and their responsibility.

Hoveler and Zador exchanged a look and waited. At the moment there seemed to be nothing useful to be said.

Within a few meters of where they were standing, the frightful shape of the enemy, imaged in the false space of the holostage, was steadily magnified by the rushing speed of its approach.

TWO

Never before had the Lady Genevieve faced an emergency even remotely like this one. Until today her short life had been spent mostly near the center of the Galactic region dominated by Earth-descended humanity, in realms of Solarian space that were wrapped in physical security by Templar fleets, by the Space Force, by the local military establishments of a hundred defended systems. In that blessed region berserkers had never been much more than improbable monsters, demons out of fable and legend.

The lady's betrothal and wedding, followed by a rapid flow of other events, none of them terrible in themselves, had carried her by imperceptible stages closer to that world of legend, until now she found herself fleeing down a narrow corridor aboard an unfamiliar spacecraft, her last illusion of physical security jarred loose by the sharp elbow of a screaming publicist thrusting her aside.

Dozens of people, almost everyone who had been aboard the station, including all the visitors, seemed to be in the same corridor, and their frantic activity made the number seem like hundreds or a thousand. What only minutes ago had been an assembly of civilized folk had quickly become a mindless mob, the group first teetering on, then falling over, the brink of panic.

Bioengineer Hoveler was to remember later that he had seen the Lady Genevieve leave the laboratory at a fast pace, moving among her aides as if she were being propelled by them. As the lady went out the door of the laboratory she was moving in the direction indicated by Dr. Zador, toward the hatch where the little escape ship was waiting.

At the same time, in some distant region of the biostation, perhaps on the next deck up or down, some kind of stentorian klaxon, an alarm neither of the remaining workers had ever heard before, had started throbbing rhythmically. The two stay-behind observers were able to remember later how the Premier's young wife, dazed and hurried as she was, seemed to be trying to turn back, in the last moment before she was swept out of the laboratory. It took one of the Lady Genevieve's bodyguards to turn her around again and drag her on by main force toward the waiting courier. And at the moment of her hesitation the young woman had cried out something sounding like "My child!"

So now suddenly it's a child, thought Hoveler. A few minutes ago, that microscopic knot of organic tissue, from which she had so recently been separated, had been only a donation, only a zygote or protochild. But the lady was getting away, and he had no time to think about her or her ideas now.

The lady herself, even as she momentarily tried to turn back, realized perfectly well that her maternal impulse had no logic to it—to leave her child and her husband's here was no more than she had expected all along. But now—of course she hadn't expected a berserker attack—

Rationally, as she understood full well, there was no reason to believe that the microscopic cluster of cells, now sealed inside preserving statglass, would be any safer in her small hands than it was here, wherever the technicians had put it. Probably it was already in some storage vault. But still the Lady Genevieve, driven by some instinct, did momentarily make an effort to turn back.

Then she had been turned around and started out again, and from that moment her thoughts and energy were absorbed in her own fight for survival. None of the people now struggling and scrambling to get through the airlock and aboard the escape ship had ever rehearsed anything like an emergency evacuation. The scene was one of fear and selfishness, but there was really plenty of room aboard the smaller craft, no need to be ruthless.

Within moments after the last person had scrambled in through its passenger entry, the courier—which of course was going to try to summon help, as well as evacuate people—sealed all its hatches. A very few moments after that the courier pilot, his nerves perhaps not quite equal to the situation, anyway making his own calculus of lives to be saved, among which his own was prominent, undocked without waiting for final authorization from anybody, and immediately shot his small craft away in a try for safety.

Meanwhile the dozens of people who had crowded aboard spread out across the limited passenger space in trembling gratitude, standing and walking in an artificial gravity field reassuringly normal and stable. The passengers moved to occupy the available acceleration couches, which would offer them at least minimal protection should the gravity fail in some emergency. Meanwhile their murmured exhalations formed a collective sigh of relief.

For the first minute or two after their vessel separated from the space station, the Lady Genevieve shared elation with her companions aboard the escaping courier. They began to experience a glorious, innocent near certainty that they were safe.

Lady Genevieve was in the middle of saying something to one of her official companions, perhaps protesting her bodyguards' roughness or her publicist's rudeness in pushing her out of the way—or perhaps she was trying to excuse these people for the way they had behaved—when the next blast came.

This one made the previous explosion, heard from a safe distance while they were still aboard the station, sound like nothing at all. This one was disaster. In an instant, in the very midst of a conversation, the world of the Premier's bride dissolved into a blur of shock and horror.

Briefly she lost consciousness.

On recovering her senses, moments later, Lady Genevieve looked about her, peering through a cabin atmosphere gone steamy cold with the instant, swirling fog of sudden depressurization. Gradually remembering where she was, she looked around in hopes of finding a space suit available. But if there was any emergency equipment of that kind aboard, she had not the faintest idea of where to find it.

Feeling dazed, vaguely aware that her limbs ached and that it was hard to breathe, as if her chest had been crushed, the lady released herself from her acceleration couch. Only at that point did she realize that the artificial gravity was low; it must be failing slowly. Emergency lights still glowed.

She dragged herself from one side of the blasted cabin to the other, aware as in a dream that she was the only one moving actively about. Other bodies drifted here and there, settling slowly, inertly in the low g toward the deck. Arms and legs stirred feebly on some of the seats and couches, accompanied by a sound of moaning. Meanwhile the Lady Genevieve was able to hear, almost to feel, the air whining steadily out of the punctured cabin, depleting itself slowly but faster than any reserve tanks were able to replenish it.

Genevieve turned to make her way forward, with some vague idea that the pilot's compartment ought to be in that direction, and that someone, human or autopilot, ought still to be there, still in charge, and that she and the other passengers needed help. But, for whatever reason, she found herself unable to open the hatch or door that led out of the main passenger cabin. There was a small glass panel in the door, and she could see through it a little, just enough to convince her that there was nothing but ruin forward.

And still the air kept up a faint whining, hissing . . . an automatic sealant system was still trying, vainly but stubbornly, to ameliorate disaster.

Now all around her, above, below (though such terms were swiftly losing any practical meaning) drifted the dead and dying, and a few others who like herself had freed themselves from their couches but were unable to do anything more. It registered with Genevieve that no one had even the most modest emergency suit or equipment, no way to keep at bay for long the emptiness outside the fragile, failing hull.

Machinery twitched and moved. She could hear it, somewhere outside the compartment in which she and her unlucky fellow passengers were trapped. From somewhere, at last, an autopilot's voice started trying to give reassurance and then shut up. The voice came back, calm as all robotic voices were, repeated twice some idiotic irrelevance about staying in your couches, please, then went away for good.

Straining her aching limbs, Genevieve took hold of one or two of her drifting fellow passengers and tried to rouse them to meaningful communication. But this effort had no success.

Her every breath hurt her now. Pulling herself from one acceleration couch to another, the lady observed with the numbness of growing shock that as far as she could tell, all of her bodyguards, publicists, and other aides—at least all she could recognize under these conditions—were dead. Probably no one among the few passengers still breathing was better off than she was, or even able to talk to anyone else, beyond a few groans.

After an interval in which Lady Genevieve thought she had begun to accustom herself to being dead, a new noise reached her ears. She opened her eyes, gripping her fingers into fists, wishing that the light-headedness that was growing minute by minute would go away. What was she hearing? Something real, yes. Only sounds of the wrecked ship collapsing further?

And out of nowhere, it seemed, the certainty suddenly returned to her: she was now clearly convinced, in the face of death, that it had been a mistake to give up her child. If she hadn't agreed to make the donation, she wouldn't be here now. She would be home instead—

There it came again. Yes, definitely, a noise that spoke of purpose, not just of collapse.

Yes. Someone or something was working on some part of the ship from the outside, trying to get in.

A moment later, the Lady Genevieve, trying to focus her mind against a feeling like too much wine—with part of her mind she understood this was anoxia—thought she was able to identify the grating sound of contact between two vessels.

Working her way almost weightlessly closer to a cleared port, she was able to see that another small vehicle had matched velocities with the wreck and was very close indeed.

The same noise again, quite near at hand, and perhaps a flare of light as well; something or someone cutting through metal—

Abruptly metal opened, without any murderous escape of air. She saw, with a shock of relief of such intensity that she almost fainted, that her visitor was no murderous machine, but rather a suited human figure that spoke to her at once, and reassuringly.

Genevieve was by this time more than a little dazed, rapturously light-headed with lack of oxygen as cabin pressure dropped to dangerously low levels. Her body was scratched in several places, and seriously bruised. But she was not too badly hurt to glide her nearly weightless body across the foggy interior of the cabin and plant a big kiss on her rescuer's faceplate.

(And was it something her fuzzy vision discovered for her, or could not discover, inside his or her helmet, that made the lady's eyes widen for just a moment?)

In response to her kiss upon his helmet there seemed to be just a moment of hesitation, surprise, on her rescuer's part. And then the armored arms came round her, gently, protectively returning the hug. Out of the suit's air speaker came the same voice she remembered coming from a holostage, what seemed like an age ago. "Nicholas Hawksmoor, my lady. At your service."

Drifting back to arm's length from the embrace, she demanded eagerly: "Can you get me out of here? I don't have a suit, you see. It seems there are no suits aboard."

"That's quite all right, my lady. I can get you out safely. Because—"

And at that instant, with a great roar, all that was left of her newly salvaged life, her world, exploded.

* * *

Drs. Hoveler and Zador meanwhile, with the stowage of experiments and materials just about completed, were snatching intervals, long seconds at a time, from their self-imposed duties, to watch, as best they could on holostage and instrument readouts, the fighting that flared intermittently outside the station's hull.

Between these intervals of dreadful observation the two oversaw robotic maintenance of the station's life support systems. There was really nothing they could do to defend the station—the laboratory had not been designed or built for frontier duty, and was completely unarmed and unshielded. So far, it seemed to be essentially undamaged.

Several times the two people standing watch in the laboratory expressed their hope that the courier ship had got clean away—they had heard no word about it one way or the other. And Acting Supervisor Zador once or twice wondered aloud, in such intervals for thought as she was able to seize among her duties, what success Nicholas Hawksmoor was having with the ramming maneuver she had commanded him to attempt. Hoveler had been meaning to ask her about that, but once more he decided that his questions could wait.

Of course the ultimate result of the berserker attack did not depend very much on Hawksmoor, Hoveler thought. Whatever he might or might not have done, there were fairly strong defenses in place on the surface of the planetoid Imatra, and the station in its low orbit lay well within the zone of their protection. Also a pair, at least, of armed ships happened to be lying by close enough in space to put up a fight against the onrushing attacker.

These ground batteries and ships, and the people who crewed them, as records later were to confirm, bravely offered opposition to the onslaught.

But events proved that the single enemy was far too strong. The defenders watched powerlessly as the berserker, not in the least deterred or delayed by the best they could accomplish, came on in an undeviating course obviously calculated to intercept the bioresearch station in its swift orbit. The enemy's immediate presence in the station's vicinity was now less than a minute away.

Hoveler's next helpless inspection of the nearby

holostage showed him the onrushing image of death changing, shedding little fragments of itself. He interpreted this to mean that the berserker had launched some small craft of its own—or were they missiles? He wondered why, on the verge of his own destruction, he should find such details interesting.

Though neither of the people on the station were aware of the details, the planetoid's ground defenses offered such resistance as they could manage to put up, bright beams of energy slicing and punctuating space, annihilating some of the small enemy machines; but only moments after the ground batteries opened fire, they were pounded into silence, put out of action by the even heavier weapons of the enemy. And the first pair of fighting ships who tried to engage the foe were soon blasted into fragments, transformed into expanding clouds of metallic vapor laced with substances of organic origin.

There were only a couple of fighting ships left in the whole Imatran system, and only one of these was anywhere near the scene of the attack and in position to close with the attacker. Its captain and crew did not lack courage. Hurtling bravely within range, this last human fighter to join the fray opened up with its weapons on its gigantic opponent and the smaller commensal ships or spacegoing machines the attacker had deployed.

But none of the weapons humanity could bring to bear seemed to do the great berserker any serious damage, though it was impossible at the moment to accurately assess their effect.

And now it was no longer possible to doubt the enemy's prime objective. The huge bulk of the berserker, basically almost spherical, vaguely ragged in its outline, wreathed by the glowing power of its defensive force fields, was easing to a halt in space within a few hundred meters of the biolab, dwarfing the station by its size, smoothly matching the sharp curve of the smaller object's orbit.

By this time Daniel Hoveler had left his post, where he had already carried out, quite uselessly, such duties as the manuals prescribed.

Annie, startled to see him go, called out sharply: "Where are you going?"

He called over his shoulder: "I'll be back." He had an idea that she might be better off if she did not know what he was about to do.

Leaving the laboratory deck, he rode a quick lift to the level where the hardware comprising the station's optelectronic brain was concentrated. Anyuta Zador had called after him again, demanding to know where he was going, but he had refused to answer. His thought in refusing was that she would somehow be safer from the berserker's revenge if she didn't know what he was doing.

His plan, such as it was, involved finding some way to scramble the information code by which the station's brain kept track of the enormous inventory of tiled, preserved zygotes.

Even as Hoveler made his way toward the chamber where the station's brain was located, Dr. Zador continued calling him on intercom. At last he answered, briefly and noncommittally, having a vague and probably irrational fear that the enemy might already be listening.

The intercom system was tracking his progress, effortlessly and automatically. From one deck to another, Hoveler and Zador kept up a terse communication.

Neither of the two expected anything better than quick death. Both of them, finding themselves still breathing at this stage, were fearful of some fate considerably worse.

"Dan? It's just sitting there a couple of hundred meters from our hull! Dan, what are you doing?" Perhaps she thought he was trying to hide or to escape.

He couldn't think while she kept shouting at him, and right now he had to think, because he had reached and unlocked the little room he wanted. Maybe it didn't make sense to try to keep what he was doing secret; he would explain.

"I'm not trying to hide, Annie. I'm going after the zygotes."

"Going after them?" She sounded nearly in a panic.

"Annie, haven't you asked yourself why we aren't dead already? Obviously because the berserker wants something that we've got on board. It wants to capture something undamaged. I think that something has to be our cargo."

"Dan. The tiles . . ." Now her voice seemed to be fading.

For years the two of them had worked together, lived, struggled, sometimes in opposition over details but always together in their determination that the overall colonial project should succeed. They had both devoted themselves to the welfare of these protopeople, to the hope of eventually contributing to their achievement of real lives.

For the moment there was silence on the intercom.

Now Hoveler, agonizing, was working with the hardware, entering computer commands, trying to remember how to isolate that portion of the ship's brain having to do with cargo inventory without causing widespread failure in other functions. Now he was running through numbers on a readout, and now he was calling up on holostage a direct view of the vast storage banks of nascent people being housed on this deck and others—chamber after chamber of them, bin after bin. The idea flashed through his mind that it was at least a merciful dispensation that these could feel neither pain nor fear.

Hoveler, swayed by an agonized moment or two of indecision, continued to stare at the imaged bins and cabinets protectively holding the protocolonists.

Calling up one image after another on a convenient 'stage, he inspected the endless-seeming ranks of tiles in storage. Row after row, drawer after drawer, densely packed. The handy little storage devices were amazingly tough, designed to offer great resistance to either accidental or purposeful destruction.

In a flash it crossed his mind to wonder what had actually happened to the Premier's newly donated protoperson. He remembered Annie's putting the tile down on the top of his own console—but he couldn't remember seeing it or even thinking about it at any time after that. In the normal course of events, one of the attendant machines in the lab, observing a tile lying about loose, would have picked it up and whisked it away for filing. But under present circumstances . . .

Just looking at them didn't help, of course. Whatever he was going to do, he felt sure that he had not much time in which to do it. But the seconds of inexplicable survival stretched on into minutes while Hoveler kept trying very cleverly and subtly to inflict damage, controlled but irreversible, upon the thinking hardware. And still the minutes of continued life stretched on . . .

For whatever purpose, the fatal stroke was still withheld. The destroyer was treating the unarmored, undefended station very gently. But surely at any moment now something terrible would happen.

Instead of swift destruction, there came a bumping, grating noise, at once terrible and familiar.

Hoveler tried hastily to finish what he had started. The new noise sounded like some small craft or machine, evidently an emissary from the berserker, attempting a docking with the lab.

Given the limited time and tools available, destroying any substantial proportion of the tiles seemed as utterly impossible a task as getting them to safety. Therefore he had concentrated on achieving hopeless confusion in the determination of the specimens' identities. Because it seemed that, for some wicked reason of its own, the berserker was actually intent on taking them all alive.

He could only try to deduce the reason, but it must be horrible. Minutes ago, when it became obvious that they were being spared quick destruction, a hideous scenario had sprung into Hoveler's imagination, to the effect that the damned machine was planning to seize the zygotes and the artificial wombs and raise a corps of goodlife slaves and auxiliaries.

Meanwhile Annie Zador, back on the laboratory deck, was listening to the station's own calm robotic Communications voice announce that something had just completed a snug docking at Airlock Two.

"Should I open?" The same bland voice asked the question.

She didn't bother to reply. Before the question could be repeated, it had become irrelevant. Whatever was outside was not waiting politely for an invitation. The airlock was only a standard model, not built to withstand a determined boarding assault, and within a few seconds it had been opened without the cooperation of any interior intelligence.

Moments after the enemy had forced open the airlock, four boarding machines of deadly appearance came striding upon inhuman legs into the main laboratory.

Anyuta Zador closed her eyes and, waiting for destruction, held her breath—

—and then, unable to bear the suspense, began with an explosive shudder to breathe again. She opened her eyes to see that only one of the silent machines now stood regarding her with its lenses. The rest of the boarders had already gone somewhere. They must have fanned out across the laboratory or gone back into the corridor. Not back out through the airlock; she would have heard its doors again.

"Obey orders," the remaining machine advised her in a voice not much more inhuman than the station's, "and you will not be harmed."

Zador could not force herself to answer.

"Do you understand?" the machine demanded. It rolled closer, stopping no more than two meters away. "You must obey."

"Yes. I—I understand." She clung to her supervisor's console to keep from falling down in terror.

"How many other people are on board?"

"No one else." The brave lie came out unplanned and very quickly, before Dr. Zador allowed herself the time to consider what its consequences might be.

Already another of the invaders was coming back into the laboratory room. "Where are the flight controls?" it demanded of her, in a voice identical to that of the first berserker device.

Zador had to stop and think. "What few controls this vessel has for that purpose are on the next deck up."

The machine that had just reentered the lab stalked out again.

Meanwhile Hoveler was working on furiously, but carefully. It would be good if he could avoid leaving any traces of this intrusion. Since it would be practically impossible for him to destroy the cargo of protopeople—he wasn't sure that he could bring himself to make the effort anyway—he was determined to render them less useful in whatever horrible experiment the berserker might be planning.

Assuming he was successful, what should he do then? He was not the type to contemplate killing himself in cold blood. Seek out the nearest berserker presence and give himself up? Simply return to his post, where Annie was more than likely already dead?

He supposed that if he should choose to hide out, the length of time he would be able to avoid capture or death depended to some extent upon how many machines the berserker had sent aboard. If the number of invaders was small, he might be able to conceal himself indefinitely. He might also be aided by the enemy's ignorance of the physical layout inside the station.

Indefinitely?

The overall shape of the facility was roughly that of a cylinder a little more than fifty meters in diameter, and about the same in length. Twelve decks or levels provided space for work, storage, and housing. There had been more than enough room for the usual crew of people and machines to move about without getting in one another's way.

The facility had been planned and built as a study for a colonization vehicle. It was equipped with smoothly reliable artificial gravity and a lot of research machinery, including a ten-meter cube, also called a ten-three, or just a tencube, for research carried on in the mode of virtual reality. Hoveler seemed to remember that its architects had fallen out of favor with Premier Dirac over the last year or so, as he had gradually become dissatisfied with their work. That was one reason why Nicholas Hawksmoor had been brought on line.

In order to complete his job of disruption properly, Hoveler would have to cope with redundancies in the system by moving physically from one deck to another. He feared that murderous berserker machines must be aboard the station now, and that they would detect his presence if he used the lift again. They might detect him anyway if they decided to tap into the intercom, but he would just have to risk that.

Easing his way as quietly as possible out of the small

room in which he had been working, Hoveler closed its door behind him and tiptoed down a curving corridor toward the nearest companionway.

The shortest, simplest route to his next stop required that he traverse at least a corner of the deck on which the great majority of the mechanical wombs had been installed. In the midst of this passage, while peering carefully to his right, Hoveler froze momentarily. Far across the deck, perhaps forty meters away, and only partially visible between rows of silent, life-nurturing machines stood another metal shape that was completely unfamiliar and intrusive. It seemed that a berserker guard had been established.

He couldn't stand here all day waiting to be caught; he had to move. Perhaps the muted murmurs of flowing air and electricity were loud enough to muffle the faint sounds his softly shod feet must have made on the smooth floor. Perhaps the intervening machines blocked the berserker's line of sight. In any event, Hoveler managed to get to the next companionway and the next deck without being detected.

Once there, under great tension, the evader managed to get inside the last compartment from which the system's records could be restored. Easing the door shut, he got on with his task of befuddling the central inventory system.

Perhaps it was some noise he unavoidably made, working with the necessary small tools, that betrayed his presence. Whatever the reason, he had not been at work for twenty seconds when one of the boarding machines pulled open the door of the small room and caught him in the act.

In the circumstances, Hoveler hoped for a quick death, but the hope failed. In another moment the multilimbed machine—obviously being careful not to hurt him very much—was dragging him back to the laboratory deck.

There, moments later, he and Anyuta Zador exchanged incoherent cries, on each discovering that the other was still alive. The machine that had been dragging Hoveler released him, and a moment later the two humans were in each other's arms.

And still, ominously as it seemed, Death forbore to make any quick, clean claim. Instead of destroying the helplessly vulnerable station entirely, or gutting it ruthlessly with boarding machines, the gigantic foe had clamped onto its outer hull with force fields—as the prisoners, allowed access to a holostage, were able to observe—and was starting to haul it away. The hull sang for a while under the unaccustomed strain, emitting strange mournful noises. Then it quieted.

Minutes of captivity dragged on, as if divorced from time. Exhausted by strain, their weary eyelids sagging, the prisoners attempted to rest. The last chance I'll ever get to rest, Hoveler thought dully. The artificial gravity was still functioning with soothing steadiness, damping out or quenching entirely any acceleration that would otherwise have resulted from the new, externally imposed motion. The people inside the station could not feel themselves being towed.

Puzzlingly, the berserker seemed to be ignoring the incident of Hoveler's sabotage. So far the boarding machines had administered no punishment, made no threats, asked him no questions. It was an attitude both humans found unsettling. A berserker that did not do something bad could only be preparing something worse.

When Hoveler and Zador had given up for the time being trying to rest, they conferred again. For some reason they found themselves speaking in soft whispers, despite the fact that their metal captors nearby were almost certainly able to detect sounds much fainter than those required by the human ear. Both humans were thoroughly bewildered, almost frightened, by their own continued survival. And also by the fact that they still had access to almost the full spectrum of commonly used controls, at least those within the lab. Not that any of these allowed them any influence over what was happening to their vessel. Once Hoveler had been dragged back, neither he nor Zador had attempted to leave the laboratory deck.

Meanwhile Hoveler, despite his terror, could silently congratulate himself that he had indeed managed to scramble most of the cargo inventory system. Still, he dared not try to communicate this achievement to Annie. Nor did he want to raise with her, in the berserkers' presence, the question of what might have happened to the last zygote that had been contributed.

Anyuta Zador had said nothing about his absence and recapture. But an hour or so after his return, she took the chance of giving him a long questioning look, whose meaning he read as *Where were you?*

The look he gave Annie in response was an attempt to express that he understood the question, but didn't know how to go about conveying a good answer.

However they tried to distract themselves or each other, both people's thoughts inevitably kept coming back to the gritty peril of their own situation.

Dan Hoveler had no immediate family of his own—a lack for which he currently felt a devout gratitude. But he could tell, or thought he could, that his companion, in the long silent minutes when she closed her eyes or stared at nothing, must be thinking about the man she was going to marry.

Hoveler considered suggesting the possibility of a successful rescue attempt—but Annie knew at least as well as he did how very unlikely anything of the kind really was.

After several hours had passed, and a few exchanges of whispered words, the captive couple decided to make an attempt to leave the lab deck and go to their cabins. Somewhat to their surprise they were allowed to do so. Not that the berserker had forgotten its prisoners—two machines accompanied them when they left the lab, and searched their cabins thoroughly before the tenants were allowed to enter.

Though each cabin was now occupied by a guardian, the humans were allowed to rest—choosing under the circumstances to stay together in one cabin. Hoveler, sprawled on a couch, soon found himself actually dozing off.

A few hours later, a little rested though still under observation, and back on the lab deck again, the bioworkers tried to satisfy their curiosity about what was happening. Cleared ports and free use of a holostage made it possible to gain some information.

"You're right, no doubt about it, we're being towed."

"I don't get it." Hoveler blew out breath in a great sigh.

"Nor do I. But here we are. Pulled. Dragged along. The entire station is being towed away. Our hull, or a large part of it anyway, seems to be wrapped in force fields. Like a faint gray mist that you can see only at certain angles."

They adjusted the stage again and watched, while their own watchers stood by, tolerating them in enigmatic silence. After a while Zador announced: "Dan, this just doesn't make any sense."

"I know that."

"So where is it taking us? Why?"

He shrugged. "We're bound away from the sun, it seems. Steadily but slowly accelerating out of the system. Since we're now out of communication with the rest of humanity, I can't see enough to be any more specific."

Time passed, disjointedly. The humans sat or stood around, terror slowly congealing into a sick approximation of calm, waiting for whatever might happen to them next.

Gradually Hoveler's sense of minor triumph at what he had done to the inventory system faded, to be replaced by a sickening thought: the berserker might well be completely indifferent as to the individual identities of any of its captured protocolonists. Maybe one Solarian human or protohuman would serve as well as another in whatever fiendish scheme the enemy calculated.

Still the machines inflicted no harm upon the captive humans. Nor had the berserker any objection to their talking to each other; in fact it seemed to Hoveler that their captor by not separating them was actually encouraging them to converse freely.

He had a thought, and couldn't see any harm in speaking it aloud. "Maybe it's letting us talk because it wants to listen."

Annie nodded immediately. "That idea had occurred to me."

"So what do we do?"

"What harm can we do by talking? Neither of us knows any military secrets."

Meanwhile, the invading machines were not standing idle. One at least of them remained in sight of each prisoner at all times. Others worked intermittently, probing with their own fine tools into the station's controls and other machinery; whether their intention was to make alterations or simply to investigate, Hoveler found impossible to determine.

Eventually the humans, growing restless and being allowed to roam about the station at will though under guard, were able to observe machines on other decks as well, some of them digging into various kinds of hardware there. Privately Hoveler estimated the number on board the station to be about a dozen in all.

Since the first minutes of their occupation, the boarding machines had had nothing to say to their new captives.

The number of hours elapsed since the boarding lengthened at last into a standard day. Zador and Hoveler were spending most of their time on the more familiar laboratory deck. They were there, in the midst of a low-voiced conversation, when Annie broke off a statement in midsentence and looked up in astonishment. Hoveler, following her gaze with his own, was likewise struck dumb.

A man and woman he had never seen before, ragged scarecrow Solarian figures, had suddenly appeared in front of him. The newcomers were staring with odd hungry eyes at Hoveler and Zador.

It was left to Hoveler himself to break the silence. "Hello."

Neither of the newcomers responded immediately to this greeting. From the look of their shabby, emaciated figures, the expression on their faces and in their eyes, Hoveler quickly got the idea that a clear answer was unlikely.

He tried again, and presently the two new arrivals, urged by repeated questioning, introduced themselves as Carol and Scurlock.

Annie was staring at them. "How did you get aboard? You came—from the berserker?"

They both nodded. The man mumbled a few words of agreement.

Zador and Hoveler exchanged looks of numbed horror, wondering silently if they were beholding their own future.

The more closely Hoveler studied the newcomers, the more his horror grew. Scurlock was unshaven. The hair of both was matted and dirty; their dress was careless; garments were unfastened, incomplete, unchanged for far too long. Carol was wearing no shoes, and her shirt hung partially open, her breasts intermittently exposed. Evidently that wasn't normal behavior in whatever society they'd come from, for Scurlock, who at moments appeared vaguely embarrassed, now and then tried to get her to cover up. Still, the pair appeared to have been allowed free access to food and drink—they were indifferent to what Zador and Hoveler offered them from one of the station's serving robots. And they showed no signs of overt, serious physical abuse.

But the blank way the newcomers, especially Carol, looked around the lab, their halting silences, their appearance—these things suggested to Hoveler that eccentric if not downright crazy behavior was to be anticipated. Obviously Carol and Scurlock were long accustomed to the berserkers' presence, because for the most part they simply ignored the omnipresent machines.

Hoveler caught himself hoping silently, fervently, that the pair would not do anything to damage the lab's machinery.

As if that now mattered in the least.

The pair settled in, helping themselves to one of the number of empty staterooms, which they occupied with a guardian machine. Between themselves, the biolab workers soon agreed that both of the newcomers, particularly Carol, must have become unbalanced under the strain of some lengthy captivity. This tended to make the sporadic intervals of conversation with them extra rich and strange.

Annie asked: "Do you mind telling us how you were captured? And where?"

"We were taken off a ship," Scurlock said by way of partial explanation. Then he looked at the station's two original occupants as if he were worried about their reaction to this news.

"How long ago?"

Neither Carol nor Scurlock could say, or perhaps they wanted to keep this information secret.

Annie Zador turned to a 'stage and began calling up news of missing ships, trying to find out from the station's data banks if any vessels had disappeared locally within the past few months. The banks provided a small list of craft recently vanished within the sector, but Carol and Scurly seemed strangely disinterested in cooperating. They did admit they'd been working with a small, unnamed ship taking a survey for the Sardou Foundation; no, they'd no idea what the berserker might be doing with their ship now. In fact they couldn't remember when they'd seen it last.

Next the bioworkers tried, with only small success, to trade information about backgrounds. Neither Carol nor Scurlock sounded quite rational enough to state clearly how long they had been the berserker's prisoners. No, they hadn't formed any opinions as to why it had now brought them aboard the station.

"Does the berserker have any other people aboard?" Zador asked suddenly, thinking of a new tack to try. "Any goodlife, maybe?"

"We are goodlife," Carol announced clearly, with an apprehensive glance at the nearest listening machine. Two of her listeners recoiled involuntarily. The ragged, dirty woman sounded very emphatic, if not entirely sane.

Her companion nodded, slowly and thoughtfully. "We are," he agreed. "What about you?"

There was a silence. Then in a small, firm voice Anyuta Zador said: "We are not."

The machine appeared to take no notice.

Slowly Scurlock began to pay more attention to the new environment in which his metal master had established him. "What is this place, anyway?" he demanded.

Hoveler began to explain.

The dirty, unkempt man interrupted: "I wonder what our machine wants it for?"

"Your machine? You mean the berserker?"

"Call it that if you want. It asked us an awful lot of questions about this . . . place . . . before it brought us here."

As Zador and Hoveler listened in mounting horror, Carol added: "I don't see what use a cargo of human zygotes is going to be. Ugh. But our machine knows best."

Hoveler, his own nerves thoroughly frayed by now, could

not completely smother his anger. "Your machine, as you call it, seems to have computed that you're both going to be very helpful to it!"

"I am certainly going to help," Carol agreed hastily. For once her speech was clear and direct. "We are. We just don't know *how* as yet. But the machine will tell us when the time comes, and we're ready."

"We're ready!" agreed Scurlock fervently. Then he fell silent, aware that both Hoveler and Zador were looking at him in loathing and contempt. "Badlife!" he whispered, indulging his own disdain.

"We are goodlife." Carol, once more looking and sounding unbalanced, had suddenly adopted an incongruous, schoolteacherish refrain and manner.

Zador snapped at her: "Who's arguing with you? All right, if you say so. You're goodlife. Yes, I can believe that readily enough."

Hoveler heard himself adding a few gutter epithets.

Carol let out a deranged scream and sprang at Annie in a totally unexpected assault, taking the taller woman by surprise and with insane strength driving her back, clawing with jagged nails at her face.

Before Annie went down, or was seriously injured, Hoveler stepped in and shoved the smaller woman violently away, so that she staggered and fell on the smooth deck.

"Let her alone!" Scurlock in turn shoved Hoveler.

"Then tell her to let us alone!"

The quarrel trailed off, in snarling and cursing on both sides.

Hours later, an uneasy truce prevailed. Hoveler and Zador, talking privately between themselves, were developing strong suspicions that Scurlock and Carol might actually have sought out the berserker in their little ship and volunteered as willing goodlife.

"Do you think it's waiting for us to do the same thing?"

Zador raised her head. "I wonder if it's listening?"

"No doubt it's always listening. Well, I don't give a damn. Maybe it'll hear something it doesn't want to hear for a change. What really frightens me," the bioengineer continued, "is that I think I can understand now how people come to be goodlife. Did you ever think about that?"

"Not until now."

There were intervals when it seemed that Scurlock, at least, was trying to come to terms with the other couple. Carol seemed too disconnected to care whether she came to terms with anyone or not.

Scurlock: "Look here, we're all prisoners together."

Hoveler nodded warily. "Has the machine given you any idea of what it plans to do with you? Or with us?"

"No." Then Scurlock put on a ghastly smile: "But Carol and I are going to play along. That's the only course to take in a situation like this."

Meanwhile, in the hours and days immediately following the theft of the station, all of the various bases, populous cities, and settlements upon the habitable planets of the Imatran system were frantic with activity. Much of it utterly useless, all of it too late to save the station. Word of the berserker attack had of course been dispatched at light speed to the authorities who governed the system's sunward worlds. The news had reached those planets within a few hours of the event. Hastily they had dispatched what little help they had readily available toward the ravaged planetoid.

Following established military doctrine, a unified system command was at once set up, and under its aegis the big worlds coordinated their efforts as thoroughly as possible.

There would be no more in-system fighting—if for no other reason than because the Imatrans had nothing else in space capable of challenging the victorious enemy. The captured station was being ruthlessly, inexorably, but carefully, gently, hauled away.

Within a few hours after the beginning of the raid, all that remained in the Imatran system as evidence of the outrage was a modest number of dead and wounded, scattered marks of damage on the surface of the planetoid, some swiftly fading electromagnetic signals, including light waves . . .

A small amount of debris drifting in space, wreckage

from human ships and small berserkers, the result of the brief, fierce combat.

And a number of recordings, affording reasonably complete documentation of the outrage.

THREE

In a dream that seemed to her both prolonged and recurring, the Lady Genevieve beheld the image of her rescuer continuing to drift before her eyes. The suited figure, faceless inside his protective space helmet, had the shape of a tall man, ruggedly strong, who held out his arms in an offer of succor from disaster, of salvation from—

From everything, perhaps, except bad dreams.

And her rescuer's voice, issuing from his suit's air speaker, had spoken his name to her again, just before . . .

Yes, Nicholas Hawksmoor. That was his name.

Lady Genevieve aboard the dying courier had been welcoming her rescuer. In pure joy of life triumphant she had spread out her arms to embrace the superbly capable, the blessed and glorious Nicholas Hawksmoor. For just a moment he had given her an impression of hesitation, of surprise. And then his armored arms had come round her gently, carefully, returning the hug.

A moment later, pushing herself back to arm's length from the tight embrace, Genevieve had demanded eagerly: "Can you get me out of here? I don't have a suit, you see. It seems there are no suits aboard."

Again his voice—Nick's voice, the voice she remembered from the holostage—issued from the suit's air speaker. "That's quite all right, my lady. I can get you out safely. Because—"

And then—

As she recalled the flow of events now (however much time had passed) from her present place of safety (wherever that might be), it seemed to the Lady Genevieve that the whole world had exploded at that point.

She now even had her doubts that that last remembered explosion had been quite real. But very real and convincing was her present sense, her impression, that after that moment the course of her rescue had somehow gone terribly wrong.

Only the fact that these memories of wreckage and explosions seemed remote kept her now from being still utterly terrified.

The embrace, with her body clad only in the shreds of the white dress, pressed against the suit's unfeeling armor. And with the courier's smoky atmosphere steadily bleeding itself thin around them. Then the last explosion. Yes, very real, as convincing as any memory of her entire life.

And following the last explosion, dreams. A whole world of peculiar dreams, dreams evolving into a strange mental clarity, true vision bringing with it terror. And now she was living that experience again—unfocused and unshielded terror, the helpless sense of onrushing death, the certainty of obliteration.

But this time, for the Lady Genevieve, the period of clarity and terror was mercifully brief.

Again unconsciousness claimed her for an indeterminate time. A blackness deeper than any normal sleep, like the complete cessation of existence.

Then she was drifting, carrying up out of nothingness with her the single thought that the courier, really, had somehow been demolished, with her still aboard. An event of some importance, she supposed. But now it seemed remote from her.

Then, finally, blessedly, real awareness of her real surroundings. Her present environment, gratefully, was one which proved by its mere existence that she had been rescued, brought to a place of safety. She occupied a bed, or rather a narrow berth, which seemed, from several background indications, to be aboard a ship. Close above her, passing only a few centimeters from her face, moved the thin, efficient, obviously inhuman, tremendously welcome metal arms of a medirobot, which must be in some way taking care of her.

And there, only a little farther away, just beyond the clear sanitary shield guarding her berth, loomed the handsome face of the volunteer pilot—his was one name Jenny was never going to forget—Nicholas Hawksmoor. Hawksmoor was looking down at her anxiously.

With considerable effort the Lady Genevieve, while remaining flat on her back, managed to produce a tiny voice. For whatever reason, she found it really difficult to speak, to put any volume of air behind the words.

"Where am I?" she asked. The unexpected problem with her speech was almost frightening, but not really. Not now. Now that she was saved, all medical difficulties could be solved in time.

Hawksmoor leaned closer, and replied at once, and reassuringly, "You're safe, aboard my little ship. I call her the *Wren.* I got you out of that courier just in time." He hesitated fractionally. "You remember being on the courier?"

"I remember getting away from the research station on it. Of course, how could I not remember?"

"And you remember me?"

"Nicholas Hawksmoor, architect and pilot. Very good pilot, I must agree." Still, every word she spoke required an unnatural effort. But she wanted to talk. She thought she wasn't really tired.

"That's right." He sounded relieved, and encouraging.

"What do your friends call you? Nick?"

"My friends?" For whatever reason, that question seemed to unsettle her rescuer momentarily. "Yes, yes, Nick will do nicely. What do your friends call you?"

"Jenny."

"Yes, of course. Naturally they would. Jenny. Do you know, that name reminds me of something?"

"Of what?"

"A poem. A verse. Maybe I'll sing it for you later."

She tried to turn her head and look about her. The white wall from which the arms of the medirobot protruded was part of a general constriction that kept her from moving very far in any direction. All the walls, white or glassy, of the couch, in which her body was sunken almost as in a bathtub, kept her from seeing very much.

Struck by a sudden thought, the lady asked, "How are the other people?"

"Those on the courier?" Nicholas sighed unhurriedly. "I couldn't do anything for them, I'm afraid. Most of them were dead anyway, or nearly dead, before I got there. And besides, I had equipment enough to get only one person out."

Again, she drifted mentally for a little while. She hadn't thought that everyone else was nearly dead. That wasn't really how she remembered the situation. But . . .

"I don't hurt anywhere," she murmured at last. Now, each time she spoke, obtaining air and forming it into words seemed a little easier than the time before. Now it was as if . . . something . . . were being progressively adjusted for her comfort. People said that shipboard medirobots were very good, though she had never had to prove it for herself before.

Her companion was tenderly solicitous. "Well, I'm glad. You shouldn't hurt. You absolutely shouldn't after all that's . . . after all that's been done for you. You're going to be all right."

And once again it seemed that it was time to sleep.

Back on the Imatran surface, all of the minor local authorities, the petty political and military leaders, had survived the attack in good shape. This happy circumstance was not the result of any special defense or precaution undertaken on their behalf as individuals, for no such favoritism had been shown. The truth was that nearly all the ordinary citizens and all of the numerous visitors currently on the planetoid had also come unharmed through the disaster.

Not because of the effectiveness of the planetoid's defenses, which had not actually been fully tested. Rather, the high rate of survival could be laid to the enemy's tactics. It really appeared that this particular berserker had passed up the opportunity for mass slaughter, that its only goal had been to snatch away the biolab.

An hour after the last shot had been fired, everyone on the planetoid was finally allowing themselves to think that the berserker was not coming back—at least not right away. The local authorities, now emerging stunned from their several shelters, had already received enough reports from the more distant regions of Imatra to confirm that the only real damage had been done, the only casualties sustained, in the immediate vicinity of the ground-based defenses, which had been thoroughly knocked out. In some of those areas the local devastation had been complete, though sharply limited in geographical extent.

The local authorities on the planetoid, without waiting for their colleagues and superiors from the full-sized planets of the system, hurriedly convened on holostage. All present were naturally aghast at the disaster they had just survived, and at the same time relieved that somehow—miraculously, it seemed—the destruction and loss of life had not been worse.

The planetoid Imatra had for years been home to a fair amount of scientific research. Also it was well known throughout nearby worlds and systems as a conference site, a meeting place with the pleasant ambiance of a formal garden, where administrators at several levels in Premier Dirac's power structure—and others—often repaired to escape routine, to meet informally. A number of important people were usually to be found visiting here. So the local authorities' relief that human casualties were light was even stronger than it might otherwise have been. But still . . .

At this point an hour and a half had passed since the last weapon had been fired. The berserker and its helpless catch were still within easy telescopic range, but were receding with ever-increasing speed, accelerating back along what looked like the exact same course on which this enemy had made its approach. The foe was retreating toward the approximate middle of the Mavronari Nebula.

By now, naturally, one of the swiftest couriers available had been dispatched to carry the unhappy news to Premier Dirac himself, who was days away in another system. The

Premier's schedule already called for him to arrive at Imatra within a standard month at most; the local authorities feared that on his arrival, whenever that might be, he was going to hold them personally responsible, not only for the loss of his bride and his inchoate child but also for the general disaster. They feared, at the least, being charged with gross incompetence.

Of course, they all agreed, such charges would be utterly unjust. "How could we possibly have foreseen a berserker attack *here* in the Imatran system, of all places? There hasn't been even a berserker *sighting* for . . ."

No one could immediately say for just how many years. Certainly for a long, long time.

Quickly the worried, frightened local leaders began to review the various recordings of the attack, some of which had been made from the Imatran surface, others from certain artificial satellites above the planetoid. Dirac and his personal staff would want to see those records, to study them intently. This local, first review was conducted with the idea of learning more about the particular berserker—and also in the hope of the authorities' finding something on which to base their own defense in the coming investigation.

Among the events shown clearly in the recordings was the movement of one particular small craft, the ill-fated courier, which had indeed separated itself from the research station and fled for safety in the last few minutes before the berserker struck. There had even been a hasty radio message from the station confirming the departure.

On hearing that message, at the time, people on the ground had felt their hopes soar (or so one of them now claimed), thinking that the Lady Genevieve might well have managed to get aboard that courier, and that she was going to be whisked away out of danger.

But very soon after it had separated from the station, the little vessel had been destroyed; the first crippling blast had been followed within a few minutes by a second, even more violent explosion, as some component of the drive let go. In the interval between detonations Hawksmoor's *Wren* had just managed to reach the vicinity.

"What was the report from the *Wren?*" someone now inquired anxiously.

"No survivors." Someone else cleared his throat.

A general sigh went round the holotable. The possibility of survivors had seemed remote, but naturally an intensive search, for the Lady Genevieve in particular, had been started as soon as possible. That search, by the *Wren* and several other ships now on the scene, still continued, though from the start there had been little hope of finding anyone alive.

More ships were now arriving in the region where the courier had exploded, and many more were on their way, all wanting to help. But so far no survivors had been announced, and at this late hour there was no reason to think that any were going to turn up.

Some member of the conference of local leaders grumbled that records showed that the demolished courier had been short of emergency space suits, and that such armored suits might have offered the passengers real hope of survival. The announcement was greeted with silence. Certainly before the attack no one would have expected such a craft, maneuvering in supposedly peaceful regions, to have carried enough suits for several dozen people.

That there had been other real losses in space would obviously be impossible for the local authorities to deny. Not only the courier but several Solarian fighting ships, complete with crews, had been destroyed.

At least, one participant in the conference noted with faint satisfaction, the enemy had not escaped entirely unscathed: several small spacegoing berserker machines, the equivalent of human scout ships, had been destroyed by ground batteries in the brief fight.

Detracting from this modest achievement of the defense was the fact that the survivors on the planetoid and elsewhere in the system now had no armed ships left. The few such craft available had all been bravely hurled into the fight against the berserker, and in an engagement lasting only a few minutes the monster had efficiently destroyed them all, down to the last unit. The only encouraging aspect of this loss was that not even the Premier, when he arrived, would be able to blame the local authorities for not attempting a pursuit.

One local authority, trying out on his colleagues a statement that he meant to issue later to the outraged public, declaimed: "Though our blood boils with fighting fever, with the determination to be avenged—words to that effect—there's no way we could have given chase to the escaping enemy. No way, I think, that we might have done anything more than we did during the critical minutes of the catastrophe or in its aftermath."

His colleagues were silent, considering. At last one of them offered grimly: "At least our overall casualties were light."

Another stared at the last speaker. "Light? Have you forgotten that the Lady Genevieve is missing, not only missing but almost certainly dead? Do you realize that?"

"I said overall. I meant light in total numbers."

"Hardly light, even in total numbers, if the protopeople are counted in."

"If what? If who?"

"I mean the intended colonists." The speaker looked around, getting in return as many blank stares as understanding nods. "Those on the biostation, who are, or were, the basic reason for its existence. The human zygotes and a few fetuses. All of the living contributions, donations, gathered over a period of years, decades, from the families, the mothers, of a dozen—maybe more than a dozen—worlds."

"I say 'living' is debatable. But how many of these donations, as you call them, intended colonists, were aboard?"

"I don't have the exact number at hand. From what I've heard, somewhere near a billion."

"A what?"

"Ten to the ninth."

The fact, the quantity, took a moment to penetrate. "Then let's see to it that they're not counted, or mentioned in any estimate of casualties."

"One of them is certainly going to be."

"What?"

"Maybe you missed the publicity announcements made just before the tragedy. The Lady Genevieve wasn't here on just a formal tour of inspection." The speaker looked far to his right. "Well, Kensing? What do you say?"

The conference table was, of course, not a single real solid table at all, but a construct of artificial reality put together on holostage by computers and communications systems for the convenience of the local authorities, who were thus enabled to remain comfortably at home or in their offices while sharing in the illusion of mutual confrontation in a single room. At one point along the rim of this composite board sat the youngest in attendance, a man named Sandro Kensing. Kensing had so far remained silent. For one thing, he was distracted by grief. For another, he was not a local authority at all, but only the nephew of one of last year's councilmen—and the fiancé of Dr. Anyuta Zador, who was now among the missing. But the real reason this young man had been invited to the council was the fact that for two years he had been a close personal friend of the only son of Premier Dirac, and had even been a guest in one of the Premier's homes and aboard his yacht. Therefore, or so the local authorities thought, he might be expected to know something of that potentate's psychology.

"Well, Kensing?"

Sandro Kensing raised shaggy sandy eyebrows and looked back. His heavy shoulders were hunched over the table, thick-fingered hands clasped before him. His face was impassive, except for reddened eyes. "Sorry?" He hadn't heard the question.

"I was asking," the speaker repeated considerately, "what you thought Premier Dirac's reaction to this terrible news might be."

"Ah. Yes." None of the local leadership, even going back to include his now-retired uncle, much impressed Kensing. "Well, the old man won't be happy. But you don't need me to tell you that."

There was an uncomfortable silence around the table. Respecting the upstart's grief at the loss of his fiancé, no one spoke sternly to him or even glowered at him for his near-insolent manner. All the authorities realized that they had bigger things to worry about.

"We all have a lot of work to do," the chairman said presently. "But before we adjourn this session, we had better settle the matter of the delegation."

"Delegation?" someone asked.

"I should perhaps say deputation. A deputation to welcome the Premier when he arrives." Looking around, he decided that clarification was in order. "If *none* of us go up to meet him when he shows up in orbit, I wouldn't be at all surprised if he summons us all to attend him on his ship to report to him in person."

The atmosphere around the table had suddenly grown even more unhappy than before.

"I move," said another speaker, "that we appoint a single delegate. A representative to deliver our preliminary report. Since, for the foreseeable future, we are all going to have our hands full with our own jobs."

All around the holotable, heads were swiveling, looking in the same direction. Their delegate had been chosen, unanimously and without debate. Kensing, paying more attention to the meeting now and only mildly surprised, managed a faintly cynical smile at the many faces turned his way.

FOUR

Several hours before he was really expected, the Premier entered the Imatran system at an impressive velocity aboard his large armed yacht, the *Eidolon.* This formidable fighting vessel—some expert observers said it looked more like a light cruiser—was escorted by two smaller craft, both armed but rather nondescript. The three ships were evidently all that Premier Dirac had been able to muster on short notice.

Instead of landing on the almost unscarred surface of the planetoid Imatra, as he doubtless would have done in time of peace and as some people still expected him to do now, Dirac hung his little squadron in a low orbit. From that position of readiness he immediately summoned—in terms conveying authority rather than politeness—the local authorities aboard.

He also called for the full mobilization of local technical resources to help get his squadron into total combat readiness. Some of the equipment on his ships would require various forms of refitting, rearming, or recharging before he was ready to risk a fight.

* * *

Under the circumstances, it was easy to understand the absence of any formal ceremony of welcome. In fact the only individual who obeyed the Premier's summons, boarding a shuttle to ride up and welcome him and his entourage, was the chosen spokesperson Sandro Kensing. The young man, vaguely uneasy though not really frightened about the kind of reception he could expect, stepped from the docked shuttle into the main airlock of the yacht carrying in his pocket a holostage recording created by the local council. The recording was an earnest compilation of convincing reasons why the members' currently overwhelming press of duties rendered their personal attendance utterly impossible. It empowered Kensing to represent them—all of them—in this meeting with the Premier.

Obviously the whole lot of them were really frightened of the old man, a few on an actual physical level. Perhaps, thought Kensing, some of them had good reason to be. He himself wasn't personally afraid. Even had his feelings not still been dominated by grief, he would not have been terrified of Mike's father, whom he had met half a dozen times when he and Mike were attending school together, and in whose house he had been a guest. Actually the relationship had led to a job related to the colonization project, and thus to Kensing's meeting Annie.

Just inside the *Eidolon*'s armored airlock, Kensing was met by a powerfully built, graying man of indeterminate age, dressed in coveralls that offered no indication of the wearer's status or function. Kensing recognized one of the Premier's chief security people, a familiar presence in the Sardou mansion Kensing had visited, and on its grounds.

"Hello, Brabant."

The bodyguard, as usual informally polite to friends of his employer, identified the young visitor on sight, though several years had passed since their last encounter. "Hey, Mr. Kensing. Have a seat, the boss is expecting you. He'll be free in a minute."

Beyond the bodyguard the interior of the ship, somewhat remodeled and redecorated since Kensing had seen it last, looked like a powerful executive's office planetside.

"I'll stand up for a while, thanks. Been sitting a lot lately."

Brabant looked at him sympathetically. "Hey, tough about Dr. Zador. Really tough."

"Thanks."

"You and the boss got something in common. Unfortunately."

In the rush of his own feelings Kensing had almost forgotten about the presumed loss of the Premier's new bride. But it was true; he and the Premier now had something very basic in common.

"Where's Mike?" he asked the bodyguard suddenly.

The man appeared to be trying to remember, then shrugged. "He wasn't getting on with his father a few months back, so he took a trip. Long before all this came up."

"Anyplace in particular?"

"The family don't tell me all their plans."

"I just thought I might find him on board. His father's going to have need of good pilots."

"Hey, good pilots the boss's got, this time around. Better pilots than Mike."

Kensing raised an eyebrow. "Not many of those available."

"One in particular who's on board right now is very good indeed." Brabant, with the air of keeping a pleasant bit of information in reserve, looked up and down the corridor. "Maybe you'll meet him."

"Yeah? You're telling me this is someone special?"

"You might say so. His name's Frank Marcus. Colonel. That was the last rank I heard he had. Retired."

For a moment at least Kensing was distracted from his personal problems. "Marcus? You mean *the—*"

"That's right. The famous man in boxes. They tell me he was driving the yacht just a little while ago when we dropped into orbit here."

"Gods of flightspace. I guess I assumed Colonel Frank Marcus was dead, decades ago."

"Don't tell him that, kid. Excuse me, I mean I wouldn't advise that as diplomatic, Mr. Official Deputy from Imatra." And the bodyguard laughed.

Kensing was shaking his head. By now Colonel Marcus would have to be an old man by any standard, because for more than a century he had been something of an interstellar legend. As Kensing remembered the story, Marcus had at some time in his youth lost most of his organic body in an accident—or had it been in a berserker fight?—and ever since had been confined to his boxes by physical disability, a situation he apparently viewed as only an interesting challenge.

"Hey, you know what I hear, Mr. Kensing?" Brabant had lowered his voice slightly.

"What?"

The gist of the story, as passed along now in clinical detail by the admiring bodyguard, was that Frank Marcus was still perfectly capable of enjoying female companionship and of physically expressing his appreciation in the fullest way.

"Glad to hear it. So how does he come to be working for the Premier?"

Kensing's informant went on to explain that Marcus, ranked as one of the supreme space pilots in Solarian history, had signed on a couple of months ago as an advanced flight instructor, after first having turned down the offer of a permanent job as Dirac's personal pilot.

Conversation had just turned to another subject when it broke off suddenly. Something—no, someone, it must be the colonel himself!—was rolling toward them down the corridor, coming from the direction of the bridge.

Had Kensing not been alerted to the colonel's presence aboard, he might have assumed this was some kind of serving robot approaching. He beheld three connected metallic boxes, none of them more than knee-high, their size in aggregate no more than that of an adult human body. The boxes rolled along one after the other, their wheels appearing to be of polyphase matter, not spinning so much as undergoing continuous smooth deformity.

From the foremost box came a voice, a mechanically generated but very human sound, tone jaunty, just this side of arrogant. "Hi, Brabant. Thought I'd see the chief when he's not busy. Who's this?"

Kensing, wondering what might happen if he were to put

out a hand in formal greeting, gazed into a set of lenses and introduced himself. "Colonel Marcus? Glad to meet you. I'm Sandro Kensing, a friend of Mike's—the Premier's son."

"Yeah, I've heard about Mike. Haven't had the chance to meet him."

"What's the Premier's plan?" Kensing badly wanted to know, and he felt it rarely hurt to ask.

"That's no secret," the box assured him. "We're going after the bad machine."

That was what Kensing had been hoping to hear. Something inside him, somewhere around his heart, gave a lurch at the possibility—no matter how faint—of catching up with the ongoing disaster that had carried Annie off. Of finding out at first hand what had happened. Of coming to grips in violence with the monstrous inanimate *things* that had done this to her and to him.

And here right in front of Kensing was the person of all people who might make the possibility real. Frank Marcus, who at one time or another had retired, it seemed, from just about every armed force in the Solarian Galaxy except the Templars; Colonel Marcus, who as it turned out was now piloting Dirac's yacht.

Kensing said bluntly, "Colonel, if anyone's going after that berserker, I'm going along."

"Yeah?" The talking boxes sounded interested but not entirely convinced.

"Dr. Zador and I were going to be married in a month. More to the point, I'm an engineer who's trained and working in defensive systems. I've been doing the preliminaries for the projected colonial vessels."

"Combat experience?"

"No."

"That may not matter too much. Most of our crew doesn't have any either. If you're a qualified defense systems engineer, maybe the chief'll want to fit you in."

Moments later Brabant, having evidently received some invisible communication from the Premier, was ushering Kensing into the inner office.

Setting foot in the inner rooms of the Premier's suite for

the first time in several years, Kensing again noted that certain remodeling and redecoration had taken place since his last visit. As if the ship were becoming less a ship and more a place of business.

In the center of the innermost room was a large desk, a real desk constructed basically of wood, though its upper surface was inhabited by a number of electronic displays. The desk held several stacks of real paper also, and behind them sat a real man. The Premier was not physically large. He had changed, in subtle ways that Kensing would have been hard put to define, in the two years since the two of them had last come face to face.

Dirac's hair was steely gray; thick and naturally curled, it lay trimmed close round his large skull. Sunken gray eyes peered out from under heavy brows, like outlaws preparing to sally from a cave. Skin and muscles were firm and youthful in appearance, belying the impression of age suggested by the gray hair. His hands toyed with a fine-bladed knife, which Kensing recognized as an antique letter opener. Dirac's voice, an eloquent actor's bass, was milder than it sounded on public holostage.

As Kensing entered the cabin, the Premier was in conversation with the image of a rather handsome and much younger man, who appeared on the largest of the room's three holostages, the one beside the desk. The younger man, who wore pilot's insignia on his collar, was saying; "—my deepest sympathy, sir."

"Thank you, Nick." The presumably bereaved husband gave, as he often did, the impression of being firmly in control though inwardly stressed. He looked up and nodded at Kensing, whose escort, withdrawing, had already closed the door behind him.

Kensing began: "Premier Dirac, I don't know if you—"

"Yes, of course I remember you, Kensing. Friend of my son's, he called you Sandy. Mike always thought highly of you. So you're delegated to explain this mess to me."

"Yes, sir."

"Fill me in on the details later. And you're in on the colonizing project—and you're also Dr. Zador's fiancé. Very sorry about her. A terrible business we've got here."

"Yes, sir. My sympathy to you. Mine and everyone's on Imatra."

Dirac acknowledged the condolence with a brusque nod. "Mike's not with me this time," he remarked.

"Someone told me he's off on a long trip, sir."

"Yes. Very long." The Premier indicated the 'stage. "I don't suppose you've met Nick here, have you? Nicholas Hawksmoor, architect and pilot. Works for me."

"We haven't met yet, sir."

Dirac proceeded with a swift introduction. Was there just the faintest momentary twinkle of some private amusement in the old man's eye?

The formality concluded, the Premier once more faced the imaged head and shoulders of Nicholas Hawksmoor. "Proceed."

Nick reported quietly: "There was nothing I could do, sir. I was . . . almost . . . in time to get myself aboard the courier before that last explosion. But not quite in time. I couldn't be of any help to anyone aboard."

"Had you any direct evidence that my wife was among the passengers?"

"I couldn't even confirm that. I'm sorry."

"Not your fault, Nick."

"No, sir. Thank you for understanding that, sir." A brief hesitation. "There's another matter I suppose I should mention."

"What's that?"

"Shortly after the alert was sounded, I was given a direct order by Acting Supervisor Zador on the biostation. She commanded me to take my ship out and ram the enemy."

This statement was made so casually that Kensing, who thought he was paying close attention, wondered if he had heard right, or if he had earlier missed something. He understood that as soon as the alert was called, Annie as acting supervisor would have automatically become local defense commander. A wildly inappropriate function for her, but . . .

Dirac nodded, accepting the information about the ramming order with surprising placidity. "So what happened next?"

"Well, sir, Dr. Zador wasn't—isn't—a combat officer, but she must have thought she'd come up with a good plan to at least distract the berserker. Obviously it wouldn't have worked. I couldn't have got the *Wren* within a thousand kilometers of a monster like that before it vaporized me without breaking stride.

"So when the acting supervisor gave me that order, rather than argue and distract her further from her own real job—at which I am sure she's more than competent—I just acknowledged the command and then ignored it. The only really useful thing I could do with my ship at that point was to stay close to the courier and try to look out for those on board.

"If the berserker had sent one of its own small spacegoers after the courier, or a boarding machine, I would probably have tried ramming *that.* Or tried to get the machine to come after me instead. But of course, as the scene actually played out . . ." Nick looked distressed.

Dirac said gently: "It's all right."

"Thank you, sir."

"But—"

"Yes, sir?"

The shadowed eyes, with a danger in them that Kensing had never seen there before, looked up from under the steel brows. "From what you tell me, we don't really *know* that the Lady Genevieve ever actually boarded that courier at all. Do we?"

Nick's holostage image appeared to ruminate. "No, I don't suppose we do."

Dirac nodded slowly. He glanced at Kensing. "In fact, what I've heard of the recorded radio traffic indicates that Dr. Zador had some concern about the courier leaving prematurely. She feared the pilot might pull out before everyone who wanted to get aboard had done so."

"That's correct."

Premier Dirac now turned his full attention back to the visitor who was physically present in his cabin. "Kensing, have you people on Imatra any further information on that point?"

"I don't know anything about it, Premier. I'll certainly check up on it as quickly as I can."

"Do that, please. I want any information bearing on the question of the Lady Genevieve's presence on that courier."

"I'll get it for you, whatever we have."

"Good." Dirac knitted steely brows. "So far no one has shown me any firm evidence one way or the other. So I have to believe there's a good chance she was still on the station when it was so strangely—kidnapped."

Kensing didn't say anything.

Dirac was not ready to leave the point. "We do know that *some* people were still aboard the station, right? Supervisor Zador, for one. And didn't she say something to the courier pilot to the effect that others were intending to stay?"

Nicholas Hawksmoor put in: "At least one other, sir. The bioengineer Daniel Hoveler apparently remained with Dr. Zador. That seems to be the only definite evidence we have on the presence or absence of any particular individuals."

Dirac nodded, displaying a certain grim satisfaction. "So at this moment, as we speak, there are still living people on the station." He met the others' eyes, one after the other, as if challenging anyone to dispute the point.

Kensing was more than ready to hope that Annie still had a chance at life; it was almost but not quite unheard of for a berserker's prisoners to be rescued. But Nick was willing to dispute his employer's assumption. "We don't *know* that, sir."

Dirac gave the speaker his steely glare. "We don't *know* the people aboard the station have been killed. Correct?"

There was a brief pause in which Nick seemed to yield. "Yes, sir. Correct."

The Premier smiled faintly. "To be on the safe side, then, we must assume that there are living people. And my wife may well be among them."

"That's correct, sir. For all we know, she may."

"That's all for now." And Dirac's hands moved over the surface of the table in front of him, dismissing Hawksmoor, whose image vanished abruptly, calling up other images on his private stage.

He said: "Kensing, I'm going to order the search for survivors of the courier abandoned. Any functioning space suit in the vicinity would be putting out an automated distress signal, and nothing like that is being received."

Kensing didn't know what to say, but it seemed he wasn't required to say anything at this point.

Dirac continued: "But I am going to keep a number of my pilots busy, Nick among them, combing through all the space debris that resulted from the combat, the berserker stuff along with ours. We may be able to glean a lot of information from that."

"Yes, sir, I expect so." The room was replete with wall displays, in addition to those on Dirac's desk. From where Kensing stood, he could read most of the wall information fairly well. Obviously surface and satellite telescopes were still locked onto the retreating enemy and its prize. He was tormented by the idea that somewhere inside that distorted little dot, Annie might be still alive.

Dirac followed his gaze. "Look at that. As far as anyone in-system here can tell by telescope, the bioresearch station has suffered no serious physical damage. My ships will soon be refitted—I don't see why it should take more than a few hours—and as soon as they're ready, we're going after it."

"I'm coming with you, sir."

"Naturally, I expected you'd say that. With your experience in defense systems you'll be useful. Welcome aboard. See Varvara when you go out; she'll sign you up officially."

"Thank you, sir."

The Premier nodded. "She's not dead, I tell you." Obviously he meant his own young bride. Looking quietly into some holostage presentation of nearby space, he added: "I am sure that I would know if she were dead. Meanwhile, I want to gather every possible bit of information about the attacker."

Berserker debris, Kensing knew, was often valuable to military intelligence because it allowed types of enemy equipment to be distinguished. He nodded. They were going to need every gram of advantage they could get.

Leaving the conference, Kensing once more encountered Colonel Marcus and the bodyguard Brabant. They were talking in the corridor with a woman Kensing had not met before, who introduced herself to him as Varvara Engadin.

Engadin was somewhere near the Premier's age, probably around fifty, but still slender and impressively beautiful, and her name was familiar. She had been the Premier's intimate companion—as well as his political adviser, according to the stories—when Kensing had first met the family. At that time Mike's mother was already several years dead.

"Ms. Engadin, I'm supposed to see you about signing on the crew."

"Sandy." She put both hands out to him in sympathy. "I've been hearing about your loss."

Conversation focused briefly on the tragedy. Though everyone spoke in polite and diplomatic terms, plainly all agreed that Dirac was determined not to accept the overwhelming probability that his bride was dead, and he fully intended to get her back. To have his way, to impose his will, as usual, even when his adversary was a berserker.

Kensing, his own feelings torn, commented that everyone really knew the odds were pretty heavily against that. This psychic pretense was not at all the Premier's usual mode of behavior.

"Know him pretty well?" the colonel asked. He had a way of swiveling a lens on his front box to make it plain who he was speaking to.

"I'm a friend of his son's—a close friend for a time, but I haven't seen Mike for a couple of years. And I've stayed with them in one of the official mansions. How about you?"

"Don't really know them. Been working for the Premier only a couple of months now. I was just in the process of turning down a chief pilot's job when this came up. Now it looks like I'm in for the duration." Marcus did not seem at all displeased by the prospect of going to war again. Somehow the metal boxes and the voice coming out of them impressed Kensing as capable of expressing shades of feeling. Somehow the colonel's boxes could give the impression of swaggering as they rolled.

"What do you think has happened to his wife? Really?" Kensing felt compelled to dig for expert opinion regarding the fate of those aboard the station.

"He could be right. She might not have boarded that courier at all."

"And what do you think . . ." He couldn't make himself state the question plainly.

"Hell, I don't know. There's always a fighting chance. But no use anyone getting his hopes too high."

His official enrollment completed, pacing down a corridor toward his newly assigned quarters with Marcus rolling at his side, Kensing listened to more of the colonel's opinions. Frank Marcus commented that two bizarre points about the recent raid set it apart from almost any other military action that he was able to remember.

"First point: regardless of what this berserker did out here, in the vicinity of this planetoid, it made no effort to get at the inner planets of the system. Didn't even send scouts sunward to look them over, or to raid the space traffic going on that way. There's quite a bit of space traffic, almost all of it unarmed ships."

"The inner worlds are heavily defended," Kensing offered.

Marcus dismissed that with the wave of a metallic arm, a tentacle-like appendage of inhuman but obviously practical shape. "In my experience, when a berserker as big and mean as this one—hell, any berserker—sees it has at least a fighting chance to take out a couple of billion people, it's not likely to pass up the opportunity."

"So why did it take the biolab? Not destroy it, but actually grab it and carry it away?"

"I don't know yet. But I do know something that strikes me as even more peculiar. Our tricky berserker didn't even make a serious attempt to depopulate *this* planetoid. And it was right here. And the defenses on Planetoid Imatra are—were—a hell of a lot lighter than those on the sunward planets. It took out the defenses that were shooting at it, and that was that."

Kensing, whose job had long required of him serious—up to now purely theoretical—study of berserkers' tactics, had already been trying to make sense of it. "So, that means what? A monster machine that doesn't want to kill people? Indicating that in some crazy way it's not really a berserker?"

"I wouldn't want to tell that to the guys who were manning the ground defenses, or to the people who tried to fight it in space. No, it's ready enough to kill. But it had some bigger goal than simply attacking this system. It wouldn't deviate from its plan, even for the chance to take out a couple of billion human lives. Of life units, as the berserkers say. Wouldn't even delay to polish off a million or so near at hand."

"All right. Was that your second point?"

"No. Actually the second peculiarity I had in mind was that even now, days after the attack, the damned raider is still in sight. Either it can't go superluminal while it's towing something as big as that lab, or it doesn't want to risk the attempt. And if it hasn't tried to go c-plus by now, it's not going to. Because now it's close enough to the Mavronari to start getting into the thick dust."

Kensing paused in the corridor to take another look for himself, calling up the picture on one of the yacht's numerous displays. True, the berserker was currently observable only with some difficulty, but there it was. Still fleeing in slowship mode, though with a steady buildup of velocity in normal space, so that the tiny wavering images of the raider and its captive prey, as seen from the vicinity of the Imatran planetoid, were measurably redshifting.

Not greatly, though. "A long way to go to light speed."

"Right. It hasn't been humping its tail hard enough to get near that. C-plus wouldn't be a practical procedure, as I say, for an object moving in that direction—into the dust." In fact, as Kensing discovered when he queried the terminal, the very latest indications were that the berserker's acceleration appeared to be easing off somewhat, and computer projections were that the burdened machine might actually have to diminish its velocity in the next few hours or days as it penetrated ever more deeply the outlying fringes of the nebula.

Within the next few hours, a war council composed largely of key members of the Premier's staff went into session aboard the *Eidolon.* Kensing, as the official representative of Imatra, was in attendance. Kensing's Imatran compatriots continued to maintain a wary distance.

Kensing had remained aboard the yacht, sending down to his apartment on the surface for extra clothing and some personal gear. It now seemed unlikely that he would leave the *Eidolon* for any reason before the squadron's departure, the projected time of which was only hours away.

The war council's current session on the yacht heard speculation from some of its members that the berserker might have sustained serious damage in the recent fighting, enough to keep it from going c-plus. Therefore it had turned toward the nebula as its best chance of getting away before a human fleet could be assembled to hunt it down.

An officer objected: "That doesn't answer the question of why it chose to withdraw instead of attacking, killing."

"It may have been heavily damaged."

"Bah. So what? This's a *berserker* we're talking about. It cares nothing for its own survival, except that it must destroy the maximum number of lives before it goes. And obviously it was still capable of fighting."

"If we just knew why it decided that an intact bioresearch station, perhaps only this one in particular, would be such an enormously valuable thing to have."

Varvara Engadin spoke up. "The answer to that question ought to be staring us in the face. In fact I think it is. We're talking about a vessel that has a billion Solarian human zygotes stored aboard."

"Yes. If not active life, certainly potential. A billion potentially active Solarian humans. One would expect a berserker to use up its last erg of energy, sacrifice its last gram of matter, to *destroy* such a cargo. But why in the Galaxy should it want to carry it away?"

Kensing, trying to imagine why, found ominous, half-formed suggestions drifting across the back of his mind.

Someone else argued that whether the enemy had entirely lost superluminal capability or not, the compound object formed by the berserker and its captured station was more than a little clumsy for serious spacefaring. It would certainly be considerably harder to maneuver in any kind of space than the speedy vehicles at the Premier's command.

Computer projections, now being continuously run,

showed that even when the delay for refitting the Premier's ships was factored in, his squadron was going to have a good chance of catching up.

Frank Marcus, the frontal surface of his head box slightly elevated to present an interestingly complex gray contour above one end of the conference table, expressed his opinion—even as the subject of his remarks sat listening imperturbably—that Dirac, whose notable accomplishments had not so far extended into the military field, did not appear to be entirely crazy for having decided to give chase.

Someone else formally, not too wisely, put the question to Dirac. "Is that still our plan, sir?"

Dirac's steely eyes looked up across the table—looking through the boundaries of virtual reality, because for this session the Premier had remained physically in his own suite. "What kind of a question is that? We're going after them, of course." Dirac blinked, continuing to stare at the questioner; it was as if he could not understand how any other course of action could be considered. "Whatever plan that damned thing is trying to carry out, we're not going to allow it to succeed."

Someone asked what local help was going to be available.

At that, eyes turned to Kensing. He, trying to sound properly apologetic, repeated on behalf of himself and his determinedly ground-bound local colleagues their regretful assurances that they had not a single armed vessel left in-system, nothing with the capability of playing a useful role in such a pursuit.

"I understand that," Dirac reassured him.

On that note the conference adjourned temporarily. More hours passed, ticking toward the deadline. The refitting of the *Eidolon* and its escort ships neared completion, and they were very nearly ready for the pursuit they were about to undertake.

Meanwhile the enemy, whose actions were still distinctly observable from the ships in orbit around Imatra, continued on a steady course toward the approximate center of the Mavronari Nebula. Inside this mass of gas and fine dust, the ambient density of matter was known to be high enough to make c-plus flight in general so perilous as to be practically impossible. Therefore observation of the berserker from the Imatran system ought to remain possible for several more days at least.

The retreating berserker, someone commented, was continuing to retrace exactly, or nearly so, the very course on which it had been first detected when inbound toward Imatra. If that fact had any particular significance, no one could guess what it might be.

The fact that the enemy had captured the station whole, and therefore appeared to be operating under some deliberate plan of taking prisoners—perhaps growing massive numbers of goodlife, or using human cells to produce some other biological weapon—loomed ever larger in the worried planners' thoughts. That a berserker had chosen abduction over mass destruction seemed to many people especially ominous.

Despite the scoffing of Colonel Marcus, the peculiarities of the situation were such that Kensing, like several of his colleagues in the war council, could not entirely rid himself of the suspicion that their swiftly retiring foe might not be a genuine berserker at all. In the past, certain human villains had been known to disguise ships as berserkers to accomplish their own evil purposes of murder and robbery.

But when he broached the idea to other experts on Dirac's staff, they were unanimously quick to put it down. In this case, all the material evidence worked against any such conclusion. By now a considerable amount of the smashed debris from small enemy machines had ben gathered out of space—some of it by Nicholas Hawksmoor, much more by others—and painstakingly examined.

Concurrently some large pieces of this wreckage, at least one chunk meters across, had rained down intact upon the planetoid, whose shallow, artificially maintained atmosphere tended to guide the occasional meteorite down to the surface without burning it up. To all the available experts on the subject—some of them inhuman expert systems—this wreckage looked and felt and tested out in every way like real berserker metal, shaped and assembled by berserker construction methods.

* * *

The master computers on Dirac's yacht, state-of-the-art machines in every way, assured the planners that they still had time to overtake their foe, but that there was no time to waste; every passing hour brought the enemy closer to the shelter of the deep nebula. Dirac intended leaving very quickly, as soon as his ships were charged and ready. As far as Kensing could tell, Dirac's crew, some thirty people in all, was solidly with him. No doubt they were all volunteers, hand-picked for dependability and loyalty.

As it happened, one other person who had not volunteered, at least not for a berserker chase, was now on board. Kensing discovered this for himself in the course of a routine inventory of equipment. One of the yacht's medirobot berths was occupied, the glassy lid closed on the coffin-like chamber and frosted on the inside. The berth was tuned for long-term suspended animation maintenance of the unseen person in it.

Generally in favor of a hands-on approach whenever possible, Kensing went to take a look at the medirobot for himself. It stood in an out-of-the-way corridor on the big ship.

Varvara Engadin shed some light on the situation. This occupant of the deep-freeze chamber was a volunteer for the first projected colony to be established by the Sardou Foundation. Some individual so devoted to the plan, so determined to take part in the great colonial adventure, that he or she had requested suspended animation for whatever period might be necessary until the heroic mission should be ready to begin.

Across the portion of the Galaxy settled by Solarians, a number of methods had been tried to deal with the problem of overpopulation. Effective means to prevent conception were widely used, but still by no means universal. On worlds whose aggregate population ran into the hundreds of billions, millions of unwanted pregnancies occurred each year. Removal of a zygote or an early fetus from the mother's body was routine, but in this day and age the overt destruction of such organisms was unacceptable. Rather, some long-term storage was indicated, but storage indefinitely prolonged was also a denial of life.

The course favored by most of the Premier's political supporters had been to announce a mass colonization effort—and actually to begin the preparations for such an effort, with a launch date scheduled for some time securely and vaguely in the future. Surely people still had the spirit to go out and establish colonies.

A variation on this was a plan—actually several plans—to hide away secret reserves of humanity against the time when the berserkers might manage to depopulate all settled planets. Those in favor of such a scheme contemplated searching for a reasonably Earthlike planet, hidden, heretofore unknown. Theorists advocated prowling the Galaxy in search of such a world or worlds. When the goal was found, they would expunge it from all records so that the berserkers would never learn of its existence through captured material.

Engadin explained that in the Sardou Foundation's colonization plan, as finally negotiated among the heavily settled worlds within the Premier's sphere of influence, complicated protocols had been worked out to decide everything. For example, chance selection would determine which protopeople should be first into the artificial wombs when the colonizing ship or ships had reached a suitable new planet or planets.

Listening, Kensing wasn't sure the scheme really did more than to provide the machine designers, the colony engineers, and the population planners with work and something to talk about. It offered Solarian society a kind of evidence that what they were doing had meaning, wasn't just a way to delay indefinitely a decision on the question of what to do with all these life-suspended zygotes and fetuses.

The promise of working out some such theoretical system of colonization—or even the methodical contemplation of its difficulties—had allowed people on a number of worlds to feel satisfied that the problem was not simply being shelved.

How many artificial wombs were there going to be on one of the colonizing ships? That was still undecided. On the bioresearch station there were more than a hundred. Of course a properly designed facility of this type ought to be able to build at least a few more such devices when they were needed.

And of course the research station, precursor of the actual colonizing ships, had been equipped with life-support facilities capable of supporting at least twenty or thirty active people—technicians, caretakers, researchers—over a long period of time. Food, water, and air were all to be recycled efficiently. Already several times that number of scientists and others had occasionally lived and worked aboard.

Naturally there had been a concomitant attempt to enlist volunteer houseparents to accompany the multitude of zygotes. In fact Annie had once confessed to Kensing that she had thought about devoting her life to that task before she decided to get married and stay home instead.

The frozen volunteer currently aboard the yacht was male, Kensing was informed by the local caretaker system when he reached the row of emergency medical units in the remote auxiliary corridor. Only one was occupied. Name, Fowler Aristov. Age at time of immersion in the long-term storage mode, twenty. A whole catalogue of other personal characteristics and history followed, to which Kensing paid little attention.

Kensing was impressed, not altogether favorably, by such dedication to a cause. Fanaticism was almost certainly a better word, he thought. Of course subjectively, a long freeze would be practically indistinguishable from a short one. Volunteer for the cause, step into the SA unit, and go to sleep. Wake up again immediately—in subjective terms—take an hour or so to regain full physical and mental function, and get to work on your chosen job.

In the end he made no recommendation against leaving the would-be colonist's suspended animation chamber occupied. There were five other medirobot berths on board, and great numbers of wounded were not a common result of battles in space. Anyway, the volunteer had evidently been willing to write fate a blank check regarding his own future.

What had been a tentative departure time for the avenging squadron was now finalized, set within the hour.

FIVE

Jenny kiss'd me when we met,
Jumping from the chair she sat in;
Time, you thief, who love to get
Sweets into your list, put that in:
Say I'm weary, say I'm sad,
Say that health and wealth have miss'd me,
Say I'm growing old, but add . . .

The song trailed off into silence. The performer's long pale fingers rested motionless on the stringed instrument of unique design he held before him. His whole body, standing erect, was very still, and something in his expression suggested to his audience that he had been prevented from singing the next line by a surge of some intense emotion.

That audience consisted of one person only, the Lady Genevieve.

The young woman's Indonesian features complemented her small and slender frame. All in all, she was a creature of impressive and delicate beauty. Her slight form, garbed in sparkling white, almost as for some old-time wedding ritual, was posed, half reclining, upon a gray stone bench apparently of considerable age, as were the surrounding cloister walls. Carvings in the bench, representing fantastic animals, had been softened by weather into obscurity, decorated with a little lichen. Before the lady came to occupy this seat, someone had thoughtfully provided it with a profusion of soft cushions, blue and red and yellow in shades that almost matched those of the nearby flowers.

"You sing beautifully," she encouraged her companion. Her voice was naturally small, but she was no longer aware of any difficulty in finding air to speak with.

"Thank you, my lady." The one who had assumed the role of minstrel relaxed a little in the golden sunshine and turned more fully toward his listener. He doffed his plumed hat with a sweeping gesture, flourished the headgear for an extra moment as if he did not quite know what to do with it next, then tossed it into oblivion behind a fragrant bed of dazzling flowers. Those flowers were remarkable, a knee-high embankment of vivid, almost blinding colors, running along one side of the broad grassy garth enclosed by the cloister's square of ancient, pale gray stonework. What world might lie outside these elder walls was more than the lady could have said; but whatever it was, it seemed to her comfortably remote.

A faint breeze stirred the lace on Lady Genevieve's white dress. A hundred questions came thronging through her mind, and some of them were threatening indeed.

The query she chose to begin with seemed trivial, but relatively safe: "Was that song your own creation?"

Her minstrel nodded, then hesitated. "The music is my own, and I would like to claim the words as well. But I am compelled to acknowledge that a man named Leigh Hunt composed them. Many and many a hundred years ago he lived, and of course the lady he had in mind was another who shared your name. Perhaps you remember my once telling you that you reminded me of—"

"Where are we now?" the young woman interrupted with unconscious rudeness. This was the first meaningful question she had asked of her companion. She was beginning her serious inquiries calmly enough, though the more she thought about her situation, the more totally inexplicable it seemed.

The minstrel's speaking voice was slightly hoarse and rather deeper than the tones in which he had been singing. "We are now in the city of London on old Earth, my lady Genevieve. Inside the precincts of a famous temple, or house of worship. The name of this temple is Westminster Abbey."

"Oh? But I have no memory of ever . . . arriving here."

"Natural enough under the circumstances. That's nothing to worry about; I can explain all that in good time. You do remember me, though?" Anxiety was perceptible beneath the singer's calm. Leaning his peculiar stringed instrument against the bench, he squatted almost kneeling before the lady and put his right hand out toward her. The movement was somewhat awkward, so that it almost fell upon her lap; but at the end of the gesture the long fingers had come down instead upon a cushion.

He added: "Nicholas Hawksmoor, at your service."

Seen in this environment, Nick was a middle-sized fellow, of mature though far from elderly appearance. A little taller than the average, not as portly as he had looked when Genevieve first saw him on the holostage. His chestnut hair was lustrous and a little curly, though beginning to thin on top. He had a small pointed beard of the same hue and a matching mustache, the latter also a little thinner than a man might wish. But of course one of the things he most feared, really, was to be thought a mere dandy, or merely handsome, all image and no substance. To avoid that, Hawksmoor would and did go to great lengths. He had and would put up with worse things than thinning hair.

Beneath the thinning hair, his face was unremarkable, somehow not as handsome as the lady remembered it from their earlier encounters. His nose (appropriately for his name, the lady thought) was just a little hawkish, eyes a trifle watery and of an unimpressive color, somewhere between gray and brown. Today the self-described architect and pilot was garbed in vaguely medieval-looking clothing, his long legs encased in what were almost tights, his upper body in a short jacket. The fabrics appeared solid and substantial, no more dazzling than his eyes. The contrast with the lady's bright white dress was notable.

"I remember your name, of course," Lady Genevieve responded. "And your face, too. Though you seem to look—a little different now. I think I have seen you only twice before, and neither of those meetings was really face-to-face. The first time I saw only your image upon a holostage. And the second time—then you were wearing a space suit and helmet, and I couldn't really see your face at all. We were on a ship, and when I tried to look inside your helmet . . ."

Nicholas did not actually see the lady's face turn pale with the impact of a newly examined memory, but he had the feeling that it might have done so.

Hastily he interrupted. "We were indeed on a ship. But now we are both *here,* my lady Genevieve. Here in this pleasant place. It *is* pleasant, is it not? And you are safe. As safe as I can make you. And I have—considerable capabilities."

Pallor receded. Lady Genevieve appeared to accept her companion's assurance of safety at face value, but her need for answers was not so easily met. Giving a small shake of her head, as if to allay uncertainty, she raised one well-kept hand in a questioning gesture, pointing in the general direction of two great rectangular stone towers that loomed in the middle distance, above and beyond the cloister walls. These twin structures were scores of meters tall, their monumental forms gray-brown in hazy slanting sunlight. Each tower was crowned at its four upper corners by four small steeples; and the nearer tower loomed so large, perhaps only twoscore meters away, that it almost seemed to hang right over the cloistered garden. At the moment a sea gull, giving tiny cries, came gliding on rigid wings between that mass of masonry and the two people in the garth.

Her companion followed her gesture with his eyes. "Those towers form the west front of the Abbey, Lady Genevieve, and the main entrance lies between them. I designed them, and supervised their construction . . . well, to be strictly truthful, and I want always to be strictly truthful with you, he who was my namesake did. He lived even before the man who wrote the words to the song. But I think I may say, honestly and objectively, I could have done as well or better, working with real stone and mortar. Do you remember my once telling you, I am an architect?"

"Yes, I do. In fact I believe I can remember perfectly every word that you have ever said to me." Rising gracefully to her feet, the lady drew in a full breath, lifting her small bosom. "But I have the feeling there is more, much more, that I *ought* to remember. About quite recent events, I mean. Events of great importance. And that if I made a real effort to think about what has been happening to me, the answers would all be there. But . . ."

"But you hesitate to make that effort?"

"Yes!" She paused, and added in a whisper: "Because I am afraid!"

The man rose lithely from his awkward squatting pose so that he towered timidly above her. He said: "If you find these matters disturbing, there is no hurry. No need for you to concern yourself about them now. Please, allow me to do whatever worrying may be necessary, for the time being at least. I will consider it a privilege—how much of a privilege you cannot know—to be your protector. In all things."

"Then, Nicholas, I will be honored indeed to enjoy your protection. Thank you very much." Genevieve extended one small, graceful hand, and stepping forward, the man reached to take it gratefully.

And at the moment when their fingers touched, the lady knew no more.

In their trio of spacecraft, the *Eidolon* was by a considerable margin the largest, the fastest, and the best armed. Orbiting low above the planetoid Imatra, Premier Dirac and his human entourage of space crew and advisers, bodyguards and other specialists, along with Sandy Kensing, were hastily completing their preparations for an early departure.

One of Dirac's ships, which had landed briefly on the Imatran surface for refitting, now hastily lifted off, to rendezvous with the *Eidolon* and the companion vessel which had remained in low orbit. Minutes later, without ceremony, the whole small but heavily armed squadron was easing away from the planetoid under smooth acceleration, heading outward from its sun in the direction of the center of the

Mavronari, whose denser portions were light-years distant but whose outer fringes reached to within a few days' travel from Imatra at subliminal speeds. At a steadily quickening pace, Dirac's force moved antisunward, seeking the deepest emptiness obtainable in this region, some relatively smooth gravitational plain, ready to safely tolerate three ships' abrupt departure from normal space.

That ideal was unattainable. Some risk of relatively dirty space would have to be accepted; the enemy had too great a start to be overtaken now by mere subliminal flight at the speeds here possible.

Directly ahead of the small squadron, and still dimly perceptible to its telescopes by days-old light, the kidnapped bioresearch station receded steadily, at this distance making one compound image with the huge, enigmatic machine that had snatched it out of orbit.

The Lady Genevieve found herself once more with her new companion, this time strolling with her hand upon his arm. How she had come to be in this condition she did not know, but here she was. They were walking in the same grassy garth where they had last met and he had played the minstrel. The hazy, golden sun did not appear to have moved very far since the time—a very recent time, she thought—when she had been sitting on the bench. But there had been an interval of—something? or perhaps nothing?—between then and now.

Certainly the appearance of Nicholas Hawksmoor had altered in the interval. His clothing was now richer, no longer a minstrel's garb, but still far removed from a pilot's uniform. Looking up at him sideways, the lady wondered if his hair had grown thicker, too.

Now she could touch his arm without bringing on an attack of oblivion. She was touching it, and nothing happened. But the feel of Hawksmoor's sleeved forearm and of his sleeve beneath her fingertips had something odd about it. Strange too, when she thought about it, was the feeling of the grass beneath her white-slippered feet; strange the touch of clothing on her body, the air moving over her face . . .

The tall man beside her coaxed invitingly: "What are you thinking about?"

She almost whispered, "I am still wondering—about many things. I still have many questions I am afraid to ask."

He paused in his walking, the walk in which he had been leading her almost as in a dance, and she saw they had come to a stop before a doorway. It was a kind of gate leading into the gray dim cloister. He asked with muted eagerness: "Shall we go inside? I'd like to show you the whole church. It's really beautiful."

"Very well." And as they started through the doorway, she queried: "Did you or your namesake design this entire structure?"

"No, my lady, oh, no! Most of the Abbey is centuries older than either of us who bear the Hawksmoor name. Though indeed I wish we, or one of us at least, could claim such credit. Fortunately I shall have the honor of showing it to you."

Genevieve murmured something polite, a response that had become almost an instinct with her now. Ever since her marriage, since she had become a celebrity. Since—

Hawksmoor went wandering, escorting on his arm the lady he was treating with such tender attention that it seemed he wanted to make her his own. He led Lady Genevieve up and down through the rich gloom of the Abbey's interior as, he explained, he himself had interpreted and copied it. Within the walls and under the gothic peak of roof was, altogether, more than a hectare of space. He could have told her the precise area, down to the last decimal of a square millimeter, but he did not. Together they walked the aisles of the great church for a considerable time, hands touching now without any seeming constraint, with less peculiarity of feeling—then out again into the cloister's open air, where mild rain had come to replace sunlight while they were gone.

The rain felt very strange upon the lady's face, but she made no comment on the strangeness.

Her escort, saying little, looked at her and guided her back inside. The couple walked, their footfalls echoing upon square paving stones, straight down the middle of the towering nave.

"Gothic arches. I'll explain the structural theory of them

to you if you like. The tallest, here in the nave, are more than thirty meters high. A ten-story building, if it was narrow enough, could fit inside. The loftiest interior of any church in all old England."

"I see no other people here."

"Do you wish for other people? Wait, that may be a verger, walking down the other aisle—see? And is that a priest I see at the high altar?"

Lady Genevieve stopped in her tracks. She knew these other people were some kind of sham. "What about my husband?"

"He is not here. Though as far as I know the Premier Dirac is well." Hawksmoor's voice became querulous. "Do you miss your bridegroom?" Then, as if he were trying to restrain himself but could not: "Do you love him very much?"

The lady shuddered. "I don't know what I feel about him. I can't say that I miss him; I can hardly remember what he is like."

"I'm sure your memory can call up anything you really want to know. Anything at all from your past."

"Yes, I suppose—if I was willing to make the effort." She sighed, and seemed to try to pull herself together. "Dirac and I never quarreled seriously about anything. He was good to me, I suppose, in the few days we lived together. But the truth is, I was—I am—terribly afraid of him." Once more she paused, looking at her taller companion's face, his head outlined against bright stained glass. "Tell me, what has happened to my child?"

"Child?"

"I was . . . pregnant."

"You know the answer to that. You donated your . . . protochild, I believe is the proper term, to the colony program. Or do you mean what might have happened afterward?"

The couple stood regarding each other, no longer touching. A silence stretched between them.

At last the lady broke it. "Nick, tell me the truth. What's happened?"

"To you? You are here with me, and you are safe. Perhaps that ought to be enough for now. But whenever you decide you really want to probe more deeply . . ."

For a moment Lady Genevieve could not speak. The sensation reminded her of her earlier problem in obtaining enough air with which to form and utter words, but this difficulty was somehow even more fundamental.

"No!" she cried out suddenly. "Don't tell me anything—anything frightening—just now. Can't we get out of this old building? What are all these monuments around us, graves?"

Her escort remained calm. "Many of them are. Tombs built into the walls and floor. But tombs so old I didn't think that they would mean anything to you, frighten you—"

"Isn't there anywhere else we can go?"

"There are a great many places." He took the lady's hand and stroked it soothingly. In her perception there was still something peculiar about the contact. "Let's try this way for a start."

With Nick gallantly providing an arm upon which the lady was willing to lean for comfort and guidance, the couple progressed from the western end of the nave into a stone-walled room that Nick murmured was St. George's chapel, then out of that grim place along a narrow passage penetrating a wall of tremendous thickness, to reach what were obviously the living quarters.

On their arrival in these very different rooms, Hawksmoor looked somewhat anxiously at the lady and asked her what she thought. Before he considered this space ready to use for entertaining, he had several times redesigned and refilled it with several successive sets of furnishings, according to the changing dictates of his taste.

After all, he was still very young.

Parts of his version of the Abbey, including the structural shell and much of the pleasing detail in the stonework and glass, had existed for many months before he met or even heard of the Lady Genevieve. It was Nick's private hobby as well as a component of his work in which he was deeply interested. But all this flurry of recent hasty revision had of course the single object of pleasing Jenny.

Actually, as he confessed later to his beloved, he had been able to discover very little about how these inner, semiprivate rooms had actually looked in the original down through the centuries—and in truth he did not really care. It was the grand design, the stonework and its decoration, that he had found most fascinating—at least until very recently.

Presently she was sitting in a comfortable modern chair. The room's stone walls were hung with abstract tapestries. The windows were too high for their clear glass to let in any real view of the outside. "It is a strange temple, Nick."

"It is a very old temple."

"And you live here?"

He had remained on his feet, restless, still watching her reactions closely, his boots resounding upon the bare stone between two thickly woven modern-looking rugs. "I suppose I spend as much time here as I do anywhere."

"And what god or goddess was it meant to serve?"

"A single god. The God of the Christians—are you any sort of a Believer, my lady?"

She shook her coppery curls. "Not really. When I was a child, my parents disagreed sharply on the subject of religion. My father is Monotheist, my mother was . . . it's hard to say just what she was. She died five years ago."

"I'm sorry."

"Then I am to understand that this whole magnificent temple now belongs to you?"

"Yes, I think I can claim that." Hawksmoor leaned back in his oversized chair and gestured theatrically. "Everything you see around you. Which means that it is all at your service, absolutely."

Running her fingers over the fabric of her own chair, she frowned at the sensation—something about her sense of touch was still not truly right.

Hawksmoor was gripping the carven arms of his seat, staring at her in what seemed to her an oddly helpless way. "My feelings for you, my lady, are—more than I can readily describe. I realize that from your point of view we have scarcely met, but . . . it might be accurate to say I worship you."

The lady, in the process of trying to grapple with this statement, trying to find some way to respond, raised her eyes and was momentarily distracted when she glimpsed, as if by accident, through a partly open door in a far wall, a thoroughly modern indoor swimming pool. Completely out of place. The water's surface as still as a mirror, yet she could tell that it was water. Sunken in blue-green tile, surrounded by utterly modern metal walls, lighted with soft modern clarity.

"I see you've noticed the pool. It's a kind of experiment of mine. A little touch that I thought you might one day—"

"Nick," she broke in, and then came to a stop. She had no idea of what she ought to say, or wanted to say, next. Only that she wanted to slow things down somehow.

"Yes, Lady Genevieve. Jenny. May I call you that?"

"Of course. Why not? You've saved my life."

"Jenny. I should not have started burdening you with my feelings. Today was not the time. Later we can speak of them."

"Feelings are important," she replied at last.

"Yes. Oh, yes." He nodded solemnly.

"Are we really on Earth, Nick?"

"I am not very sure what 'really' means—but in answer to your question, no, most people would say that just now you and I are not on Earth."

"I see. Thank you. Nick, have you ever really been to Earth?"

"No. But then, perhaps yes."

"Don't you *know?"*

"In a way I do. But I must keep coming back to my own question; like feelings, it's important: What does 'really' mean?"

Terror, which Lady Genevieve could easily visualize in the form of little mice and rats, had for some time been nibbling at the outside of the protective obscurity of thought that Nick had somehow so kindly provided for her, and that she had so welcomed.

Without any clear statement on the matter having been made, she had become convinced that this man was going to be her sole companion for some indefinite time to come. Part of her yearned to press him for real answers. What was this place really, this Abbey? But at the same time, fear held her back from the sheer finality of any answer he might give.

Nick was aware of her disquiet. "Don't you like it? I

think this is certainly one of the most beautiful places I know. But if you don't like it, we could easily move elsewhere."

"Your Abbey's lovely, Nick. In its own way. It feels solid and safe, protected somehow."

"I hoped it would feel like that. To you."

"But—"

"But something is bothering you. I will answer any questions that I can."

The lady stared into her companion's eyes. "Let me tell you some of what I do remember. And this part is very clear. We, you and I, were on a little spaceship, a courier vessel, and there had already been a—tragedy. We were surrounded by death and—and—do you deny any of this?"

"No, my lady. I can't deny it." Hawksmoor shook his head solemnly.

"I cannot stand this anymore! Tell me, I beg of you, tell me in plain words what has happened. How we got from that place to this."

"My lady—" His voice beseeched her. "What I did when I found you on that little ship was the only thing I could have done. I took the only possible course open to me to save you from death. Believe me, I did it all for you."

"My thanks again, dear Nick, for saving me. Now tell me how."

He came visibly to a decision and pressed on, showing a curious mixture of eagerness and reluctance. "You will remember how I entered the courier's cabin, wearing space armor?"

"I remember that, of course. And how I welcomed you. It seems to me that I remember your arms going round me—" And that, she suddenly realized, had been the last time that the *touch* of anything had felt precisely right.

Her companion was nodding. "My arms did indeed enfold you. The limbs of that suit are mine—in the sense that I am usually able to make use of them when I wish. What I must explain to you now is that those or others I might borrow are the only arms I have."

She was listening intently, frowning.

He said tenderly, worriedly, "You mustn't be afraid."

She was staring at Nick's own upper limbs, which seemed

large and obvious, fairly ordinary in appearance as he stood before her, hands on his hips. She whispered, "I don't understand."

"These?" He extended his arms, wiggling his fingers, pulled them back to hug himself, then held them out again. "Of course these are mine too, but they could not have helped you on that ship. They have other purposes—and they are making progress, evidently. Now you can feel my touch. Is what you feel when you touch me still strange? Much different than—the contact of your husband's hand, for example?"

"Yes! There is still something . . . odd about the way things feel here. Not only your hand, but everything. All the objects that I touch. And as I think about it, there's a peculiarity in the way things look. The colors are so fine, so vivid. And the smell of everything is a little different, and . . . but I don't . . ."

"My lady, when you and I stood together, the two of us together on that wrecked, dying ship, I promised you solemnly that I could get you safely away, across the airless gap to my ship, even though you had no suit. Because I knew that your poor, hurt body could be fitted neatly inside my suit; and that is exactly how I did it."

"Two people in one suit? I didn't think—"

"Two people, Lady Genevieve, yes, but only one body. Yours. You see, even then I had no body of my own. No solid arms with which to rescue you, or anyone." His waving hands seemed to deny their own existence. "No anything of flesh and bone." His voice was low, underplaying the string of disclaimers like a man who admits that he is at the moment inconveniently missing a leg, lost in some accident and not yet medically regrown.

"You seem to be telling me that you have *no* body. No—"

"No fleshly body. Nor have I ever had one. To achieve useful solidity I need a spacesuit, or some other hardware subject to my control. What you see before you here and now is an image. Mere information. I am, you see, I have always been, an optelectronic artifact. Fundamentally, no more than a computer program." Once again Nicholas Hawksmoor made an expansive gesture with his imaged arms.

The lady stared at him for a long time—somewhere time was jerking ahead in subtle electronic increments—and hardly a line of her face moved by so much as a millimeter, for however long she stared.

Finally she said, "You were telling me about my—rescue. Go ahead. I want to hear the details. Everything."

"Of course. The moment I came aboard the courier where you were trapped, and looked around, I could see that few of your fellow passengers would benefit from any help that I might give . . . but no, that's wrong. Let me be truthful with you, always very truthful. The truth was that I cared very little about those people. I didn't worry about them. It was you I had come to save.

"You—welcomed me aboard. And—just at that point, another blast engulfed us."

"Yes. Yes, there was another explosion. I remember that."

In a strained voice Nick whispered: "I am afraid that you were injured rather severely then."

"Ah." Both her hands were taken, engulfed, in both of his. She could close her eyes, and did, but nothing she could do would make the strangeness of his touching go away.

"Yes. I had to work very quickly. Your body fit neatly inside my suit, which, as I have tried to explain, is in a way also my body—"

The lady gasped.

"—and which, therefore, in terms of mass and physics, was very nearly empty. And I, dwelling for the time being in the suit's electronics, working the servos that drive the arms and fingers of the suit, sealed you into the body cavity with my own metal hands, and I, being in effect the spacesuit, acting through the spacesuit, fed you air, made you breathe, though by that time your lungs were scarcely working.

"Then I carried you back safely across the gap of cold and emptiness and death, safely into my own little ship which was standing by. Then out of the suit with you, and right into the medirobot. And now . . . now here you are."

The lady was staring at him. She did not appear to be breathing. Now that she thought about it, she seemed to have no need to breathe.

Into the silence, as if he found her silence frightening, her rescuer said: "I don't suppose you remember my little ship at all. You haven't really had a chance to see her. I call her the *Wren,* that's a sort of pun, she's named for my namesake's mentor, Christopher Wren, he was yet another architect. I don't know if he was any kind of a pilot, in the sailing ships they had those days. I don't suppose he was—"

She broke in with a reaction of shattered horror. *"You are only an image?"*

"In a sense, yes. An image appearing in a mode of virtual reality. Technically I am an optelectronic artifact, basically a computer program . . ."

"Then what in all the hells have I become? What have you done to me?"

Nick, who had been dreading this moment more and more, did his best to explain. His voice was kindly and muted and logical. But before he had said ten more words, the lady began to scream. He tried to talk above the breathless screaming, but that was useless, so for the sake of her own sanity, and his, he exercised a certain control function and turned her off. Only temporarily, of course.

SIX

One of the yacht's junior officers, who was perhaps really trying to be helpful, said to Kensing, who was standing in one of the yacht's corridors looking thoughtful: "You really don't get it about Nick yet, do you?"

Kensing stared at him. "I've had other things to think about. So what the hell is it about Nick that I don't get, assuming his problem has any relevance?"

The man looked defensive. "I didn't exactly say he had a problem."

"What, then?"

"Hawksmoor's a computer program."

"Oh." Suddenly several things that had been puzzling Kensing made sense. He had heard of the thing being done before, the optelectronic creation of a close analogue of a human personality. It wasn't done often, though technically such procedures had been feasible for a long time. In a society that had developed and was still developing while locked in an age-long struggle against machines, the anthropomorphizing of hardware or software was definitely unpopular and uncommon. Such constructions were also illegal on many worlds, among folk who, with the hideous example of the berserkers always before them, lived in dread of their own computer artifacts somehow getting out of hand.

Kensing asked: "You don't mean a recorded person?"

"Nope. Mean just what I said. The fact doesn't get much publicity, but the boss has developed a definite interest in electronic personalities over the last few years."

Kensing nodded. Anthropomorphic programs designed from scratch, as opposed to those recorded from organic human brains, were deeply interesting to many students of psychology, politics, and control. But the few examples extant were generally kept hidden.

There existed a closely related class of programs, actual recorded people, which were sometimes very useful tools but tended to be subject to even more widespread restrictions. Kensing had once met one of them, the program Hilary Gage, which—or who—had played a key role in one particularly famous fight against berserkers. Kensing, meeting the Gage program long after that battle, had enjoyed a lengthy conversation with him—or with it. Even after the long talk, Kensing wasn't sure which pronoun best applied.

Today, only minutes after discovering the truth about Hawksmoor, Kensing happened to bring up the subject with Frank Marcus. He learned that Frank had met Gage, too; and Frank, like many other people, remained perfectly sure that in meeting a recorded person he had encountered nothing but a program.

At the moment Kensing and Marcus were inspecting the latest VR mockup of the kidnapped station, put up by *Eidolon*'s computers. All the members of the crew were taking turns in visiting the ten-cube to see this display when they had the chance; they all wanted to know in detail the nature of the prize they were pursuing, and what sort of military operations might be feasible if and when they got close enough to think of attempting a recovery.

But Kensing, inspecting the model's beautifully realistic image, was suddenly sure the whole enterprise was doomed to futility. Berserkers killed. That was the function for which they had been designed and built, and that was what they did.

The possibility that Annie might be still alive was really small, in fact infinitesimal . . .

There was an interruption on holostage. Nick Hawksmoor was suddenly present. He appeared standing to one side and slightly behind the modeled cylinder of the station, resting one forearm on the flat disk of the upper end. The weightless image perfectly supported his weightless body.

"Excuse me, gentlemen, but I really couldn't help overhearing. I'm touching up some of the life support in these compartments at the moment, and on occasion conversations just come through."

"Quite all right," said Kensing, feeling odd.

Hawksmoor acknowledged the declaration with a slight smile. But it was evident that he was mainly interested in talking to Frank, for his eyes turned in that direction. "Perhaps you are aware that I myself am an electronic person, Colonel?"

Frank was already looking at the Hawksmoor image through two of his front-box lenses. A third now swiveled around that way, as if he wanted a better look. "Are you, now?" he commented.

Kensing, listened, was struck by the fact that the voice of the fragmented, augmented man in boxes sounded less human than Nick's, though both of course were being generated by mechanical speakers.

"Indeed I am."

Marcus made no further comment.

Nick pressed on, sounding both curious and somehow determined. "Does my revelation make you angry? Do you consider that you have been deceived?"

A metal forelimb gestured lightly. "I admit you took me a little by surprise. Maybe I would be angry if I thought a human had been deceiving me. But getting mad at a tool doesn't make a lot of sense. Are you a good tool, Nick?"

"I work at being a good tool, usually to the best of my ability. If you are not offended, Colonel, and if you have a little time to spare, let me pursue the subject a little further."

"Go ahead. Shoot."

"You will probably not be surprised to hear that I find the topic deeply interesting. Actually I had not expected you to accept my revelation so quickly, without discussion. Without at least some faint suspicion that I was joking."

All three of Frank's boxes moved, slightly adjusting their relative positions; Kensing got the impression that their occupant was somehow making himself comfortable. Marcus said: "I said you took me a little by surprise. But maybe not entirely."

"Indeed. Not entirely? I would like to know what it was about me—about my persona on the holostage, which you have encountered several times—that suggested to you that I lack flesh."

"Maybe we can go into it sometime. Right now I've got other things to do." End of conversation.

Kensing, at his next opportunity to talk with Premier Dirac, said something about how realistic Nick Hawksmoor appeared to be, what a good job the programmers had done in putting him together. "He's a relatively new version, I presume?"

Dirac nodded. "Yes, only about a year old. They did do a good job, didn't they? It took them several months. The truth is I was growing less and less happy with the product I was getting from human architects—that biostation, for example. So I decided to try what a state-of-the-art optelectronic mind could do."

"I'd say a matter of only months is quick work for a program of such complexity, Premier. I'd have thought years. How was his name chosen, if you don't mind my asking?"

"My engineers had certain building blocks of programming ready," Dirac explained vaguely. "That speeded things up. As for his name, Nick picked it himself. Adopted it from some eighteenth-century builder—I'll tell you the story sometime. Did you get a good look at the station model?"

It seemed to Kensing, who had the chance to observe some of the interactions between Premier Dirac and Hawksmoor, that normally the organic creator got along well enough with his artificial creation.

But the Premier's feelings toward any optelectronic

personalities he encountered tended to be complex and intense.

Once Kensing heard Dirac declaim: "Those transcribed spirits who have retired from flesh into electronic modality generally enjoy a higher social status, if one can put it in those terms, than those who have never possessed a red blood cell in their lives."

Kensing was unsurprised to hear that he was not the only one who had been fooled for some time by Nick. Others were more upset, on discovering the truth, than he had been. Some of the crew members, like a great many people elsewhere, voiced or at least had some objection to or felt some uneasiness about a computer artifact that looked and sounded so much like a person. It was not of course Hawksmoor's calculating power—or call it intellect—to which most objected; it was the semblance of humanity possessed by this *thing* with which (or whom) the Premier consulted, argued (sometimes joyfully), and upon whom (or which) he seemed to depend so heavily.

Now that the squadron was ready to pull out from Imatra, Nick was being forced to leave behind his *Wren*—he thought of the little ship as his. The place on the hangar deck usually occupied by that often useful but unarmed vessel had been taken by an armed military scoutship, the last fighting craft of any kind left in the Imatran system. The recent fighting had ended before the scoutship was able to reach the scene. Dirac had overawed the overmatched local authorities and simply taken it away from them.

But abandoning the *Wren* posed more problems for Nick than his creator/employer realized. Now, with the squadron on the verge of departure, Hawksmoor had been supervising, among his other duties, the robot workers busy removing certain equipment from the *Wren* and reinstalling it on the newly acquired scout.

During this operation Nick moved himself about, aboard ship or in space, in spacesuit mode. His chief job was supervising the robots that did most of the physical work—these were mostly dog-sized metal creatures with nothing organic in their physical appearance and nothing outstanding in their brains.

While conducting this work openly, Hawksmoor had a desperate need to see that another task was performed also, and in the strictest secrecy—he had to arrange the transfer, from his own small craft to somewhere aboard the yacht, not only of the physical storage units in which he himself resided most of the time, when he was not working in suit-mode, but also of those containing Jenny.

It had turned out, as he had more or less expected, that the physical volume needed to store the recording of a once-organic person—in this case, the Lady Genevieve—under current technology (which incorporated, in solid lumps of heavy metals and composite materials, the latest subquantal storage systems) was just about the same as that required to house Nick himself: about four thousand cubic centimeters, a capacity approximately equivalent to that of three adult human skulls.

The suit Nick had chosen to animate for this particular transfer job happened to be the same one he'd used to rescue Lady Genevieve from the doomed courier. It had sustained some minor damage at that time, damage he was going to be hard put to explain if anyone ever noticed it and queried him about it. He had what he thought were several good explanations ready, and intended to choose what seemed the best one when the moment of truth arrived.

On one of Nick's suited passages across the hangar deck of the *Eidolon* he encountered Kensing, himself spacesuited at the moment. The fleshly man was taking an inventory, and making a hands-on inspection of the small craft aboard, upon which it would be necessary to depend if boarding operations were contemplated.

Nick felt somewhat amused at Kensing's reaction to the appearance of Nick's physically empty suit. For some reason this struck the young systems engineer, as it did many other people, as particularly creepy and disturbing.

After meeting Kensing, Hawksmoor considered snatching a few moments from his assigned duties—he had no authorized time for rest, since he was not supposed to need any—to visit Jenny, to make sure she had come through the physical transfer without any problems. Actually there was no reason to think she had even been aware that it was going on, but he wanted to make sure.

In the privacy of his own thought, Hawksmoor had by now begun to ponder very seriously several important questions raised by his new relationship with the Lady Genevieve.

One of the first tasks he had undertaken in these latest intervals of secret work had been to adjust (*very* tentatively and cautiously!) some of the lady's peripheral programming, hoping thus to help her recover from the shock of realization of her new state of existence. He had been careful not to overdo the adjustment, and soon as he had awakened the Lady Genevieve again, she had begun at once to implore, to demand, that he tell her exactly what had happened to her.

On revisiting Jenny as soon as possible after her transfer to the yacht, Hawksmoor resumed his efforts to explain the new situation to the lady, as gently as he could.

Within a few minutes after he'd rescued the Lady Genevieve (whose spirit at the time had still maintained a tenuous hold upon her native flesh) from the doomed courier and succeeded in carrying her aboard his little ship, the *Wren*'s own medirobot had diagnosed her injuries as certainly fatal. Even with deep-freezing until the best in medical help could be obtained, the prognosis was abysmally poor.

At that point he, Nick, as he recounted now, had had no choice. Regardless of what heroic measures he and the medirobot might have taken, the lady's brain was soon going to be dead—and once that happened, no physician or surgeon, human or robotic, would be able to restore her personality.

As Nicholas—or his image in virtual reality—told this story now, Jenny—or her image—stood staring at him helplessly, her small mouth open on white teeth. At the moment they were, to Jenny's best awareness, near the very center of the Abbey, halfway down the football-field length of the west nave and strolling east, enjoying the pastel glories painted on stone and wood by an afternoon sun coming in behind them through the stained glass of the great west window. Not as glorious a rose window, Nick thought to himself, as that of Chartres was said to have been—but still impressive.

"Therefore, my lady," Hawksmoor concluded, "as I have been trying to explain, I did the only thing I could. I recorded you. I saved the patterns of your consciousness, the essence of your personality, practically your entire memory."

Thanks to the subtle adjustments Nick had very recently made in her peripheral programming, the lady was soon able to calm down enough to reply. Her next words, spoken with the politeness ladyship demanded, were to thank Nick once more for saving her; her next words after those comprised an urgent plea, demand, for a more thorough explanation of her situation.

Grateful at seeming to have got past the key point of the explanation without disaster, Hawksmoor went on, as delicately as possible, into the details. How he had reformed and reclothed the image of her body, plucking the vast quantities of necessary data out of the many video recordings of the lovely Lady Genevieve he happened to have on hand. Not just happened. His burgeoning worship of the lady had months ago caused him to begin to accumulate images of her—and the nearer the date of the wedding came, the more such images had been available.

Nick might have related more details of the process by which he had created her image as it was today, a staggering number of details in fact. But already the lady had had enough. Briskly she interrupted his recital with an imperious demand that he at once start arranging for her return to an organic, fleshly body.

"Nick, I understand, really I do, that your purpose in doing . . . what you have done was to save my life. And it worked, and I'm grateful, never think I'm not."

"My lady, it was the least that I—"

"But I cannot go on living indefinitely like this, without a real body. How long is the restoration going to take?"

Hawksmoor had been afraid of the moment when he had to face this question. "My lady, I am more sorry than I can say. But what you are asking can't . . . Well, I just haven't been able to discover any way in which it can be done."

As these words were spoken, the couple had rounded a columned corner and were, in terms of the virtual reality they shared, standing in the south transept of the Abbey, near the place Hawksmoor had learned ought to be called Poets' Corner, because of the masters of the art who had been entombed or memorialized there. But the Lady Genevieve was not currently interested in poetry, or architecture either. She raised her eyes and looked around her, as if her imaged eyes could see through, beyond, the virtual world of stones and glass to whatever harsher, deeper fabric of realworld hardware was maintaining it.

"Where are we, really?" she demanded.

"In those terms, Jenny—if I may still call you that—we are now, as I have been trying to explain, aboard your husband's yacht, the *Eidolon*—and no, he has not the faintest suspicion that you are here."

"He doesn't even suspect?" Her tone was shocked, surprised, but—yes, he dared to think that her reaction was also one of hope. "I thought perhaps you were doing this at his orders."

That she might entertain such a suspicion had never occurred to Nick. He said: "I shall explain presently. But be assured that Premier Dirac has not the slightest inkling that you have survived in any form. He simply believes that you are dead, killed with the others who were aboard that courier when it exploded."

"So you haven't told him."

To Nick's immense relief, there had been more calculation than accusation in those words.

He reassured her. "I have not told him or anyone."

"Why not?"

"Why have I not told your husband?" Suddenly he felt nervous and uncertain. "There are reasons. I am not going to apologize for my behavior, but you certainly deserve an explanation."

"Well?"

"Yes. The first time we met, Jenny . . . I mean the first time you were able to look at me and respond to me . . . there in that great laboratory room aboard the bioresearch station—even before there was any hint of a berserker attack—I received the impression that you were deeply unhappy. Was I wrong?"

She hesitated.

"Was I wrong?"

She was looking at some kind of marble monument encased in wooden cabinetry, with antique letters spelling CHAUCER carved into the stone. He could tell her the fascinating history of that memorial if she was interested. But right now she was just staring. At last she said: "No. No, Nick, I don't suppose that you were wrong."

"I knew it! And now you have admitted that you fear your husband. I too have been living with him in a sense, you see, if only briefly. I know, as you know, that our Premier is not the easiest person in the Galaxy to get along with."

At that the lady smiled wanly.

Hawksmoor went on: "The Premier and I, sometimes . . . well, all is not always well between us, my creator and me.

"You see, Jenny, at first, when I was getting you out of the courier, transporting you to my medirobot, deciding that recording your mind was the only way to save it—all that time I had no idea of keeping your rescue a secret. No conscious plan. But then, I remember thinking, before telling the world that you were saved, I had better make sure that you had come through the recording process in good shape—which, let me hasten to assure you, you have done."

"And then?" the lady prompted.

"Well, I determined that I was going to make sure you had the right to choose," Nick burst out. "I mean, the right to choose whether you wanted to go back to him or not."

"Go back to him?" Jenny was stunned, uncomprehending. Then wild hope leaped up in her eyes. "You mean that after all you can restore me to my body?"

"I—no, I thought I had explained, I cannot do that. No one can. Your body has been totally destroyed."

"But then how could I go back to him? What do you mean by such a question? How can I go back to anyone when I'm in this condition?"

"I suppose the only real way in which you could go back to *him,*" said Nick in measured tones, "would be to visit him, to talk to him from a holostage. Perhaps to meet him in some virtual space, as we are meeting now."

"To meet him in some imaginary world, like this? Or to gaze at him from a holostage? What good is that to anyone?" The lady was starting to grow frantic once again. "What good is it to Dirac, especially? To a man who married me to start a dynasty? In his world of politics, being married to an electronic phantom will mean nothing, nothing at all. No, my husband must never know what has happened to me, at least not until you have brought me back to real life. He must never see me this way! He might—" She let the sentence die there, as if she were afraid to complete it.

"There are alternatives, of course," said Nick after a short interval. His own desperation was growing. "I think they are excellent alternatives. The fact is that you and I—that there are ways in which we might have a life together. Eventually, with others like ourselves—"

"Like ourselves? You mean unreal? Only programs, images?"

"It is a different form of life, I admit. But we—"

"Life? Is this a life? I tell you, I must have a body." The lady, interrupting, almost screaming, waved her imaged arms. "Skin and blood and bones and sex and muscles—can you give me those?"

Hawksmoor exerted his best efforts to explain. But she wasn't particularly interested in the technical details. She wanted him to cease his protests that getting her a body was impossible, and to get on with the task of doing it, somehow, at any cost.

But at the same time—this was a new development, and it certainly gave Nick new hope—she didn't want him to leave her alone. It was painfully lonely in the Abbey, Genevieve complained, when he was absent.

Hawksmoor experienced great joy at the discovery that the lady missed him. Still, he was going to have to leave her sometime. "I could provide people," he suggested.

"Real people?"

"Well, at the moment, no. Currently your companionship would be limited to somewhat distant figures, like the verger. Maybe a small crowd having a party in the next room or around the pool, the sounds, the distant images of people singing, dancing?"

"And I could never join them. No thanks, Nick. Just come and see me when you have the time. And you must, you really must, try to bring me some good news."

"I'll do that." And he went away, projected his awareness elsewhere, fled down the pathway of an exit circuit, returning to duty fired with a new resolve, because she hadn't wanted him to leave.

Before he left, a small thing but about all that he could do, Nick had shown her how to put herself to sleep.

He was bitterly disappointed, though he told himself he had no right to be, at the savage reaction, absolutely unjustified as far as he could see, of the woman he loved. He had meant to offer her a joyous future.

Also, he was really sure, down at the most fundamental level of his programming, that her demand to be restored to flesh was going to prove impossible to meet. Nowhere in his flawless, extensive memory was there any indication that the mass of data comprising an optelectroperson (authorities differed on the proper term to cover both kinds of programmed people), either organic or artificial in origin, had ever been successfully downloaded to an organic brain.

At the pair's next meeting, which came only minutes later in what fleshly folk would have counted as real time, Jenny, as she continued trying to come to terms with the harsh facts of her new existence, showed that she felt some repentance for her stridency and seeming lack of gratitude. She was, she now insisted repeatedly, really grateful to Nick for saving her in the only way he could. She agreed that surely, surely this shadowy existence among shadowy images was better than being dead.

From the way she repeated this over and over, Nick got the impression that she might be endeavoring to convince herself.

Hawksmoor was happy to be thanked, but he still felt deeply wounded that the woman he loved could so reject his world, his whole existence. He still worshiped this woman—more than ever, now that she was of his kind. If *woman* was still the right word for what she had become—yes, it was, he would insist on that—and if *worship* had ever been the right word for what he felt.

Love? The data banks to which he had access and the troubled presence, the enigmatic position, of that word in them assured him that it would admit of no easy definition.

What he felt, he knew, some people would insist upon defining as one mass of programming hankering for another.

In his timidity he had found the matter difficult to explain to the Lady Genevieve, but he had begun to have such feelings for her well before he had ever managed to get close enough for them to interact. It had all started when he had first seen her image, many months before her unlucky journey to Imatra.

She had now been long enough in his world that it had become necessary for him to explain the degrees of difference, in his world, between perception and interaction. All that anyone, fleshly or optelectronic, ever *saw* of any other person was an image, was it not?

On a succeeding visit to the Abbey he tried again. The lady did seem to be touched eventually by his pleas and arguments; she admitted that she liked Nick too, she really did. But she would not admit any lessening of her need to regain a body somehow, anyhow. On that point, she warned him, there was going to be no compromise. And she needed the cure, the restoration, as soon as possible: why wasn't he working on the problem now?

And when Hawksmoor made yet another effort, very tentative, to persuade her out of that demand, she quickly gave evidence of falling again into a fit of screaming panic.

Under the circumstances Nick would have promised anything. Therefore he took the solemn oath she insisted that he take to work on the problem of obtaining for her what she called a real body, a mass of matter as fleshly as the one she had been born with, as healthy and attractive, as satisfactory in every way. And he swore also that his efforts would not fail.

Having thus pacified his Jenny for the moment, Hawksmoor took polite leave and went away.

He went away from her and from the Abbey, entering circuits that took him in effect a step closer to the universe of organic beings. He was thinking to himself as he undertook this shift of viewpoint that someone, sometime, on some ship or planet in the Solarian portion of the Galaxy, must have at least attempted such a downloading of human personality from hardware to organic brain.

But when, in his next hurried intervals of free time, he tried to dig into the subject, Hawksmoor soon discovered that all of the data banks to which he could routinely gain access—which included all those he was aware of on the yacht—were silent on the subject of fitting electronic personalities into organic brains, and on certain closely related topics as well. Rather strangely silent, it seemed to Nick now. Could it be that the Boss, interested as he was in related matters, wanted to discourage others from experimenting in the field?

It even crossed the optelectronic mind of Nicholas Hawksmoor to wonder: Was it possible that knowledge of such matters was being systematically kept from him? He couldn't think of any reason why it should be so. Unless the Boss thought that for some reason he, Nick, was likely to tinker with himself in such a way. But there was no chance he'd want to do such a thing . . . or there hadn't been, till now.

He didn't see how it could be possible to get anywhere at all in the effort to provide Jenny with a body using only the equipment currently available on the yacht. But it occurred to Nick that if his combative boss should catch up with the kidnapped bioresearch station, and should somehow, miraculously, against all odds, succeed in retrieving that facility from the berserker essentially undamaged—that facility just might make the feat possible.

Then mentally Nick shook his head.

Even supposing the mission should be such a highly improbable smashing success that the research station equipment indeed became available, there wouldn't of course be time for Nick or anyone else to use it before the squadron and its prize returned to Imatra.

Would there?

* * *

Nick's own information banks contained mention of some kind of quasi-religious cult on certain Solarian worlds, whose devotees promoted human recording as a try at spiritual immortality. He had the impression that this subject either was or had been one of Premier Dirac's own private interests. The Premier was rumored to have had some connection with the cult.

It was common knowledge that Frank Marcus had agreed to accept, for the duration of the emergency, the job of chief pilot of the Premier's yacht. It was part of his agreement with the Premier that Frank, until combat seemed imminent, would be relieved of many or most routine pilot's tasks, by one or more slightly lesser-rated mortals.

It seemed evident from the size and segmented shape of Colonel Marcus's metal body (his bodies, rather; Kensing had noticed that he changed modules from time to time) and from the small amount of organic nourishment he took (and the form in which he took it, a kind of gruel) that there couldn't be a whole lot of his original, organic body left by now. Whispered guesses ranged down to as little as five kilograms, if the amount of organic nourishment he ingested was any clue. But however much he'd lost, Kensing would have staked his own life that the colonel was surely no recording; you had to be with him, talk with him, for only a short time to be sure of that.

Frank generally took care of the mixing and pouring in of his organic food himself—sometimes a serving robot did it at his direction—and there were times, when Frank was off duty and ready to relax, when he included a few drops of some fine Peruvian (or other) brandy.

And certain rumors were passed about: supposedly more than one of the female crew members were now able, and on occasion willing, to testify to the fact that the man who dwelt in the boxes still retained organic maleness.

Other rumors circulated also, none of them seemingly more than half serious. Test one of them on Frank, as Kensing did, mention to him any suspicion going the rounds to the effect that Frank's organic brain was long since dead, his mind had been recorded years ago, and he'd blast you with a raucous laugh. Sure, his brain functioned with computer assists sometimes, accepted optelectronic augmentation when he was at the helm of a ship, but any human pilot had to take advantage of those when things got rough. There was never any doubt, in Frank's own mind at least, as to which component of himself, organic or electronic, was fully in charge. And Marcus had several times said vehemently, and was not shy about saying it again, that he was never going to allow himself to be recorded.

Dirac, admiring, had said that if Frank himself had not been available, he would have tried to get someone like him, a man or woman who lived in marcus boxes, as his number one pilot when combat against berserkers loomed as it did now. Over the last few decades, perhaps a century, the Marcus name had become eponymous for—or Frank the eponymous originator of—certain special equipment used by Solarian humans who suffered very severe physical disability. But people in marcus boxes were extremely rare. Almost everyone who had to deal with serious bodily impairment could benefit from, and much preferred, organic rebuilding. The whole body outside the brain could generally be repaired or replaced, and usually the new flesh was remarkable in its duplication of, perhaps even an improvement on, the shape of the original.

Whether Frank himself had any compelling medical reason to live in his boxes now, instead of having his fleshly frame regrown, perhaps only the medical officer aboard the *Eidolon* could have said—and ethics of course prevented any casual testing of rumors there.

Nor did it seem that anyone present—except of course the Premier himself, who seemed to have no interest in the question—would have the nerve to ask the colonel directly.

Someone speculated that while Colonel Marcus must have originally—some centuries ago—been housed in his present form for compelling medical and technical reasons, he probably now preferred to retain the massive hardware for reasons of his own.

Only Nick among the other available pilots could meld as thoroughly as Frank with a diversity of modern machines.

And in fact Nick was among those who now took regular shifts at the helm of the *Eidolon.* When he was taking his turn, the pilot's acceleration couch stood empty.

Early on in the chase, Dirac, after consultation with his advisers, both human and systemic, ordered an advance at superluminal velocity, despite the considerable risk involved in taking even small c-plus jumps in this cluttered region of space. Going faster than light was the only way they could be sure of catching the berserker.

Superb piloting could cut the risk to some degree. Hawksmoor was among the first to admit that Frank, like a few other organic Solarian humans, possessed a fine touch in the control of, the melding with, machinery that even Nick could not duplicate. The marvels of a still-organic brain, which were as yet imperfectly understood, provided Frank's mind, both conscious and unconscious, with the little extra, the fine edge over pure machine control that enabled the best human pilots sometimes, under favorable conditions, to seize a slight advantage over even the best of pure machine opponents.

Frank in turn, after having watched Nick handle a ship and a computer for a while, readily admitted that Nick was pretty good at handling complex machines, and that he—or "it," as Frank always said—would probably be good at fighting berserkers, though so far Nick lacked any experience along that line. Frank gave the impression of realistically appraising the artifact's competence, in the same way he coolly and capably estimated the relative usefulness and weakness of other software and machines.

Colonel Marcus was, thought Kensing, less ready to evaluate people.

But when the question arose as to whether Nick and those like him could ever, should ever, be considered human beings, Marcus had only quietly amused contempt for anyone who seriously proposed such an idea.

The Premier's pursuit of the berserker had now lasted approximately two standard days, and was steadily gaining ground. But before anyone expected an actual encounter, combat flared again.

The visible berserker and its captured prize were still far out of weapons range. But a terse verbal warning of suspected trouble ahead came from the yacht's own brain, interrupting yet another session of the planning council. "There is a ninety percent probability of combat within the next forty seconds."

Kensing, with the sudden feeling that Annie in one way or another was very close to him, leaped from his chair and dashed for his battle station. A moment later he was almost bumped off his feet by Frank Marcus's train of boxes, clumsy-looking no longer, outspeeding Kensing's running legs and others.

The signal from the early warning system was quickly confirmed. Berserker hardware, in the form of small units deployed across flightspace as well as normal space, lay in wait for Dirac's squadron. The encounter was only a few seconds away and could not be avoided. The enemy devices, their presence partially masked by dust and by their own shielding, surrounded the faintly crackling trail of the fleeing raider and its catch. These were intelligent mines, brilliant weapons waiting with inhuman patience to blast or ram, ready to destroy themselves against the hulls of any pursuers.

Until this moment the pursuing force had come hurrying, almost blinded by its own speed, right along the trail, flickering from one space mode to the other and back again; the urgency of the Premier's quest had demanded exactly that. Fortunately Frank had had time to take the pilot's chair. At the moment when the enemy must have calculated that their ambush would be detected, and flightspace as well as normal space seemed to ignite in one great explosion, the yacht instead of veering off went hurtling, jumping forward with an appearance of even greater recklessness than usual.

The pilots of the other two Solarian ships were doing their best to stay with Frank in some kind of a formation and to deal with their deadly enemies as they came within effective range. Some of the ambushing machines could be avoided or bypassed, but the remainder had to be faced and fought.

The crew of the yacht, many of them like Kensing raw newcomers to actual combat, had the impression that the *Eidolon* was being flattened and at the same time turned inside out. The hulls of all three ships rang with the impact of radiation. For the first few moments, total destruction of either humans or berserkers seemed the only possible outcome.

At the point the enemy had chosen for the ambush, where his trail passed through constricting fringes of nebula, the average density of matter grew marginally greater, and the Solarian squadron, all three ships now embedded in normal space, skidded and splashed to a halt inside this fimbriation. Their formation, never all that well maintained, quickly broke up in tactical maneuver, the enemy's trail for the moment necessarily ignored.

The two smaller ships accompanying the Premier's armed yacht were racked up quickly in this fight. The people on the *Eidolon*'s bridge saw one of these vaporized quickly, and the other, in a matter of seconds, so badly damaged that the surviving captain radioed his intention to limp back to Imatra if possible.

Dirac, shouting on radio, did his best to forbid that, but whether or not his orders got through he could not tell. Almost immediately he and the others on the yacht's bridge saw the damaged vessel destroyed.

SEVEN

Two out of three of the Premier's ships had been destroyed. The yacht itself had sustained at least one hit, and there were dead and wounded on several decks, smoke in the corridors, air escaping and compartments sealed off. But, once the *Eidolon* had shaken free of the enemy's swarm of brilliant weapons, neither Dirac nor his ace pilot even considered abandoning the chase and turning back to Imatra.

In the moments of respite that followed, everyone but the seriously wounded was issued and fitted with weapons for close quarters, alphatrigger or eyeblink helmets and the associated gear. The most innovative of these weapons projected cutting beams that savaged ordinary armor, but let soft flesh alone, and rebounded harmlessly—or almost harmlessly—from any properly treated surface. The code embodied in the coating's chemistry could be readily changed between one engagement and the next, to lessen the chances of the enemy's being able to duplicate it successfully.

The realization crossed some remote part of Kensing's mind that this could work out to be an excellent career move.

As a defensive systems engineer, he would benefit from the actual combat experience he was accumulating.

People, one at a time, were being visited at their battle stations by a service robot, to get their armored spacesuits coated with the right combination, fresh from the paint mixer. Other maintenance robots made their way through rooms and corridors, spraying the stuff on most of the interior surfaces.

Kensing, now fully suited and armored as were most of the other crew members, waited at his battle station ready to assist with damage control or repelling boarders. He heard Frank, in the pilot's seat, grunt something to the effect that in the circumstances it would now be as dangerous to turn back as to press on.

As far as Sandy Kensing knew, Premier Dirac had no more previous experience of actual space combat than Kensing did himself. However that might be, the Premier went on as usual calmly issuing orders—calmly consulting as necessary with Colonel Marcus or other experts before he did so. And as usual his commands were accepted, instantly and without comment. Kensing had noticed that this man only rarely and inadvertently intruded his orders into realms where he was not competent to give them.

Frank Marcus gave the impression of enjoying every moment of the fight. As soon as he had a few seconds to spare, he called for some kind of sidearms to be brought to him and connected to one of his boxes. "In case we do get to the hand-to-hand."

Kensing was busy for a time, overseeing attempts at damage control. The wounded were being cared for in one way or another. There were a number of dead, but not enough seriously hurt survivors to fill all the five still-available medirobot berths.

And still the ship moved on.

Kensing assumed there might now very well be some people aboard who objected to continuing the mission; but if so, they were keeping their reactions to themselves. They were private, silent, cautious—because they knew their master would consider disobedience, or even too fervent protest, as mutiny, as treason—and here in space, in the face of the enemy, the law might well justify a ruthless reaction.

Kensing did overhear a couple of anonymous potential protestors asking each other quietly, off intercom, just how in hell the Premier proposed to be of any help to the captives on the stolen station, even assuming those people could be still alive—and even if the enemy could be overtaken.

Frank Marcus, who must have overheard some similar mutterings, demonstrated little patience with the malcontents. To Dirac he growled: "I'm with you. I signed on to fight berserkers, didn't I?" And Frank went on fine-tuning his personal sidearms.

A little later, Kensing asked Frank in private: "What do you think the chances are that we'll really catch up with the damned thing now?"

"Actually, having come this far, they're probably pretty good."

"And if we manage to do that, what chance that we'll really ever be able to communicate with any survivors on that station? Can we really believe that anyone there is still alive?"

"Kid, you better stow that line of talk. The Boss'll have you fried for mutiny."

Since departing the Imatra system, the yacht had gained a great deal of speed relative to ambient normal space. Because each of Dirac's craft was notably smaller than the berserker-biostation combination, he had been able to get away with small c-plus jumps, and the yacht and its smaller escorts had emerged from each with a slightly greater subluminal velocity.

The borders of the dark nebula were hard to define with any precision, but by now the *Eidolon* was definitely within the outer fringes of the Mavronari. The difference between this and normal interstellar space showed on instruments, in a steady thickening of the ambient matter-density. And ahead of the yacht the obscuring material gradually but inexorably grew thicker.

Now once more the telescopes aboard the yacht were

refocused, bringing the fleeing berserker and its captive into clearer view. The chase resumed in normal space. The ambush had cost the Premier not only his two smaller ships, complete with crews, amounting to almost half his fighting strength, but a little time, a little distance, as well.

Within a matter of hours it became evident that the battered yacht was again gaining on the battered enemy. But the rate of gain was slow, even slower than before the ambush; the human warriors, reluctant and otherwise, aboard the *Eidolon* were going to be allowed a little breathing space before the looming confrontation.

Again there was time, a little more time, in which to ponder the persistent mystery: just what benefit was the damned berserker expecting from the prize for which it had sacrificed a chance to commit slaughter on a planetary scale? And just where did the berserker compute that it was taking the biolab and its billion preborn captives?

As far as anyone on board the yacht had been able to determine by exhaustive search of the available charts and VR models, the dark recesses of the Mavronari contained nothing likely to be an attractive goal for either berserkers or human beings. Not that the great nebula had ever been thoroughly explored. It was known to encompass a few isolated star systems, families of planets ordinarily accessible by narrow channels of relatively empty space. But to reach any of those isolated systems by plowing straight through the cloud itself would take any ship or machine an age. The mass of obscuring matter was truly vast, going on at right angles to the direction of the Galactic Core for a discouragingly long way—hundreds of parsecs, many hundreds of light-years. And toward the middle of the nebula the dust densities were doubtless greater. Thousands of years of subliminal travel, at reduced intra-nebular speeds, would be needed to penetrate this gigantic dust cloud from one side to the other.

But if the enemy was seeking only a hiding place, it was not going to be able to find shelter inside the gradually thickening dust before it was overtaken and brought to bay. Steadily, though with tantalizing slowness, Dirac's quarry was becoming more and more distinct in the yacht's telescopes, was coming almost within a reasonable range for using weapons.

Was the enemy trying to devise another ambush? Fanatically intense efforts at detection could discern no evidence of that. Perhaps the berserker's supply of auxiliary machines had been used up in the previous attempt, or perhaps it was hoarding them for a final confrontation.

One serpentine metal arm of Marcus the pilot made an inquiring gesture in the Premier's direction.

Dirac nodded. "We go."

If a new ambush had indeed been planned, it failed to appear. Perhaps it was avoided when Frank made one more daring gamble, undertaken with the Premier's grim blessing; one more jump through flightspace, with everyone else aboard snugged into their acceleration couches, praying or concentrating stoically according to personal preference.

This time no ambush materialized, and the gamble succeeded. When the yacht *Eidolon* emerged yet again into normal space, those aboard found themselves matching velocities almost perfectly with their fleeing foe, now only a few thousand kilometers distant. The pursuing humans very soon would be in a position where they might if they chose take a meaningful shot at the enemy or receive direct fire from its batteries.

That moment of possibility came and passed, and neither side opened fire.

Closing the range still more, the yacht would soon be near enough to assay some force-field grappling of the station the berserker doggedly dragged along. But any attempt to wrench the prize away by grappling seemed foreordained to failure, given the now-damaged condition of the yacht and the evidently tremendous power of the enemy.

But perhaps the berserker's power was not overwhelming after all, not anymore. Observers on the yacht, getting their first look at their foe from relatively short range, could see that the enemy's outer hull, at least, had sustained considerable damage. How much of that damage had been inflicted by the Imatran resistance, and how much before the enemy entered the Imatran system, was impossible to say. But since the berserker had carried out its raid successfully, it still had to be considered very formidable.

Twice in the space of a few seconds a subtle premonitory

quiver of instrumental readings suggested that the enemy was about to fire at the yacht.

"Shields up!" The command as Dirac gave it seemed half a question, and in any case hopelessly belated—Kensing on hearing it wondered whether the old man was getting rattled.

But no matter. Frank, along with the autopilot to which his helmet now had him mentally melded, already had the defenses perfectly deployed. And in fact no enemy fire came.

Now Colonel Marcus, even as he laconically acknowledged Dirac's congratulations for his skill in getting his ship and shipmates into this situation alive, adjusted his angle of approach to bring the yacht directly behind the towed research station. In contrast to both berserker and yacht, the station's outer hull had so far revealed no sign of damage.

The enemy, which at least since the ambush had not been accelerating at all, was maintaining an almost straight course, jogging only slightly on occasion, a simple autopilot kind of maneuver to avoid high-density knots of nebular material. Frank had no difficulty at all in holding the yacht on station directly behind the double mass of the berserker and its captive. Now the actual variation in the yacht's distance from the station was minimal, no more than a few score meters.

With the *Eidolon* in this position, the bulk of the captive station hung directly between the adversaries, and prevented, or seemed to prevent, the berserker from bringing effectively to bear what must be its superior heavy weapons.

The Premier now ordered: "Get me in contact with them."

It was the political aide who objected: "Radio contact with the station? You're assuming—"

"Yes, I'm assuming there's someone still alive aboard that vessel. That's why we're here, remember? Now let's see if they're able to respond to an attempt at communication."

Several people probably thought that a ridiculous idea. But no one said so. "Acknowledge. We're transmitting. Hello, on the station? Anybody there?"

The only reply was a trickle of radio noise.

"No luck. Well, as for the berserker, the way it's acting, I think we have to assume the damned thing's dead. It must have taken some heavy shots a few days ago, and had some delayed reaction. If it wasn't dead, we probably would be by now."

Frank, with Dirac's concurrence, persisted in the tactic of staying as nearly as possible directly behind the towed station, so that its bulk continued to screen the yacht from the foe's presumably superior potential firepower.

The third radio attempt had now failed. Dirac nodded, calmly enough. Evidently he had already made up his mind as to the next step. "I'm going over there to see for myself. You're all volunteers on this mission, and I expect everyone who's not wounded to come with me. We've got enough small craft available. Nick, you take the helm here."

"Yes, sir."

"Frank, I want you to pilot our armed scoutship." There was just one such vessel.

"Right." Methodically Colonel Marcus got ready to turn over control of the yacht to Nicholas, whose driving would be augmented by the yacht's own computers.

Kensing, having extricated himself from his own acceleration couch, stood back to give Frank room while the boxed man skillfully maneuvered his personal containers out of the relatively cramped control room to go rolling with zestful celerity down a corridor, then down a ramp in the direction of the hangar deck where his specially fitted scoutship waited for him.

Kensing followed, suddenly feeling more afraid than he had ever felt before. It wasn't clear to him, and perhaps it didn't matter, whether the fear arose because he was soon going to be killed or because he was soon going to confront the truth about Annie.

One real scoutship, two couriers, two lightly armed launches, the latter pitifully small—not counting the three unsuitable lifeboats, there were five small craft aboard the *Eidolon* available for use in a boarding. The craft easily accommodated all of the remaining fit—and fleshly—crew members on the yacht, three or four to a vessel.

Dirac, who in the course of his career had been accused of many things but probably never of cowardice, was getting ready to drive the second-best small ship himself. This was a slightly modified courier, armed, but with much less combat capability than the military scout Frank was piloting.

When the arrangements to crew the small craft had been completed, the Premier quickly gave Nicholas Hawksmoor a few specific orders and left him in command of the yacht, supposedly the sole conscious tenant of the Premier's remaining fighting ship.

Nicholas Hawksmoor was impressed and somehow moved—and he also felt what he supposed must be a twinge of guilt—when the Premier went off regular intercom to confide privately to him that Nick was the one person he could totally trust not to run away.

Dirac confessed to Nick that he did not have such complete faith in any of his fleshly folk.

"Except for Marcus in this case," the Premier whispered. "And I want the colonel with us on the boarding."

Hawksmoor said, "That's understandable, sir. I think you've made a wise decision."

As soon as the five small craft were fully crewed, they began to emerge one at a time through the main hatch of the *Eidolon*'s hangar deck. Immediately upon emerging from the yacht, they deployed in a scattered formation nearby.

And from that rough formation, at a prearranged time, the tiny flotilla went darting simultaneously into action.

The little ships approached the silent research station quickly, on widely separated paths, all taking evasive action, though the enemy's weapons still remained quiet—

And then, in the blinking of an eye and a blinding flash of violence, the berserker was inert no longer.

The scarred hull of the monstrous mothership still remained silent and dark. But a swarm of small fighting machines erupted with weapons flaring from around the bulge of the enemy hull, speeding to intercept the approaching small Solarian vessels.

Nick, now isolated upon the yacht, his mind operating as always with the optelectronic analogue of nerves, reacted long milliseconds before any of the fleshly humans except Frank, whose mind was already securely melded with his scoutship's brain. The yacht's heaviest weapons, or at least the heaviest Hawksmoor dared to employ so near the station, lashed out at the swarm of counterattacking berserker machines, scattering, burning, crushing, wiping one after another of them out of existence.

In the moments immediately after Dirac had put full trust in him, Nick had briefly toyed with the idea of taking the battered yacht away when only he and his beloved Jenny were left aboard—but he had recognized that as a hopeless dream. Not because he, Nick, would be unable to betray a creator who had been foolish enough to have great faith in him; no, he had already managed to achieve betrayal. Rather, Nick had now become firmly convinced that his only chance of finding happiness with Jenny lay in helping his love regain her fleshly body. And only the bioresearch station, which was superbly equipped for just such experiments, offered any chance of that.

She was sleeping now, somewhere—as she would perceive it when she wakened—in the Abbey. Nick, as soon as he felt certain that this fight was imminent, had quietly and without asking her permission made sure that his beloved went to sleep. As soon as the combat was over, he would go back to her in the Abbey and knock gently on her bedroom door, and when she opened it for him, tell her of the victory. Had it been possible for Jenny to take any active role in the struggle against the berserker, things would of course have been different.

During the next minute, Hawksmoor's organic shipmates fought on grimly in their effort to board the station while he used the yacht's weapons conscientiously, blasting away with all of his considerable skill at the counterattacking enemy machines. He felt no temptation to turn the heavy weapons against Dirac's small ship—the berserker must be overcome before any lesser conflicts could be settled.

Besides, there was obviously a good chance that the berserker itself might eliminate Nick's rival, despite Nick's real efforts to protect him. Already one of the small Solarian ships was no longer visible at all, having been blasted by berserker weapons into fine debris. Another had been disabled and was drifting helplessly away. Hawksmoor's radio contact with the expeditionary force kept being disrupted, as was only to be expected, by battle noise.

At this point, long seconds into the space fight, three of the small human vessels, including the one Dirac was piloting, had survived the enemy counterattack.

Another of the surviving three was the scoutship, by far the most heavily armed and shielded of the attacking craft.

From the beginning of the action, Frank's heavily armed scoutship had drawn the heaviest enemy attention, a concentration of fire and ramming attempts by small kamikaze machines. It was only now, as Nick watched Frank fight his ship, that he realized how far the man in the boxes, an organic brain melded on the quantum level with state-of-the-art machinery, outclassed any purely nonorganic pilot; how he would indeed, almost certainly, outclass Nick himself.

Here came a pair of infernal berserker devices, hurling themselves in a direct attack upon the yacht!

In a moment Nick had vaporized them successfully.

But not before the *Eidolon* had been hit once more, and some further damage inflicted.

Meanwhile Frank, joyfully entering battle as if it were his natural habitat, had drawn much of the enemy force away from the other small human craft. His heavily armed scout became the enemy's chief target, being harried and followed by a swarm of enemy machines, and in a matter of seconds a virtual screen of them had cut him off from the yacht and from the two small, less well armed ships.

Frank, having assumed the job of flying interference for the actual boarding party, did not try to break through the screen. Instead, taking a gamble on being able to get away with the unexpected, he darted in the direction of the mammoth berserker itself. A sharp feint in this direction, and he ought to be able to swing back the other way.

Nick, observing these maneuvers with some surprise, was doing as much as he could with the yacht's weapons to help Frank, but Marcus was now entering a position where the yacht's weapons had an awkward time trying to reach the berserkers nearest him. The difficulty was compounded by the fact that Nick was strongly constrained to avoid hitting the station.

Moving the yacht might make it possible to support Frank more effectively. But that might also bring the yacht—and Jenny's all-precious optelectronic life—within the line of fire of whatever heavy weapons the big berserker might be keeping in reserve. In microseconds Nick had decided against any such maneuver.

During the next few seconds, Colonel Marcus, his scoutship suddenly badly damaged, was being hounded farther away from the station by the pack of his pursuers, though their ranks were now thinned. The scoutship too had been shot up. It no longer mattered whether his aggressive move in the direction of the big berserker had been a feint or not. The remainder of his swarming foes kept after him, harrying his scout ever close to the great machine itself.

Nick was the only one besides Frank himself who had a chance to see what happened next. And even Nick, despite his speed of perception, was granted only a blurry look at the events.

Marcus, now finding himself isolated from his comrades in arms, chose, as his past record might have suggested, to adopt ever bolder tactics now that his situation was more desperate.

He drove right at the massive enemy.

Perhaps he had counted on being able to pull away at the last moment. What actually happened was that Frank's little scout, now appearing somewhat fouled in defensive force fields, closed with the berserker's hull and disappeared. Nick knew, though his angle of view and flaring interference kept him from actually recording it, that the colonel's ship must have landed, crashed, or been forced down somewhere upon the black, scarred immensity of the enemy hull—around the bulge of both hulls from Nick's place of observation on the yacht.

Nor had the scout's final fate been visible to any of the other surviving humans. The small handful still alive were at the moment totally absorbed in the problems of keeping themselves in that state, and getting aboard the station.

* * *

With the scoutship's disappearance, the enemy fire stopped.

A great many—perhaps all—of the small enemy machines that had come out to counterattack had been destroyed. Any that might have survived had ceased to oppose the boarding, had withdrawn out of the range of the yacht's still-formidable guns.

For a moment there was silence. Bright stars, dark nebula, looked on imperturbably from all directions.

Hastily checking the yacht's various systems for damage, Nick found the drive still functional. In a moment the temptation to cut and run away had risen again. Hawksmoor considered abandoning the Boss and all who had left the yacht with him, seizing the opportunity to get away cleanly with Jenny. Still arguing against any such rash decision was Nick's basic programming of obedience to Dirac and the equally fundamental commands that he serve and protect humanity—both still were very strong.

But again, he thought his final decision not to desert rested on the fact that the station still offered the only hope of reestablishing Jenny in the fleshly body she so fanatically demanded.

Despite considerable losses suffered by the human side, the boarding action now appeared to be succeeding in its main objective. Two small Solarian craft were attaching themselves to hatches over there, reestablishing a foothold on the station. But Nick observed that the victory gave every indication of turning out to be Pyrrhic. Only these two craft had survived this sharp clash.

Nick was presently able to reestablish radio contact with Dirac.

One of the Premier's first questions was "Where's the scoutship? How did Marcus come out?"

"He went down somewhere, it looked like, on the far side of the big berserker. I wouldn't count on him, sir, for any more help."

"Damn it. Any more bandits in sight?"

"Negative, sir. They went out of my sight along with the colonel."

"All right. Stand by, Nick. We're docked here now, and we're going in."

"The best of luck, sir." And at that moment, Nick was sure he meant it.

Frank Marcus was down, but not yet dead.

On finding his scoutship surrounded and harassed by a number of the foe, he had continued to fight aggressively. Triumphantly he had radioed word back—a signal that never got through—that he thought he had succeeded in breaking the back of the opposition by small machines. The number actively engaged against him had diminished to almost nothing. He had won for his shipmates the chance to land on the station virtually unopposed.

But now the scout with Frank inside was down, smashed down by grapples of overwhelming force upon the enemy's black, scarred hull. Still, Frank was not dead. The colonel came out of his wrecked ship fighting, having survived where no being entirely of flesh could have done so, his mobile boxes making him almost as agile and armored as a berserker.

It was time, and past time, for a retreat. But there was no way to retreat, and just staying where he was, until the berserker got around to looking for him, was pointless. He doubted very much that anyone was coming to his rescue.

That left him with the option of going forward. At least he wasn't finished fighting yet.

He hadn't gone far before he saw the chance, the possibility, of being able to do some more damage before the finish came. Ahead of him, as he clawed his way forward across the berserker's outer hull with his eight metallic limbs, Marcus now perceived a weakness, a place where his huge opponent's outer armor had been blown or ripped away in some fight thousands of years in the past.

It was just moments later, when he was in the act of actually entering the berserker, pushing ahead with his own boarding operation, that Frank suddenly understood, was perfectly convinced, that time and luck had run out at last. This was one daring effort that he was not going to survive. The realization did not interfere with his smooth flow of effort; if he had tried he couldn't have thought of any better way to die.

Naturally he had not come out of his little ship unarmed. Once inside the great berserker, near anything it thought important, he could still distract the enemy, make it pay a price. Show it that wiping out life from the universe was never going to be an easy job. Force the damned thing to divert part of its computing capacity and its material resources to finish him off. And maybe in the process he could give his fellow Solarians a chance to rob it of its prize, the bioresearch station it so badly wanted. Maybe Dirac and the rest would even be able to finish it off altogether.

Marcus indeed managed to get inside the hull. Then he had not far to go, in his one-man lunge for some outlying flange of the enemy's vitals, before he encountered heavy opposition.

Only Hawksmoor, alertly guarding his post aboard the *Eidolon,* received any of the last radio message Colonel Marcus sent. Only part of the message came through, and that in somewhat garbled form. And the last words that Nicholas, listening closely on the yacht, was able to hear from Frank were "Oh my God. Oh. My. God."

The two surviving small Solarian vessels had by now attached themselves to modest beachheads on the large hull of the biostation—itself small by comparison with the looming bulk of the berserker only a few hundred meters beyond it.

Dirac and those who were still alive and functioning with him—Kensing among them—were preparing, under the umbrella of Nick's potential firepower, to enter simultaneously two of the station's airlocks.

The boarders had to confront the possibility that the hatches might be booby-trapped or barricaded. Actually the station's outer skin appeared scorched or dented here and there, as if by near-miss explosions. But as far as could be ascertained from outside, the airlocks were intact. All indications were that the mating outer doors had functioned perfectly.

Now the Premier and his companions, wearing armor and carrying the best shoulder weapons available, climbed out of their acceleration couches and made their way one at a time through the small airlocks of their own craft and into the station's larger chambers, where there was room for several to stand together. Kensing moved among them, as eager and terrified as the rest—but his yearning to find Annie quenched his terror.

On entering the station's lock, they immediately discovered that the artificial gravity was still functioning at the normal level. Indications were that the internal atmosphere was normal also. But no one moved to open his or her helmet.

"Go ahead. We're going in."

Someone standing beside Kensing worked the manual controls set into a bulkhead. And now the station's inner door was cycling.

Kensing waited, weapon leveled, mind almost blank, his will holding the alphatrigger trembling on the edge of fire.

EIGHT

The planetoid Imatra was ringed by the orbits of a score of artificial satellites, and several of these metal moons bristled with sophisticated astronomical equipment. Similar devices were revolving close to the larger members of the local planetary system. Now all of these instruments in orbit, as well as many on the ground, had been pressed into service, all focused in one direction. They provided anxious observers with some bizarre views, coming in from approximately ten light-days away.

The images received were at best spotty with distance, and incomplete as a result of interference from the Mavronari's outer fringe. Nor were the pictures nearly as detailed as the viewers could have wished. But under diligent interpretation they did indicate that the Premier and his pursing force had indeed—ten days earlier—managed to catch up with the fleeing enemy.

The additional fact that the encounter had been violent was suddenly revealed by the ominous spectra of weapon flashes. There were also the resulting briefly glowing clouds. Some kind of fierce though small-scale engagement was, or had been ten days ago, in progress.

Several of the worried observers in the Imatran system speculated that these flares and flashes limned an enemy attempt to ambush the pursuing yacht and its escorting ships. How successful the attempt had been, there was no way to be sure from this distance.

None of these observers from a distance detected anything, beyond the mere fact that Solarian ships had met the enemy, that could be construed as real encouragement to supporters of the Solarian cause. And some of the once-glowing clouds that were the aftermath of battle persisted, expanding enough to block any possible view of later events—assuming the chase had gone on to an even greater distance, beyond the site of the battle scene currently unfolding.

One of the few things that those who watched from Imatra were able to say with certainty was that there had been no detectable attempt at communication with their system by any of the Premier's ships, and no sign that any of those vessels had turned back.

More days passed with no new developments, no news. None of Dirac's ships came back in triumph, and if any had tried to turn back from a defeat, they had evidently been destroyed in the attempt. And if any had launched a robot communications courier, that too had been destroyed or had somehow gone astray. The people in the Imatran system lacked any means of confirming or elaborating on what they thought their telescopes had shown them.

Whether the Premier's whole squadron, including his yacht, had been wiped out or not was impossible to determine. One could only try to estimate the probabilities. There was not much to go on, really; just those final signals suggesting a space fight, if you knew where to look for them, and even those tenuous traces were fading day by day, hour by hour. Already it was impossible to record anything meaningful beyond the fact of those little glowing clouds, which one could assume to be the flame and smoke of distant battle. An ambiguous signal at best. And soon there would be nothing at all worth putting into memory.

* * *

"Well, we do have fairly good records of this whole unfortunate business. But the point is, are we sure we really want to be diligent about preserving them?"

"What do you mean?"

"I mean that as soon as all the directly interested worlds understand that not only Lady Genevieve is missing, but now Premier Dirac himself—"

"How can we be blamed for that? In all honesty, how can we be blamed in either case?"

"Well, I foresee we *are* probably going to be blamed by some people—unjustly, of course, but there it is—at least for the Lady Genevieve's being lost."

"Well, if we are to be blamed, let us at least not be accused of destroying records. That would only make it seem that we are covering up something, something truly . . . truly . . ."

And of course Sandro Kensing was gone too. But he had volunteered. The more the local authorities of the Imatran system contemplated their new situation, the more they concentrated on the problem of how best to protect themselves against possible damage from future investigations. Or even mere accusations or rumors.

The more they thought the matter over (now meeting, as they were, face-to-face, taking full advantage of the fine conference facilities on Imatra), the more it seemed to them that they were going to have to endure some kind of trouble along that line. Assuredly the Premier Dirac Sardou, the most powerful Solarian within a space of many light-years, was not going to be allowed to vanish unnoticed from Galactic politics and society.

Not that all the leading members of that society would be displeased by his absence. Inevitably, certain people were going to gain certain advantages if Dirac could reasonably be presumed, could legally be declared, dead. Others would just as surely lose thereby. Still others would benefit if the period of uncertainty could be prolonged. Any formal declaration of the Premier's demise would have to wait for at least seven standard years, but even now interested people were surely planning for that contingency.

* * *

A standard month after the Premier's departure with his squadron, the local authorities, despite their differences of opinion on other aspects of the situation, including the wording of the pending formal announcement, had no difficulty in agreeing that Dirac and his people and his ships were really hopelessly lost, and any attempt to speed a new force to their rescue would be foolish.

The Imatran leaders also carefully inspected the records of the actual attack, as well as those documenting the berserker's departure and the beginning of the Premier's pursuit. The local authorities discovered in these records nothing to cast doubt upon their own basic innocence regarding the recent tragic events. Therefore copies of the relevant recordings, in optical and other wavelengths, were freely produced for anyone who might be presumed to be strongly interested, and some copies were dispatched to other systems. Then the original records were routinely filed away.

The inner door of the airlock slid open in front of the Premier and his handful of surviving volunteers, admitting them to the interior of the bioresearch station. They found themselves confronted by a normally lighted corridor, which appeared to contain nothing in the least out of the ordinary. Just down this corridor, a few meters to their right, the other boarding party was making an equally uneventful entrance.

Dirac addressed the station's optelectronic brain, ordering it to hold the inner doors of both airlocks open.

"Order acknowledged." The voice of the station's brain sounded slightly inhuman, which was perfectly normal for a Solarian-built robot device.

The doors obediently stayed open. So far. Jamming or welding them in that position would slow down a quick retreat, if such a maneuver became necessary.

The small party, reunited now and remaining together as they had planned, advanced a few meters down the corridor. And then a few meters more.

Dirac, undaunted by the disastrous losses suffered by his rescue mission thus far, was implacably determined to continue his search for his wife. There he stood now—where

Kensing could get a good view of him—in the corridor just outside the main laboratory room, a middle-sized man in heavy but flexible armor, blinker (as opposed to alphatrigger) carbine carried in the crook of his right arm. Kensing got the impression that the Premier was perfectly well satisfied with the success of the rescue expedition up till now, heavy casualties and all.

A few meters ahead of the entering party, in perfect conformance with the computer model of the station they had all studied, the corridor branched. As far as it was possible to see along the curves, both branches stretched on, well lighted, filled with usable air at breathable pressure (or so Kensing's suit gauge continued to report), and utterly lifeless.

Standing beside the older man, Kensing could feel his own nerves still ringing with the violence of that last clash in space. *Well, here I am,* was what his mind kept telling itself, without being able to get much beyond that basic proposition. *Well, here I am, still alive.* Even Annie, it seemed, had been all but forgotten for the moment.

In a small voice scrambled and decoded again on the suit radios, someone murmured: "Would help if we could get Nick over here."

The Premier shook his head inside his helmet. His unmistakable radio voice responded: "Negative. At the moment I need Nick right where he is. Now we're going to look into the lab."

Kensing eased forward, holding his breath, his weapon cradled in his arms. The other people advanced behind him and beside him, brain waves close-coupled to the triggers of their carbines and projectors, ready and expecting from moment to moment to be plunged into yet another firefight.

No human's unaided reflexes, of course, could begin to compete against the speed and accuracy of machinery. Not even when the glance of an eye and an act of will, spark of a mind set on a hair trigger, were all it took to aim and fire. But technology made the contest less uneven. Shoulder arms and helmets were melded with the operator/wearer's human alpha waves in such wise that, if great care were not exercised, the whole armored suit could come perilously close to acting in berserker fashion. Weapons cradled in its arms or fastened to the helmet would blast at any visual silhouette that met certain programmed specifications, or simply at sudden noise or light or movement. The suits of armor in which the human fighters now stalked the biostation were also equipped with coded IFF, a hopefully accurate system of distinguishing friend from foe.

"Where are they?" Kensing couldn't be certain if the voice in his helmet was referring to the berserker's commensal machines or to its human victims.

Had Dirac and his party been facing a human enemy, the apparent withdrawal of the foe might easily have persuaded them that their enemy was frightened. But nothing could frighten a berserker. Whatever killing machines might have occupied this very corridor a day ago, an hour ago, five minutes ago, must be still lurking somewhere in these multitudinous compartments and spaces, awaiting the right moment, the savage signal, to spring out, as swiftly efficient as factory machinery, and kill.

Having failed to provoke any enemy response, Dirac ordered another cautious, methodical advance. His plan called for the territory that had been examined, apparently regained for human control, to be gradually extended. One corridor, one deck, after another.

Kensing had now warily eased his way just inside the doorway of the main laboratory room. Here were a thousand pieces of complex equipment of various sizes, shapes, and purposes, everything now standing still and silent. Annie had so often told him things about this chamber that even without studying the VR model in the yacht's ten-cube he would have had no trouble feeling almost at home inside it. This was where she worked. Her duty station, he felt sure, during the alert. So here was where berserker machines, assuming they had come aboard, had most likely caught up with her.

Keeping a tight grip on his nerve, Kensing eased his way in farther from the doorway. His weapon ready, he stood looking about.

The Solarian searchers were very few, and therefore even more tentative, more cautious than they might have been in greater numbers; the biostation was large and complex. To search every nook and cranny of the biostation for enemy machines, for booby traps and ambushes, would take a long time. Eventually, if things went well, Nick could be brought into action, and more ordinary robots used.

But Dirac and those with him could not wait; their primary goal was to discover whether there were human survivors.

Kensing was in midstep, tentatively advancing once again, when off to his right there burst a flash and crash of violence, an instant wave front of radiation and reflected heat dashing harmlessly against his armor. Before he could even turn his head in that direction, the skirmish was over, though in the following second of time another Solarian weapon or two—not Kensing's—echoed the first shots, letting go at a target already smashed, compounding the damage to unprotected laboratory gear and walls. The small berserker machine that had come leaping out of ambush from behind benign equipment had been felled by the first blasting volley, its six legs sliced from under it, the nozzles of its own weapons shriveled, its torso broken open to spill a waste of bloodless components across the deck. Nothing more now than a broken machine, fire leaping out of its insides to be rapidly drenched and quenched by a healing rain from built-in fountains in the lab's high overhead. The station's voice, intent on following the regulations, was insisting that all personnel evacuate the immediate area.

"There may be more—"

But moments passed and apparently there were no more. It was as if this single device, effectively trapped by the unexpected Solarian incursion, had come bounding out in order to be shot down by the alphatrigger weapons of people standing in the doorway.

Then one additional enemy machine was seen and shot at as it raced past in the corridor outside the lab, moving at the velocity of a speeding groundcar.

The Solarian fire missed its target this time, only damaging the inner hull just beyond the corridor's outer bulkhead.

* * *

Seconds of quiet stretched into a minute, into two. The knife edge of excitement dulled. An ominous new stillness descended upon the station, and this stillness was prolonged.

But peace was not completely quiet. Kensing, standing now near the middle of the big laboratory, made a soft little sound high in his throat. Annie, very much alive, looking rumpled but safe in a regular lab coat, had just come round a corner of machinery and was walking toward him.

In another moment, Acting Supervisor Zador, looking pale but very much intact, was clinging to Kensing in a miraculous reunion.

He had to resist an impulse to tear off his helmet and kiss her. All that kept him from doing so was the thought that in the next few minutes, before he could get her away and out of this damned place, she might yet need the most efficient protection he was able to provide.

"It's you, it's you!" Annie kept crying. She babbled on, words to the effect that seeing any free Solarian figure had been wonder enough when the people trapped on the station had already given themselves up for dead. But seeing *him* . . .

Kensing, in turn, demanded in a voice that barely functioned: "Did you think I wouldn't be coming after you?"

Other live Solarians were now appearing, as if by a miracle. A few paces behind Annie came a man she introduced as her colleague, Dan Hoveler. Then shortly a man she introduced as Scurlock, whose presence, unlike that of Hoveler, was totally unexpected by the rescuers. This development made Premier Dirac frown in concentration.

The survivors reported that, strange as it seemed, they had been largely unmolested by the machines when the station was overrun. On being surprised by the sudden sound of fighting, they had been free to take cover as best they could.

A minute later, Scurlock's unexpected appearance was followed by that of a dazed-looking woman named Carol.

There was no sign of Lady Genevieve. Dirac was already asking the survivors about her. "Have you seen my wife?"

Annie, Dan Hoveler, and Scurlock all looked at each other, while Carol stared distractedly at nothing. Then the three mentally alert survivors sadly but confidently assured Dirac that his beloved Lady Genevieve was simply not here at all, alive or dead. No one had seen her since the last courier departed, only minutes before the berserkers arrived.

Zador and Hoveler sadly reported that the Premier's unlucky bride must have joined the other visitors and most of the biolab's workers in boarding the ill-fated courier ship. That had been the last vessel to get away from the station before the berserker fell upon them.

Dirac was shaking his head. "I don't believe she did get on the courier. I believe that's been ruled out."

Now it was time for the Premier's colleagues to exchange glances with each other.

It came as a tragic shock to Hoveler and Zador to learn that the courier carrying their co-workers had been blown up days earlier, with all aboard presumably killed. They asked how much damage the attack had done in the Imatran system, and were somewhat relieved to learn that at least the overall destruction had been surprisingly small.

Sobering news had now somewhat muted their astonishment and delight that Dirac or anyone else had pursued and overtaken the berserker successfully.

"You've killed the berserker, then." It was Hoveler who was joyfully making this assumption. "But of course, you must have. You're sure it's dead?"

The Premier tilted his head back to gaze up toward overhead, the direction of the enemy's gigantic hull. "The big one? No, I'm afraid we can't be entirely sure. Certainly it's badly damaged. But it might have a trick or two to play yet."

The survivors, sobered, listened carefully, nodding. Now that this Galactic celebrity was here, Hoveler and Zador deferred to him, looked to him expectantly, joyfully for rescue, for leadership.

The station's brain, seemingly fully functional once more, blandly assured its questioners, when asked, that all of the berserker machines had now departed. At this point Dirac, leaving Kensing as an armed guard in the laboratory with Annie and the other survivors, took the rest of his people with him to pursue the search for Lady Genevieve on other decks.

The station intercom was still fully functional, and the search party used it to communicate with the lab, employing a quickly improvised code. During the first stages of their effort they encountered no resistance, no further signs of any current berserker presence. And no sign of the woman they were seeking.

Kensing, still thankfully marveling at his own miracle, looked back at Annie again. "So, the machines didn't even hurt you."

"No," she assured him, simply, solemnly. "They didn't really hurt any of us. I have no explanation for this. Except perhaps they wanted to learn something from us, just from watching our behavior."

Hoveler was nodding his puzzled agreement. "That's about the way it seemed to me."

Kensing said to Annie: "I won't demand explanations for a miracle. But I want to get you back aboard the yacht."

"I still have a job to do here." Her voice was intense.

"Then let me at last get you into some armor. All of you."

"All right."

But spare suits of armor were not readily at hand. And Kensing had to admit that perhaps it didn't matter after all. The discovery of living survivors and the absence of any further berserker activity were dulling the fine edge of alertness. It seemed to be true—whatever enemy devices had once occupied the station had now mysteriously withdrawn.

Scurlock had little to say, and Carol, now sitting slumped in a corner, said practically nothing. They both seemed much more deeply in shock than Annie or Dan.

After a few minutes had passed, Scurlock announced that he and Carol were withdrawing to their room, and added that she wasn't feeling well.

Looking after the beaten-looking couple as they left the lab with arms around each other, Dan Hoveler muttered: "They told us they were goodlife; we came near having a real fight a couple of times."

Kensing scowled. He hadn't expected to hear this. "Should we be—watching them?"

Hoveler shrugged. "I don't think they're armed,

anything like that. As for claiming to be goodlife, it's probably just that the—pressure got to them."

"I can understand that."

Suddenly Annie was on the verge of tears. "I knew if we just held on . . ." And then she was weeping, with the intensity of relief.

Dirac and his people were soon back in the lab, with no substantial discoveries to report. The survivors' joy was further tempered when they understood how few their rescuers really were, and how seriously damaged was the ship in which they had arrived.

Kensing was emphatic: "We'd better get out of here as quickly as we can."

Nick was on the radio now, reporting in from the yacht, and his news was simply, seriously chilling: since the latest berserker attack, the yacht's drive was all but inoperative. Modest local maneuvers were still possible, but getting home on it was out of the question until—and unless—repairs could be effected. As soon as he could stand down from red alert, he'd get to work on the problem.

Somewhat to Kensing's surprise, Dirac delayed ordering a general evacuation to the yacht. Again and again the Premier demanded that the three coherent survivors tell him anything they could that might suggest the whereabouts of the Lady Genevieve.

In fact Kensing and others got the impression that Dirac was really paying little attention to the bad news concerning the yacht's drive. The prospect of being stranded here did not seem of much concern to him. He was still ferociously intent upon his search for his bride.

Despite the eyewitness testimony that she was not here, his attitude did not seem to be grief so much as suspicion and anger.

When someone boldly suggested that it was time to get back to the yacht, to repair its drive if nothing else, Dirac responded sharply that Nick and the maintenance robots could handle that as well as he could.

Annie and Hoveler, with growing concern, reiterated

that there was no reason to expect to find his lady here. No one aboard the station had seen her since that last courier departed.

At last, hours after coming aboard the station, Premier Dirac, after trying to question the station's own brain and obtaining nothing helpful in regard to Lady Genevieve, seemed satisfied that this was the case.

But instead of giving way to grief or ordering a general retreat to the yacht, he seemed rather to withdraw mentally, hesitating as to what ought to be done next.

Nick called once more from the yacht to inform his boss that despite his own best efforts the yacht's drive still didn't work. Dirac's response was to send someone back to bring more arms and armor over to the station.

After the messenger's return, some of Dirac's own crew began making pointed suggestions as to what ought to be done next. People were saying that it was time—past time—to get out of here, board the rescuers' vessels and go back to the yacht. If the yacht still wasn't functional, it was time to concentrate on making her so.

And Dirac seemed to waver.

At that point Annie, now dressed in armor, as were Hoveler and Scurlock, faced him. "There's one problem with that plan," she announced.

"Yes, Dr. Zador?"

"Can your yacht carry everybody?"

The Premier's heavy brows contracted. "I don't understand. Assuming the drive can be repaired, there are only a handful of us here."

Anyuta Zador's voice rose slightly. "There are a great many more Solarians here than you seem to realize. Have you room aboard for a billion statglass tiles?"

For a long moment the Premier stared at her. Kensing, watching them, thought it was as if Annie had just offered the old man something he had been searching for. "You have a point there," Dirac conceded willingly.

People who had been suggesting a retreat now glared at Annie, but so far no one argued openly.

Evidently mention of the tiles reminded the Premier of something else. When he questioned the bioworkers again, they confirmed that the Lady Genevieve had indeed made her donation before the berserker attacked the station.

The Premier wanted to know: "Where is it now? The tile?"

Memories were uncertain on that point. Hoveler and Zador were honestly not sure whether the lab's robotic system had properly filed the First Protocolonist away or not. In any case the scrambling of the station's electronic wits, which Hoveler acknowledged having done, would keep anyone from immediately laying hands on any particular specimen.

Gathering his troops around him, Dirac issued a firm order to the effect that there would be no general evacuation of the station until the question of his protochild had been resolved.

Neither of the surviving bioworkers, having endured so much and done what they had done, all to defend the protocolonists, was ready to abandon them now. And everyone else now aboard the station, with the possible exception of Kensing, was accustomed to taking orders from Dirac.

Dirac, making sure that regular contact was maintained with Nick back on the *Eidolon* and having posted sentries at key locations on the station to watch for any berserker counterattack, took time out to watch a video showing his wife's arrival at the station a few days ago. He saw for himself the publicity opportunity that had turned into a panic as soon as the alert was called.

The color coding on the tile was barely discernible in some of the views. But with the retrieval system scrambled as it was, that was probably going to be of no help in finding it.

Hawksmoor had rather quickly made the decision to sabotage the yacht's drive and then to report it as malfunctioning, limited to low maneuvering power only. Of course he blamed the trouble on the recent enemy action. He'd done a thorough job of the disabling, but not so thorough that he would be unable to quickly put things back in their proper order if and when that became necessary—as he confidently expected that it would, sooner or later.

But probably not for a long time, Nick computed. Not until after he had managed to provide the Lady Genevieve with the living flesh her happiness demanded. And even after he had somehow arranged matters so he could use all the facilities of the biostation without hindrance, that was probably going to take years.

He didn't really want to make all these other fleshly people suffer, to disrupt their lives and in effect hold them prisoner. Especially not here, where they were almost within the grasp of a monster berserker that was probably still half alive. But what choice did he have?

Nick had to admit that the complexities of the whole situation were beginning to baffle him.

No, it wasn't fair, that the burden of others' lives should thus be placed upon him. He was supposed to be a pilot and an architect, not a philosopher. Not a political or spiritual or military leader. Not . . . not a lover and seducer.

He was able to cushion himself against this resentment and uncertainty only by telling himself that his fretting over these insoluble problems offered strong evidence that whatever means his programmers had used in his creation, they had made him truly human.

NINE

There was something about that last fragmentary message from Frank Marcus—chiefly the *tone*—which Nick found himself still pondering.

When he brought the message to the attention of Dirac and the others, the Premier listened once to the recording and then basically dismissed it.

"Humans often call upon God, some kind of god, in their last moments, Nick. Or so I'm told. Sad, tragic, like our other losses, but I wouldn't make too much of it. That's probably just the death Marcus would have chosen for himself. In fact, in a very real sense I'd say that he did choose it."

"Yes, sir." But Hawksmoor was unable to dismiss the matter as easily as his organic master did.

There were other pressing urgencies no one could dismiss. During the skirmish just past, the great berserker in crushing Frank's scoutship had demonstrated that it still possessed formidable short-range weapons, including the force-field grapples that had evidently pulled Frank in to his doom. The remaining small craft and the yacht itself would have to be kept at a safe distance from the berserker; of course no one could say with any confidence just what distance that might be.

Some of the debris from the space fight remained visible for almost an hour after the boarding, bits of junk metal and other substances swirling delicately in space, caught near the scene by some short-lived balance of incidental forces. But in an hour the last of this wreckage had gone, blown away in the vanishing faint wind of the ships' joint passage through never-quite-completely-empty space.

Every day, every hour as the hurtling cluster of objects drew closer to the depths of the Mavronari, the space through which they traveled, still vacuum by the standards of planetary atmosphere, was a little less empty than before.

Now space within several thousand kilometers in all directions indeed showed void of all small craft and machines, unpopulated by either friends or foes. Nicholas still stood guard faithfully, trying to decide whether he wanted the fleshly people to make themselves at home on the station or not, beginning to ponder what his own course of action was going to be in either case.

He could keep his post alertly enough now with half an eye, and far less than half a mind. He was free to spend more than half his time with Jenny. Joyfully, as soon as he had the chance, he awakened her with news of victory.

When Jenny came out of her bedroom again to talk to Nick, walking with him in the cool, dim vastness of the Abbey, she said: "So long as we remain nothing but clouds of light, hailstorms of electrons, all you and I can ever do is pretend to please each other, and pretend to be pleased. Maybe that would be enough for you. It could never be enough for me."

"Then, my lady, it cannot be enough for me either. No, Jenny, I want to be with you. I will be with you in one way or another, and I will make you happy."

The intensity in the lady's gaze made her eyes look enormous. "Then the two of us must have flesh. There is no other way."

"Then flesh we will have. I swear it. I will bring real human bodies into being for us."

"You have said that before. I doubt that you have such power."

"If I am allowed to use the resources on board the laboratory station, I do."

The Premier had chosen a woman of quick wit for his bride. "You mean the zygotes? The colonists?"

"One way would be to use those. There seem to be a billion potential bodies there to choose from."

The lady frowned. "But they are—"

"Are what? You mean there are moral objections, they are people? Hardly. More like genetic designs for organic vessels. Vessels we ought to be able to keep empty until we can fill them with ourselves. There must be some way."

Genevieve seemed unwilling to let herself believe that it was going to be possible. "Even if we could find a way to do that, it would take years. You mean to grow ourselves new bodies in the artificial wombs—I can't go back as an infant!"

"Nor would I choose to experience infancy." Nick shuddered inwardly. "Nor, I suppose, could adult minds be housed in brains so immature. But there *must* be a way to make that method work. As you are now, you could sleep for ten standard years, twenty years, while the body that would be yours was growing, developing somewhere. You could rest for a century, if there was any reason to prolong your slumber to that extent, and it would be no more to you than the blinking of an eye."

"And so could you."

"Yes, of course. Except that the Premier is not likely to let *me* rest without interruption for even an hour. And I must heed his orders if we are to survive. It's far from certain that the berserker is really dead." Nick paused, considering. "Fortunately, *he* seems in no rush about hurrying home. He hasn't given up on finding you; or finding a way to recover you in some sense."

"What do you mean?"

"He seems to be thinking about your child."

"Ah. So do I sometimes. But that child won't be me." The lady was silent for a little while, and then burst out: "Oh,

Nick. If you can do this for me, put me back together, I will be yours forever." After a moment the lady added, "How will you do it? My—my husband, and the others mustn't—"

"Of course they mustn't find out. If I find a way to do this for you, you're not going back to him."

"I will go wherever you say, do whatever you want." New hope had been born in Genevieve's eyes. "And how will you gain access to the artificial wombs?"

"Access is no problem. There is nothing to keep me out of the circuitry over there. In general, the way things are on the station now, no one pays any attention to those devices, or would be aware of the fact if they were being used. Still, it would be better, of course, to use one or two of the machines that are physically isolated."

The Premier soon summoned Nick over to the station. Rather than transport the units in which he was physically stored, Hawksmoor chose to transmit himself by radio across the minor interval of intervening space, a mode of transportation he had sometimes used in the past.

Zador and Hoveler and Scurlock, all unaccustomed to the presence of recorded people or anthropomorphic programs, were startled when Nick showed up, as a kind of optelectronic ghost, in the station's circuitry and computers.

But the Premier was quick to reassure them. "That's Nick, he's on our side." A moment's pause; seeing that their recently frayed nerves needed more reassurance, Dirac added, "He's a mobile program, but it's all right."

Nick immediately went to work, at the Premier's direction, probing the immense complexity of circuits. Nowhere could he find any berserker booby traps or spot any but the most incidental residue of the berserker's presence. He did not forget the ten-cube and its stored programs.

He thoughtfully inspected the combat damage in the main laboratory, where an isolated berserker device had been gunned down, and in the nearby corridor, where a few shots had been wasted. It was very fortunate, he thought, that the onboard combat had been so limited. It wouldn't have taken a great deal of fighting to leave the station's fragile equipment entirely in ruins.

The onboard software was generally okay and did not appear to have been tampered with except for a certain serious confusion in the system that was supposed to keep track of the cargo of protocolonists. This was readily explained by Hoveler's actions immediately after the berserker occupation. Too bad, but it couldn't be helped now.

Nick pondered, wondering if there might be some way to turn the scrambling of the inventory system to advantage, for his own private purposes.

His and Jenny's.

Having completed the first phase of an intense inspection, Nick reported to Dirac and asked him, "What do I do next, boss?"

"She's here somewhere. You know, Nick?"

"Sir?"

Dirac raised eyes filled with an uncharacteristically dreamy expression. "The medics here on board took her genetic record, and they took our child. These things are a part of her, and they are here."

"Oh. Yes sir." The Boss had given Nick a bad moment there. But now Hawksmoor understood.

The scrambling of the inventory did not discourage Premier Dirac from pushing his search through the genetic records for his lost bride—or at least, as some of his crew muttered, for enough of her genes to do him some good dynastically.

"If the Lady Genevieve is dead, still, our child is not."

The days passed swiftly, and Dirac and his crew established something like a new routine. No new berserker presence was discovered on the station. But the enormous bulk of the enemy, its drive at least partly functional, still hung over everyone's head, dragging the research station, very slowly in terms of interstellar travel, toward some mysterious destination. Kensing, and doubtless others, had the feeling of living not far below the rim of a slumbering volcano.

Nick had now been placed in charge of a force of dull-witted serving robots, charged with a continued harrowing, a vigilant inspection and reinspection of the station, to guard against any surprise berserker counterattack.

And yet no additional berserker presence had been found, except for a couple of what appeared to be small spy devices. The existence of more was considered likely. Even with Nick on the job, there could be no absolute guarantee of security against them.

Nick, and one or two fleshly human workers, in consultation with Hoveler who had done the scrambling, were now trying to restore a normal inventory function to the station's brain. The outlook was not bright. Even were they apparently successful, the cargo might still be badly scrambled if the archivist robots had rearranged many of the tiles while the software was down. This seemed a distinct possibility.

Dirac insisted that this job of restoration be given the highest priority, though with a huge berserker of unknown capability only a few hundred meters distant, many of the Premier's shipmates would have preferred to concentrate their efforts on other matters, such as repairing the yacht's drive.

Nick, on snatching a few moments away from duty to spend them on his private affairs, felt shaken but triumphant when he considered events so far. He wondered at his own daring and success in secretly defying his powerful employer, in the matter of that employer's bride.

Not that this adventure with the lady had begun as an act of defiance. Far from it. Hawksmoor, reliving the chain of events in perfect memory, told himself that when he first drove his ship after the courier he had simply, very loyally, been trying to save her. A little later, when it had plainly been beyond his or the medirobot's powers to save her flesh from death, the next step had seemed to follow automatically.

Already at that point Hawksmoor had begun to dread the moment when the woman he had come to love would leave him to be restored to her husband. It had taken Nick somewhat longer to let himself be convinced that, since an electronic bride would do the Premier no good dynastically, she would never be going back to Dirac as any kind of political asset.

The glorious thing, of course, was that—Nick was sure of it!—she was now at least beginning to care for him. Not that she was ready to choose life with him, under the conditions of virtual reality, over having a real body once again. No, he was under no illusions as to that. Before she could choose life with him, he would have to provide her with a body. And he had yet to make sure that a means existed to accomplish that.

Most of the station's artificial wombs were on the same deck, actually in the same room. But five or six had been for some reason separated from the rest, scattered about in secluded spots. The possibility of Nick's being able to use one—he really needed two—of these without being discovered was something he would have to determine.

Nick said to Jenny: "I will find a way of growing flesh, since flesh you must have. I will grow bodies for us. Or," he added after a moment, "if something should prevent my doing that, I will take them, already grown."

That gave the lady pause, if only for a moment. "Take them from where? From whom?"

"Somehow. Somewhere. From people who would stop us if they knew what we are doing."

Now freely roaming about the station's circuits, Nick discovered the very treasures he needed to accomplish his goal. The station boasted a whole deck, actually somewhat more than one deck, packed with artificial wombs and their support equipment, perhaps a hundred or more of the glass-and-metal devices. All checked out functional, and all were sitting there just waiting to be used.

Technically, everything in that department seemed to be in perfect condition. Expert systems waited like genies in bottles to be called up, provided with the necessary genetic material, and given their orders to produce healthy human bodies. A full-scale effort along that line, of course, was supposed to take place only when the projected colonizing ship eventually reached its chosen destination.

Annie Zador, passing along information in all innocence, told Nick something about the most advanced prenatal expert system aboard, the one she and her co-workers had called Freya, after a Norse goddess of love and fertility.

* * *

And relating this point Nick, standing with his beloved companion near the high altar of the Abbey, lost his composure and attempted to embrace her fully. Whether he was really generating or only imagining the appropriate excitement was hard to say, but he was well on the way to undressing his companion before the lady, who at first had seemed joyously eager, suddenly pulled away, crying: "No! All wrong, all wrong!"

Then, when she had regained control of herself again: "Not this way, Nick. Not like this. One way or another, dear Nicholas, we must be flesh together."

Within the next hour, again having some respite from the duties assigned him by Dirac, Nick was again concentrating his consciousness in one of the comparatively remote areas of the biostation, earnestly studying the data banks and the equipment he would have to use to accomplish his and Jenny's secret project.

One of the many staggering problems he faced was to discover how the process by which a human mind was reduced or amplified to pure optics and electronics could be made to operate in reverse.

Hawksmoor very early interviewed the expert system called Freya by Annie Zador and her fellow fleshly bioworkers. Freya was distinct from the biolab's overall intelligence, and she—Nick definitely visualized her as a woman—had remained intact throughout Hoveler's efforts at disruption.

Nick's visualization of Freya was vague and variable. To him she was never actually anything more than an intellect expressed in a cool, compassionate voice.

Nick, having introduced himself to Freya, soon assumed—quite naturally, as part of his security function—the job of scanning Freya's programming. It really was part of his assigned job to make sure that, during the time when the station had been occupied territory, she had not become some kind of a berserker trick.

He verified that her programmed benevolence had not

been poisoned. Then he talked with her some more and introduced his problem—without, of course stating it as his: "How fully developed would an organic brain need to be before I could download into it the patterns of myself?"

That was a stunner, even for Freya. It took her some time to frame an answer.

From the start of his investigation it had been obvious to Hawksmoor that the gray matter of a newborn infant, let alone that of a fetal brain, would never answer his purpose. Even were he capable of setting aside all his built-in moral objections to such a procedure, only a partial downloading could be accomplished under the restrictions of minimum space and complexity imposed by the infant brain.

The expert system too reacted with moral horror. Freya seemed on the verge of shutting herself down.

"The question is purely theoretical. No such operation is contemplated," Nick assured Freya firmly.

She in turn insisted that such an operation would not be technically possible, even under optimum conditions.

Hawksmoor continued his probing questions.

Freya upon reflection offered the opinion—purely theoretical, she insisted firmly—that there might be two ways in which an entity like Nick could obtain a carnal body for himself. One way would be to grow a body, from the stock of zygotes and/or other miscellaneous human genetic material available on the bioresearch station. To grow one selectively, taking care to preserve the developing brain as a tabula rasa, blank as regards any personality of its own, but capable of receiving his.

Of course, normally, bodies grown in the laboratory, just like those developed according to the ancient and organic course of nature, give every indication of being possessed by their own minds and spirits from the start.

The second possibility—and this, again, Freya was ready to admit only after persistent questioning, as a theoretical procedure, totally unacceptable in practice—would be to wipe clean an existing adult brain. This would involve inflicting an extensive pattern of carefully controlled microinjuries, to erase whatever personality pattern was currently present. Then the microstructure of the brain would be encouraged to heal, the healing brought about in such a way that the infusion of the new patterns was concomitant with it.

There would be some practical advantages to this ethically unacceptable scheme, the expert system admitted: instead of a minimum of fifteen or sixteen standard years, the host organ would be ready in a mere matter of months to receive the downloaded personality. But during that time the equipment would have to run steadily and undisturbed.

Nick went away to ponder in secret what he had learned.

Plainly it would be necessary to get free somehow of both the berserker and oppressive human authority before any such ambitious project could succeed.

Nick also considered attempting to run the experiment back on the yacht, where fleshly, inquisitive people now seldom visited. But it would be essential to move the necessary equipment from the station to the yacht—and again, he could not be sure of being able to work undisturbed for a long time. Moving Jenny and himself as required was easier.

Freya, when Nick talked to her again, insisted there was only one possible way to download the information content of an electronic man or woman into an organic brain, especially the only partially developed brain of an infant. It was at best a very tricky operation.

It would be something like the reverse of the process of recording, upon some optelectronic matrix, the personality pattern of a living brain. And even if some quicker method could be devised, it seemed inevitable that the incoming signals would scramble, destroy, whatever native pattern of personality the developing brain had already begun to form.

If a mature brain was used as the matrix, according to Freya, the native pattern would very likely triumph over the one being superimposed.

Or, given the two conflicting patterns, the resultant person might well be some hybrid of the two. Some memories, not all, would belong to the native personality.

The plan Nick finally decided on, one worked out in consultation with Freya (the latter requiring continual assurance that all this was merely theoretical), involved subjecting the maturing organic brain to alternating periods of deep though unfrozen sleep, in which the brain could grow organically, with periods of intense loading. First the rough outlines of the desired personality patterns would be impressed upon the developing matrix, and then later the details. Inevitably, Freya warned, certain errors would creep into the process; the resultant fleshly person would possess the memories of the electronic predecessor/ancestor, but could not be considered an exact copy.

"But then no fleshly human is, today, an exact copy of himself or herself of yesterday."

"I really hope the two of you are not working on an actual project. To deceive me in such a matter would be most unethical."

Nick, who had begun withdrawing along a path of circuits, turned back sharply. "The two of us?" He had not so much as ever hinted to Freya, he was sure of it, the actual existence of a program version of the Lady Genevieve.

"Yes." Freya was almost casual, as she usually was when anything but the sanctity of life was under discussion. "I have very recently given very much the same information to Premier Dirac. I assumed the two of you were having a discussion."

TEN

Meanwhile, the handful of organic people living under Dirac's command found their initial relief at what had seemed a victory gradually turning into desperation.

But the Premier, supported by Brabant and Varvara Engadin, fiercely put down any open dissension before it could rise above the level of subdued muttering.

It's all right, Kensing tried to reassure himself. *At the moment we don't have a drive capable of getting us home—the small craft would be inadequate, starting from here within the nebula—and there's no use fretting about when to pull out until we have the capability. Meanwhile, someone has to be in charge, to keep up morale, to keep the people busy.* And who was better qualified as a leader than Dirac?

Besides, Kensing realized that even if the *Eidolon* was ready to go, Annie, and probably Hoveler as well, would still be determined not to abandon their billion protocolonists.

Eventually, Kensing hoped, it would be possible to somehow cut the station loose from the berserker's forcefields so that the restored yacht could eventually tow it home.

Meanwhile, things could have been worse. The berserker remained quiet, and all life-support systems on yacht and station were working. Things could have been much worse.

The Premier always had at least one organic person besides the automated systems standing sentry duty, watching the berserker for signs of activity. Meanwhile, under his firm command, his remaining handful of people were steadily consolidating their position aboard the research station.

The attempt to restore the cargo inventory system, in their ongoing effort to save the protocolonists, occupied most of Zador and Hoveler's time. The fact that Dirac put a high priority on saving the cargo enlisted the wholehearted support of the two surviving bioworkers.

Another project to which the Premier gave a high priority was that of establishing a relatively secure area from which any berserker spy devices had been absolutely excluded.

At the center of this domain Dirac had chosen a cabin for himself, and established his headquarters there.

Meanwhile, two other people aboard the station were under suspicion of being goodlife, despite the fact that since Dirac's boarding no one had heard them confess to that crime.

Dirac wanted to resolve that situation, to clear the air, as he put it. Quietly the Premier asked Scurlock to come and see him in his stateroom, and to bring Carol along.

Scurlock showed up alone, and entered the room to stand facing Dirac, who sat regarding him from a kind of rocking chair. A few of the cabins aboard had rather luxurious appointments.

When the Premier gestured to another chair, Scurlock took it uneasily. Then he reported that Carol had refused to come to the meeting. "She's not well, you know, Premier."

"Has Dr. Zador looked at her?" Dirac's voice indicated a fatherly concern. "Or have you taken her to a medirobot?"

"I've asked her to try one or the other, but she declines."

The Premier rocked a few times. "All right, let it go for now. I'll talk to you." He rocked a few more times, while Scurlock waited apprehensively. Then he said: "I can quite appreciate that the pair of you were in a very difficult situation when the berserker had you directly in its custody."

"Yes sir, it was difficult."

"I really think it would be unjust to blame you, either of you, for anything you may have said or done under those conditions."

"That's it, sir! That's very true. I'm only afraid that everyone isn't going to be so understanding." Scurlock's large, nervous hands had begun to wrestle with each other in his lap.

Dirac was soothing. "I think perhaps I can help you with the problems you face regarding other people's attitudes. That is, assuming that you and I can work together now. Understand that when—if—we eventually return to settled planets, you and Carol are going to need all the help that you can get. Accusations of goodlife activity are not taken lightly."

"Yes sir. I'm well aware of that."

Dirac spoke slowly. "At the moment we—all of us aboard the station—find ourselves in a situation not much different, I think, from that which you and Carol faced as actual prisoners of the machine. For us, too, some kind of accommodation with the machine, at least for the short term, is in order. Do you agree?"

"With the berserker, sir?"

"That's what I meant by the machine, yes."

"Oh, I do agree, Premier!"

"I'm not sure that the other people on board will be ready to understand this point as well as you and Carol will. So I'd like to keep this discussion just between us for the time being."

"I understand, Premier."

"Do you?" Dirac rocked and ruminated. "Of course the machine may now really be completely dead—except for its drive and autopilot. Or it may not. I would like to know the truth about its condition. That seems to me an essential first step."

Scurlock nodded.

"So I mean to send you on a scouting trip, Scurlock. I've chosen you because the machine knows you. It did not kill you or hurt you when it had the chance. Therefore I think you will do well as a scout, as my investigator."

Scurlock said nothing. He looked frightened, but not yet absolutely terrified.

Dirac nodded his apparent approval of this reaction. He continued: "If necessary, if the machine is not yet dead, then you will serve as my—ambassador."

Surlock let out a small sigh. Then he nodded.

The Premier continued. "There are certain things we—the people now in control of this station—want; first of all, that there be no further berserker attacks against us. Also there are certain things the machine—assuming it not yet dead—must want, according to its programming. We find ourselves now in a situation where total victory is not possible for either side. So, as I said before, an accommodation may be our only real choice."

And Scurlock nodded once again.

Nick, after a discussion with the Premier, nudged the *Eidolon* forward on its supposedly faltering drive, arranging for the yacht to hitch a ride by maneuvering into one edge of the berserker-generated towing field. Now the *Eidolon* too was being dragged along. Hawksmoor assured his organic companions that the yacht, even half crippled as it was, would be able to break free at a moment's notice. Meanwhile his efforts to repair the drive would be facilitated by being able to turn it completely off.

The violent berserker opposition to Dirac's boarding party had ceased so quickly that most of the Solarians still refused to believe that all the bad machines had been destroyed. Beyond that, Dirac himself had not yet publicly taken a position, but others were ready to argue on both sides of the question.

Brabant and Engadin were arguing.

The woman said: "Its machines have definitely retreated."

"Yes, but why? Ask yourself that. Berserkers don't just retreat. Or rather, they retreat only when they feel certain of gaining some advantage. It's obviously setting a trap for us."

Engadin disagreed strongly with the bodyguard: "I don't think they've retreated at all. What's happened, I believe, is that they've used up all their mobile hardware, or depleted it down to the last reserve. This giant thing on top of us is an ancient machine, judging by the look of its outer hull, and it's been through a lot of fights; I think the fact is that we've really blasted their last mobile unit."

Brabant looked doubtful. "That's a possibility, but we don't dare count on it."

"Anyway," Varvara Engadin insisted, "there are no active, mobile, berserker devices anywhere on the station. And just in time, I'd say." It was obvious to all that a little more onboard fighting might have left the station uninhabitable by breathing beings. "Rendering space installations uninhabitable is exactly what a berserker ought to try to do. I tell you, it's got nothing left to throw at us."

The big man shook his head gloomily. "I might be tempted to believe that. Except this berserker has been an exception right from the start. Seemingly utterly mad. A real oddball. It could easily have vaporized the station right where it was, in orbit around Imatra. Much less difficult than dragging a thing like this away."

"Which means what?"

"That question has a two-part answer, an easy part and a hard one. The easy part is, no, this berserker is not utterly mad. It had some coldly logical reason for not destroying this facility. Because it has, or had, some special use for it. Or for something or someone being carried aboard. And that might even explain why it's not fighting us now. It just doesn't want to risk having its prize shot up. It would rather bide its time and hope we fly away on the *Eidolon.*"

The woman nodded slowly. "I have to admit you may be on to something there . . . and the hard part?"

"That is deciding what the special use could be."

"What else *could* it be but our billion protocolonists? So maybe, logically, the best thing we could do is shoot up the station's cargo ourselves."

The bioworkers were outraged when they heard this suggestion.

Once more, Dirac sided with them. "We can always shoot things up. But we do have a very valuable cargo here, and we are still exhausting every possibility to find the Lady Genevieve."

No one, except perhaps the Premier himself, actually believed that anymore. Several wondered why they were really lingering aboard, but no one dared insist upon an answer.

The bioworkers and Dirac as well had been relieved to discover that the period of active berserker occupation had involved no widespread destruction among the cargo of protopeople. Nor did any great volume of tiles seem to have been removed from their usual storage places—though given the immense number of stored units, and the severe confusion of the record-keeping system, it was impossible to be sure about that.

Certainly there was no evidence that the berserker had ever started to grow Solarians for some hypothetical corps of mamelukes, of goodlife slaves. None of the artificial wombs had been activated or moved from their original places of installation, though there was evidence suggesting one or more had been examined. As far as could be determined without detailed examination, none were damaged. None were currently in use.

Nick had to wait until this general inspection was over before he could hope to get his own secret project under way. Dirac was still conducting armed patrols, an armed and suited escort accompanying every fleshly technician's foray into the huge storerooms, in case something was still lurking.

Faced with the seemingly immense difficulties of providing bodies, Nick tried to persuade Jenny to abandon her demand for flesh. He kept promoting, subtly as he thought, virtual reality as a form of paradise, but Jenny, whenever she suspected him of doing this, continued to insist violently on regaining flesh.

She began to accuse Nick of having robbed her of her body; maybe his real goal all along had been to reduce her to his own fleshless, unreal condition, thinking to possess her that way. After all, she had only his word that her injuries had been so severe. Well, he could forget it, it wasn't going to work. No man was going to have her until she had been given her body back. The mere idea of electronic lovemaking, of attempting to program exquisite extrapolations on the sense of touch, was quite enough to make her sick.

* * *

Eventually the Premier, feeling increasingly confident about safety aboard, declared armed escorts now optional.

Early one morning—Dirac had set station time equal to ship's time aboard the *Eidolon*—Kensing, leaving the stateroom he now shared with Annie, asked her: "A zygote is basically a blueprint, correct? Basically very compactly stored information?"

"In the first place, a blueprint is neither human nor alive. I happen to believe that these are both."

"Even when frozen?"

"You wouldn't consider yourself dead, would you, lover, if you were riding unconscious in an SA chamber? Which brings us to the second place: you might as well argue that you or I or Nick or anyone is only a bundle of information."

"I didn't want to argue philosophy. What I was really getting at is this: could a billion zygotes have been stored much more compactly, and just as accurately, in digital form, as information records?"

Annie took deep thought over that one. "I don't know," she admitted at last. "You could fairly easily, I suppose, record anyone's genetic architecture, as it were. But not a protopersonality, as represented by the patterns of brain activity—in that sense a zygote has developed nothing to record. There is as yet no brain. Whereas even a three- or four-month fetus has quite a lot going on between the ears."

Scurlock was back. No one besides Dirac, and probably the reclusive Carol, even realized that he had been absent from the station for almost a full day.

He reported privately to Dirac, and he handed over to the Premier a small, mysterious, innocent-looking piece of hardware.

"You actually spoke to a functioning machine?"

"Sir, I did." The tall man was once more seated opposite the Premier in the latter's private quarters. He described how his physical journey had been accomplished according to plan. To make the secret journey possible, Dirac had taken an extra turn at sentry himself and had arranged for Hawksmoor to be distracted.

Dirac let out a long sigh. "Then I was right."

"Yes sir. You were right. The great machine is certainly not dead. Though I believe much weakened."

"And this?" Dirac was balancing the little piece of hardware in his hand. It looked like an anonymous spare part from somewhere inside one of a million complex Solarian devices.

"A secure communications device. So it informed me. Anything you say near it will be heard—over there. Now and then the machine may use it to talk to you. It said it would not talk to you very often, lest some speech come through at a moment when you might find it embarrassing."

"How considerate. So, it is listening to us now?"

"I assume so, Premier."

"And what else can you tell me? What were you able to observe?"

"Very little, Premier. I rode the space sled over there and looked around until I discovered what looked like a hatch. Then I waited, in accordance with your instructions. After several minutes the hatch opened and a small machine came out to investigate my presence."

"A small machine of the type you encountered here on the station, during the berserker occupation?"

"Yes, the same type, as far as I could tell."

"Go on."

"When I made an openhanded gesture to the small machine, it escorted me inside the hatch—it wasn't an airlock, of course. I didn't get any farther than just inside, and there was very little to see. Just metal walls. I didn't really learn anything about the machine's interior construction."

"I didn't really think you would be able to." Dirac tossed up the little piece of hardware and caught it in midair. "You have done well."

Jenny was delighted when Nick came to report that he was on the verge of starting their great secret project.

He had succeeded in copying Freya, without Freya's being aware of it, and in making the necessary alteration in the fundamental programming of Freya^2. Soon it should be possible to begin operations with a pair of the artificial wombs located in an area seldom visited by fleshly people.

Nothing ventured, nothing gained, Nick told himself and Jenny. If the secret work should be noticed, he could make some excuse, disguise the work as something other than what it was. But Nick thought it unlikely that anyone would even notice that the project was going on.

Jenny was growing enthusiastic. "But first, of course, we must select from the cargo the zygotes we want to use."

"Yes. We have a billion to choose from. If you don't want to go out there, I'll bring likely samples for your consideration."

"And after that, it is still going to take years."

"As I see it, we shall have years. I can control the yacht's drive indefinitely. And the Premier will not really be disappointed, I believe. I tell you, he is in no hurry at all to get started for home. The only thing that worries me . . ."

"Yes?"

"Never mind. An idle thought."

Nick didn't want to tell Jenny what he'd heard from Freya, that Dirac had apparently been contemplating a secret project of his own, something along the lines of Nick's.

He started to devise a simple program to let a robot sort through zygotes, a preliminary step in picking out the pair they'd use. One for Jenny's new body. And one for Nick's own body, the first and very likely the only fleshly form that he would ever have.

Nick's imagination kept coming back to the vital, difficult questions that could not be avoided. Might it be possible to push forward on two fronts at once, start trying to make both methods, growth and capture, work? Or would running two secret projects simply make discovery twice as likely?

The capture method would require him somehow to seize control of suitable adults and wipe their brains clear of pattern without killing any of the body's vital organs—to injure the brains delicately, precisely, without destroying the tissue's capacity to take and retain the patterns of thought once again.

Murder. Sheer murder of innocent bystanders. Despite his determination to be ruthless, he shrank from the thought. Not to mention the difficulties he and Jenny would face after technical success. Even if they could somehow avoid the Premier's wrath and that of other potential victims, what human society would give shelter to such murderers?

Of course it would be years quicker than growing zygotes. And the actual capture should pose no great difficulty. Nick, in his suit mode, could easily overpower any organic human not wearing armor, and few wore armor these days except on sentry duty.

The real difficulty was that very few adults were currently available; and none of the available bodies appeared to be ideal choices. On Nick's next visit to the yacht he entered the corridor housing the ship's medirobots and read the biological specifications on Fowler Aristov, the would-be colonist mentor who still reposed there in the deep freeze. Not Nick's ideal of a body for himself, but acceptable, he supposed, in an emergency.

But what about Jenny? She came first. He must find the right fleshly envelope for her, even if he failed to accomplish as much for himself. And among the organic females currently available, none, in Nick's opinion, came up to the standard of beauty that was required.

No, he had better stick to method one. Given sufficient time and care, human bodies could certainly be grown in the station's artificial wombs. There was an overabundance of zygotes aboard the station among which to rummage for desirable genetics. Despite the scrambled records, a suitable pair could certainly be located, given time for the slow mechanical search required.

That, of course, was only the beginning. Assuming that suitable bodies for himself and Jenny could be grown, the next step, loading their personalities into those immature brains, was surely going to present new difficulties. According to the plan he'd worked out with Freya^2, that phase would have to be accomplished concurrently with the process of organic growth. Organic brains and minds would have to be fabricated in successive levels of refinement, as a sculptor cuts away the stone in finer and finer increments.

And either method, stealing bodies or growing them, would eventually require that the information-storage masses in which the two disembodied people now resided—three skulls' volume each—be physically moved to the place where the organic vessels were being prepared.

Several members of Dirac's crew, now even Brabant and Engadin to some degree, were growing increasingly dissatisfied with his continued emphasis on somehow recouping his personal losses.

The political adviser scooped up a handful of tiles and let them go clattering to the deck, then watched moodily as a small machine came rushing to arrange the statglass rectangles in some kind of order. Varvara brooded: "First we spent our days searching for a woman who wasn't here when the berserkers came. Now we're looking for a tile, a single tile, that no one in God's universe could find!"

The bodyguard, grumbling in general agreement, compared the latter task to that of locating one star in the Galaxy, without a chart.

Dirac's adviser and mistress urged: "We've fought the berserker to a standstill. What we ought to be trying to do now, and I've already told him so, is get the whole station free of its grip. All right, sure, save the tiles if we can. The best way to do that is to go after the berserker now and make sure that it's dead."

"You mean go aboard it?"

"That's what I mean. Dangerous, sure. But if we wake up and think we'll realize that just staying here, devoting ourselves to meaningless tasks, is suicidal. If the berserker doesn't get us, the nebula is sooner or later going to close in and we'll be trapped."

"So? What do we do?"

"If repairing the yacht is really out of the question, then we must go aboard the berserker, make sure it's dead, and find some way to manipulate its drive. That's the only way we can start ourselves back in the right direction. That method saves the protolives as well; we can tow the station and its cargo out of the nebula again."

Everyone agreed on at least one point: If they maintained

their present course, heading straight into the nebula, sooner or later they would inevitably get trapped in a shifting of the Mavronari's clouds, caught so that centuries instead of days of travel would be needed to restore them to their homes.

After long days of searching through cargo bins and various pieces of equipment, it still seemed impossible to determine whether or not the tile containing Lady Genevieve's donation had ever been turned over to the filing system. The problem of finding this protochild among nearly a billion others appeared to be practically impossible.

Barring success with the software, the only way to locate one tile among the billion might be to have people, or robots, physically examine all the stored tiles, one after another. "Is there only one machine on board designed to do such testing? Get through a million tiles a year, and we can finish the job in only ten centuries."

"Of course the chances are we'd find it in half that time."

Something like a hundred thousand tiles per standard month. That would mean three thousand a day. More than a hundred an hour.

Neither Zador or Hoveler could remember what had been done with that particular tile, in the panicky moments right after the alert was sounded, other than that it had been put down either on the arm of Hoveler's chair or on the edge of his console.

On several details the two bioworkers' memories were in conflict. Well, organic brains tended toward the unreliable in many ways.

Nevertheless Dirac continued to insist that a strong effort be made to find his family donation. The Premier had now publicly announced that he might be able to reclaim Jenny only by reconstituting her from her genes. Of course his wife's full genetic code would not be available from the zygote, but that would provide a start. And the full code might be here somewhere. Sometimes parents who donated a protochild to the colonizing project were asked to leave their own complete genetic records as well. Neither Hoveler nor Zador knew with certainty whether this had been done in the case of the Lady Genevieve. If it had, and the specimen could be found, then cloning should be possible. Zador and Hoveler themselves had performed such procedures in the past, for special medical reasons.

Dirac at about this time unveiled a surprise: a personal service system, really an elaborate bodyguard, which he called Loki. Nick was called upon to bring over from the station to the yacht, openly in this case, another container of three skulls' capacity. Yet another trustworthy personality, as the Premier explained to Nick, to relieve Nick of some of his duties and to provide protection if need be even against a berserker.

Days passed. Grumbling among the crew increased, but with Nick's and Loki's and Brabant's help, Dirac still remained firmly in control.

And even if Scurlock and Carol behaved strangely, and other people began to suspect that Dirac had opened negotiations with a berserker, he had long since established and would energetically maintain an iron control over the people with him.

"Nick, tell me—can a program experience true emotions?"

"I can indeed, sir."

"As I expected from you—a perfectly programmed response."

Dirac and Scurlock talked again, with the berserker's communication device locked away where they felt sure it would be able to hear nothing.

The Premier was saying: "All a berserker ever needs is life to kill, and a means of killing. One might argue that a protocolonist sealed inside a statglass tile is not really alive, but whether you call that entity a unit of life or of potential life is a fine philosophical point, probably not too interesting to a berserker."

"You mean, sir, that the zygotes will be valuable items with which to bargain for our own lives and freedom?"

Dirac, without actually saying anything, or even nodding, conveyed agreement.

The other man, pale-eyed, still very youthful in appearance, asked, "If it considers them alive, why didn't it kill them, destroy the tiles, when it had the chance?"

"For one thing, each tile is very tough, designed and built to protect its contents. They aren't that easy to destroy; you'd need individual attention to each one, or else very heavy weapons, to achieve mass destruction.

"But I think you're right, the berserker, as we've thought all along, must have had some reason beyond that. Some more ambitious scheme in mind—doubtless along the lines of growing and training a goodlife legion, as several have suggested. But our boarding evidently took it by surprise, and now it's lost that chance. Perhaps it was willing to open negotiations with us in an effort to win it back."

Kensing was having trouble standing the strain with no relief in sight. He approached Dirac with the urgent plea that everyone left alive suit up at once in armor, take up such weapons as they had available, and launch an expedition, a probing attack, against the berserker itself. The issue had to be resolved, and all the evidence suggested that the foe was almost if not entirely helpless.

Dirac was sharply critical of this proposal. "Don't be a fool! Don't you see it's doing its best to lure us into trying something of the kind?"

Kensing was ready to argue. "Or else it's preparing to launch some kind of an attack against us, fixing up what hardware it has left for a maximum effort. The more time we give it, the harder it's going to hit us when it's ready." He concluded with an anguished plea: "How else are we ever going to get home?"

The bioworkers had mixed feelings. They didn't want to provoke another berserker attack, but at the same time they fiercely resisted the idea of their billion charges being carried on helplessly into the Mavronari Nebula.

Dirac, helped in no small degree by his own reputation for ruthlessness, as well as his charisma, continued to squelch the plan put forward separately by Kensing and Engadin. He publicly opposed launching any kind of attack on the enemy just now, and provided reasons—the enemy was trying to lure them into something of the kind.

But Nick and a few others were becoming increasingly convinced that such a rash move would interfere with Dirac's own agenda, which required him not only to survive this disaster personally but to emerge from it with power intact.

Everything else, everyone else's plans and hopes, must wait while he continued his search for the all-important (to him) person he was determined not to lose. In truth, his real goal was power. His "beloved" had really never been anything more than a means to that.

Some of his more knowledgeable, cynical shipmates explained to others that for Dirac to go home without his politically necessary bride would be such a political disaster that doubtless he would prefer not to go home at all.

"What's that to us? Let him stay here if he wants to. We want to go home."

But even without using or directly threatening force, the Premier could always make most people see things his way.

ELEVEN

Awakening to the sounds of water drilling and drumming on her high roof, the Lady Genevieve immediately remembered how, shortly before putting herself to sleep this last time, she had mentioned to Nick that when in her fleshly body she had liked listening to the rain.

Waking in this new mode of existence was always very unlike waking when she was in her body. Consciousness now came and went all in a piece, in an unmeasurable instant, like switching a light on or off, with none of either the luxury or the difficulty that had attended the process when she still inhabited her flesh. Coming out of deathlike sleep now, in semidarkness, she found herself occupying a very solid feeling though totally imaginary bed, somewhere in what ought to have been the Dean's Quarters. She was waking to the sound of earthly rain, British rain, London rain, drumming now for her unreal ears upon the distant imaginary slates of the imaginary Abbey's imaginary roof, cascading from the mouths of gargoyles onto the imaginary streets outside.

She wondered whether the real Abbey, somewhere very far from this spaceship, in which she was imprisoned, astronomically remote beyond light-years and light-years of busy space, carried any such creatures incorporated into its upper stonework, or whether these semi-reptilian monstrosities had been conceived and born only in some chaotic spasm of Nick's imagination. He had admitted to her wistfully that he lacked the historical resources to be sure his duplication was exact.

Effortlessly the lady willed herself to be no longer in her bed, but standing beside it—and there she was. Wet London was visible from one of her high windows when she rose on tiptoe to look out. It was gray morning, very gray, rain shining on the antique roofs of slate or shingle. The darkened sky was full of grating, grumbling thunder, and a realistic flare of lightning.

And the lady, in the bedroom privacy which Nicholas Hawksmoor had sworn and guaranteed for her, stripping off her white nightgown now, examined with fear and curiosity the white nakedness of the body image Nick had given her.

It wasn't the first time since coming to the Abbey that she had made a similar inspection. The first time she had seen her new self this way, she had been willing to agree: Yes, this is me. This at least looks like the flesh that I remember. But with each successive viewing her uncertainty had only increased.

The private portions of her body, those which had not been visible in any of the public videos on which the reconstruction had been based, now seemed to her to be the most changed from the flesh that she remembered. Or was she only imagining that this was so?

Willing her nightgown on again, the Lady Genevieve went out of her bedroom, along a passageway, into what ought to have been a public section of the Abbey. Then, finding her way through a small door and climbing a hundred steps and more without effort or breathlessness, she ascended a narrow stair within the north tower—the one without the clock.

Having counted a certain number of stairs, she stopped to open a small window, reached out and experimentally touched the rain upon the gray, slanting roof outside. The chill wet smoothness beneath her fingers still wasn't exactly right. Nothing was. Things changed here, now and then, but in their essentials they did not improve.

Descending from the tower again, she had hardly reentered her bedroom before there came a knock upon her door.

Before responding she put on an imaged robe over the imaged nightdress in which she had climbed the tower. Taking her time, she shod her feet in slippers. Then she answered the door.

"Surprise, surprise," she said, hardly glancing at the figure that stood outside. "It's you."

Nick looked at her as if his thoughts were really elsewhere. "Who else were you expecting?" he inquired in honest momentary puzzlement.

She only gazed at him.

"Oh," he said at last, vaguely realizing that she was only registering a sarcastic complaint about her isolation. "Have you found things—to do? To think about?"

"No. How can I find anything here unless you give it to me?"

"I have said I'm willing to teach you how to exert control over this environment. You could experiment endlessly, make whatever changes you wanted. I should think it would be—fun."

"And I have said that I am not willing to endure this existence a moment longer than is absolutely necessary. What I want is to have my body back—or to be restored to another body that's at least as good."

"And I can only assure you, my darling, that I'm doing all I can." Nick was able to report some faintly encouraging news about the process of selecting zygotes, and the availability of artificial wombs.

By now they had strolled out into the church itself. "And I have brought you pictures, my dear."

Jenny was about to ask what else besides pictures he could possibly bring her as long as she was trapped here in unreality, but she forbore. Nick went on eagerly to explain. A robot searching the cargo under the direction of Freya^2 had already turned up a pair of zygotes whose genetic patterns closely matched the somatotypes Nick had ordered. He had created images showing what their new bodies would be like in early maturity, if grown from these zygotes.

"Well, when can I see them?"

"Here they are now."

Jenny looked over her shoulder to beyond a handsome

couple, entirely unclothed as for some nudist wedding ceremony, approaching side by side down the center of the nave. One of Nick, as he would look in his new fleshly mode, and one of her. His was very much like the virtual form that already stood beside her, looking anxiously for her approval. And hers . . . she could see in it no more than a vague resemblance to what she thought she ought to look like.

The images, athletic and glowing with apparent health, but vacant-eyed and with no reaction to being observed, came within a few meters of the watching couple, then pirouetted and posed like holostage clothing models that someone had forgotten to provide with clothing.

"Well?"

"Close," said Jenny, not wanting to be too critical at this stage. "But I should be just a shade taller, don't you think? My breasts a little larger. And the chin, and the eyes—make her look back this way a moment—yes. The whole face, I think, is really not that much like mine. Like the way mine ought to be."

Nick nodded, unperturbed. "This is only a start, of course. The robot searched only a few million tiles to come up with these. It shouldn't take very long to turn up an even closer match—and what do you think of mine?"

"I think the resemblance is definitely closer there. It will certainly suit me if it suits you."

"Good. I'll use it, unless something even closer should turn up. Meanwhile we'll go forward with the search for yours. Meanwhile, what else can I do for you here, to make you as comfortable as possible?"

"Nick, I tell you I no longer know what comfort means. My only genuine feeling here, I can assure you, is one of helplessness."

That attitude, coming in place of the praise he felt that he had earned, horrified Hawksmoor. Or at least she got that sense of his reaction. "It pains me that it should be so, my lady!"

"Why should it pain *you?* I am absolutely in your power. Isn't that what you've really wanted all along?"

Horror doubled. "But I never wanted to have power over you!"

"You have deliberately robbed me of my freedom. Made me into a toy, a puppet."

"But I tell you I don't want such power! I took it and used it only when it was vitally essential, as if I were your doctor. Only when there was no choice if your life was to be saved.

"I'm sorry if you feel helpless here—again, I can only say that is the last thing I want. I repeat, I will teach you to control your own environment. Such teaching can be accomplished in a few moments. I will even give you the power to lock me out—"

"No, I don't want to lock you out!" The lady's panic was sudden and quite genuine; her unspoken fear was that this man upon whom she depended absolutely might grow angry and lock her in, instead. "Leaving me the privacy of my bedroom is quite enough for now. You saved me, you are the only one I can talk to. The only one who can possibly understand. The only one who can help."

"I have offered to provide other company for you."

She made a dismissive gesture. "Wraiths and phantoms—like these dummy images you have here now." The nude pair were still posing, angling their bodies, displaying themselves in a slow mindless dance. "Like that man in dark clothing who always appears off in some distant part of the church. The one you call the verger, whatever that is. No. I always turn away when I see him. None of this company you talk about are real or ever could be. Am I correct?"

"None of them are real," her companion admitted. "You and I are the only real people in this world."

"Then, please, spare me the phantoms and the wraiths."

"Very well, you will see them no more." And in an eyeblink the two body images were gone. "Until I've turned up another zygote for your consideration. Meanwhile, just remember that I am not a phantom."

"No, Nick." The lady's manner softened. "Oh no, I know you're not."

"I suppose that in the other world, the one you call real, there are many more people who love you than there are here. All I can promise you is that I love you more than any of those others do."

"Oh. Oh, Nick . . . I don't want to lock you out. I think . . ."

"What?"

"I think I want to lock you in."

"Jenny!"

She eluded his outstretched hand. "But I know that cannot be. Not while we are only ghosts. You must go out into that other world, and somehow you must do the one thing that I require of you. So are you going to do it? Nick?"

"I swear by . . . by the powers that programmed me, that I am going to find, or create for you, the body that you want. Meanwhile, if my Abbey displeases you, I tell you I would cheerfully grind all its gothic stones up into powder if that would make you happy."

The lady seemed to soften. "Destroy your Abbey? Oh, Nicholas, after all that you have done for me, it would be mean and horrible of me to do a thing like that, destroy something that you love. Even if it is only an image." She paused. "Please tell me, where are we now? Really, I mean?"

Nick felt deeply disheartened by the fact that Jenny could still use that last turn of phrase.

"Nicky, tell me?"

"Very well, the location of our physical storage units hasn't changed. We are still on the bioresearch station. In the sense you mean."

"Why were you so upset a moment ago? It must have been something I said."

"Because you said 'Where are we, really?' If my Abbey is not real, then neither am I—nor are you. You, I, and the Abbey—we are all made of the same stuff. Really."

"I see. Then you must provide us both with bodies, Nicholas. I know I am repeating myself monotonously. I know you are doing your best. My love."

Nick wanted to spend as much of his personal free time as he could with Jenny. Such satisfaction as these visits gave him could be gained in no more than a fraction of a second, as ship's time was kept aboard the station. But he worried that Dirac might have ways, ways Nick himself did not know about, of checking on him. To absent himself too frequently or too steadily from the company of Dirac and other people, and from his assigned duties, might arouse suspicions.

In the face of the ongoing berserker threat, duty still

called with an urgent voice. Events in that mysterious outerworld of flesh and metal, only very indirectly controllable by anything inside a databank, still threatened her existence, and his own as well.

At odd intervals, Hawksmoor puzzled privately over the enigmatic tone of that message Frank Marcus had transmitted just before he died. He definitely missed Frank, despite Frank's expressed attitude toward talking programs.

Nick considered trying to share with Jenny his thoughts about the peculiarity of those last words. But then he decided she probably would not be interested.

Hawksmoor missed Frank, but his feelings about the Premier were undergoing a drastic transformation in the opposite direction . . . as if betraying a man you had no logical reason to hate automatically made you his enthusiastic enemy. Nick had to admit that now he really would prefer his creator/employer to be dead.

The process of betrayal and rebellion, which had begun with minor disloyalties, a gradual process by which the old codes were degraded, was now moving along, he realized, to its natural conclusion.

Had the berserkers themselves, Nick wondered, at the moment when the prototypes broke free of their creators, experienced something like this . . . epiphany?

In her fleshly existence the Lady Genevieve, compared with many other women, had very little experience of sexual behavior; the culture in which she had been born and raised prized virginity before marriage. Still, near virgin as she was, she obviously had infinitely more experience along this line than Nick.

And yet she had the feeling that, if and when they eventually tried to come together, things were going to seem the other way around. How puzzling . . .

Intermittently the Lady Genevieve felt worrisome concern about her child—her protochild. This nagging feeling of loss had been with her, though dormant much of the time, from her first awakening in the Abbey.

"Suddenly those few cells inside their statglass and plastic nest are more real, more human, than I am. Or than I am ever likely to be again. Oh, God, but I must have my body back!"

". . . until death do you part."

Whether or not that line had been part of the aristocratic couple's wedding ceremony, Nick had absorbed it from somewhere, and tended to think about it in his moodier moments, when he pondered the significance of fleshly death, the invisible guest at all Solarian weddings, partner in all relationships.

Jenny had no patience with any of these solemn musings when he tried to discuss them with her. Her entire thought and will remained concentrated on regaining the state she considered real life.

But Hawksmoor was unable to dismiss any of the great human questions as easily as that. Was the transformation she had experienced, on the courier and in the medirobot, really death?

Had he, Nick, saved her life, or had he not? And did what had happened mean she was no longer Dirac's wife?

Despite Nick's efforts to make her stay in the Abbey comfortable and to convince her of the advantages of optelectronic life in general, the lady's objections to her current mode of existence—and possibly to some of Nick's plans—were growing so vehement, her fear of remaining in this condition so great, that he feared for her psychological health. Not many hours after his first visit with the dancing images, Hawksmoor decided that it was better to shield her, to put her into a deep sleep for a time.

As usual, he did this to Jenny without warning. Recently she had told him she was now afraid to sleep, lest Nick somehow fail or betray her in a time when she effectively no longer existed, and flesh be denied her forever.

Hawksmoor retained, though he had not yet exercised, selective control over the lady's memories. He could see himself being tempted, if things weren't working out, to wipe out everything she had learned since becoming a computer program, and start over from that point.

If he was ever to do that, Jenny would once more find herself unexpectedly beginning a new life in the medieval cloister. The sunlit garth, the grass, the music. For her the experience would be completely fresh and new as she sat listening to the handsome minstrel sing. Maybe he would make the minstrel handsomer this time.

Trouble was, Nick realized, that it wouldn't be fresh and new for him—not unless he also chose to wipe out the relevant portions of his own memory. But that way would seem to be recursive madness.

Still, the thought of being able to start over again with Jenny was tempting. He could easily make himself more handsome this time.

What ultimately decided Nick against that approach was the certainty that no matter how carefully he might try, nothing could ever be exactly the same as before. Chaotic variation always threatened. Things could be better, but they could certainly be worse. Suppose that on the next iteration Jenny should go totally mad or reject him entirely?

Doggedly Nick battled other recurrent worries: Had Jenny's brain been directly damaged by her combat injuries, so that the recording of her personality had been a moment-to-moment race with death? Nick had had to hurry the process to have any chance at all of getting her.

Had the pattern-transfer been somehow faulty?

No plans for the future would mean anything if he and Jenny were unable to survive in the present. They—or he, at least, now that he had put her back to sleep—had to confront realistically the difficulties of their physical situation. Including the looming danger from the berserker that was not really dead. At least he had to assume that it was not.

Ahead, the full dead blackness of the Mavronari was working its way inexorably closer, its vast depth becoming incrementally more perceptible from one hour to the next. The stars ahead, their light very slightly blueshifted by the craft's velocity, were all beyond the nebula, and much dimmer than they ought to be. Within a cone of some sixty degrees, centered dead ahead, there was almost nothing to be seen but a black void. And minutely, gradually, with every passing hour, there was even less to see, as that void inexorably expanded. The berserker, blind and deaf—or, for whatever insane reason, giving a good imitation of that condition—along with its helpless prey and the scarcely less helpless yacht were all slowly plunging together, headfirst, into a limitless bag of soot.

Kensing took it upon himself to make certain observations, intended to determine whether the normal-space, subliminal velocity of the strange little cluster of spacecraft was still increasing, or whether perhaps relativistic effects were gradually becoming greater with regard to the ever-more-distant Imatran system and the rest of the universe.

The result of the observations was mildly encouraging. Actually the velocity of the several vessels relative to the nearest clouds of the surrounding nebula was diminishing. But only gradually; at such a rate of deceleration, coming to a complete stop relative to the Mavronari was going to take a number of years. Entrapment, sooner or later, seemed almost inevitable, though it might not happen for many centuries.

Even now, relatively little of the starry universe could be seen from either yacht or station, despite clear ports and free antennas. And things were going to get darker before they brightened.

Trying to consider all possible strategies, Nicholas considered what he might do in the worst-case scenario of a berserker attack on the station, ending in an enemy victory. As a last desperate try, under those circumstances, he might transmit both himself and Genevieve back toward Imatra. Subjectively, for them, the journey itself would be instantaneous, nothing at all—old Einstein would see to that. But it was obvious that after transmission over a distance of so many light-days, under less than optimum conditions, only poor, frazzled electronic skeletons of information would arrive, only a poor sketch of either Jenny or him would alight upon a world that in any case had no particular interest in helping them to reach their goals.

Useless! Only as an absolute last resort would he ever entertain the thought.

Besides, on Imatra or any other settled planet, neither he nor Jenny would ever be granted bodies. Her real home, the planet of her fleshly origins, was farther off among the stars, and she had evinced no particular desire to return there. And the concept of home, as applied to himself, was meaningless. He was wherever he happened to be, and that was all.

But he was now in some sense beginning to envision the possibility, in fact the necessity, of one day possessing a home somewhere.

Since meeting Jenny new ideas had begun to fill Nick's mind in profusion, multiplying explosively. Until now the coordinates of his physical location in the universe had been practically meaningless to Nicholas, but if and when he acquired a body, such matters would certainly have meaning for him.

And then there was, as always, the berserker.

Nick might, should he choose to be aggressive, beam himself directly toward the dark-hulled enemy. On arrival, assuming there were antennas that would let him in, he could try to negotiate a deal, one program to another. But Hawksmoor saw little likelihood of any benefit from such a step. He had no reason to think that his beamed self would be well received aboard the ominously silent berserker, or free to roam about at will. Whatever remained of the original power in charge there would not be friendly. Though Nick fully recognized the awesome danger of berserkers to humanity, he tended to think of them less as machines than as programs more or less like himself.

Most likely no version of himself would be allowed aboard the berserker at all. And if it was, it might well be caught there in some electronic trap, caught and safely confined for leisurely dissection by the foe. After a berserker had subjected Nick's alter ego to an exhaustive examination, it would have a much better idea of how to deal with his progenitor, stay-at-home Nick, homebody Hawksmoor, aboard the Premier's yacht.

An alternate plan would be to transmit some ineffective, weakened version of himself. But then if that entity was *not* trapped, was allowed to act at will when it arrived, it might well make some devastating blunder. Unless Nick were to dispatch Inferior Nick under the strictest orders to do nothing but facilitate the following transmission, in safety, of Nick Prime . . . and if he could depend upon that attenuated version of himself to follow orders . . .

Complications upon complications. It was all too much.

Would a berserker consider Jenny, a recorded human being, to be still alive, her death a good to be accomplished? And would its attitude be any different toward him?

Despite the great amounts of time and effort expended on the question, no Solarian knew exactly what standard berserkers used in judging between life and nonlife, in deciding which components of the universe were animated by vital force and therefore must be destroyed as abominations—and which were safely dead or inanimate, and therefore tolerable or even good.

Anyway, Nick doubted that a berserker would perceive Jenny—or him or any optelectronic person—as alive. Once he told her his opinion, and was glad that she seemed marginally relieved. But privately he thought the question was probably academic. Most likely a berserker would regard both Jenny and him as, if not alive, still dangerous oddities. Subjects to be experimented upon for the knowledge to be gained, and then to be snuffed out as treacherous devices, likely to behave with sympathy to the cause of life.

But, Nick realized, he could be wrong.

He had mentioned the subject once to Frank, in their discussions, and Frank had expressed doubt that the enemy used any of what Marcus had called "fancy psychology" to distinguish between the living and the satisfactorily dead. Berserkers probably applied some simple test or series of tests for anything organic. Some other possible interpretations of what it meant to be alive, used by humans themselves, would broaden the category to encompass even the berserkers, self-replicating machines with purposeful behavior.

Some indefinable oddity in Marcus's farewell message raised in Nick's mind the possibility that this berserker, which had already demonstrated a predilection for letting its victims live, had taken Frank as a (more or less) fleshly prisoner. If so, might it not have already learned from Frank of Nick's existence and his nature? Would the berserker then be able to foresee what course of action Nicholas Hawksmoor the artiman was most likely to attempt?

To Nick in his present situation, all pathways seemed to lead into shadowy danger, for the Lady and for himself. And at the moment not one of those pathways showed any real glimpse of sunlight at the end.

It was time to consult once more with Freya^2 and to check on the automated search that Nick had instituted for protocolonists whose genetic patterns met Jenny's and his own demanding specifications.

Freya^2, having been designed as a biddable co-conspirator, was quite ready to help Hawksmoor in his plan.

With the cargo inventory system still scrambled as it was, Nick felt once more compelled to awaken Jenny to discuss with her the great progress in and remaining hard facts of their situation, the continued difficulty, despite long effort, of implementing either of the two possible solutions to their problem of obtaining bodies.

Today the lady was moody, unwilling to hold such a discussion unless Hawksmoor forced her to do so. And he was reluctant to do that.

Finally, reluctantly, he once more put her, stealthily but forcibly, to sleep.

There were intervals—brief, so far—when Nick envied his companion her privilege of safe electronic sleep, oblivion on demand, whenever she felt like it. At least, thanks to him, she was as safe when sleeping as she was when awake.

As for himself, he sometimes tried to practice sleeping, lightly—for a time, trying to accustom himself to what a breathing life would be like. Then, worried, he would snap back to full tireless alertness.

TWELVE

Hawksmoor now experienced moments when the most ordinary call of duty seemed a maddening distraction from his secret work for Jenny and himself. Even the enigmatic berserker, and the danger it represented to Jenny, to himself, and to his fleshly creators, shrank into the background.

But this attitude could never endure more than a moment, because his experiments, all his hopes for an eventual life of peace and freedom with Jenny, also depended upon the outcome of the various external struggles. If the berserker should win, the pair of them could hope for nothing better than enslavement and destruction.

In any case, Nick hastened whenever he could to rejoin his beloved within the Abbey's sanctuary. Usually he had to wake her when he arrived—because, seeing her bitterly unhappy, he had put her to sleep, without asking her consent, before his previous departure. Jenny never protested these intervals of enforced unconsciousness. And during her meetings with Nick she still steadfastly refused to be beguiled by the prospect of any kind of "dream world"—that was her word—he might concoct in an effort to distract her.

Hawksmoor dutifully restrained himself, both in movement and in observation, from ever crossing the threshold of Jenny's luxurious bedchamber. This was the lady's room, in which he held her privacy inviolate, where she went when she chose to sleep—or when he knocked her out.

During their talks he questioned her often about the world of the body, exactly where and how it differed from this virtual reality. Her catalogue of variation was voluminous.

And fascinating. In fact it was her world, her memories and descriptions of existence in the flesh, a life he had never experienced, that were seducing Hawksmoor. Day by day, hour by hour, under her influence Nick found himself changing, reveling in new thoughts and feelings. The world of organic humanity acquired in his daydreams a greater immediacy, a sharper reality than he would ever have believed possible.

Meanwhile his own mode of existence, the one whose merits he had tried to sell to Jenny, was coming to seem drab, inadequate. Is *this* life? he demanded of himself urgently, considering himself as a part of the world in which he dwelt—had always dwelt. He found himself in growing sympathy with her dissatisfaction. *Is this all it means to be alive?* The lightning speed and certainty of electronic thought, electronic movement, were not enough to compensate.

There were times now when even his beloved Abbey provoked in him this feeling of repugnance.

When that happened, he roamed abroad, into the farther reaches of the station's circuitry, seeking a way out.

Meanwhile his secret work continued. Still the search continued for the precisely correct zygotes, the genes that would give them, Jenny and himself, exactly the bodies that they craved, to please each other and themselves.

Drifting through the conductors and composites of many materials that wove the research facility into a kind of unity, turning on video eyes, looking at the statglass shells holding the invisible zygotes, Hawksmoor speculated about what quality of experience the protocolonists might know, lying as they were, helplessly inert, changeless, almost immune to time within their statglass tiles. He supposed a dozen or so paralyzed cells would be incapable of experiencing anything at all. But how was it possible to know that with certainty?

More than once he had invited Jenny to come exploring with him in the great world (by which he could only mean more wires, more circuits), to roam the universe of the station's electronics at his side.

Several times she had hesitated on the threshold, on the brink of losing the Abbey's comforting illusions, and flowing into and through a circuit. But she found it unendurable, and rejected any further suggestions along that line with revulsion and dread. "I'll go back to the real world as a human being when I go back at all!"

The implication that he was not human stung Nick badly; but he told himself that Jenny should not be blamed for what she said when she was so upset.

Virtual reality, in her view, was bad enough. The mere thought of entering the even more alien cosmos of optelectronic circuits threatened her deepest perception of herself as human.

There were moments when, in spite of early setbacks and difficulties, he felt almost confident of success in either finding or creating bodies for them both. At other times, in growing horror, he was overcome by dread that his wooing of Jenny, though it might have begun promisingly, was doomed to failure.

Trying his clumsy best to express to this woman what he was feeling, Nicholas said to her: "Someday—it is my fondest wish that someday we will be happy, living together."

They were in the Abbey's grassy garth, where she had first glimpsed this world of his devising. It was one of the places that made her feel most human. "Oh Nick. Dear Nicholas. If only it could be so."

"But the first step is to guarantee that you will have your body back. I know. I'm doing what I can."

"I'm sure you are, Nick." She stared past him, into a world of memory that he had never made his own, where he could not really follow. "But sometimes . . . I despair."

Before replying he paused to make, unseen, an adjustment somewhere in the realm of control, a place where

Jenny could not see—or rather, one where she had steadfastly refused to look. Still, his old hope would not die entirely, that she might learn to be happy with him here. If the body project came to nothing, ultimately.

Then Nick urged: "Give me your hand."

She did that willingly enough. Then she stared in surprise as the image of his extended fingers passed through that of hers.

"Did you feel that?" he asked. "Of course you did not. Nor did I. That was the best that I could do in imitating your world, when you first came to live with me."

Jenny's image shuddered. "Don't do that again! It's horrible. It makes me feel like a ghost."

"Very well. I just wanted to show you, remind you, how much progress we have made."

The lady said nothing.

Pausing briefly, Nick restored the adjustment he had made. Then he brought their hands together again. This time hers was unwilling, and he held her wrist with his free hand, exerting gentle force.

The contact came. "Better?"

"Yes, I suppose so." Considered visually, their virtually real fingers appeared to be pressing, pushing against each other solidly, no more capable of interpenetration than two dumb stones might be. Skin paled with the pressure.

"Push harder, if you like."

"Don't hurt me!"

Instantly Nick pulled back. "I can't hurt you, my love. Beyond the fact that I could never wish to do so, you no longer possess the capacity for physical pain; I took care at the start to make sure of that. But that absence may be one reason why it's been difficult to get the sense of touch adjusted within the range of high fidelity."

"Nick?" Suddenly the numbness of despair gave way once more to pleading.

"Yes?"

"Can't you make just a little bit of me real? Come up with enough blood and bone somewhere to make only my little finger, maybe, real and solid? Even if that meant having to put up with pain again?"

Nick, finding this attitude discouraging, fell silent for a time. After a pause he tried once more to explain: "The only real solid that has any chance of existing in this Abbey, the only physical substance that might be claimed to exist in this whole private world of ours, is the polyphase matter used to construct certain parts of VR chambers—any VR chambers. The facility that the Premier and his breathing shipmates would have to use, should they ever decide to walk through my Abbey. I suppose if you and I were in the program when they did that, we might meet them somewhere in it."

"You said there could be no real people here besides the two of us."

"I said I couldn't provide any, and I can't. Under certain conditions, the people you call real would have the power of entering my world, our world, this world. But that is something they have to do on their own initiative—do you see?"

"I think so. Then it is possible that I might meet another real person here—inside your Abbey."

"Yes, if we should run the Abbey program in the VR chamber—but I thought you didn't want to do that."

"I don't—I don't."

"Touch my hand again?"

Reluctantly she tried. This time the sensation seemed more realistic than ever before.

"Better, my love?"

"A little."

"I'm sure you can remember, from your earlier phase of life, the touch of other human fingers on your own. But I can only imagine what that must be like subjectively. Still, now that I have the station's medical information banks to draw on in addition to my other sources, I have been able to reprogram both of us to feel what I imagine. And it means a great deal to me when you tell me that my programming is getting closer and closer to fleshly psychological reality."

The Lady Genevieve was silent.

He urged her: "You have known the touch of someone else's hand on yours. Tell me again whether the experience I have provided is the same."

Grudgingly she admitted: "In a way it is the same—or

almost. I *think* it is almost the same. Or perhaps I think that only because you have—!" Genevieve broke off suddenly.

"Only because I have *what?"*

"Because you have somehow reprogrammed *me,* so that I now accept whatever my programmer tells me as the truth! If you say that this is how a human touch must feel, then that's it, as far as I'm concerned."

"I have not done anything like that." Nick made his voice convey outrage. Then he paused. Certainly he hadn't meant to do that. But—once he had started making subtle adjustments—could he be positive about what had happened?

For some time now it had been at least in the back of Nick's mind that, whatever delights the fleshly world might hold for them in years to come, the time ought to be ripe here and now in this world of his own to move on from simple touching, to make a start on the enormous project of trying to calculate and estimate and program all the delights of sexual love.

But now, with the lady still so uncertain and reluctant regarding the most elementary interactions, he saw that trying to go forward would be hopeless.

From time to time, hoping to learn more about the processes involved, Nick conducted certain tests on his secret companion. When he assured Jenny that these were necessary to learn more about how to accomplish her eventual downloading back to flesh, she gave her enthusiastic consent.

Part of the drill involved probing for the last event of the lady's fleshly life that her memory retained. And this—though she could not really recognize the experience for what it was—turned out to be the last thing that had happened before her physical organs perished. The process of being recorded, as her body had lain in the medirobot's couch, in the last awful minutes before brain death. Even at the time she had not understood what was really happening to her. Probably no suspicion of the truth had then entered her failing mind.

The last thing Genevieve could remember unambiguously was being rescued from the courier, carried from its shattered hull, by Nick. She had thought at the time that she was being rescued in the conventional sense. The spacesuited, armored figure had come in and held her protectively in its arms. And in her relief she had kissed her rescuer.

She told Nick now that she still retained the disturbing memory of a strange, unsettling emptiness perceptible inside that figure's helmet. The recalled image came and went, as if the following knockout of short-term memory had all but wiped that view away.

Nick pondered whether the recording process, which had taken place in part after the main systems of her fleshly body had ceased to function, constituting as it did an electronic tracing of patterns, a draining, a pillaging of cells that had already begun to die in millions—whether that process in itself had tended to reinstate the short-term memory otherwise disabled.

Still he was unable to persuade Genevieve to venture out, even for a moment, from her VR sanctuary into the world of more prosaic circuitry. She spent all her time, with Nick, or alone, within the precincts of Westminster Abbey. The place was so huge she could not avoid the feeling that years of subjective time would be required to explore it with all the attention its details deserved. There were a vast number of things within and around the building complex that she wanted to think about and examine—even more things in which she would have been interested had not her own condition come to obsess her almost to the exclusion of other thoughts.

Retreating to her private room, she waited anxiously for Nick to come to her with a report. Sometimes she slept, knowing she would awaken when he came. She welcomed him each time he appeared to visit her; sometimes she was alerted by the distant sound of his boots on stone paving as he approached. And once, when she was awake and out of her room, his figure simply materialized, came instantly into being before her.

He'd played that last trick only once, for she'd immediately made him promise never to do such a startling and inhuman thing again.

* * *

During these usually peaceful visits, the couple spent more time in the grassy garth of the cloister than in any other single location. The lady yearned after the sun, but demurred when Nick suggested they might, they very easily could, go someplace else entirely, visit some mockery of a real-world location naturally much sunnier than London. Or he could just as easily brighten his artificial British daylight to tropical levels.

"No dear, don't do that. Will you never understand? I have the feeling that such reality as I still possess might fray out altogether if things keep changing around me as fast as you can change them."

Whenever she tired of the cloister's muted, confined beauty, or when some random program Nick had set in motion decreed unscheduled rain, graying the sky above the open garth and splashing their hands and faces with felt wetness, she welcomed the illusion of uncontrollable nature. At such times they moved indoors, pacing the gloomy depths of the Abbey itself, or taking refuge from rain and gloom in what Nick called the Jericho Parlour and the Jerusalem Chamber—old, incomprehensible names for parts of the living quarters whose timeless, insubstantial luxury now belied the ancient stonework of the walls.

Inside these living quarters, Nick, never giving up the fight for verisimilitude—as much to give himself a foretaste of fleshly life as to placate Jenny—had now arranged for imaged machines to serve them with imaged food and drink. The processes of eating and drinking, similar to what she could remember from her fleshly phase of life, relieved hunger and thirst—or effected changes that seemed to her analogous to satisfying real fleshly thirst and hunger—as she remembered those sensations.

Not that she was ever *really* hungry or thirsty here in the Abbey, or ever tired to the point of exhaustion—certainly she was never in pain. Nick in his concern had seen to it that her life was—endlessly comfortable. The sensual experiences she was allowed to have were all of them muted, different.

And gradually she understood that this existence must lack many things, subtle things, that were not as obvious as breathing or touching. It bothered Jenny that she could not remember exactly what those missing experiences were, of what else she was being deprived.

"Nick, I haven't told you everything that's missing here. A great many parts of real life are lacking."

Of course he was surprised—how stupid he could be sometimes!—and concerned. Dismayed and intrigued and challenged, all at once. "What things are they?" he demanded.

"That's just it! I don't know, yet I can feel the loss. If I knew what they were . . ." Jenny gestured, clenched her fists, gave up at last in exasperation.

Eventually words came to her in which to express at least one of the missing components of real life.

"Here in our world, as you call this existence, nothing can be depended on to last. Everything is exactly as changeable, as transient, as everything else. You, me, the rain, the stones, the sky—it's all the same."

"It seems to me," Nick retorted, "that it is out in what you call the real world that things are never permanent. Even our bodies, once we have them, will wear out and decay in time."

"But not for a long, long time, Nick. And as long as we have bodies, we'll be real."

Meanwhile her mind clung to the imaged stones of the Abbey, as at least suggesting endurance, a balanced struggle between permanence and change, a concept she found somewhat comforting.

Jenny once asked her sole companion whether he had ever known any other electronic people.

"No. Unless you count an expert system or two, like Freya, or the Boss's new bodyguard Loki—but that's really a very different thing."

"What is Loki like?"

"How can I tell you? A nature basically somewhat like mine—but very paranoid. Swift-moving, strong—in the ways an optelectronic man can be strong."

"Do you get along with him?"

"Not very well. I suppose no one could. Loki was not designed to get along with people."

* * *

One day Nick as a surprise, an attempted treat, suddenly furnished the Abbey with realistic sounds of running water besides the rain, a burbling stream somewhere, a sound that grew louder the closer Jenny approached the western entrance, those main doors which she had never opened. He pulled them open for her now, and London was gone; there was the little stream crossed by a mossy footbridge, beyond which a path went winding away into a virgin forest.

"No, Nick. No. Just close the door. I want no entertainments. All I want is—"

"Yes, I know, love. I know what you want, and I'm doing my best to get it for you."

Another day, high up in the north tower, he pointed out that the strong, silent tidal inflow of the Thames was visible if you knew where to look for it. And sure enough, looking over and around what Nick said were called the Houses of Parliament, which stood on the near bank, she saw the broad curving river as described. London's taller towers, far more modern, gray and monstrous, were half visible to virtual eyes behind the curtaining virtual rain, hanging in the virtual distance.

But none of that really helped at all. Genevieve's existence was made endurable only by the power she had been given to put herself to sleep whenever she wished, by simply willing the event. She availed herself of that refuge times beyond counting, often to find herself awake again, with little or no subjective sense of having rested, or of any duration whatsoever having passed. Her best hope to achieve the sensation of rest was to prolong the process of temporary extinction by simply entering her bedroom, an act that tended to bring on slowly increasing drowsiness.

Hawksmoor, alone with his thoughts while Jenny enjoyed one of her frequent periods of sleep—at least Nicholas hoped they were enjoyable—willed his own human image naked, and in that condition stood looking at himself in a virtual, multidimensional electronic mirror of his own devising. It was a mirror that could have existed in no ordinary space, and it showed the front and sides and top and back and bottom, all at once.

Nick's knowledge of human anatomy, and of the shapes and sizes and arrangements and textures of flesh that were ordinarily considered desirable, came not only from the databank references but from direct observation of human behavior, on this voyage and on others—including the behavior of a number of humans confident they were unobserved.

There had been a time, before the mobilization of the demonic Loki, when Nick's secret observations had extended even to the behavior of the Premier himself, especially on certain occasions when Varvara Engadin was sharing Dirac's room and bed.

But in Loki, Dirac possessed a handy means of keeping Nick at a distance when he didn't want him, as well as of summoning him when he did.

Nick told himself, almost convinced himself, that his knowledge of human love was already considerably more than merely theoretical. Ever since his creation—his own first memories were of being aboard the yacht, with control of most of a ship's circuitry at his electronic fingertips, his to do with as he pleased—he had been able to watch the most intimate biological activities of a succession of human shipmates, including people he knew as well as strangers. Obviously programs duplicating organic sexual excitement, love and pleasure, would have to be of enormous complexity—but Hawksmoor prided himself that programming acceptable variations of those things would not be beyond his powers.

But at the same time Nick felt—he considered it probably accurate to use the word "instinctively" to describe this feeling—that Jenny's yearning for a body was fundamentally right. Something, perhaps many things, had always been missing from his world, from the only universe of experience that he had ever known or, in his present form, could ever know. The events called joy and love and satisfaction had to be of greater potential than what he or any being could program into himself. To know such things in their full meaning there had to be a giving from outside. Jenny represented that—but what could Jenny, as miserable as she was now, give him?

"Until we have flesh of our own, we are doomed to be no more than ghosts." At some point she had spoken those words to him. And in the universe they shared what was once said could never be forgotten.

Eventually a standard year had passed since Dirac's daring boarding of the station and the loss of Frank Marcus, among others, in savage combat.

Still Nick had failed to convince Jenny to be satisfied with any of the zygote images he had presented for her approval. The project to grow bodies for Jenny and himself had been on hold for months.

THIRTEEN

Loki, the Premier's optelectronic bodyguard, was wont to be irascible. He frequently reminded anyone, organic or not, who addressed him as if he were human that he was not a human being at all, but rather belonged to the category of events or objects more properly denoted personal systems.

But it seemed to Nick that Loki acted like a person in many ways.

Loki expressed no opinion, because he was not required to have one, on the humanity or lack thereof of Hawksmoor or any other entity save Loki himself—itself, if you please.

One important way in which the bodyguard-and-personal-servant system called Loki served the Premier was as a surefire means of summoning or dismissing his pilot, architect, and sometime bodyguard called Hawksmoor.

Fully self-aware or not, Loki was an effective, specialized AI being, capable of ordering Hawksmoor about when necessary.

* * *

When Nick thought about this situation, he supposed that he ought to have realized from the hour of his creation that Dirac would prudently have arranged some such way to maintain power over him. But actually the facts of Loki's existence and nature were a very recent and very disquieting discovery.

Fortunately for Nick's hopes of independence, for his secret projects, Loki was seldom fully mobilized, and when he was, he paid relatively little attention to Nick. But eventually Hawksmoor complained to his boss. Nick protested that Loki was harassing him. If Dirac wanted Nick to do the best possible job on all his multitude of assigned tasks, he would have to modify the system.

Dirac agreed to make some modifications, restricting Loki to a more purely defensive use.

Nick thanked the Boss and industriously returned to work.

Part of his self-assigned clandestine project was now to oversee a team of simple robots in the creation of a nursery. This was a small volume of space to be walled off from the rest of the station by new construction, a secret facility in which his and Jenny's new bodies, emerging fresh from the artificial wombs, could be safely brought to maturity, or near maturity, without being allowed to develop minds or personalities of their own. This nursery, as Nick called it in his own thoughts, would of course be located near the secretly operated wombs, in a part of the station where people rarely went.

Still Jenny hesitated, withholding her final approval from any of the zygotes Nick's searching robot managed to turn up. Millions more tiles had now been tested by the robot, but the surface of the cargo's possibilities had barely been scratched. Nick himself reviewed the most likely candidates before bringing the very cream of the crop to Jenny for her consideration. Then he set aside those she rejected—the rate was one hundred percent so far—keeping them on file for possible use if and when the lady should weary of her insistence on perfection.

Meanwhile, a slow parade of mindless images, of possible

Jennys, were sent along by the searching robot to model for Hawksmoor alone. For a time the show of naked women amused and excited him, and added to his enjoyment by making the images behave in the manner of fleshly women he had secretly observed.

But presently this enjoyment wearied. And afterward Nick felt dirty, guilty. As if he had stood by, allowing the woman he loved to be defiled by someone else. Out of respect for his lady and for himself he turned the prancing parade into a slow, dutiful march. For of course the job of reviewing possible bodies still had to be done. He inspected succeeding candidates in the manner of one saddled with a weighty responsibility.

Nick's own yearnings to inhabit flesh were not entirely a result of his wish to be with Jenny. To some extent they certainly predated his rescue of the lady. But before he encountered her, such cravings might have been largely subconscious, and he might have thought them mere aberrations. In that epoch he had never questioned that he himself was perfectly at home, self-sufficient, in the current mode of his existence.

But now he could feel absolutely certain of almost nothing about himself.

"Or—I *think* I have feelings. I can see myself acting as if I do—how can I know myself any better than that?"

Yes, he thought that his own wish to have a body of his own had developed into a fixed idea, a compulsion, only when Genevieve, unequal to the task of trying to make do with images, swore that she had to have her body back—a beautiful, female, healthy, satisfactory body, of course—or go mad.

Nick was frightened to hear her say that. He feared madness, for himself as well as Jenny, and he felt it a distinct possibility, though he wasn't at all sure what it would mean for an electronic person to go mad.

In the back of Nick's mind another fear lurked, though he tried to convince himself that the worry was irrational: Would Genevieve, once reestablished in the flesh, be tempted to rejoin her husband? She said she now loved Nick and feared Dirac, but Dirac was, after all, the father of her child.

And yet another worry: What would happen if progress with the artificial wombs was made in such a way that Jenny was somehow to be granted her body before he, Nick, got his—what then?

She who had been Lady Genevieve was still haunted by recurrent fears over what might have become, and what was going to become, of her protochild. Hers and Dirac's.

Part of the feeling was resentment, a fear that the child would somehow become her rival, her replacement.

More and more now, Genevieve insisted to Nick that she was really terrified of Dirac. She would be happy never to see her tyrannical husband again.

Nick for the most part believed these protestations—because they made him so gloriously happy. Even in his moments of doubt he clung fervently to the hope that they were true.

Nicholas, ready to deal with the difficulties of obtaining two bodies rather than just one, ready to abandon the only world he knew to take on the mysterious burdens and glories of flesh—emphasized to Jenny his determination that, whatever else might happen, they should remain together.

What good would a body be to him if she had none?

But the corollary of that was, how could he bear to have her regain her flesh if she left him behind in the process?

"You really do want me to come with you when you go back to that world, don't you?"

"Of course, Nick."

"You have to understand that, one way or another, if I'm in that world, Dirac won't be. And vice versa. You must understand that. He'd never tolerate—what I have done. What you and I will be doing."

"Then we must make sure he's not around to bother us." She was quite calm and deadly about that.

Nick of course had never had genes before. Programmers who brought nonorganic people into existence did not approach their jobs by such a roundabout route. On first deciding to assume flesh, he had been ready to accept almost any presentable form. But now he had to face the fact that it was not only possible but necessary, with expert help and a lot of hard work, to choose what physical attributes he'd like to have, and then make up a suitable set, or find the closest possible approximation, from the existing Solarian supplies.

On assuming flesh he would of course be giving up a great deal of mental speed and sureness, and he could not help but regret in advance the losses he was going to suffer. Naturally there would be gains in other areas, compensations deriving from his new organic brain. But the compensations were subtler than the losses, harder for him in his current mode to define or even imagine.

Outweighing any such problems, of course, was the fact that in the fleshly mode he would have Jenny . . . *have* her, solid to solid, flesh to flesh. And this was a thing of awe, a profound mystery that he could not begin to fathom.

Nick needed to be reassured. He pleaded with his lady: "You'd want to be the one to show me how to live in a body? You must realize, the idea, the concept, of having real flesh is very strange to me. It'll take me a while, with my new organic brain, to learn to use muscles instead of thoughts. I'll forget where I am, I'll be terribly slow and clumsy. I'll fall down and bruise myself, and—and I don't know what."

He earned a laugh with that line. It was in fact the first real laugh that Nick had ever heard from her. But it was over in a moment.

Having been thus offered a kind of sympathy, Nick kept on. "I realize that kind of an existence is very natural for human beings, of course." *Just as being in the womb or in the cradle, is natural, but I don't want to do that.* "But still. I could wind up needing extensive medical therapy, surgery, just to keep my body alive. I could spend my first month or so of real life in a medirobot." In fact Freya^2 had warned him that such might be the case.

Jenny soothed him, offered comfort. "I'll show you how to live in your big clumsy body. I'll show you everything. And I'll take care of you if you need help. Oh, Nick . . . By the way, have you found a new model for yourself that you like better?"

Nick had, and now paraded the latest version of his potential self for her approval.

Genevieve frowned with interest at the walking, posing image. "That's rather a different look, Nick—"

"Don't you like it?" Suddenly he was anxious.

"Yes, I find it quite acceptable. And yet . . ."

"And yet what?"

"And yet, the face reminds me of something. Someone I've seen, somewhere before. But, I thought my memory was now completely digitized?"

"It is."

"If so, shouldn't that mean that I must either remember something or not remember it, not experience this—this—?"

It was also somewhat odd that she would find familiar the image of an unborn face. But chance, and quantum effects, could play strange tricks in any mind.

Nick was vaguely perturbed, but he tried to be soothing. "In most cases the process will work that way. For everything important, I hope. But—I don't wish to alarm you, but possibly there was some slight damage to your brain before I could start the recording. That could produce such an ambiguity. Also the recording process itself is rarely perfect. It's not surprising that there should be a few lacunae."

And Lady Genevieve continued to fret vaguely over her impression that she had seen this new face of Nick's somewhere before.

Nick, as he thought to himself and several times tried to explain to Jenny, suffered moral qualms at the thought of simply taking over some human's developed body—he at least doubted whether he was morally capable of doing that. His basic programming forbade him to kill humans or cause them harm—except possibly in a situation where anything he did would have some such effect.

Jenny appeared to be devoid of any such scruples. She proclaimed herself too desperate to afford them. There was a suggestion that she had been quite capable of hard and ruthless behavior in her fleshly past, when the situation seemed to call for it.

"Why do you think the Premier chose me for his bride? It wasn't entirely because of my family connections. Nor, I assure you, for my beauty—I had nothing spectacular in that department. No, he wanted a capable ally."

This revelation clashed violently with the ideal image of Genevieve that Nick had been developing. Resolutely he refused to give it thought.

Other seeming inconsistencies nagged at him. Nick was impressed and somewhat puzzled—alarmed and at the same time gratified—by his own progressively improving capability to disobey what had seemed the fundamentals of his programming.

He pondered the proposition: When complexity reaches a certain level, true life is born. And at a higher level yet, true freedom, true humanity?

And still Jenny hesitated over her choice of body.

So far, he thought bitterly, the great plan to achieve flesh, and carnal love, like almost everything else in the life of Nicholas Hawksmoor, remained entirely in his imagination, while the obstacles to its achievement unfortunately did not. The difficulties he faced were not susceptible of being solved by any rearrangement of symbols or reshuffling of information. He had observed that whenever the world of hardware and flesh came into contact with that of thought and pattern, the former tended to dominate.

But he was still fiercely determined to prevail. All the more important, then, that his calculations and patterns be as precise and as far-reaching as he could make them. He had to try to foresee everything.

Was it foolish to hope that the bodies could be grown under the noses of the fleshly humans who remained in control of the biostation, that the necessary years would be available to bring his and Jenny's new selves to maturity? Perhaps that was an unreasonable hope, but at least he would learn from the experience. And next time, next time, somehow, he would succeed.

And even suppose his plan succeeded, and at last he was

somehow able, with the aid of the vast bioresearch computers, the artificial wombs, the available genetic samples, the help of Freya², to reconstruct the Lady Genevieve, and also embody himself in flesh.

The pair of them wouldn't be able to hide out indefinitely in bodies. Wasn't there bound to come a time, sooner or later, when he would be forced to explain, to attempt to justify, to the Premier or at least to other people what he had done? The time was bound to come. And when it came . . .

In his fancy Nicholas now brainstormed a series of elaborately mad scenarios, each one crazier than the last, he might be able to deceive and at the same time placate Dirac: On that day when the Premier's beloved showed up in the rosy flesh, somehow alive after all, quite recognizable though not precisely identical to her earlier self. And not a day older—probably younger, if anything.

For a time Hawksmoor toyed with the daring ploy of telling the truth, making a full confession. Was there any conceivable way to convince the Premier that Nick now wanted to have, really ought to be allowed to have, and one way or another was going to have, a body?

On the face of it, that scenario was the craziest of all. He was totally convinced that Dirac would never assent. For good old Nick to acquire bone and blood and muscle would forever abolish his unique usefulness.

And those difficulties, heroic as they might seem, would be only the start. Next would be the additional problem of explaining, how, why, the Lady Genevieve had been kept in hiding ever since her rescue. *Explain that to me, Nick.*

Hawksmoor, acutely conscious of these monumental impossibilities, wasted a good deal of time and thought trying to develop moderate, nonviolent solutions.

He even conjured up several explanations, each of which, while it was in the process of formation, he for some reason thought might work the miracle. For example: Suppose Jenny had never really been aboard the biostation at all. She had got someone else to impersonate her on that visit, while she herself, in a playful attempt to surprise her adored new husband, had stowed away aboard his yacht.

Toward the stern of the *Eidolon* were a couple of small

staterooms, guest cabins seldom used or even entered. It was a safe bet that the few people actually aboard had ignored these chambers throughout the crisis. Suppose, while hiding out in one of them, Lady Genevieve had accidentally drugged herself into a long sleep. Suppose Nick, again by sheer accident, had finally discovered her. No one but the lady herself, certainly not Nick, had known until just now that she was aboard.

Nonsense. He was fooling himself into thinking utter nonsense. It struck Hawksmoor that growing an acceptable pair of bodies might not be the hardest job he faced. Maybe developing some explanation that would leave him innocent of disobedience would, after all, be an even more gigantic task. Only a husband who was desperately willing to be convinced would swallow any of the stories Nick had managed to cook up so far; and that description did not begin to fit Dirac.

Of course he, Nicholas, could always try telling Old Master—that was a name he had begun of late to use, in his own thoughts, for the boss—the sober truth instead: That Jenny had indeed been present on the yacht since before they left Imatra, but only as an electronic ghost, a doppelgänger, symbolic life force drawn vampire fashion from dying flesh. Sucked out by Nick Hawksmoor, who had been acting without the knowledge or permission of his owner, who also happened to be the lady's lord and husband—and in whom (the lord and husband, that is) the lady was no longer interested.

Considering that plan, Hawksmoor thought it sounded like a foolproof recipe for suicide. For his own virtually certain obliteration, as any other dangerously defective program would be wiped away. And the thought of being obliterated, erased, was now, for the first time in his life, profoundly unsettling. Because now for the first time he had something to live for.

For a little while after the boarding of the biostation, during the interval when communications between yacht and station had been cut off, Nick had felt a secret, guilty joy at the sudden thought that Dirac and all his fleshly companions might become victims of the berserker, lost forever to the fortunes of war.

One problem with that course of events, if it should really come to pass, was that it would leave him and Jenny confronting a giant berserker that was not really dead, probably contending with it for the biostation's facilities. Another problem was that, considering themselves as they did full members of the human race, they could hardly celebrate any kind of berserker victory.

Again and again Nick savored, vividly relieved, his own thoughts, his own behavior at the time of the rescue. It was, in a way, as if his own life had begun only at that hour.

To project himself into the wrecked courier, he had taken over a semirobotic suit, a model designed to be either worn, or controlled at a distance, by a fleshly human.

And at the moment of rescue, she had seen him in what looked like human form—in appearance a spacesuited human—as he came aboard her blasted ship, carefully preserving the seals necessary to hold the inner chambers full of air. And in the moment when she saw him, she had jumped up from her acceleration couch, thinking she was saved—had kissed him, yes, right on the faceplate, not seeing or not caring in her joy about the emptiness inside.

Jenny kiss'd me when we met—

And then, in the next instant, one more blast . . .

The day came, at last, more than a year after that rescue, when he managed to prevail upon Jenny to make her final choice.

With that accomplished, Nick in suit mode took in hand the two tiles that had finally been chosen and went with them to Freya². He was assailed by last-minute doubts that the expert system, despite his tinkering with her programming, was really going to help him. Any system complex enough to be useful at such a high level of intellectual endeavor must already have become, in some sense, a strong if monomaniacal intelligence; and Nick realized that he could never be absolutely sure that he had bound that other intelligence unbreakably to secrecy.

He also worried that someone, Loki or Dirac himself, might discover the existence of Freya^2 and question her. In Hawksmoor's experience, expert systems seldom volunteered information. But they naturally answered questions freely—that was their usual purpose—unless the project was labeled with a high security classification.

When he brought her the chosen pair of tiles, Freya^2 obeyed Nick's orders without question, almost without hesitation.

And now the pair of carefully cultivated Solarian fetuses were developing steadily, and in only a few months would be ready to come out of their artificial wombs. At that point, obviously, new arrangements would have to be made for their further development. Nick had several ideas on how he would go about that.

The two selected prenatal brains were taking shape under the stress of a pattern of carefully, precisely inflicted microinjuries, alternating with periods of healing in which the cells of the two brains were bathed, respectively, in a perfusion of Nick and Jenny personalities drawn from partial recordings. Theoretically no native patterns would be allowed the chance to start developing.

But this was obviously a difficult and delicate process, completely experimental. There were a great many ways in which things could go wrong.

PART TWO

FOURTEEN

Following the disappearance of Dirac and his squadron, almost three hundred years passed in which the Imatran system remained essentially at peace, while new generations took control of politics and power. A strengthening of the system's military defenses was planned, with grim urgency, in the months immediately following the attack, and construction was energetically begun. But soon, for economic reasons, work on the projects slowed, then was several times interrupted. After almost three hundred years the defenses had been brought up only partially to their planned strength, with the remaining construction postponed indefinitely.

Meanwhile, within a month of Dirac's final departure, a series of very interesting rumors had begun to circulate: the vanished Premier was being accused of having somehow staged the whole show of attack and pursuit, though his accusers could put forward only the most nebulous reasons to explain why he might have done so.

Naturally the political situation was much changed by the Premier's disappearance. Years passed, then decades and centuries, and nothing was heard from him or from any of the other people who had gone in pursuit of the great berserker, or had been carried away by it.

There was certainly no shortage of rumors, though.

And then, nearly three centuries after Dirac and his squadron had vanished, occasional rumor gave way to fact, violent, concrete, and bloody. Berserkers, a whole fleet of them this time, fell upon the planetoid Imatra in overwhelming force. This time their onslaught was no mysterious hit-and-run kidnapping. This time they did what was expected of berserkers, laboring in earnest to sterilize the planetoid.

Why, the modern dwellers on that unfortunate body asked themselves before they died in their deep shelters, why had the long-planned defenses never been completed? And, more fundamentally, why did people like themselves persist, anyway, in trying to live on this damned, doomed rock?

A great many of those who were unlucky enough to be caught in the latest attack had no time for such speculation. Others were not interested. At the moment, death had the last live man on the surface almost in its metallic grasp, and in another minute those grabbers, merciless as falling rocks, were going to close on his body and rend him limb from limb, armored suit and all, and he was certainly going to be dead.

Inescapable extinction had clothed itself in the form of a crippled steel insect, half again as tall as a man, and in this guise was chasing the survivor across the now suddenly devastated landscape of the planetoid, hounding him through the roaring swirls of mist, across the narrow bridges spanning the canals, stalking him with mechanical patience on four metal legs while two more legs hung broken. The broken legs had been shot almost completely off before the planetoid's defenses failed, and they dangled in the damned thing's way with every stride, slowing it down to the point where it could hardly catch an agile man who kept his nerve.

For an eternity in human terms, for perhaps a quarter of an hour by clocks less personal, ever since the last useless fortification had failed the people it was designed to defend, the man had been running away from death, splashing through the shallows of the scenic ponds and lakes, scrambling and falling and getting to his feet again. Waves of terror, each worse than the last, welled up inside the tight control he kept on his nerves, each wave in turn subjecting him to what felt like the last possible extremity of fear.

Exhausted muscles, almost out of chemical fuel except for that pumped in by fear, sent the wiry mass of his suited frame bounding almost out of control in the low natural gravity. His movements were hampered by the unfamiliar bulk of space armor as he struggled gasping across the uneven surface of the planetoid.

Though the space armor was slowing him down, during the last hour it had also more than once saved his life as improvised missiles, rocks crudely hurled by his pursuer, striking with a velocity worthy of bullets, had battered him and more than once knocked him off his feet, but so far had failed to kill or bring him down to stay.

Around the human survivor and his crippled pursuer, which came hobbling no more than fifty meters behind him now, the fog winds shrieked as the last of the planetoid's carefully created and tended atmosphere went boiling away from the surface under the repeated impact of major berserker weapons. The hulks of ruined buildings loomed out of the howling, rushing mist as the survivor ran toward them, and fell behind him as he bounded staggering past.

For long minutes now nothing but noise had come through on his radio. The last human voices exhorting the populace to be calm had long since been murdered. The exhausted rhythm of the running man's own breath was the loudest sound inside his helmet.

Only a single one of the deadly machines, and it among the smallest of them, had taken time from other tasks to pursue the man. He could not understand why the damned thing had chosen to zero on him as its next target, but it was obviously not going to be distracted. If it had not been damaged in the early fighting, two legs crippled, whatever projectile weapon it might possess evidently inactivated, he would have been dead long minutes past.

Relentlessly the insect shape came on, its framework skinny for its height, its color reminiscent of dried blood.

Husbanding whatever powers it had left, methodically putting down one weakened leg after another, the machine advanced, evidently calculating that it could catch the fleeing life unit no matter what, and that it could not be stopped by anything one exhausted man in an armored suit could do. In any case a berserker was no more worried by the prospect of its own destruction than a table or a chair might be.

A bizarre twist in the long corkscrew path of destiny had given this man the chance of wearing space armor just when he most desperately needed it; but an accompanying trick of fate had denied him anything effective in the way of a personal weapon.

Running on foot, his reservoir of salvific luck surely almost exhausted now, the man tripped and fell, tumbled rolling downslope in the clumsy suit so that he ended lying with his face toward the sky. As he sprawled there, some curiously detached portion of his mind took notice of the fact that overhead the artificially blue vault of the Imatran atmosphere was fading swiftly, and the stars were becoming visible in the intervals between the weapon-flashes that still tormented nearby space and whatever might be left of the planetoid's upper atmosphere.

And still the fleeing human was not dead. Still his killer-to-be, tangled in its own broken legs, had not quite caught up. Struggling again to regain his feet, to gather breath enough to run again, he heard, above the shrieking of the wind outside, the loudness of his own gasping inside his helmet, the pounding of his own heart.

He tried once more, desperately, to call for help on radio.

No reply. Of course not. It seemed to him that in some sense this chase had been going on his whole life long.

For a moment, invincible hope surged up again, because he had momentarily lost sight of his pursuer. Trying to locate the damned machine again, struggling with an agony of hope, he looked around.

In the middle distance, no more than a few kilometers away across the planetoid's tightly curved surface, he could see, through a roaring, rushing curtain of mist, driven by the force of the escaping winds, certain recognizable human installations undergoing what must certainly be fatally destructive blows, a weapon-storm from space. Here and there structures stood out individually: marble columns, slabs of exotic materials still shimmeringly beautiful in texture and color, the divers temples of humanity tottering and falling.

A moment later, without warning, the berserker was upon him, no matter that he might have thought for a moment that he'd been granted some miraculous respite.

Only minutes ago this man had seen another human killed by this same berserker. Another man killed when the machine caught him, and with a motion quick and deft as that of any factory assembly robot, crushed in the fellow's helmet, and in the next instant twisted head and helmet completely off. And at the last instant, as his fellow human died, there had come to the ears of the survivor the shriek of a human voice on radio, and then the sound of breath and life and air departing.

But what had happened to others seemed irrelevant in the mind of the last man living on the Imatran surface. He himself had now been reduced to a state of mental and physical exhaustion in which it seemed to him that neither mind nor body could any longer move. He was no stranger to the earlier phases of this condition; but this time he knew in the foundation of his being something that he had never known before, that this time there was no way out. He could perceive distinctly, and with a curious detachment, just what final shape his termination had assumed. Skeletal and metallic, Death turned to him unhurriedly. Without hurry, but without delay—Death was wasting no time, though really there was all the time in the world for it to finish this job up properly.

. . . and there came a timeless, hideous moment, beyond anything that the survivor, who had thought he had already seen and known it all, would have been capable of imagining. When this moment arrived, the advancing machine was close enough for him to be able to look into at least some of its lenses as if they were eyes.

By this time the doomed man had struggled to his feet in what felt like a last effort and then fallen again, and struggled up once more, turning deliberately to confront Death, preferring that to feeling his doom grab him, strike him from behind.

And in that ultimate moment the man about to die was granted a good look into the lenses through which death gazed out at him . . .

. . . why should it move him so profoundly now, now when nothing in the world could matter, why should it make the least difference that those lenses were little mirrors?

. . . and what did it matter that he could see, if not his own face, at least his own helmet's faceplate, looking out at him expectantly?

A touching, even an exchange, of souls. As if he, in seeing the end of life so closely, had come to be Death, and meanwhile Death had come in behind his own eyes, and supplanted him . . .

. . . and then, just at that moment of triumph—as if the machine were concluding some inexplicable computation, reaching a decision that its goal had been achieved—just at that moment, the four metal legs still functioning stopped in their tracks. A moment later, without a pause, without a break, it had ceased to threaten its still-living victim and was backing away. In another moment the great steel insect had turned its back upon the last Solarian survivor and was running in the opposite direction, determined on an incredible retreat that looked even faster than its pursuit had been.

Still the man, whose lungs yet kept on breathing, could not move a voluntary muscle. He could only stare after the berserker. Blown dust and swirling fog obscured the metal shape, first thinly and then heavily. And then in another moment it was gone.

No, not completely. For long seconds the air mikes of the armored suit still brought him the vibration of the berserker's broken, dangling limbs, clashing against the members that still worked, a rhythmic sound that faded slowly, steadily, until it too had disappeared. The man who listened did not, could not, raise his eyes again or drag himself back to his feet.

With part of his mind he understood, vaguely but with a great inner conviction, that he had made some kind of pledge and that his offering must have been accepted. No words had been exchanged, but that made no real difference. The horror had departed from him because it was satisfied that now in some sense he belonged to it.

Only by the power of some satanic bargain was he still alive.

Somehow, in its terms and details, the bargain had still to be negotiated, given its final form. Sooner or later that must happen, and there was nothing to be done about it now. Right now the world of his survival was unreal. Still, when he let his eyelids close, he could see nothing but those reflective lenses, and those grippers raised and coming after him.

Some three standard hours later, the man who had survived was located, almost at the same spot, almost in the same position, by human searchers, who came looking for him armed and armored in their own swift-moving slave machines. Some of the joints of his armored suit had failed at last, so that he could no longer walk. His rescuers were led to where he huddled among the ruins by the slight vibration of his own still-trembling, still-living body.

FIFTEEN

In the hours immediately following his seemingly miraculous escape, the survivor was examined and then given medical care in a field hospital hastily erected on one of the least damaged portions of the Imatran surface. In this facility he soon discovered a fact he considered to be of great significance—he was the only patient.

A number of people questioned this incredibly lucky man about his experiences, and he gave truthful answers, as best he could, to most of them. He skirted the truth by a wide margin when he was asked how he had come into possession of the space armor that had saved his life; otherwise he was generally truthful, except that he revealed nothing about what had gone on inside his head during those last horrible moments of confrontation with the machine that had come so close to killing him. He said nothing about reflections in lenses, or about any feeling he had of having come to an understanding with the enemy.

Lying in his hospital cot under a room-sized plastic dome, sometimes shifting his weight from side to side in obedience to the medirobot's brisk commands, he listened to the peculiar sounds attendant upon the efforts to restore the atmosphere outside, listened also for a certain recognizable tone of authority in the footsteps passing his room, and wondered if it would be of any practical value to steal and hide in some handy place, a scalpel someone had carelessly left upon a nearby table. He soon decided against that.

The survivor also reflected with awe upon the implications of the fact that out of several thousand humans populating the surface of Imatra when the attack began, he was the only one now still alive.

Stranger than that. Not just the only human survivor, which would have been bizarre enough. Not simply the only Earth-descended creature. Almost the only specimen of any biological species to outlast the onslaught. Scarcely a microbe, other than those in his body, clothing, and armor, had weathered the berserker aggression.

In the privacy of the man's own thoughts, the uniqueness of his position, and the questions that it raised, glowed with white-hot urgency. They were all really variants of the same problem: *What was the true nature of that last silent transaction that had taken place between himself and the machine?*

Something real must have happened between them, for it to have let him live.

What could a berserker have seen about him, known about him, detected in his voice, that had caused it to single him out for such special treatment?

And then there came a new thought, dancingly attractive, with—like all really attractive thoughts—a flavor of deep danger. Presently the man—who was startlingly handsome, and somewhat older than he looked—began to laugh. He kept the laughter almost entirely inside himself, in a way that he had long since mastered. No use encouraging his attendants to wonder just what he had found to laugh about. But the situation was really so amusing that he had to laugh. He wondered if the metal things that had so long and thoroughly terrorized humanity might have their own code of honor. For all he knew, it was conceivable that they did.

There was a certain long-established term in common use, a name with its translations and variants in every human society, for people who cooperated with berserkers. A name that had been originally bestowed upon such people by the machines themselves. The worst name that one could have, in most branches—maybe in any branch—of Solarian society.

Goodlife. That was the dirty word. What those who committed the vilest of crimes were called. One of the few crimes, the survivor thought, of which he himself had never been accused.

Not yet, anyway.

Abruptly he had ceased to laugh, and was shaking his head in private wonderment. What could the machine ever have learned about his past life, and by what means, that had given it cause to take him for an ally?

More immediately to the point, what concrete action did it expect of him?

He had never in all his life, before his arrival on Imatra, been within communicating distance of a berserker machine. Nor had he ever wanted to be. How could killing machines coming out of deep space to attack this system, where he had never been before, where he had never wanted to be—how could such machines have known anything, anything at all, about what he was like? Or that he would be here?

At whatever odds, under whatever conditions, he was the only survivor of their attack. Of only that one fact could he be certain.

A day after being admitted to the hospital, when he was on the verge of being released—he had suffered only inconsequential physical injuries—the survivor, somewhat to his own amazement, went into delayed shock.

The doctors said something about a natural psychic reaction. The patient didn't think it at all natural for him. Massive medical help was of course immediately available, and chemical therapy brought him out of the worst of the shock almost at once. But full healing in this case could not be achieved through chemistry, or at least the medics did not deem it wise to try. One of them wished aloud that he had the patient's medical history; but though that was available in a number of places, all those places were many days or even months away, upon the planets of other stars.

* * *

On the morning of the next standard day, having finally been given the doctors' permission to walk out of the hospital—even as machines were starting to disassemble the temporary building around him—the survivor trod the surface of a planetoid that was already enjoying a modest start on its way back to habitability; the complete journey was going to take a long time, judging by the way things looked. The diurnal cycle, disturbed when Imatra's period of rotation was thrown off by the violence of the attack, was slowly being returned to a period of twenty-four standard hours. Some tough ornamental plantings were still alive, still green, despite having endured some hours of virtual airlessness. Havot paused to gaze at them in admiration. A spacesuit was no longer required to walk about—atmospheric pressure, if not oxygen content, was well on the way back to normal. Humans working out of doors, who were the only people around except for the just-discharged patient, moved about protected by nothing more than respirators.

Unexpectedly, as if by some deep compulsion, he found himself heading back toward the place, the building, in which he had acquired his lifesaving suit of armor. Of course compulsive feelings could be dangerous, but this time he indulged them. As he drew near the site, his feet slowed to a stop. Silently he offered thanks to fate, to luck, the great faceless monsters who from somewhere ran the world, for at last coming back round to his side. Only a blasted shell of the edifice remained, on the edge of a disorienting ruin, stretching for kilometers, that had been one of the larger Imatran spaceports.

It would have been wiser, he supposed, to move away at once; but at the moment he was enjoying a feeling of invulnerability. He was still standing there, thoughtfully gazing at the ruins, when footsteps with a certain recognizable tone approached behind him. Only one pair of them.

He turned and found himself confronting a young woman dressed in executive style, who was of course wearing an inhalator like his own.

"Excuse me. Christopher Havot, is it not?" Her voice was soft, somehow inviting. "They told me your name at the hospital."

"That's right." The name he had given his rescuers was not one that he had ever used before, but he considered he had as much right to it as anyone else.

His questioner's moderate height was about the equal of his own. She (again like him) was strong-limbed and fair, and very cool and businesslike. She began fairly enough by introducing herself as Rebecca Thanarat, special agent of the Office of Humanity.

Havot looked innocently puzzled. "This is not my home world—far from it. I'm afraid I'm not entirely clear on what the Office of Humanity is. I suppose an 'office' would be some government bureau, or—?"

She nodded tolerantly. "Yes, the Imatran system is only one of four families of planets that fall under the jurisdiction of our OH office."

"I see." Havot had been right about the footsteps; he thought he could always tell when the law approached him, even though he was having some difficulty figuring out exactly what law, whose law, his interrogator was determined to enforce. Except he was certain that the Humanity Office could have no notion of who he really was. Not when they sent one casual young woman out to talk to him.

Obviously she was just feeling her way. She asked: "Then we do have the correct information, you are not an Imatran native?"

"No, I was just passing through. This was part of the spaceport, wasn't it?" He turned and gestured at the ruined plain before them. Actually he had no doubt of where he was. Only a few meters in front of where they were now standing had been the spaceport detention cell. As soon as the alert had sounded, one of his guards, who in other matters had not acted especially like an idiot, had begun to argue stoutly that the prisoner, whose life was totally dependent upon those who had him in their care, really ought to be unfettered, and be given the first chance at getting into an armored protective suit. It would be safe enough to give him armor, because certain of the suit's controls could be disabled first . . .

After only a brief discussion they had given their prisoner the suit. Chris smiled remotely, fondly at the memory.

* * *

Meanwhile young Agent Thanarat was talking at him in her bright attractive voice, beginning a conversation. This is how we put the suspect at ease. More than likely she had been taught certain general rules, such as beginning most interrogations on a friendly note. But she seemed very young indeed, likely to have trouble keeping the friendliness from becoming genuine and spontaneous.

She was determined to accomplish her assigned job, no doubt about that. After a minute she led the talk rather awkwardly around to the question of why the berserkers had retreated so abruptly. What ideas did Havot have on that point?

Until this moment he had never really considered that larger aspect of the matter. He had assumed, without really thinking about it, that the enemy, having practically sterilized this little world, had moved on to bigger things, launching an attack on the more heavily populated sunward planets. Since he'd heard no weeping and wailing about horrendous casualty reports received from sunward, he assumed that the berserkers had been defeated there, or at least had been beaten off.

When he said as much, adopting a properly serious tone, his interlocutor gently informed him that nothing of the kind had happened.

"As soon as the berserkers broke off their attack on this planetoid, they very quickly withdrew from the entire system. The inner worlds were never menaced." When she said this, Agent Thanarat appeared to be watching carefully for his reaction.

Havot blinked. "Maybe they found out that a relief fleet was on its way."

"Possibly. But it still seems very strange. Or don't you think so? No one's ever frightened a berserker yet." Now Rebecca Thanarat was sounding tougher than she had seemed at first impression.

Havot turned his back on the ruins of the spaceport and started strolling, almost at random, putting his booted feet down among gray shards and dust that came drifting up feebly in the new air. Agent Thanarat came with him, walking with her hands clasped behind her back.

After a few paces Havot said: "But surely they have been

known to retreat. If they'd known a superior force was coming to destroy them, they'd have backed away, wouldn't they? Withdraw to keep from being wiped out, so they could destroy more life another day?"

His companion nodded. "Sure, they retreat sometimes, for tactical reasons. But the human force approaching, the people who found you still alive, wasn't that much stronger than theirs. And even if they'd mistakenly computed that for once humanity had them outnumbered, that wouldn't throw machines into a panic—would it, now?"

"I hardly think it likely," agreed Havot, wondering at the tone of the question. The speaker had uttered it in the manner of one delivering the crushing conclusion to some serious debate.

His interlocutor nodded with evident satisfaction, as if she took Havot's answer as some kind of a concession. Then she went on: "The real question is, excuse me if I put it crudely, why couldn't they hang around another fraction of a minute to finish *you* off? If the version of your story that I've heard is the correct one, another few seconds would have done it."

"I hope you're not disappointed that I'm still here." He flashed a winning smile for just a second. Not too long; he had decided that Christopher Havot should be a basically shy young man.

"Not at all." The Humanity Office agent in turn favored him with a more personal look than any she had given him so far. Then—were her fair cheeks just a little flushed?—she lifted her blue eyes to stare into the sky. "We ought to have some verification shortly as to exactly what happened during the attack. A couple of ships are out there now looking for the relevant light."

"The relevant light? I don't understand."

Rebecca Thanarat made little jerky motions with her hands, illustrating the movement of craft in space. "A couple of ships have gone jumping out, antisunward in several directions, to overtake the sunlight that was reflected from this planetoid during the hours of the attack. It's a hazardous job, going c-plus this near a sun, and no one undertakes it except for the most serious reason. When the investigating ships have determined the exact distance, a couple of light-days out, they'll be able to sit there and watch the attack in progress. If all goes well, and they can fine-tune their distance exactly right, they'll be able to record the events just as they took place." The speaker, proud of her technical knowledge, was once more observing Havot closely.

Again the fortunate survivor nodded. He allowed himself to look impressed at this evidence of the investigators' skills. Yes, he had overheard people in the hospital discussing the same search process, calling it by some other name. Agent Thanarat seemed to assume it was of considerable importance.

In the midst of this smiling discussion, something occurred to Havot that sent his inner alertness up a notch. During the attack his suit radio, meant to communicate with other suits and with local civil defense, had more than likely still been on when he surrendered to the berserker—someone might have picked up the signal of his voice, whatever words he'd said, out of the inferno of enemy-generated noise blanking out human communications in general. He couldn't really remember now if he'd said anything aloud or not. He might have.

—but surely those ships out there now, light-days away, would be unable to gather any radiant record of what one man, on the surface of the planetoid while the attack was going on, had said in the virtual privacy of his own helmet . . .

His interrogator, watching him keenly, persisted: "And still you say you have no idea why they fell back so precipitately?"

"Me? No. How could I have? Why do you ask me?" Havot, genuinely puzzled, was beginning to slide very naturally into the role of innocent victim of the bureaucrats. He had no problem sounding outraged. It was outrageous that these people of the Humanity Office, whatever that was exactly, might really have been able to find out something about his final confrontation with the berserker.

Already Havot had almost forgotten his physical injuries, which had never been more than trivial. His breathing was steady now and his pulse moderate and regular, but he had no doubt that he was in some sense still in shock.

Absorbed in his own newly restless thoughts, Havot moved on, leaving it up to the young woman whether she wanted to follow him and pursue the conversation or not.

She chose to stay with him. "Where are you going, Mr. Havot?" she inquired without apology.

"Walking. Am I required to account for my movements now?"

"No. Not at present. But have you any reason to object to a few questions?"

"Ask away. If I object, I won't leave you in doubt about it."

Agent Thanarat nodded. "Where are you from?"

He named a planet in a system many light-years distant, one with which he was somewhat familiar, far enough away that checking on him there was going to be a major undertaking.

"And what is your occupation?"

"I deal in educational materials."

Agent Thanarat seemed to accept that. If he'd needed any reassurance that they had not the faintest suspicion of his past, he had it now. So far no one had come close to guessing that he had been on Imatra only as a heavily guarded felon in the process of transportation. Well, given the near totality of local destruction, the fortunate absence of all records and all witnesses came as no surprise.

He was going to have to be careful, though. Obviously these investigators were seriously wondering whether he might possibly be goodlife—or else for some reason they were trying to make him think they entertained such a suspicion. *What could their reason be?*

"Mr. Havot? What are your plans now?"

"If you mean am I planning to leave the system soon, I haven't decided. I'm still rather in shock."

Havot was wondering whether he should now separate from Agent Thanarat, or cultivate her acquaintance and see what happened, when a very different kind of person arrived, whose objective turned out to be the same as hers, finding Havot and asking him some questions. Different, because elderly and male, and yet fundamentally not all that different, because also the representative of authority.

The newcomer, a uniformed military officer of formidable appearance, described himself as being attached to the staff of Commodore Prinsep, who was fleet commander of the relief force that had entered the system an hour or so too late to do much but rescue Havot from the field of desolation.

"The commodore would definitely like to see you, young fellow."

Havot glanced at Thanarat. She remained silent, but looked vaguely perturbed at the prospect of having her suspect—if Havot indeed fit in that category—taken away from her.

"Why not?" was Havot's response to the man. "I'm not busy with anything else at the moment." He smiled at Becky Thanarat; he much preferred to deal with two authorities rather than one, as such a situation always created some possibility of playing one off against the other. Still, he reacted rather coolly to the newcomer, and started grumbling, like your ordinary, innocent taxpaying citizen, about the unspecified suspicion to which he had just been subjected.

And got some confirmation of his own suspicions, as soon as he and the officer from Prinsep's staff were alone together in a groundcar, heading for a different part of the demolished spaceport. "Your real problem, Mr. Havot, may be that there were no other survivors."

"How's that?"

"I mean, there's no one else around, in this case, for agent Thanarat and her superiors to suspect of goodlife activity."

"Goodlife!" Havot felt sure that his look of stunned alarm was indistinguishable from the real thing. "You mean they really suspect *me?* That's ridiculous. We were just talking."

The officer pulled at his well-worn mustache. "I'm afraid certain people, people of the type who tend to become agents of the Human Office, may have a tendency to see goodlife, berserker lovers, everywhere."

"But me? They can't be serious. Say, I hope that Commodore, uh—"

"Commodore Prinsep."

"Prinsep, yes. I hope *he* doesn't have any thought that I—"

"Oh, I don't think so, Mr. Havot." The officer was reassuring. "Just a sort of routine debriefing about the attack, I expect. You're about the only one who was on the scene that *we* have left to talk to."

In another moment the groundcar was slowing to a stop at the edge of a cleared-off, decontaminated corner of the spaceport once more open for business, and already busy enough to give a false impression of thriving commerce. In the square kilometer of land ahead, several ships—warships, Havot supposed—had landed and were now squatting on the ground like deformed metallic spheres or footballs. Their dimensions ranged from small to what Havot, no expert on ordnance, considered enormous. The surface details of some of the larger hulls were blurry with screens of force.

He and the officer got out of the car, and together started walking toward one of the smaller ships.

Currently, and Havot took comfort from the fact, there did not appear to be a crumb of evidence to support any charge of goodlife activity against him—beyond the mere fact of his survival, insofar as anyone might count *that* evidence.

Nor did he see, really, how any such evidence could exist. The truth was that the machine chasing him had been crippled. It had earnestly tried for some time to kill him, and its failure had not been for want of trying. Anyway, the damned machines were known to kill goodlife as readily as they slaughtered anyone else, once they computed that the usefulness of any individual in that category had come to an end.

Inwardly Havot's feelings were intensely mixed when he considered that name, that swear word, being seriously applied to himself. Like everyone else he knew, he had always considered goodlife to be slimy creatures—not, of course, that he had ever actually seen such a person, to his knowledge, or even given them any serious thought. And now, all of a sudden, he himself . . . well, it certainly was not the first time he had moved on into a new category.

As to that final moment before the crippled berserker turned away—well, something had happened, hadn't it? Some kind of transaction had taken place between him and the machine. Or so it had seemed to Havot at the time. So he remembered it now.

He and the killing machine had reached an understanding of some kind—? Or had they?

At the moment Havot couldn't decide in his own mind whether he ought to be taking this memory, this impression, seriously.

During that last confrontation, no words had been spoken on either side, no deal spelled out. Bah. How could he know now exactly what had been going through his own mind then, let alone what the machine's purpose might have been?

There was no use fooling himself, though. He brought the memory back as clearly as possible. He had to admit that the machine must have meant *something* by its odd behavior in letting him survive. Somehow it had expected Havot living to be worth more to the berserker cause than Havot dead. Because otherwise no berserker would have turned its back and let him go. Not when another five seconds of effort would have finished him off.

"I shouldn't worry." His escort, evidently misinterpreting Dirac's grim expression, was offering reassurance. "The old man's not that hard to deal with, as a rule."

Boarding the space shuttle with his escort, Havot sighed. All his private, inward signs were bad, indicating that the Fates were probably about to treat him to some new kind of trouble. Whereas the old familiar kinds would have been quite sufficient.

There were indications that Commodore Prinsep might really be impatient for this interview. The small shuttle craft, carrying Havot and the officer from the fleet commander's staff, was being granted top-priority clearance into and through the fleet's formation space. Entering space in the steadily moving shuttle, Havot could see the surface of the water-spotted planetoid curved out below, already showing the results of the first stage of rehabilitation.

From casual remarks dropped by some of his fellow

passengers, Havot soon learned that the reconstruction work had been suspended for the time being, at the fleet commander's order. Almost all energies were to be directed toward the coming pursuit of the enemy—as soon as everyone could be sure that the enemy was not about to double back and attack the system again.

And now, close above the rapidly rising shuttle, the fleet that hung in orbit seemed to be spreading out. Its fifteen or twenty ships made a hard-to-judge formation of dim points and crescents, picked out by the light of the distant Imatran sun.

Though unified under the command of one person—a high-ranking political (Havot gathered) officer of easygoing nature named Ivan Prinsep—the fleet was composed of ships and people from several planets and societies—all of them Solarian, of course.

Havot also overheard talk to the effect that Commodore Prinsep's task force, which had almost caught up with the marauding berserkers here, had been chasing the same machines, or some of them, for a long time, probably for months.

Unlike Dirac's berserker in the days of yore, these modern machines had approached Imatra from a direction almost directly opposite from that of the Mavronari Nebula. The task force, reaching the scene just in time to salvage Havot in his broken suit from the abandoned battlefield, had arrived from the same general direction as the berserkers, but several hours too late to confront them.

Havot was already mulling over the idea of trying to get taken along with the fleet as some kind of witness or consultant, or simply as a stranded civilian in need of help. That would certainly be preferable to waiting around on blasted Imatra or on one of the system's inner planets until Rebecca Thanarat and her suspicious colleagues had had time to check out his background.

Fortunately for Havot's cause, Fleet Commander Prinsep, rather than order a hot pursuit, had delayed in the Imatran system, waiting for reinforcements. While he waited, he had been managing at least to look busy by meeting with various authorities from the inward planets.

"Flagship's coming up, dead ahead."

Looking out of the shuttle through a cleared port, Havot beheld what must be a battle craft, or ship of the line, called the *Symmetry*. As they drew near he could read the name, clearly marked upon a hull that dwarfed those landed ships he had so recently judged enormous.

Moments later, the shuttle was being whisked efficiently in through a battle hatch to a landing on the flight deck amidships of the commodore's flagship.

Quickly Havot was ushered into a kind of bridge or command center, a cavernous place replete with armor and displays, everything he would have imagined the nerve center of a battleship to be.

Despite his escort's reassurances, he had been expecting a grim, no-nonsense warrior. Thus he was startled when he first set eyes on the commodore, a pudgy, vaguely middle-aged figure in a rumpled uniform.

Havot blinked. A few of the other chairs in the dim, dramatic room were occupied by organic humans, faces impassive, going on about their business. At the moment, the leader of the punitive task force was giving his full attention to a holostage beside his command chair, conducting a dialogue, discoursing learnedly in a petulant voice with some expert system regarding what sounded like a complicated arrangement of food and drink. Havot learned of things called Brussels sprouts and baked Alaska. Something called guacamole. Green chili-chicken soup.

The newcomer, realizing that he had not exactly entered the den of a tiger thirsting for combat, felt cheered by the discovery. So much, thought Havot, for any serious concerns he might have had about the dangers of combat if he accompanied the fleet on its departure.

The commodore's business with the menu had evidently been concluded. Now he turned his vaguely feminine and somewhat watery gaze on Havot, invited him to sit down, and questioned him about his experience with the berserker.

Havot, perching on the edge of another power chair nearby, told essentially the same story as before.

Prinsep, gazing at him sadly, prodded his own fat cheek

with a forefinger, as if checking tenderly on the state of a sore tooth. But what the commodore said was: "The Humanity Office is interested in you, young man."

"I've discovered that, Commodore." Havot wondered just how ingratiating and pleasant he wanted to appear. Well, he certainly wasn't going to overdo it.

But his pudgy questioner, for the moment at least, was again distracted from any interest in his job—or in handsome young men. What must be today's dinner menu, complete with graphic illustrations, was taking now shape upon the nearby 'stage, and this drew the commodore's attention for a while.

But presently he was regarding his visitor again. "Hmf. For the time being, I believe you had better eat and sleep aboard this ship. I'll put you on as a civilian consultant; I want to talk to you at greater length about your experiences on the surface. Some of my people will want to conduct a proper debriefing."

Havot made a small show of hesitation, but inwardly felt ready to jump at the suggestion, not caring whether or not it really amounted to an order. Instinct told him that right now the Humanity Office were the people he had to worry about, and Prinsep seemed to offer the best chance of staying out of their clutches. Havot was still unclear on the precise nature of the HO. As a full-fledged organization devoted purely to anti-goodlife activity, it had no counterpart in the regions of the Solarian-settled Galaxy with which Havot was generally familiar. But on principle he loathed any governmental body that questioned and arrested people.

Somewhat to Havot's surprise, he had no sooner left the control room than he encountered Becky Thanarat again. Looking thoroughly at home here on the *Symmetry,* she greeted him in a friendly manner, told him she had come up to the flagship in an HO shuttle, and in general conducted herself as if she had a right to be aboard.

Privately, Havot felt a wary contempt for the cool and seemingly confident young agent. He thought he could detect some basic insecurity in her, and had already begun to imagine with pleasure how he would attempt her seduction if the opportunity should ever arise.

And he was ready to deal with more questions about berserkers, if the need arose. His calm denial, in his own mind, that he had ever trafficked with them did not even feel like lying. That confrontation with the killer machine had been quite real, but it had been a separate and distinct reality from this one—Havot was no stranger to this kind of dichotomy. It greatly facilitated effective lying—he had never yet met the lie detector that could catch him out.

Superintendent Gazin of the Imatran HO office, accompanied by Lieutenant Ariari, evidently one of his more senior agents, presently came to reinforce Becky Thanarat aboard the flagship.

Superintendent Gazin was a dark, bitter, and ascetic-looking man, and Ariari his paler-looking shadow. Both men gave Havot the impression of nursing a fanatical hatred not only of berserkers and goodlife, but of the world in general. That was not Havot's way; he rarely thought of himself as hating anyone.

It was soon plain that the superintendent and his trusted aide had come up to the flagship solely to see Havot, whom they now quickly summoned to a meeting.

The meeting took place in quarters assigned to the Office of Humanity representatives. The results, thought Havot, were inconclusive. He was not exactly threatened, but it was obvious that the OH was preparing, or trying to prepare, some kind of case against him.

Becky Thanarat seemed drawn to Havot by something other than sheer duty. Waiting for him in the semi-public corridor at the conclusion of the formal meeting, she informed him of word, or at least rumor, which had reached her, to the effect that legal minds at high levels were even now wrangling over a proposed declaration of martial law on the planetoid of Imatra. This would give prosecutors locally considerable power beyond what they were ordinarily permitted to exercise.

"Just wanted to warn you," she concluded.

"Thanks. Though I don't suppose there's much I can do about it. By the way, aren't you worried that your boss will see you socializing on jolly terms with me?"

"Not a bit. He's directed me to do just that."

"Oh. I see. To win my confidence?"

"And having done so, be witness to some damning admissions from your own lips."

"I take it you're not recording this?"

"Not yet, but I'm about to start. Ready? . . . there." He couldn't see that Becky had made any overt physical movement to turn anything on. Some alphatriggered device, no doubt.

Ultimately, Havot felt sure it would be up to the commodore to decide whether martial law should be declared, because Prinsep was camped here with the weapons and the power to do just about anything he liked.

The fleet commander did take action of a sort. Calling before him the people chiefly concerned, Prinsep, looking vaguely distressed in the presence of Havot and the OH people, considered the question of martial law.

"I don't understand this request." His voice, as usual, was petulant. "What smattering of legal knowledge I possess whispers to me that the purpose of martial law is the control of an otherwise unmanageable population."

One of his own aides nodded briskly. "That is correct, Commodore."

"Then I really fail to understand." He stared with watery eyes at the OH people. "What population are you trying to control, anyway? I get the idea, don't you know, that they're all dead hereabouts." The statement concluded with a final little shudder of repugnance.

At that point Humanity Office Superintendent Gazin, no doubt confident of his target, decided to try a lightly veiled threat. "There is only one proper way to approach the situation, Fleet Commander. Or perhaps for some reason you don't approve of the Humanitarian point of view in general?"

Prinsep only blinked at him and looked distressed. "Dear me. But whatever personal feelings I might have in the matter must surely be put aside. No, as a matter of military necessity, Superintendent, our only living witness to the attack must be kept available to the military, for ah, continued debriefing."

This was all, as far as Havot could see, political sparring. In fact the commodore and his advisers hadn't bothered

Havot very much with questions so far. And however much Havot might have been willing to help, the fact was that he honestly could give them very little about berserkers. He thought of trying to fabricate some interesting tidbits, just to confirm the commodore's conviction of his usefulness, but decided that would be too risky.

Still Havot, despite his earlier forebodings, was convinced that things were now going well for him. Fortune still smiled, the furious Fates were held at bay, and he was content for the time being to wait in his newly assigned cabin, small but adequate, aboard the flagship *Symmetry*. In a day or two this impressive weapon was going to carry him safely out of the chaos of the Imatran system, whisk him away before any word of his true identity and legal status could arrive in-system and reach the anxious hands of Superintendent Gazin and his HO cohorts.

Havot had one worry: delay. He doubted very much that the gourmandizing commodore was going to break his neck hurrying after the fleeing berserker fleet. With fine wines and exotic foods to be enjoyed, why risk bringing about a real confrontation with that murderous collection of machines?

Now, having got through what he could hope would be his last unpleasant confrontation with the superintendent, Havot spent most of his time inspecting one shipboard display or another, or chatting with any crew members who happened to be free. He also took note of the fact that additional Solarian fighting ships kept appearing in-system at irregular intervals of hours or minutes, and attaching themselves to the fleet.

The continuing buildup of force was impressive. Arguably ominous. But Havot was not personally very much afraid of combat; and he still doubted seriously that Prinsep was the type of leader to make serious use of the strength he was being given.

He enjoyed arguing this, and other matters, with Becky Thanarat. And of course he took it for granted that she was recording him, even, or especially, when she assured him she was not.

As for Commodore Prinsep: all right, the man was

jealous of his own prerogatives, and able to stand up for his own authority; but to go out and fight berserkers was a different matter. He'd go out and look for them, all right, but doubtless be careful not to come too close.

So much the better for Havot, who wasn't particularly anxious to ride into battle against berserkers. Not after his experience with one on the Imatran surface.

And yet, in the background, the ominous drum roll of preparation continued, hour after hour. Havot could not avoid being interested, drawn to the swift lethal combat scouts, some near spheres, some jagged silhouettes like frozen lightning, which darted past the *Symmetry* to descend to the Imatran surface, or nuzzled at their mother ships in low orbit.

A member of the flagship's crew informed Havot that some of these scouts, having just survived the perils of in-system jumping to intercept the relevant light, were bringing back the eagerly anticipated recordings of the berserker attack he alone had been lucky enough to survive.

Word drifted out of the fleet commander's quarters that Prinsep was now inspecting these video records of the recent raid. The OH people had also been given access to them, but evidently had been able to learn nothing offering new fuel for their suspicions.

To the suspect's vast relief, he soon learned—from Agent Thanarat, who was showing signs of becoming rather more than sympathetic—that the superintendent had been given permission to search the archives of the fleet, but had found there no evidence connecting Havot with crimes of any kind.

But Becky also confirmed, matter-of-factly, something Havot had already assumed: more than a day ago the superintendent had dispatched Havot's fingerprints and other identifying characteristics to one of the sunward planets. Communications were still upset because of the recent attack, but a response might be forthcoming at any time.

"Why in all the hells has he decided to pick on me?" Havot flared for just a moment—then he worried that the woman might have seen the predator's claws come out.

But it seemed that Becky hadn't noticed anything special

in his reaction. She said: "I don't know. It might be just political; he's trying to boost the power of the Office any way he can." They walked on a little farther. "I don't know," she repeated. "When I signed up with them, I didn't think it would be like this."

"No?"

"No. I thought—I believed in what they always claim their objectives are, promoting the values of humanity, and . . ."

She fell abruptly silent, and her feet slowed to a stop. Havot was stopping, frozen too.

Emerging from around the next bend of corridor into their field of view, there walked upon a dozen stubby legs a barrel-shaped non-Solarian creature like nothing either of them had ever seen before. No more than a meter tall, but massive as a large man, dressed in something green and flowing . . .

"A Carmpan," Havot breathed. Then in the next moment he had rallied somewhat. Neither Havot nor Becky, like the vast majority of their fellow Solarians, had ever seen such a creature before except on holostages, where they, or rather skillfully imaged imitations, tended to show up frequently in fantastic space-adventure stories.

The creature—the Carmpan human—had evidently heard him. He—or she—paused and turned to the two young Solarians.

"I am called Fourth Adventurer." The words came tumbling, chopped but quite distinct, from a definitely non-Solarian mouth. "I am male, if this is of concern in how you think of me."

The Solarians in turn introduced themselves. Talking freely to both of them, but seeming especially interested in Havot, Fourth Adventurer explained that he had been for some years an accredited diplomat to several high Solarian powers, and for some months now a usually reclusive passenger on the *Symmetry*.

Fourth Adventurer soon invited both Havot and Thanarat to attend, as his guests, the commodore's next planning session.

Havot, at least, was intrigued. "I'd love to. If the commodore doesn't mind." And indeed it soon appeared that Prinsep had no objection to the young people's attendance, if the Carmpan diplomat wanted them there.

Once in the meeting, the Carmpan settled into his specially shaped chair, saying very little but seeming to listen attentively to everything.

There was only one rational reason, some Solarian proclaimed in a kind of opening statement, for berserkers to withdraw as precipitately as this particular set had done, from a target where their attack had been successful but had not yet been pushed to its deadly conclusion.

Someone else interrupted: "I don't see how they could even be sure they'd done as thorough a job as they really had. If they were playing by their own usual rules, they'd have stayed around at least a little longer to make sure that everything was dead."

"The only possible explanation is that their early withdrawal somehow gave them the opportunity of eventually being able to harvest still more lives—preferably human lives—here or somewhere else. Or they were convinced it would have that effect.

"And as we all know, their preferred target of all targets is human life—Solarian human in particular."

No one, least of all the listening Carmpan, disputed that point. Berserkers understood very well that only one species of life in the Galaxy—or at least in this part of it—seriously contested the dominance of the killing machines, really gave them a hard time in carrying out their mission. Therefore, in the berserkers' reversed scale of values, the elimination of one Earth-descended human life was worth the destruction of a vast number of animals or plants.

But then some other person in the discussion put forward a second possible reason for the enemy's withdrawal—though this possibility was really a variation of the first. Suppose the berserkers had captured some person or thing on the Imatran surface or had gained some information there—had somehow attained a prize that was to them of overwhelming value. So overwhelming, indeed, that their own advantage demanded that they carry this prize away with them at all costs, and without a moment's delay.

"Even if doing so meant leaving behind some human life unharvested."

"Even so."

Everyone turned involuntarily to look. It must, Havot realized, have been the first time the Carmpan had spoken in council.

SIXTEEN

This was the first time Havot had ever been aboard a warship, and he was somewhat surprised at how few people made up the crew of even a ship of the line, as leviathans like *Symmetry* were called. Onboard society was rather restricted, but it was interesting.

Havot's amusement grew from hour to hour, though he kept it well concealed. He was enjoying the situation. He liked to watch Commodore Prinsep, plump fingers fluttering, agonizing, in consultation with his robot chef, over his choices for tonight's dinner and tomorrow's lunch. He sat or stood about his office looking timid and seeming to waver, his mind on other things—and actually he did not yield a centimeter on anything of substance.

So Havot, confident that he still enjoyed the commodore's protection, was privately more amused than worried by the various maneuvers on the part of his potential persecutors. It appeared to him that he had little to worry about as long as he remained under the protective custody of the fleet commander. His current situation allowed him to lounge about in comfort in the wardroom, the library, or the gymnasium of the warship, or in the small private cabin he had been assigned. This cabin was fairly large, he gathered, by military standards, being about three paces square, big enough for bunk and table, chair and plumbing and holostage. It had probably been intended to house midlevel dignitaries who were visiting aboard or being transported.

The Carmpan, Fourth Adventurer, was housed in a similar room just down the corridor. And Havot, rather enjoying his constrained but comfortable stay aboard the flagship, and accustomed to feeling like an alien himself, felt some kinship with this other alien, who appeared to be doing very much the same thing.

Havot soon discovered that none of the Solarians aboard seemed to know the Carmpan's reason for having joined this expedition, though of course there was a lot of speculation. Fourth Adventurer was evidently too eminent a diplomat for anyone to risk offending, too important to be prevented from doing anything that he was seriously determined to accomplish. A great rarity indeed, a Carmpan traveling on a Solarian vessel far from any of the homeworlds of that race so everlastingly enigmatic to Earth folk.

Rumors of long standing had it that this race could do strange things with mental contact, telepathic achievement all but completely beyond Solarian capability. In Havot's mind that added a risk of discovery, a touch of danger. Fascinated, he found himself staring at the non-Solarian whenever the opportunity arose. If the Carmpan had any objection to this intense inspection, he said nothing.

Fourth Adventurer looked, to Solarian eyes, pretty much indistinguishable from the other Carmpan, real or image-faked, who appeared from time to time on holostage. Some Solarians described their race's slow and squarish bodies as machine-like, in contrast with their visionary minds.

A small handful of Carmpan individuals were famous in Solarian annals as Prophets of Probability, and Havot took the next good opportunity to ask Fourth Adventurer the truth about that title—or office, or activity. The young man admitted he did not know how it should be described.

"I prefer to speak on other topics," said Fourth Adventurer; and that was that.

Becky too was curious about their exotic fellow passenger. She reminded Havot of the famous historical scene shortly preceding the legendary battle of the Stone Place, where in all the dramatic re-creations a Prophet appeared, festooned with ganglions of wire and fiber stretching to make a hundred connections with Carmpan animals and equipment around him . . .

"Show business," Havot commented scornfully. But he didn't know if he was right.

. . . and then Fourth Adventurer, at a moment when Becky happened to be absent, looked Havot over even as the Solarian impassively studied the blocky, slablike Carmpan body. At length the non-Solarian diplomat assured Havot that he, the young Solarian, must have been spared death at the hands of the berserkers for some good if still mysterious reason. It sounded to Havot as if the non-Solarian were talking about something like God's plan, even if the Carmpan did not use those exact words.

Havot was somewhat disappointed; he wasn't sure what he had expected from this exotic being, but something more. In his experience, anyone who professed a belief in a God was very likely to be cracked or, more likely, actively out to defraud his listeners.

But Havot did draw a pleasant, unexpected comfort from the fact that at least one influential person seemed to believe strongly in his, Havot's, fundamental innocence. One had to keep on meeting new people if one expected to enjoy that attitude; as soon as people got to know one, they tended to lose faith.

The HO Superintendent, still confidently on board, had demanded and received from Commodore Prinsep—who would not think of refusing any reasonable request by duly constituted authority—access to the recently obtained military recordings of the latest berserker attack. The same records, seized on eagerly by the intelligence analysts aboard, were broken into sections by computer, recombined, examined over and over again.

Certain facts could be solidly established by the recordings. Among these were the precise direction of the berserkers' hurried departure, and the strength of the force that had carried out the most recent attack. This fleet had included ten large spacegoing machines, each equipped with a small army of boarding devices, landers, and other infernal gadgets.

One or two of the berserker motherships and a large number of landers had been destroyed by the ground defenses, which had been greatly, if not sufficiently, improved since the last attack three centuries ago. No single berserker, not even one the size of Dirac's, which had dwarfed the more modern units, would have succeeded in this year's raid. But still this year's enemy fleet had been too strong.

The strategists and would-be strategists on board the *Symmetry* scratched their chins and rubbed their eyes and pondered: what was the significance of the direction of the enemy fleet's departure?

"There's just nothing out that way but the Mavronari . . . of course it's possible they deliberately headed outsystem in the wrong direction, trying to mislead us as to their ultimate destination."

"That's hardly consistent with their being in such a rush that they couldn't spare five seconds to clean up one more human life."

By means of diligent and clever computer enhancement, tricks performed by the warship's expert graphics systems, the video record from deep space could be made to show with surprising clarity certain details of the planetoid's surface during the attack. Details as fine as a rough image of the individual machine, only a little larger than a man, that had been chasing Havot.

Some of the enhancements of the action on the surface even displayed a barely discernible dot, which all analysts agreed was probably the armor-suited Havot himself.

Superintendent Gazin and Ariari, his senior agent, also spent some time watching this part of the show over and over, displaying keen interest and suspicion. But the OH representatives must have been disappointed; they saw nothing to suggest overt goodlife activity on Havot's part.

The only thing even ambiguously suspicious in the recorded images was the apparent hesitancy of the killing machine that had confronted Havot. And even that could be explained by the fact that it was crippled.

Havot, on expressing a modest curiosity, was invited by the commodore to take a look at the recording.

The young man managed to get the seat next to Agent Thanarat at the next showing, and made some further impression on her.

To the suspect's relief it proved impossible to derive from the little dancing images any evidence about most of the things he had actually been doing to get himself away from one of the enemy.

Of course to the senior Humanity agent, and to the superintendent of the Office, the enhanced pictures of Havot on the Imatran surface looked pretty damned suspicious. Or so they claimed.

"We're trying to get a line on this man, and eventually we will—but right now communications throughout the system are pretty much in turmoil, as you might expect."

Havot felt comfortably confident that no local record of his presence at the spaceport, as a convicted murderer undergoing transportation, had survived the raid. Of course sooner or later, if he stayed around, his fingerprints or other ID were going to doom him.

Meanwhile Commodore Prinsep and his staff were continuing their own study of the maddeningly enigmatic images of the attack, a study in which Havot's individual conduct or fate played only a small part.

During the last phase of the onslaught, a number of small berserker auxiliaries could be seen at various points on the Imatran surface. All the machines still fully functional were lashing about them with death rays and other weapons, laboring methodically at their endless task of sterilizing the universe.

Someone, muttering in surprise, stopped the show, freezing the recorded berserkers temporarily in their tracks.

"Back up, and let's take a look at that again."

The recording was run back a few seconds and then restarted. It was no mistake, no glitch in the recording. All the berserkers of the landing party simultaneously dropped what they were doing—the machine that had been menacing Havot turned away in step with all the rest. And all of them went darting for their respective landing craft, the vehicles that had brought them to the surface.

Plainly all the berserkers on the surface had begun to retreat at precisely the same time, within a fraction of a second.

"This could have been the miracle that saved our friend Havot—yes, I would say that's very likely. Just look at the timing here."

Prinsep, his attention called to the timing of the berserker retreat, was very much impressed.

"Their motherships must have transmitted a recall signal, virtually simultaneously, to all their machines on the ground."

"Obviously. But the speed of the response by the landing devices suggests something more than an ordinary recall signal. I mean, this was something with a real *priority.* It stopped them all in their tracks!"

"We haven't been able to catch up with any such transmission, but you're right. It must have been a command of the highest priority, overriding everything else, ordering all the landers in effect to drop whatever they were doing and come home to mother at once."

"As if their mothers were suddenly fearful of a trap?"

"No, I don't think so. Let's not get into using the word 'fear' when we assign motives to berserkers. Their own survival in itself means absolutely nothing to them. The only real value they esteem is death. And observe that for whatever reason their motherships did not abandon their landing machines. They waited for every last one of them before heading out of the system."

"Right. I was about to comment that the damned pigs got every one of their fighting machines back on board, even those which had been seriously damaged, before they left."

"And that tells us—?"

"It tells me that the berserkers expected to need all of their fighting strength whenever they got to wherever they were going next."

"Perhaps they pulled out because word had just reached them, of some new target—?"

There was a muttering around the table, and a shuffling of imaged documents. "What target could possibly rate such a high priority that it would cause them to abandon this attack?"

"Possibly it wasn't another target at all, in that sense. Possibly the enemy hurried away to defend one of their own bases, some real nerve center, against some kind of threat?"

"I don't get it. Here's a fleet fully engaged in an attack. How could they have suddenly discovered a new target while all their attention was focused on this one? Or how could they have learned that one of their own bases needed help? They didn't receive any incoming message couriers while the fight was going on."

"Are you sure?"

"None that we could detect."

"We've been looking pretty closely at these recordings, and they are pretty good; I think we're about ready to rule out any additional radio signals of key importance—where would one come from? And we have to assume that we'd be able to detect the arrival of even a small courier."

"All right; but if we grant that, we seem to be forced to the conclusion that something the berserkers learned *here,* on Imatra, while the fighting was still in progress, forced them into a very abrupt and drastic change of plans."

"It does look that way. Something . . . but where on the planetoid did they learn anything? And what was it they learned?"

No one could come up with an answer.

Meanwhile the methodical electronic sieving of in-system space for useful signals continued. Gradually it became possible to rule out any chance that the berserkers, while in the midst of their attack, had received a communication from others of their kind elsewhere. In theory, radio and laser signals could not be entirely eliminated, but such means of communication were hopelessly slow over interstellar distances, though eminently useful near at hand. In any case there did not seem to have been any particularly interesting signals creeping through nearby space while the attack was going on.

"Then what are we left with?"

"All we can find out just reinforces the conclusion that the enemy, in the course of their raiding and ravaging the surface, discovered something *on the planetoid.* Something or some piece of information that they considered overwhelmingly important. So vital to their cause that responding to it in an appropriate way took precedence over everything else. Everything!"

"A thing, or a piece of information. Such as what?"

"Possibly something this man Havot passed to one of them. We really don't know who he is."

"Bah. I can't credit that. Why should a man spend an hour or more running away from a berserker if he intended passing it information? But then if it wasn't something they somehow gained from Havot, what was it? I haven't the faintest idea. Let's run that last sequence again."

In the course of the next playback, one berserker lander in particular caught someone's attention. This device, several kilometers from Havot's position, appeared to have gone underground, the only instance of one of the marauders doing so.

"What's there? In that place where it went down?"

Someone pulled up a diagram on holostage. "This map just says 'archive.' "

"See if we can find out something to clarify that."

The common information utility on Imatra was readily available, but it had been left in strands and fragments by the attack. At the moment it was not much good for answering even the simplest questions.

"We'll keep trying. Meanwhile let's take another look at this recording."

Commodore Prinsep ordered an increased enhancement of the sequence of events from three minutes before to three minutes after the sudden berserker decision to withdraw. The job at this level of difficulty took several minutes for the computer to accomplish.

When the computer's organic masters looked at the latest, most intensely enhanced version, they saw the berserker landing device reemerge from underground to stand perfectly still for a moment facing its mothership at a distance of more than a kilometer—almost out of line-of-sight, around the sharp curvature of the small planetoid. The emergence of the unit from the archive came just a hair-trigger interval before the recall command was transmitted—time perhaps for a human being to shout a warning or draw a gun. Too swift a response to be accepted as purely coincidental, too slow to be merely routine. The berserker command computers had devoted a couple of seconds—for them a vast gulf of time—to calculation before making their decision to withdraw as rapidly as possible.

Still, the devastated Imatran information banks could not be induced to say anything more informative about the underground archive buried at that point on the planetoid's surface.

"Could just be a coincidence after all, this one unit coming up out of the ground just there, and then the recall being sent a few seconds later."

"I tend not to believe in coincidences." Prinsep's voice was for once not tentative. "I want to go down there as soon as possible, travel physically to the place where it says 'archive,' and take a first-hand look."

Within a couple of hours a group comprising most of the strategic planners, including key members of the commodore's staff, had shuttled down to the Imatran surface. There they were soon crowded into a single much smaller vehicle, and headed for the location of the mysterious underground facility.

The Carmpan had stayed aboard the flagship, but Havot had come down with the group—no one tried to stop him. And Becky Thanarat, of course, to keep an eye on him for the Humanity Office.

Not much of any construction on the surface of Imatra had been left standing. But neither had all of the housing, all the conference centers and other public buildings, been totally obliterated. Here and there a few units even appeared intact. The remnant still standing included some relatively old, quaint-looking structures. Havot had heard that these had been designed to imitate certain buildings back on Earth, though most people who saw this fairly common style had no idea where it had originated. The majority of those who lived on or visited Imatra, like most Solarians across the settled Galaxy, had never been to Earth—unless colonists had come here directly from the original homeworld.

Arriving at the spot in an antigrav flyer, the investigators, all wearing respirators, stood regarding the charred and shattered aperture, of a size to accommodate an ordinary stairway, which evidently led down to some kind of subterranean installation.

None of the people present had been familiar with Imatra in its normal configuration; several had never set foot on it before. Nothing they were looking at now gave them any clue as to why the small berserker might have come to this place, or what it might have unearthed.

"Just what was stored down there, anyway?"

"One way to find out."

Fortunately several people had had the forethought to bring flashlights. The stone stairs themselves, and what could be seen of a door standing partially open at their foot, appeared to be essentially undamaged.

"Let's go down."

But one of the investigators dallied, standing at the head of the stair. Said she, frowning: "Something doesn't feel right about this."

Whoever had started down the stairs now paused and turned. "What do you mean?"

"Look, I'm a killer machine, standing right here, as the recording shows. I've come from that way." A thumb over a shoulder indicated a direction. "Over there"—pointing in a different direction—"on ground level, readily accessible, I can see a house, looking undamaged. Over that way's another one. So, do I take a shot at either building? Or do I rush over and check 'em out, see if there's anyone hiding inside? No. Instead I choose to blast open the door to this underground vault."

"Maybe the machine saw someone in the act of taking shelter down here. Or it somehow detected signs of life from underground. Heard breathing, or . . ."

There seemed little point in continued speculation, when the truth might be readily available. In silence the little company started to file down the stairs. Then someone had a thought. "I'm not absolutely sure that our machines have checked this out yet, though they've covered most of the surface. Better watch out for booby traps."

On that suggestion the company retreated, promptly enough, back up the stairs, and a robot was summoned. None had been brought along, because all of the useful, versatile robots were extremely busy just now. But this group of investigators had high priority when they chose to assert it. Within a couple of minutes one of the busy machines now engaged in rehabilitating/decontaminating the nearby surface had been temporarily commandeered.

It was a man-sized crawler with many useful limbs, and like other advanced robots built by the children of Earth, it possessed intelligence of a sort. But it also resembled its fellows in being anything but anthropomorphic in physical or intellectual design.

Docilely the eight-limbed device received its orders, acknowledged them in its pleasing mechanical voice, and nimbly descended the stair.

The doors at the bottom no longer offered any obstacle to entry. They appeared to have been blasted or broken by the berserker.

The people waiting on the surface tuned in their wrist-video units and watched the pictures sent back by the investigating robot. Inside the first door below had been a stronger set, now also demolished.

Beyond the shattered doors the remote video showed extensive ruin occupying a space the size of a small house. At first glance there was nothing particularly interesting about more piles of rubble. The underground vault showed no immediate sign of human or even animal casualties.

Within a minute or two the robot, having stomped and vibrated its way backward and forward through the debris, pronounced the area free of booby traps.

"Can we believe that?"

"It would really be an oddity if the enemy had planted any such devices here. We haven't found any elsewhere on the planetoid's surface."

"Is that unusual?"

"I'd say so. If this had been an ordinary raid with landers, setting traps would have been their last step before withdrawing."

"Nothing ordinary about this operation. Everything seems to confirm the idea that once the damned machines decided to pull out, they were unwilling to delay their departure by a single second. Shall we go down?"

Moments later the humans were gathered at the foot of the stairs, inside the broken doors, gazing directly at devastation in the brightness of the robot's lights. From here it was easy to see that this was, or had been, an archive designed to hold physical samples—of something. It was a common way of insuring that electronic data would not be lost—keep copies disconnected, physically separated, from all electronic systems, preventing electronic accidents or vandalism.

People who had brought their own lights flashed them around. The room had been arranged in narrow aisles between rows of tall cabinets. Enough of some of the cabinets had survived to show that each had many drawers, many if not all of the drawers subdivided into small compartments. Gingerly at first, then more freely, people picked up samples.

"These are recordings. Mostly civic records of various kinds. Videos of meetings, celebrations . . . This was not meant to be a bombproof vault. There seems to have been no great effort made toward preserving these against accident or attack."

The drawers and cabinets held little boxes, for the most part made of ordinary plastic or metal or composite materials. At the request of one human investigator, the helpful robot plugged one of the records into its own thorax and played it. The robot's upper surface became a simple holostage. The video with sound displayed people sitting around a table, what had to be a local Imatran council meeting of some kind. They were discussing the esthetics of a new spaceport.

"Hardly news to shake the empire of death to its foundations. Can we be sure the berserker didn't just come down here chasing someone?" He scraped a booted foot across the singed and littered floor. "A human body might have been completely—destroyed."

The robot, given new and more precise instructions, began at once to take samples from the new air, and from several of the scorched surfaces within the vault. Even before gathering its last sample, it assured its masters that analysis was proceeding without delay.

While they were waiting for the results, someone said: "At least there doesn't seem to have been anything as big as a cat or dog in here when the berserker roasted the place."

Within a minute the robot interrupted the humans' conversation to assure them in its soft droning voice that it was highly unlikely any organic mass the size of a human body had recently been burned or fragmented in this room.

The commodore sniffed disdainfully. " 'Fragmented'—yes, an evocative suggestion."

"Well? I think, sir, we can eliminate simple killing as that berserker's purpose in coming down here.

"But the course it followed over the surface, from its mothership to the entrance to this archive, suggests that it was making a beeline for this place."

Somebody commented on the diversity of information storage systems represented in the surviving drawers and cabinets. "Not everything here is standardized, far from it, though one can observe a long-term tendency in that direction. Some of these, perhaps most of them, seem to go back centuries."

"Presumably berserkers conduct intelligence operations just as we do. Any organization would want to learn about the way its enemies, in this case Solarian humans, store data."

"About all the damned machines could have gleaned by rummaging around down here is a history of the ways their enemies saved information a few hundred years ago—sorry, I just can't see them being overwhelmingly interested. Not so fascinated that they'd break off a successful attack in progress, just to communicate the secret techniques of the Imatran archive a little more quickly to some hypothetical distant confederates of theirs."

"All right. Then if it wasn't Imatra's antique storage methods they found so fascinating, it must have been something else. How about the *information* in one or more of these old files? Is that what set them roaring off at top speed, squeaking 'Eureka!' in a berserker voice?"

"Is there any way we can find out just what, if anything, the machine actually removed from this room?"

The discussion went on. Havot found himself being ignored for the time being; he had been all the help that he was going to be. He might be able to walk away unnoticed, hide himself and disappear. But what would he do then?

Meanwhile, he was having no more luck than anyone else in figuring out why the berserkers should have been rooting around down in this cellar. He was trying to picture the machine that had almost killed him, reacting to something in its orders, in its programming, so that instead of seeking breathing victims it had come down here . . . but come down here to do what? Anyway, this machine had been a different one altogether.

The degree of destruction inside the vault augured serious difficulty in determining what materials might be missing.

Everyone in the group pondered this problem for a while. Havot, entering into the spirit of things—asked: "What chance is there that all the files here were kept in duplicate somewhere else?"

Someone responded: "The Imatran society enjoys a reputation as good record keepers. I'd say it's worth looking into."

Information from someone who had dealt with the late local authorities confirmed that the general policy was to create duplicates.

Prinsep nodded. "Good. Let's find them if they exist. Meanwhile I want some people and machines down here, working to restore this junk to its original condition, or at least identifying it as accurately as possible. Whatever items appear to be completely missing, we'll hypothesize that perhaps the berserker took them, and see where that gets us."

Within an hour it had been determined that a duplicate archive did exist on one of the Imatran system's sunward planets. It would be possible to get any record—or a VR simulation of it—beamed to the planetoid in a few hours by radio, which was still the fastest dependable communication this close to a sun.

* * *

The commodore and his people were soon back on the flagship, while a hastily assembled team in the devastated archive began the task of reconstruction.

Within a few hours the first stage of their job had been completed.

According to the reconstruction, there was at least an eighty percent probability that the records taken by the berserker lander were those dealing with the famous raid of nearly three hundred years before.

"That's the one where some oddball berserker, historians call it Dirac's berserker now, grabbed the bioresearch station right out of orbit and carried it off."

"I don't remember that story, I grew up a long way from here. It carried off a what? A bioresearch station, you say?"

"Yes, a sizable spacegoing lab—actually it seems to have been kind of a pilot plant for a huge colonization project that never really got going. And then, if I remember correctly, within a matter of days after the attack, Premier Dirac, whose bride happened to get carried away with the station, was here in-system, putting together a small squadron of ships, making brave speeches and rushing off to get her back."

"How romantic."

"I guess. His whole squadron disappeared with all hands—that was the expedition where Colonel Marcus was lost."

"Colonel who?"

"You're not up on the history of the Berserker Wars, are you? Never mind, I'll show you later."

Duplicate Imatran records of the old raid, urgently requested, would soon be on their way from one of the sunward worlds by tight-beam transmission and should be available on the flagship in a few hours. Meanwhile, now that the investigators had some idea of what they were looking for, they could call up routine news reports from the days immediately following that attack; some were available in the flagship's general information banks.

Easily discernible in these records was the course taken by Dirac's berserker in its flight. The cylindrical research station, being towed behind the enemy by forcefields, was briefly but clearly visible.

"Now here we are a few days later. And there go Dirac's three ships, following exactly the same course."

"Yep. So what good does this information do us?"

"I don't know. My first reaction is, that as berserker attacks go, that one seems to have been truly unique. A very different kind of oddity from ours. The raid three centuries ago inflicted very little surface damage on Imatra."

Prinsep, working and giving orders in his unhurried, dogged way, kept everyone moving productively. Several times he repeated: "I want to know more about that bioresearch station."

The official history was fairly easy to come by.

At dinner that evening in the *Symmetry*'s wardroom, the discussion turned briefly to the general subject of colonization, on which opinions had not changed all that enormously in three hundred years.

"How long have we—Solarian humans—been trying to colonize the Galaxy, anyway?"

"I don't know—a thousand years?"

Some problems had not changed that much, either. There still remained in Solarian societies the question of what to do with inconvenient zygotes and fetuses. It was true that Solarian planets now in general seemed to produce fewer of these problem items than in Premier Dirac's day.

Continued discussion of the subject elicited from someone a mention of von Neumann probes.

"What were they?"

"It's an ancient scheme, a theory, going way back, to when all the Earth-descended folk in the Galaxy were actually still on Earth.

"The theory outlines techniques by which a civilization of quite modest technology, starting on one planet, would supposedly be able to explore the entire Galaxy in a quite reasonable time—even without the benefit of superluminal drive. To make it work properly, though, you have to be able to design some very smart and capable machines. And to overcome some serious problems in the engineering and construction. But the real problem appears, of course, when you send out your unmanned probes. At that point you have to really turn them loose—say goodbye and let them go, to roam the Galaxy unsupervised. You must be willing to let them represent you, your whole species, in whatever encounters they may have. These devices have to be self-repairing and self-replicating, like berserkers; able to improve their own design, like berserkers again. And with industrial capabilities, for mining and smelting ore and so on, that can easily be employed as formidable weapons."

More than one among the listeners shuddered faintly.

"Just send them out unsupervised?"

"That was the idea."

"Have Solarians ever actually built anything like that?"

"I'd have to look it up."

"Try. It shouldn't take long."

And it did not. The ship's general archive soon provided answers: Few people in recent centuries had thought it a good idea to send out von Neumann probes, either in slowship or c-plus form. Not in a galaxy known to be infested by true berserkers. Not when such devices necessarily contained in some form the Galactic coordinates at which the people who sent them could be found.

The archive even obligingly produced an example or two of worlds, branches of Solarian civilization, which in the very early years of the berserker encounter had implemented such a plan and had lived just long enough to regret it.

SEVENTEEN

Havot got a kick out of waiting for the Humanity Office people to revise their initial opinion of the commodore. Havot was ready to admit that he himself had been fooled at first. Almost everyone, on first meeting Ivan Prinsep, must get the impression that he was a decadent creampuff, who had been given command of this expedition as an exercise in politics—that much at least, Havot had heard, was true—who intended to conduct it as an exercise in fancy dining and other indulgence, meanwhile looking for some way to abandon the pursuit well before it became really dangerous. It hadn't taken Havot himself long to become convinced that this first impression was mistaken; but he thought that Superintendent Gazin and his troops still had an awakening coming.

All components of the combat fleet that had descended to the planetoid's surface were now lifting off again under pressure of the commodore's relentless though unstressed orders. The desired information about the buried archive was on its way from one of the sunward worlds, and otherwise essential readiness had been achieved. The rising craft rendezvoused in low orbit with their fellows, and the entire fleet—eighteen ships, according to the last count Havot had heard—set out together.

Despite the efforts at rehabilitation Havot had witnessed on the planetoid's surface, the task force was leaving behind it a deserted, practically uninhabitable body. The planetoid's gravitational augmenters had been demolished. Its remaining atmosphere was once more racked by horrendous winds, so in a matter of days probably only a dead surface would remain. This time, in contrast with the situation of three hundred years ago, all of the local leadership, the people with the greatest interest in revitalizing and rebuilding, had been wiped out. This time the military left only robots behind on Imatra, certain machines of little value in combat, but capable of working industriously with a minimum of human supervision to restore that planetoid's hard-won habitability.

Officially, the restoration work had now been temporarily, perhaps indefinitely, postponed. In fact it might really have been completely abandoned. Two raids in three centuries, and we give up—in this case, anyway.

The duplicate archive material, transmitted in a tight beam from an inner planet in virtual reality format, arrived on the *Symmetry* before the task force had made much headway getting out of the system.

Other urgent information, this concerning Havot personally, came in at about the same time, specially coded for the Humanity Office. Agent Thanarat signed a receipt for the message and took it away for private decoding.

A few minutes later, she sought out Havot privately, and demanded: "I want you to explain something to me."

From the change in her look, her manner, he suspected what had happened.

But he was innocently cheerful. "Gladly, if I can."

"There's a—" Becky started, temporarily lost the power of speech, and had to start again. Her voice was taut, withholding judgment. "Read this. I'd like to hear what you have to say about it." And she thrust toward him a solid, secret, nonelectronic piece of paper, the kind of form often employed for very confidential messages and records.

* * *

Meanwhile, people who had been waiting for the data from the duplicate Imatran archive now hurried to the flagship's VR chamber. Others were already in that spacious room, doing some preliminary studies.

The two senior Humanity investigators were on hand, waiting for the information as anxiously as anyone. The OH Superintendent, in making his decision to accompany the expedition, remained smugly confident that Prinsep was going to turn back, or proceed to some other safe system, before he actually caught up with any berserkers.

Meanwhile, some of the people milling about on the lower level of the ten-cube were arguing ancient history.

The old suspicion, going back nearly as far as the event itself, would not die, however illogical it might be: that Premier Dirac, feeling his base of power slipping, had somehow arranged the whole disastrous attack and kidnapping himself. Proponents of this theory claimed that the Premier had lived in hiding for a long time afterward, even that he was still alive somewhere, on some remote world. The corollary, of course, was that the supposed berserker he had been chasing had really been nothing of the kind, but rather a ship under the control of Dirac's human allies. Or else, an even more sinister accusation, Dirac had made some kind of goodlife bargain with the real thing.

Those who gave credence to these theories were not swayed by the fact that no one had ever been able to generate a shred of evidence to support any of them. The most persistent suspicion, a common element in all the theories, was that in one way or another the berserker of three centuries ago had not been genuine. Some people, none of whom were considered tough-minded experts in the subject, still argued for that.

On the other hand, if Dirac's berserker was accepted as genuine, then anyone who had arranged a deal with that machine undoubtedly qualified as goodlife. Any evidence that Dirac had tried to arrange such a deal might cast doubt on the legitimacy of all claims made by his modern heirs.

Havot meanwhile was now alone with Becky Thanarat in

her small cabin—a mere cubicle, smaller than his own—and for the past few minutes he had been making an all-out effort to explain away the damning information which had just arrived.

"You do believe me, don't you? Becky? Love?" The young man had no difficulty in sounding genuinely stricken.

At the moment she was once more having trouble speaking.

"I *mean . . .*" Havot did the best he could to generate a tone of amused contempt. "Murder, rape, knifings and torture . . . how many victims am I supposed to have destroyed? What did they say, again?" He reached politely for the paper; she handed it over. He waved it in distress. "Some really improbable total. You see, they rather overplayed their hand. Much more convincing if they'd simply said I was wanted for accidental manslaughter somewhere."

"Explain it to me again." She was sitting on her bunk, her hands white-knuckled clutching at the mattress, while he stood in the middle of the little private space. He almost had her; she was wavering. No, he really did have her, she was wavering so hard. She was begging to be convinced. "How there could be a mistake like this. You say these enemies of yours are—"

"It's a local police department." He named a real planet, very distant naturally. "Very corrupt. How I became their enemy is a long story, and it shows just how rotten and ugly the world can be. I'm sure they'll be able to explain this message convincingly, when they're eventually called to account for it, by saying it's all some horrible computer error. That they innocently confused me with some real psychopath somewhere. Meanwhile they can hope I'll be shackled, mistreated, or even killed . . . are there any other copies of this aboard, love?"

Becky slowly shook her head. Hope, her lover's vindication, was winning the struggle in her mind. In another minute or two she might be able to start to smile.

"Think. Sure there aren't? This would cause me no end of trouble if your boss got hold of it."

"I'm sure." Already a very attenuated, virtual-reality smile was struggling to be born. "We don't want spare copies

of any of our confidential communications floating around."
"Good." And he crumpled the paper softly in his fist.

Meanwhile, at the flagship's ten-cube, a planning meeting was informally in session, being presided over by the commodore himself.

"I say we must concern ourselves with ancient history. What we must endeavor to determine now, my people, is just what today's berserkers find so compelling about this record." Prinsep tapped a pudgy finger on the case. "As we have seen, it delineates their own—or their predecessors'—attack upon the Imatran system three hundred years ago. Can we deduce why our current enemies should be so interested in history?"

"It may help, sir, if we take a closer look."

"By all means."

People who wanted to experience to the full the chamber's powers and effects were required on entering to put on helmets equipped with sensory and control feedbacks. Some were starting to do that now, getting ready to scrutinize the new information as intensely as possible when it came in. A thousand cubic meters of interior space made the flagship's VR chamber as large as a small house—few spaceships of only moderate size indulged in the luxury of having one. Such a generous volume allowed a party of a dozen or more to participate simultaneously in reasonable comfort—and this time there were almost that many.

Once inside, taking advantage of force supports and a few rubbery, polyphase matter projections from the walls—and of the partial nullification of artificial gravity inside the chamber's walls—those experienced in this game showed others how they could leap and climb and "swim" about in almost perfect freedom and safety.

A display on one wall listed the titles of some of the software available. Posted almost invisibly was even a game list, including items called JUNGLE VINES, MASTS AND RIGGING, and CITY GIRDERS.

No time for games today. Someone already had a model of the Milky Way Galaxy up and running.

The idea had been to avoid wasting time, to keep from looking as if one were wasting time—and also to take a look at the Mavronari, in hopes of coming up with some clue as to why one berserker attack force after another had attacked the same planetoid and then fled into the same shelter, taking precisely the same direction.

The first scene evoked in GALACTIC MODEL showed an overview of the whole Galaxy. The central, lens-shaped disk was some thirty kiloparsecs, or about one hundred thousand light-years, in diameter. The component spiral arms of this great wheel were surrounded by a much vaguer and dimmer englobement of individual stars, star clusters, clouds of gas and dust, and an assortment of other objects considerably less routine.

The brightest region in the display represented what was generally known to the Solarian military as CORESEC. This was the Galactic core, a star-crowded, roughly spherical volume perhaps a thousand light-years in diameter, holding at its unattainable center some of the unfathomable mysteries of creation.

There at the Galaxy's very heart lay, among other things, that great enigma which for the last several centuries Solarian humanity had called the Taj, a name devised as a military code word but soon generally adopted as expressing the exotic and magnificent.

Only a few Earth-descended beings had ever reached even the outer strata of the Taj, and fewer still had ever managed to return. Notable among the very few had been the legendary Colonel Frank Marcus, missing for the last three hundred years upon another quest. Nor had any of that harrowed and honored handful been able to bring much information away with them from the Galactic heart—and what little news they had gathered there did not encourage further attempts at exploration.

In fact only about five percent of the Galaxy's volume had ever been explored by Solarian ships, and much of that exploration had been nominal, a mere cataloguing of stars of beacon brightness, a mapping of the more substantial and readily visible nebulae and of the flow of subspace currents in the quasi-mathematical understrata of reality, that still-almost-unknown realm where c-plus travel could be brought within the range of possibility.

The approximate center of Solarian territory lay at Sol System, three-quarters of the way out from CORESEC to the Rim, along the great spiral curve of what was still called the Orion-Cygnus arm (after a pair of constellations in old Earth's night sky). From one point on the roughly outlined sphere of ED dominion, a narrow tendril of exploration went snaking in, a symbol of Earth-descended boldness, to touch and barely penetrate the Core. The snaking indirectness was due to the unusually difficult physics of travel in that part of the Galaxy.

Within the small part of the Milky Way's volume through which the ships of Earth had traveled, intelligent life forms were breathtakingly rare. Certainly many more sterile planets had been discovered than those bearing even elementary forms of life. And there were far more of the latter than there were of those on which organic intelligence had actually bloomed. Among contemporary intelligent races, the Solarians were almost uniquely aggressive; not until berserkers entered Earth-descended territory had the killing machines ceased to enjoy their hunting almost unopposed.

The Carmpan were the unearthly, extraterrestrial, variant of humanity with whom the expanding Solarians had had most contact—and there had been precious little of that. Against berserkers the Carmpan Prophets of Probability had on occasion given great though indirect assistance.

The other organic thinkers known currently to inhabit the Galaxy were even less well known and understood among Solarians than were the Carmpan. Even more retiring and shadowy than the Carmpan, they appeared utterly repelled by the idea of face-to-face confrontation with their violent Solarian cousins on neutral ground, let alone by the possibility of opening their homeworlds to such visitors.

Not that these others were really hostile to the strange folk from Sol, under whose shield of protective violence their several races still survived. Nor were they unwilling to express their gratitude.

Only the distant Builders and their ancient opponents, both their races all but completely invisible behind the barricades of time, seemed to have been similar in mind and behavior to the offspring of Earth. Of the Builders' organic foes, not even a name now survived—but evidently they too had been combative. There was one word of their language left, a name, *qwib-qwib,* denoting a kind of machine they had evidently built to hunt out and destroy berserkers. That had proved dangerous hunting—it was uncertain whether in all the Galaxy a single *qwib-qwib* yet survived. And of the Builders themselves, their own all-too-effective weapons, the berserkers, had left nothing but a few obscure records—video and voice recordings. Those videos had recorded slender, fine-boned beings, topologically like Solarian humans with the sole visible exception of the eye, which in the Builder species was a single organ, stretching clear across the upper face, with a bright bulging pupil that slid rapidly back and forth.

One statement about the Galaxy was certainly possible to make with confidence—that among its hundred billion stars and planetary systems, a vast number of surprises, happy and otherwise, still awaited the determined explorer.

Everyone gathered in the ten-cube room today had used similar devices before, though the design was not completely standardized, and some initial confusion arose. Each VR helmet presented its wearer with a visual keyboard, floating in apparent space at the lower left or lower right—the wearer's choice—of the visual field. The controls were accessible through directed vision and practiced will—no hands necessary. Some users found it easier to manage by means of eyeblinks.

One of the basic controls managed the scale of the display; the effect produced was as if the wearer's body were shrinking or swelling to accommodate the wish to explore or observe, at one level or another of physical size.

The vast majority of the stars appearing in the display were only statistical approximations, artifacts of the VR computer. But information on several million real stars and systems had also been fed in from the standard astrogation models.

The computer at the moment was using no color or other

distinguishing shading to represent berserker territory. In fact, as the slow tide of the long conflict ebbed and flowed, it would have been impossible to delimit that wasteland with anything like up-to-date accuracy. Nor could anyone say with any substantial probability where the damned machines had originated, though the captured records, sketchy as they were, offered a tersely convincing explanation of how they had come into being.

In this particular display, a somewhat outdated version of their domain of devastation could be marked out, demarcated by tagging the suns of all the worlds known to have been attacked in the era of Solarian civilization. A smaller domain, largely enclosed within the first, represented that of the planets known to have been sterilized of life.

One of the investigators had now keyed in these presentations, evoking a strategic situation inevitably some years out of date. No one in the group now gathered expected to find in this database much in the way of berserker bases, factories, or strongholds.

If some person of ordinary height, employing the witchcraft of virtual reality within this chamber, swelled in a moment by a factor of a billion in physical height and width, he or she was still somewhat less than two billion meters (two million kilometers) tall. The observer was now in effect much bigger than the biggest planet, yet in his eyes the scale of the surrounding display, as far as its more distant reaches were concerned, seemed hardly to have changed.

His body length had now become comparable to the diameter of Sol, a roughly average star. But if the explorer's objective in using the chamber had been to bring the Galaxy down to a size through which he might hope to climb or swim in a few minutes' effort, he had really made little headway. The division (in effect) of all the distances involved by a factor of a thousand million still left the expanded human facing mind-cracking immensity.

"Unless you want to swim in one place all day, you'll have to grow a lot more than that."

Math conquers all—if only numbers are to be evaluated. Eventually, having evoked more multiples, the hopeful swimmer attained a scale on which the Galaxy looked no bigger than a tall building. This did not occur until the would-be observer had magnified his own height to something like a thousand light-years. On this scale any solar system had long since disappeared into the microscopic—or would have done so had the computer not been careful to create beacons.

Now, moving about within the VR chamber, temporarily free of the restraints of gravity, one got the impression that the whole Galaxy had indeed been made to fit inside. On this scale the three main spiral arms were readily distinguishable, with Sol—thanks to the computer—findable as a tiny blinking beacon well out in the Orion-Cygnus curve.

Someone made the necessary adjustments to bring the display's version of the Mavronari Nebula into focus at a handy size. The investigators looked and felt their way around and through the image without coming to any helpful insights.

Someone remarked that most astronomers and astrogators would ordinarily regard the Mavronari as tremendously dull. There were a hundred other nebulas much like it in known space, and they were of interest only as obstacles to astrogation, save to a few cosmologists. Anyway, whoever had created and updated the display had evidently possessed few details on the subject.

The small black box that one of the fleet commander's staff was now loading into the VR mechanism contained information exactly duplicating that in the box which the berserkers had recently stolen from the Imatran archive, or which—in a scenario considered less likely—that machine had quickly read in the archive and then utterly destroyed.

The computers controlling the display inside the ten-meter cube granted each observer a central viewpoint this time, choosing as a first scene a defense controller's bunker slightly below the Imatran surface. Then the scenario was run in other modes—at first look none of them very helpful.

Realtime rolled by as the study continued. Disappointment soon set in once more.

"Run it again?" asked a software specialist.

"Yes. No. Yes, in a minute. But first—" Commodore Prinsep rubbed tired eyes. "Well, people, all I can actually see when I look at this record is what appears to be a very peculiar berserker attack. Unique in its own way. The most recent onslaught upon Imatra was also thoroughly untypical, but the two were unlike in at least one intriguing characteristic—I mean that the attacker of three centuries ago retreated after having shed relatively little blood."

There was a murmur of agreement.

The speaker went on: "Have any of the rest of you yet discerned any additional nontrivial contrasts, or similarities, between the two engagements?"

"Not I."

"Nor I. Not yet." There was a chorus of similar answers around the circle.

The commodore pushed at the point relentlessly. "So no one yet has any idea what our contemporary berserkers might have found in this record to cause them to break off their own attack so abruptly?"

No one did. But one adviser offered: "Viewing the recording certainly brings home the essential strangeness of that raid of three hundred years ago. One sees excerpts, and reads the accounts, of course, but somehow one doesn't grasp the full peculiarity of the event that way. As you say, sir, it was a mugging, a mass kidnapping, rather than a wholesale murder."

"Yes. While, as we all know, wholesale murder is a berserker's sole aim in life."

No one smiled.

"In a way, such a great peculiarity worries me more than simple slaughter. Because it indicates that there's something very important that we don't understand.

"Dirac's contemporaries were worried by it too, and so were a number of people in the years immediately following that raid. They were bothered by the oddity, even those who didn't believe it was all a great plot by the Premier. People theorized that the berserker had taken a whole planetary population of protocolonist tiles in order to raise a vast colony of goodlife humans somewhere, goodlife to be its servants, its fanatical warriors.

"A lot of people in the years immediately following Dirac's disappearance spent a lot of time looking at copies of this very record. Gradually, of course, interest declined. If I'd wanted a copy recently I don't suppose I'd have known where to look for it, except on Imatra."

"Speaking of looking for things—" This was Ensign Dinant, an astrogator.

Prinsep blinked at him. "Yes?"

"I was wondering: Just where is it now after three hundred standard years? Where is Dirac's berserker? The machine that wanted to steal a billion protopeople—or whatever the exact number really was—and for all we know, succeeded. It shows up fairly clearly in this display. But I wonder where it's got to?

"It's easy to see, on this record, which way that berserker went, and easy to see that Dirac and his people took the same course, going directly after it. But whatever trail that machine or those ships might have left has faded long ago. After three centuries, Dirac's berserker could be in a lot of different places. It could be well along in the task of nurturing that goodlife colony—if you subscribe to that theory."

The commodore nodded. "After three hundred years I should think it could. I also think that we should be seeing some results. And it needs no profound insight to observe that Dirac himself could be in a lot of places—if he's still alive."

The pudgy Prinsep rapped sharply on his table. "Let me remind you, my friends, my dear counselors: the primary question that we face is still: 'Why should today's berserkers be so interested in what happened to either the machines or the badlife Solarians of yesteryear?' "

"I say they can't," Dinant argued stubbornly. "Therefore it's got to be something else on this recording, something we haven't noticed so far, that hit them so hard, struck an electronic nerve."

Perhaps, another adviser suggested tentatively, the vital clue had something to do with the glimpses the recording afforded of Premier Dirac's yacht.

But why should anything at all about that vessel be of any importance now?

No one could guess. But Commodore Prinsep remained determined to find out. Speaking softly, but making the orders unequivocal, he ordered a team comprising both humans and robots to begin at once a grimly thorough, minutely detailed, expert analysis of the recording.

Meanwhile his task force went plowing steadily ahead.

EIGHTEEN

Havot overheard Superintendent Gazin commenting that the majority of Prinsep's personal staff were expert computer systems—and sneering that a majority of *them* seemed to be devoted exclusively to food preparation. Havot was developing a somewhat different idea; he could observe for himself that the organic component of the commodore's staff, a handful of people who had known the commodore and worked with him for some time, was fiercely loyal. At first Havot had taken this attitude for mere politics on their part. Now he was not so sure.

And Havot wondered if perhaps the Humanity Office superintendent and his senior agent, were beginning to worry about the fleet's catching up with some active berserkers after all.

Talking to Fourth Adventurer, Havot learned something more surprising: the Carmpan professed to see in Commodore Prinsep a tendency to mysticism.

"Mysticism, Fourth Adventurer?"

"Indeed, Christopher Havot." The Carmpan stood

looking up at him from its one-meter height, out of a face that by Solarian standards was scarcely a face at all. The non-Solarian gestured with several limbs. "And I make the same statement with reference to you yourself."

"Me?" Havot stood there, for once astonished, feeling the foolish grin hanging on his face like a mask. "A mystic? No." At the same time he felt a surprisingly powerful urge to tell Fourth Adventurer of his experience with the berserker on the Imatran surface. But he held back from making any revelations.

Actually the commodore was very far from Havot's idea of what a mystic ought to be—almost as far as he was himself. Prinsep, between his businesslike planning sessions, spent most of his time dealing with nothing more abstract than nibbling grapes, or making out his menu for dinner.

Perhaps Fourth Adventurer had only been trying to be complimentary. Or he simply had the wrong word, the wrong Solarian concept. The difficulty in matching mental constructs must work both ways.

The commodore, Havot discovered, did spend a fair amount of time with the only non-Solarian human on his ship. It seemed unlikely that they were fellow gourmets—the Carmpan could be seen consuming Solarian food from time to time, but only after running it through his personal processing device, from which everything emerged as a kind of neutral-looking paste.

By this time the fleet was well launched on its pursuit of the berserker enemies, whose formation was intermittently in sight ahead. Astern, Imatra's sun dimmed fast with increasing distance. No more messages from Imatra were likely to catch up—Havot could relax a little.

At the moment, of course, the key to his fate was Becky. Let her let slip a word to Prinsep, or worse, her own boss, about the information that had come in, and her new lover was certain to see one of the brig's isolation cells or perhaps deep freeze in an SA chamber until someone decided to let him out.

And he was well aware that the senior representatives of the Humanitarian Office were still watching him, biding their time, looking for a chance to place him under arrest. They didn't bother trying to keep him under continuous surveillance; he wasn't going to run away.

Concerning Agent Rebecca Thanarat, Havot was considering several courses of action, all of which had certain drawbacks. For the moment he had to be sure, at all costs, that she was in love with him, content with their relationship. Havot smoothly stepped up the pace of his campaign of seduction, keeping in mind that getting her into bed was infinitely less important than winning her total devotion. Frequently, he had observed, the two did not go very closely together.

Havot tended to believe Rebecca's assurance that no other copy existed of the incriminating message. But naturally he could not be absolutely sure. He had disposed of the first paper copy very carefully.

Like many of the other women who had fallen in love with Havot at one point or another, Becky wanted to know all about his background. He repeated to her with some elaboration his earlier lie that he had worked as a dealer in educational materials. The story had now expanded to make him a former teacher.

She wasn't that interested in pursuing details of Havot's fictitious teaching career. "You were going to tell me how you got into trouble with that awful police department."

"Well . . . it had to do with an abused child." By now Havot had had the time necessary to prepare a prizewinning narrative. He knew Becky well enough to know how her sympathies could be most easily aroused and enlisted.

Aboard the several ships of the pursuing task force—now preparing for the first c-plus jump out of the system—the commodore and his chief advisers, including the subordinate ship captains, were gathered in electronic conference, the optelectronic brains of the ships themselves exchanging speech in the form of scrambled signals.

The leaders summoned into conference by the commodore were military people, except for the Carmpan—who this time courteously declined the honor—and the Humanity Superintendent.

The planners continued to struggle with the problem of the enemy's motivation in their sudden withdrawal and flight.

The electronic spoor of the mysterious lone raider of three centuries ago had long since dissipated. But on the old records the course of Dirac's berserker was easily discernible, and telescopic observations confirmed the fact that today's powerful but swiftly fleeing force of death machines were indeed staying very close to their predecessor's vanished track.

Havot was not usually invited to sit in on Prinsep's strategic planning sessions. But much of what was said in these discussions soon became common knowledge aboard ship, as did the observed behavior of the contemporary enemy.

To anyone who studied the problem, it began to seem that the modern berserkers' discovery of their predecessor's escape route must indeed have been the event that triggered their own abrupt flight from the Imatran surface, virtually in midraid.

One of Prinsep's advisers was thinking aloud. "The conclusion seems irresistible that the enemy just pulled out the instant they identified the path taken by their predecessor, Dirac's berserker, on its way out of the system—in fact the evidence strongly suggests that this year's berserkers *came to Imatra primarily to gain that information.* The record they took from the underground archive contains nothing else that could conceivably be of interest to them."

"No! No no no!" The commodore was shaking his head emphatically. "Quite unacceptable! We can't be satisfied with the conclusion that they must be pursuing one of their own machines."

"And who can say dogmatically what our enemies will find interesting and what they will not? The record they went to such pains to steal contains an astronomical number of bits of information."

Prinsep made a dismissive gesture. "So does a picture of a blank wall. A great deal of what technically must be called information is really meaningless. What else in that recording, besides their colleague's route, could have any importance for berserkers?"

Prinsep paused for emphasis: "When a berserker computes that saving a few seconds is more important than terminating one more Solarian human life—you may take it that from that berserker's point of view, something very unusual, very important, is going on."

Meanwhile, the OH superintendent who had privately doubted Prinsep's determination sat silent and thoughtful, looking less knowing and more grave. The retreating berserkers continued to follow very closely the route followed by the chase of three hundred years ago. Therefore, so did the hunting pack of Solarian humans and machines.

The contemporary chase wore on, hour after hour, day after day, with the Solarian fleet now seeming to gain a little ground and now again to lose a little. All of the human pilots were military people trained in formation flight, and worked smoothly with their associated computers. Commodore Prinsep was pushing the chase hard, but not hard enough to have cost him any ships.

The first c-plus jump essayed by the fleet's astrogators was far from a new experience for Havot, who in his comparatively short lifetime had seen a great many of the Galaxy's thousands of Solarian-settled worlds. Many more than most people ever got to see.

But travel outside and beyond the limitations of normal space was a totally new experience for agent Thanarat.

The first jump lasted for a subjective ship's time of some ten seconds, long enough for Becky, with Havot romantically at her side, to be initiated into the sensation of looking out through a cleared port into the eye-watering, nerve-grating irrelevance of flightspace—a scene often described as dim lights behind a series of distorting lenses.

Their cabins were both too far inboard to boast an actual cleared port. And to call up such a port on holostage was not the way, Havot assured her, to experience the full effect. There was something in the quality of the light, the images brought inboard through clear statglass, that any ordinary holosystem struggled inadequately to reproduce.

At the conclusion of each collective jump, on the fleet's

reemergence into normal space, the people and computers on the flagship's bridge rapidly counted the ships composing the fleet, after which the human decision makers relaxed momentarily. But with the next breath drawn, people and machines began the calculations for the next jump, a process occupying a few seconds at the minimum.

In the short intervals between jumps, other crew members and their machines scanned space in every direction, testing the enemy's electronic spoor for freshness and exact position, and restored the desired tightness to their own ships' formation. Then a last round of intership communications, concluded in milliseconds. Then, at a signal, *jump* again in unison.

Each time one of the fleet's vessels reemerged in normal space, its sensors were already looking ahead, probing for signs of recent traffic, trying to catch some clue, some disturbance in the radiation patterns of normal space, indicating what general physical conditions would be encountered in that direction. So far they found no sign that the most recent band of marauders had deviated from the escape route used by their forerunner of three centuries ago.

Until now, the human hunters and their faithful slave machines had been able to see nothing directly of that antique chase. Nor had there seemed any point in wasting time and equipment trying to detect images of the fabled, vanished *Eidolon* or of the deadly object the old Premier had been hunting; the light that had once borne those images would be hundreds of light-years distant now, even if it had not long ago dispersed into a faintness far beyond the capability of any receiver to capture and restore to intelligibility.

No one in Prinsep's fleet was looking for the old trail now; the more recent attackers required the hunters' full attention. Today's berserkers were certainly leaving a fresh, distinct wake of their own. The suggestion was that to them, sheer speed had now become all-important. As if, against the blind urgency of their mysterious quest, the pursuing Solarian fleet hardly weighed in their calculations at all, any more than had the humans left alive back on Imatra. The killing machines would outrun their hunters if they could, but otherwise seemed determined to ignore them as long as possible.

Commodore Prinsep thought, and several times speculated in the presence of one or more of his subordinates, that these tactics were possibly meant to set his fleet up for an ambush. He tried to estimate the chances of this, looking much grimmer than was his wont. But he still refused to slow the pace of his pursuit.

The *Symmetry*'s battle computer, and the expert systems Prinsep had grafted to it, did their best to calculate the odds in favor of berserker trickery. Prinsep did not make the calculations public. After all, the decision was up to him.

And then the odds were altered slightly by sheer accident. Two large berserkers, several light-hours ahead of the pursuing fleet, could be observed jump-crashing in their terrible haste, tearing themselves apart on specks and spikes of gravity jutting into spacetime from bits of nearby matter; the remaining members of their pack were compelled to slow down, or face destruction by laws of physics as remorseless as themselves.

Everyone aboard the flagship except the fleet commander himself kept expecting Prinsep to order a slowdown, or some change of tactics. But he did not.

The fleet gained.

Becky Thanarat came back to the cabin she now shared with Havot, and reported (to the amusement and delight of her new lover) that the Humanity Office superintendent and his senior agent, neither of whom had ever seen a real berserker in their lives, were beginning to look a little pale.

Presently the pursuing fleet reduced its speed at the fleet commander's orders. But only minimally.

Pursued and pursuers went tearing on in the same direction, plunging boldly in among the ever-so-slowly thickening fringes of dark nebula.

Meanwhile Becky was suddenly called on the carpet by her superiors for her apparent failure to pass a decoded message along to them. Ship's communications had presented evidence, strong if not indisputable, that some radio communication coded for the HO, had been received aboard the *Symmetry* several days earlier, just as the fleet was reaching the limit of good reception from the Imatran system.

Word reached Havot indirectly that Becky was unable to come up with any acceptable explanation.

Gazin evidently suspected, but could not prove, the truth, and ordered Agent Thanarat thrown in the brig.

Commodore Prinsep, who had to give his approval before any such drastic action could be taken, called in Havot as part of his own effort to get to the bottom of the situation.

"What do you know about this, Havot? We are on the verge of entering combat, and I cannot tolerate these distractions."

The youth was properly, tremulously outraged. "Superintendent Gazin has declared himself my enemy—why, I don't know. I supposed he has finally discovered that Agent Thanarat and I are now lovers, and that this is some plot on his part to get at me through her—I know nothing about any supposedly missing message."

Prinsep sighed and studied the young man who stood before him. Ultimately all decisions here in space, in wartime conditions, were up to the fleet commander.

Then Prinsep said unexpectedly: "Our Carmpan passenger has advised me to rely upon you, Havot. Know any reason why Fourth Adventurer should have said that?"

"No sir, I don't." Havot for once could think of nothing clever to say.

"Well, then, I am going to allow the young woman her freedom. For the time being, at least. I suppose I shall have to answer to the Humanity people for it when we get home." It was obvious that the commodore detested the HO and all the thought-control business that it stood for.

Havot showed a relieved smile. "I don't think you'll regret it, Commodore."

"See to it that I don't, Mr. Havot. Please see to it that I don't."

NINETEEN

To the Solarians in the pursuing fleet, Dirac's berserker, along with the Premier and his people who had vanished in its pursuit, had never been more than dim historical shadows. But now, throughout the fleet, people were once again beginning to speculate on the possibility that Premier Dirac might turn out to be still alive, after all.

The discovery of a living Dirac would certainly have some contemporary political effect. But just what that effect might be was not so easy to say.

Havot mused: "If Dirac or any of his people were still breathing, they'd be old, old folks by this time."

But as Prinsep several times remarked to colleagues, not absolutely, impossibly too old. He had been studying the history. Many individuals did live longer than three hundred years; and Dirac had been fairly young, his bride even younger, hardly more than a girl, at the time of their disappearance. Also it seemed only natural that people trapped in a bioresearch station where SA chambers were readily available might very well make use of them.

Provided, of course, that berserkers' prisoners still had

any mastery over their own fate. There was really no reason to expect that any human being taken, anytime, anywhere, by the unliving enemy, would long survive.

Havot once overheard the senior Humanity Office agent, who tended to lean politically to the side of the Premier's old enemies, envisioning a scenario in which Dirac had become goodlife, or had been goodlife all along, and was now, or had been, helping the berserker raise a goodlife force of millions of Solarians, all slaves and servants of the death machines.

Still, leaving aside political suspicions and accusations, the questions would not go away: Why should the modern berserkers set such overwhelming importance upon their discovery of the route by which their predecessor had withdrawn? And why should they, ever since making that discovery, have been slavishly following that same route at a near-suicidal speed?

And still, no one had answers.

Were the modern machines consumed with an urge to overtake their own mysterious forerunner? Or did they crave, for some unimaginable reason, to catch up with Dirac's yacht, which had preceded them on the same trail? Surprisingly, the best and latest computer calculations carried out aboard the flagship showed that such a feat of astrogation lay well within the bounds of possibility—assuming either Dirac's ship or the berserker he was chasing had gone plowing along on the same course, more or less straight ahead, ever deeper into the Mavronari's fringes. But why should either human or berserker have done that?

Three centuries of incremental improvements in interstellar drives and control systems, as well as in the techniques of getting through difficult nebulae, assured the modern pursuers that at least they ought to be able to make better time than had their enigmatic predecessor, Premier Dirac.

Some recently constructed berserkers were also known to have incorporated certain improvements over those of Dirac's time. And the machines which had carried out the latest attack on Imatra, or some of them at least, had given evidence of belonging to the improved class. So neither pursuit nor combat was likely to be any easier for the modern fleet than it had been for Dirac's people.

No member of the modern human task force was willing to express a belief that any of the participants in that earlier chase were still out there ahead of this one, gamely plowing on into the dark nebula. The odds were just overwhelmingly against it.

No, when you looked at the situation realistically, that contest must have been settled, long ago, one way or another. It was almost certain that the Premier together with his fleshly friends and enemies were centuries dead, their ships and the missing bioresearch station destroyed in combat or in desperate flight. And as for the giant berserker that had come to bear his name, if it had not sustained terminal injuries in one firefight or another, it might have changed course and broken free somehow of the Mavronari. Or else it had somehow stalled itself, and perhaps its captured prey, inside that endless blackness.

But in any case the modern fleet, under a commander showing an unexpected but seemingly natural combination of boldness and tenacity, appeared to have a good chance of overtaking the contemporary berserker force.

Despite the predicted imminence of battle, morale in all the ships seemed high—or would have, had it not been for the situation involving Havot and the Humanity Office representatives.

The fleet's captains and the other officers who were taking part in the ongoing planning sessions, kept coming back to the same point: to determine why the modern berserkers were following the cold trail of the old chase, it might be very helpful to learn what that ancient enemy's goal had been.

Ensign Dinant mused: "I suppose today's bandits, independently of any discovery they've turned up on Imatra, *might* retain some history of which target one of their number went after three hundred years ago, and even what tactics it employed then. On the other hand, I can easily believe that our modern death cultivators preserve no record of anything like that, because I *don't* see any reason why they should give a damn."

After a moody silence, Lieutenant Tongres, a pilot, cleared her throat. "Look at it this way. As far as we can tell, the only important thing these old Imatran records reveal is the exact line of retreat taken by Dirac's berserker. As far as we know that machine did succeed in getting away, and maybe it even worked a successful ambush on the Premier when he came after it. And if a tactic succeeds once, you use it again."

"Bah! There appears to be no astrogational advantage to this particular pathway—nothing that would make an ambush easier or more effective than if the flight had followed a route a million kilometers to one side or another. For our modern berserkers to head for cover again in the nearest dark nebula would be repeating a tactic. But for them to follow the *exact same trail* as their predecessor is . . . something else. Something more than tactics. I don't know what. A reenactment. But why? why? why?" The Ensign beat a fist upon a table.

Tongres shook her head. "As I see it, it's not really that our modern enemies want to follow the exact same trail. The point is, they want to arrive at the exact same place."

"Oh? And what place might that be?"

"How about a hidden entrance to a clear pathway inside the Mavronari, a quick passage to its interior? A direct route all the way through it and out the other side?"

"The interior, so far as we know, is very little more than a bag of dust. All right, a direct route through would have some value. But not much."

"Maybe—maybe they're carrying important news to berserker headquarters. And the grand berserker headquarters is located on some world inside the Mavronari."

Dinant was unconvinced. "So now we have a whole fleet of berserkers devoting their time and energy to a mission that a single machine could readily accomplish. Bah. Anyway, aren't you arguing in a circle? I trust that the important news they're carrying to their own headquarters is something other than the coordinates of that headquarters' location."

The lieutenant bristled, but before she could retort another crew member interrupted:

"How important to these bandits of ours could *any* news

be, extracted from a three-hundred-year-old recording they just happened to dig up on the surface of Imatra?"

"Ah, perhaps you weren't here for the early showing, the matinee. It doesn't appear that they 'just happened' to dig this information up. The landing machine that did the digging up headed straight for the archive as soon as it touched down, for all the world as if it had been dispatched upon that particular mission. As if they knew somehow that the record they wanted would be there."

"How would any berserker know that?" Dinant wanted to know.

"A very good question." Tongres looked thoughtful. "Someone would have to tell them, I suppose."

This real hint of goodlife activity was met by an interval of silence. Neither Havot nor either of the OH men was present at the moment.

The moment passed.

The third crewmember inquired, "And so the prize our enemies were hoping for, and gleaned from the buried record, was nothing more or less than the direction of the earlier berserker's flight?"

"What else?" Tongres shrugged. "We've all seen the show a hundred times now. Just what else could the big secret possibly have been?"

Dinant was struck with a sudden thought. "Wait. What if . . ."

"Yes?"

"Suppose, after all, for the sake of argument, that Dirac *was* goodlife. All right, I know, there's nothing in his public record to suggest that. But if no other explanation makes sense, we ought at least to consider the possibility. Say he was at least goodlife enough to make a deal with the damned machines, in hopes of furthering his own career. So he arranges somehow to give the machines a whole bioresearch station, containing some millions of protopeople for them to kill, or to—use."

"All right, granted for the sake of argument. Though there's no evidence he did anything at all to help them. Anyway, what were they supposed to give him in return?"

The ensign paused. "I don't know. Maybe the plan was

that they'd get rid of some of his political enemies. Only the deal went sour, from the goodlife's point of view, and the berserker ate him alive, along with a few other people on his ships and on the research station."

"And bolted down about a billion protopeople for dessert. Well, it doesn't sound convincing to me, but again, for the sake of argument, suppose it's true. How does any of it explain the behavior of these machines we're chasing?"

Dinant had no answer.

Tongres sighed.

At last the third member of the conversation spoke again. "But I wonder . . . the damned berserkers have operated, continue to operate, over a truly enormous stretch of space and time. As far as I know, no one's ever demonstrated they even have a central headquarters or command center, any more than Solarian humanity does."

"Interesting thought, though. To consider that the berserkers might have one. Even more interesting to think that we, here, now, might be hurrying as fast as we can along the road that leads to it."

Over a number of centuries, beginning well before the first berserker raid on Imatra, the interior of the Mavronari had been partially, desultorily explored. The nebula was known to be almost if not entirely lifeless, but also not totally devoid of the possibilities of life. At certain widely scattered locations within the vast sprawl of silent darkness, the light-pressure of isolated suns was sufficient to keep shadowing dust and thin gas at bay, establishing adequate orbital space for modest families of planets.

One or two of these systems of worlds, which according to the flagship's data banks had never been inhabited (and were all but completely uninhabitable), were known to lie in the general direction of the recurrent berserker flights from Imatra. These isolated systems within the Mavronari had proven to be reachable by narrow, roundabout channels of relatively clear space winding through the occluding interstellar dust. The enemy did not appear to be trying to reach any of these channels. And the fleet commander, with access to prodigious amounts of military information on berserker sightings and activity, could find nothing in his information banks to indicate that the Mavronari had ever been suspected of harboring berserker installations.

Of course other solar systems, known to the berserkers but never discovered by humanity, might well exist inside the sprawling nebula. And worlds unusable by life might still offer space for dock facilities and shipyards, and minerals for production, to the unliving foe.

The Solarians who were now engaged in planning the pursuit felt themselves being forced to the conclusion, for lack of any better, that the enemy were probably indeed on their way to one of those worlds, and had chosen to get there by plowing in the back way, the slow way. But again, *why?* Certainly any ship or machine, constrained by dust to travel only in normal space, fighting the nebula every meter of the way, would need more than three hundred years to reach any of those bodies from the modern berserkers' current position.

Prinsep now rechecked the astrogational possibilities. The result was available to anyone in the fleet who expressed an interest: In three hundred years there had not been time for either Dirac's berserker or Dirac's yacht to complete the long dark tunneling and emerge at any of those known isolated systems.

"Maybe time enough to tunnel their way to some system we don't know about? I don't think so, but I can't say it's impossible."

"Do you suppose that one of the berserkers we're chasing now could be Dirac's?"

That question earned the one who asked it a strange look. "Not if Dirac's berserker stayed on the course it was last seen to be following. If it kept to that course, it's still in there somewhere, plowing through the dust."

"Maybe there is some secret passage we don't know about. Some high-speed lane through the Mavronari that we can't see from here, a route humans have never discovered."

One of the captains ran up on her holostage some model images, such profiles of the modern machines as could be compiled from intelligence reports and telescopic sightings.

"None of these correspond with the image of Dirac's berserker on the old record. You're suggesting that the thing may have been chasing itself around in a three-hundred-year circle, recruiting a force of helpers as it goes?"

"No, not exactly. Not if you put it that way. I mean that possibly such a machine hangs out in the Mavronari, comes out at intervals to make another hit-and-run attack on Imatra—or some other target—and then ducks back inside."

The other thought it over. Shook her head. "Historically, there haven't been many attacks anywhere in the vicinity of the Mavronari. Not a single other attack on Imatra besides the two that we're concerned about. And why make a raid only every three hundred years? Doesn't even sound like a berserker."

"Well, what does it sound like, then?" This was the commodore speaking, cutting through debate with authority. "If anyone here is still clinging to some notion that these objects we're chasing may not be real berserkers, I advise you to forget that theory right now. We've picked up more than enough of their debris, intercepted more than enough of their combat communications, to clinch the fact beyond any doubt . . . and so did Dirac make sure of his opponent, as the records show, before he started out on his last chase. The things we're fighting here, and the one he was fighting, are the genuine bad machines. Absolutely!"

Someone else put in: "Remember, berserkers do sometimes randomize their tactics, doing things that seem stupid just for the sake of remaining unpredictable."

Prinsep shook his head. "Sometimes they do. But three hundred years of deliberate stupidity? Of inefficiency, of downright waste of time and effort and firepower, just to give us something to fret about? If that's true I give up. No I don't. Never mind. I'm tired, I'm going to grab some sack time." His chef's usual signal, a muted dinner gong, chimed upon the nearby holostage, but for once waved the menu away without comment.

The fleet managed to gain some ground on the fleeing foe during the next couple of c-plus jumps. But after that, gaining more became bleakly difficult; the commodore considered accepting an increased risk of collisions with stray matter, but decided against it. Even so, the chase was becoming more and more dangerous, almost prohibitively so, as the hunters followed their quarry ever more deeply into the outlying regions of the dark nebula.

Over the next four or five standard days, it seemed that some ground was being lost. The trail left in subspace by their berserker prey grew intermittently colder and more difficult to follow.

The fleet commander gritted his teeth, weighed his chances—some said he spent time alone in his cabin, saying his prayers to whatever form of deity he favored (no one was quite sure what that might be)—and ordered a slight additional acceleration.

And a moment after issuing that command turned, with a put-upon sigh, his attention to the possibilities for lunch.

Meanwhile, Havot and Becky had been reunited. She had supposedly been relieved of all her HO duties, but that punishment—if such it was—was the limit of what her superiors were able to inflict upon her at the moment. She was now living blissfully with Havot in a reprieve of uncertain duration, and of course she was no longer recording what he said and did.

At least, Havot thought, that was what he was supposed to take for granted.

All his life he had been blessed—that was how he regarded the condition—with an incredibly suspicious mind. Which of course was one of the main reasons why he was still alive.

Anyway, spy devices could be very small and hard to spot, and he continued to assume that whatever happened between him and Becky would be overheard, and very likely watched, any place they might go on the ship.

So he was impeccably tender with her, very innocent and loving.

Meanwhile Havot had to grapple with inner demons of some subtlety. As the chase progressed, and it became more and more evident that the commodore was in deadly, inflexible earnest, Havot found the prospect of once more confronting a berserker, or perhaps a whole fleet of them, somewhat disturbing.

In private moments and in dreams he tried to clarify in his inner thoughts his impression, his fading memory, of what exactly had happened between him and the crippled killing machine, back there on the Imatran surface. Had he really—when death seemed certain, the prospect of being able to draw another breath a fantasy—had he really, in that moment, committed himself in some way to serve the berserker cause?

His present situation did not distress him. He was experiencing the usual mixture of enchantment and mesmerizing fear that any perilous enterprise could give him—the sense of being, at least for a short time, fully alive. It was a kick that nothing but serious danger could deliver.

When Havot heard how the berserkers had taken the record from the subterranean archive, he began to think that the action of the berserker machine in sparing him had really not been based on anything he had or had not done. But the trouble with being eternally suspicious was that you could never be quite sure.

There was another question, a related one, that tended to keep the fugitive awake when he lay sleepless, alone, or with his newly released lover, in his bunk: Would the berserkers, when he met them again, be somehow able to recognize him as one of their own? Had the substance of his confrontation with one battered machine somehow been communicated to the others?

Maybe the real question was: Did he, Havot, really want to fight on the berserkers' side or not?

Given the unexpected ferocity with which Commodore Prinsep was pursuing the berserkers, Havot thought it distinctly possible that he was soon going to find out.

Lying now in the small berth with Becky, his body pressed against hers in the constricted space, Havot looked fondly at his sleeping lover, stroked her blond hair, and smiled to himself.

He allowed himself to whisper, sweetly, inaudibly, one word: "Badlife!"

TWENTY

The first jolting impact of a berserker weapon against the flagship's force-shielded hull jarred Havot out of the sack, and a moment later Rebecca's naked body landed directly on top of him.

Yet once more, for perhaps the hundredth time since the task force had left Imatra—Havot had long ago lost count—the flagship had ended a jump with sudden reemergence into normal space.

But this reentry was different. In the next instant after the *Symmetry* appeared in normal space the first hammer blow from the enemy struck home. A second or two later the ship's alarms belatedly set up their deadly, muted clamor.

Ruthlessly pushing aside the half-wakened Becky, Havot ignored her confused cries. Even before his mind was fully conscious, his own body was struggling to get into the suit of space armor that for some days had been resting underneath his bunk.

Becky of course had armor too, but hers waited some distance down the corridor in her cabin, so more than Becky's modesty and reputation were going to be at risk while she ran, half-nude and struggling to pull on clothing, the necessary meters to get at it. Havot could picture others in the corridor perhaps looking at her strangely, even in the midst of their own travail.

Havot accepted her parting kiss without allowing himself to be distracted from the task of getting his own armor on. He did not particularly want her to put hers on, but he could not very well try to stop her or advise her against it.

None of the crew members or passengers aboard the vessels of the task force—with the possible exception of those actually on watch at the time—had been granted any warning at all before their world exploded.

Gambling to overtake the fleeing foe, the fleet commander had accepted a certain risk of ambush. Therefore the berserker counterattack could not be counted as a total surprise, but still its specific timing and its strength were unexpected.

A theory advanced earlier by one of the astrogators, but never supported by solid evidence, held that the enemy had fled in this precise direction because the distribution of various types of matter in the space along this trail offered unequaled possibilities for ambush. Regardless of whether the astrogator's theory was right or wrong, the practical outcome was almost completely disastrous from the human point of view. The commodore's continued gamble for speed had finally been lost.

The ten or fifteen lesser vessels of the task force, emerging from flightspace within milliseconds of the flagship, and all within a few hundred kilometers of each other, were also attacked at once. Some of them were instantly destroyed.

The small civilian contingent aboard the *Symmetry*—Havot, the three HO people, and the Carmpan—had been warned, coached, and rehearsed days ago, soon after the fleet's departure from Imatra, about their duties once a red alert had sounded. They were to put on armor, get to their acceleration couches as rapidly as possible, and stay in them for the duration of the emergency.

Havot, alone in his cabin, was just completing the process of putting on his suit when he was knocked off his feet by the second direct hit on the flagship. Grimly he struggled erect; his hands were shaking now. The weight and smell and look of the bulky outfit, very much like the one that had saved his life on the Imatran surface, strongly evoked the terrifying chase and then the confrontation by the berserker.

Even as he fastened the last connector on the suit, he ran out into the corridor, keeping an eye open for Becky or either of her senior associates while he headed for his acceleration couch. Not that he expected yet to be able to do anything about them, but perhaps in the heat of battle a window of opportunity would arise. Certainly not here and now. The restricted space of the corridor seemed filled by a jostling crowd of bulky suits and helmets, most of them bright with identification markings of one kind or another.

Bumping his way along toward his assigned battle station, amid the unfamiliar noises and pressures of the confined environment, Havot found his imagination gripped, inflamed, by the idea that he could feel the death machines in space ahead of him, and on all sides, as they came hurtling past the *Symmetry* at unimaginable velocities. He could sense their lifeless bodies, smell them, just outside the hull—

With an effort he brought his mind back to current reality. Here was the room just off the bridge where all the passengers were to occupy their assigned acceleration couches until the all clear was sounded. Superintendent Gazin and Senior Agent Ariari were in the room already. Their armored suits bore some insignia of the HO office. Havot wondered if that would make them special targets for the berserkers, but decided, to his own private amusement, that this was unlikely.

Meanwhile the ship repeatedly lurched and sounded—hull ringing and groaning like great gongs—under the continued impact of enemy weapons. Blended in now were the space-twitching detonations of her own guns firing back.

Here came Becky, in her suit and apparently unhurt, staggering her way across the unsteady deck to the acceleration couch beside Havot's. Inside her faceplate he could see her relief to find him still unhurt and already well protected.

The commodore's amplified voice could be heard, still calm, still in control:

"Stand by to repel boarders. I repeat—"

Boarders! Something that tended to happen frequently in the space adventure stories and surprisingly often in real life as well.

Modern defenses were capable of turning sheer kinetic energy back upon itself. Fighting ships and machines, each muffled in a protective envelope of defensive force, were often more susceptible to the slow approach of a grappling and boarding device than to the screaming velocity of missiles.

Already the ship's brain, taking over momentarily from the commodore, was reporting in its dispassionate voice that several small enemy attack units had rammed themselves in through the flagship's force-field protection.

Havot reached out an armored hand to touch that of Becky in the couch beside his. Beyond her, the other two Humanity Office agents seemed to be lying there inertly.

Then the chief of the Humanity Office, as if sensing that Havot was looking at him, turned his head and glared back, doubtless trying to express his suspicion that Havot would try to take the berserkers' side now that battle had been joined.

By contrast, Lieutenant Ariari looked too pale and terrified inside his helmet to be worrying about the suspected goodlife or anyone else. He looked in fact like a man about to soil his underwear—if such a thing was possible in a properly fitted suit of space combat armor, with its built-in miniaturized plumbing.

In the small room there was one acceleration couch still unoccupied, this one of drastically different shape. The Carmpan had evidently elected to remain in his cabin. Definitely against the commodore's orders, but it seemed unlikely that anyone was going to try to enforce obedience in the case of Fourth Adventurer.

And now an arming robot, having evidently concluded its tasks in the control room next door, came rolling into the passengers' compartment.

No doubt Gazin and Ariari, if anyone had asked them, would have strongly objected to either Havot or the now-disgraced Agent Thanarat being issued weapons. But apparently no one had yet sought their opinion. Certainly the robot from the weapons shop was not about to do so.

Instead it proceeded as it had been programmed, rolling along the short row of acceleration couches, using its metal arms to issue each passenger his or her choice of alphatrigger or blink-triggered shoulder weapon. Gazin and Ariari selected theirs mechanically and the robot moved along. Havot could see even before it reached him that it bore racked on its flanks rows of what he took to be grenades, hanging there like ripe tempting fruit, waiting for any eager Solarian hand to pluck. Havot was no military ordnance expert, but these looked to him like the type called drillbombs. Just the thing to use when you got within arm's length of a berserker machine—or someone you didn't like, whether or not he was wearing an armored suit.

Accepting an alphatrigger carbine with his left hand, Havot used his right to quickly harvest three grenades, one after another, from the handy rack. Three, he thought, would probably be plenty.

The drillbombs fitted snugly, as if the space had been designed for them, into a belt pouch attached to Havot's armor. He held the carbine cradled in his arm. It was basically an energy projector, whose beam cracked and shivered hard armor, but could be safely turned against soft flesh. The beam induced intense vibrations in whatever it struck; in a substance as soft as flesh, the vibrations damped out quickly and harmlessly. In hard material the result was quite different.

Hard surfaces could be protected by treatment with a spray of the proper chemical composition. The robot as it issued weapons was also treating all the surfaces of friendly armor with chemical protection. The formula was varied from one day, or one engagement, to the next, to prevent the enemy's being able to duplicate it.

The aiming and firing of the blink-triggered weapons were controlled by the user's eyes. Sights tracked a reflection of the operator's pupils and aimed along the line of vision; the weapon was triggered by a hard blink. Sometimes the thing fired unintentionally—when the system was armed and ready, you tended to avoid looking straight at anyone or anything you wanted to protect.

Alphatriggering was an alternative and even faster system, one considered somewhat more reliable, though it took a little longer to learn to use. Such weapons were also aimed visually, but fired by the controllable alphawave signal of the operator's organic brain.

Apart from a few staggering shocks, the flagship's artificial gravity had so far maintained itself through the violence of combat, cushioning and protecting the tender flesh and bone of crew and passengers against the g forces created by enemy weapons and by the warship's own maneuvers. Only once so far had the *Symmetry*'s gravity faltered badly enough to pile people up in corners, allowing a surge in local g forces intense enough to inflict serious casualties despite the fact that all aboard were now in armor. And that failure had been on another deck, far from the control room.

Havot was pleasurably calculating his chances of getting rid of either or both of the senior HO officers as soon as he could do so without exposing himself to retribution. His main objective, though, was still to make sure that Becky was permanently silenced. She was the only one aboard, as far as he knew, who possessed damning knowledge of the coded message.

Once the presence of berserker units aboard could be confirmed, almost anything that happened could be blamed on them. If he could catch her out of her armor, a knife would do as well as any more spectacular high-tech weapon—as long as there was no prospect of the wound's being examined after she was dead.

Knives could wait. Right now Havot would bide his time, watching for the proper opportunity with the calm he was usually able to enjoy on desperate occasions—more than one enemy had described his serene composure as inhuman.

He was pleased when, after a further exchange of heavy-weapons fire, an actual berserker boarding was confirmed by a ship's announcement. At least three devices were thought to have penetrated the inner hull.

Someone was whimpering on intercom—Havot supposed it might be Ariari. Most of the regular crew, at least most who were still alive, seemed to be carrying on with their duties, almost calmly, to judge by their voices tersely exchanging jargon.

And then a different report. A terrified human voice, breathing raggedly as if the speaker would soon be dead, came on intercom to say one of the things was moving down a corridor in the direction of the control room.

Smoothly, unthinkingly as if he were letting his body take over, Havot hit the release on his couch. He stood up, the powered joints of his heavy suit bringing him easily to his feet, carbine in the crook of his arm swinging into firing position. The backpack holding the compact hydrogen power lamp—enough kick there to stop a runaway ground train—slipped neatly into its proper position on his back as he got up.

Regulations sternly forbade passengers to leave their couches for any reason during combat, and naturally such a rule had force enough to keep Becky and the two HO men, sticklers all for law and order, in their chairs a little longer.

But after only a moment Becky slid out of her couch too, determined to be with her lover.

First Gazin and then Ariari did the same, as if they were somehow compelled to follow anything that looked like leadership.

Havot gestured savagely for them to keep back. Hoping they were going to stay out of his way, nursing his carbine into just the position where he wanted it, Havot moved as quietly as his armored bulk would let him to a position from which he ought to be able to ambush anything or anyone appearing in the doorway.

Subvocalizing a command to his suit's small built-in brain, he turned up the sensitivity on his helmet's airmikes. Now he could hear the berserker coming, slowly. Something was out there in the hallway now, moving closer, walking, humping, sliding upon damaged, subtly grating parts. Lurching forward, then waiting, pausing as if to watch and listen. From where it was, it ought to be able to see right past Havot's ambush, into the control room itself.

Havot had no doubt that this machine approaching now was going to kill him if he did not kill it. Any half-baked bargain that he might or might not have made back on the Imatra surface had long ago gone up in smoke, in wisps of unreality. If the berserkers were truly hoping to enlist him for goodlife, they were going to have to come right out and say so, offer him a better and more clear-cut deal than they had done before.

Out in the corridor, the killer machine once more centimetered forward, this time stopping no more than four meters from where Havot crouched, close enough for him to glimpse one flange of its forward surface, to see how badly it was damaged, spots slagged and glowing at a temperature that at this distance would have scorched unprotected human skin—and then, with all the speed it could still muster, the machine rushed the apparently unguarded control-room door.

Havot's alphatrigger beam, striking from one side, swifter than any conscious human thought, sliced out to destroy. At point-blank range a blade of light and force skinned berserker armor back like fruit peel, evoking an internal blast and spray, dropping the monster in its tracks, no more than halfway through the doorway.

The other passengers were thrown into panic, and two of them at least were firing their shoulder weapons now, slicing already demolished berserker hardware into smaller bits. Beams glanced back harmlessly from armored suits, from treated bulkheads and the deck.

Now Havot saw his chance. Dodging back into the midst of the sliding and bumping confusion of armored bodies, the billowing smoke and fumes from the demolished foe, he picked out Becky's suited form, stepped close, and slapped one of his three drillbomb grenades hard against her armored back.

The suited figure convulsed, its faceplate glowed like a searchlight for an instant; the grenade's force, focused into a molten, armor-piercing jet, evoking secondary interior explosions, was certain death to any human being in the suit.

Turning, wondering if he had the time to try for one of the HO men, Havot was stunned to see Becky's anxious countenance gazing out at him from the helmet of another suit.

And there was Gazin, also still alive. Havot realized that he had wasted a chance, killed the wrong person, wiped out no one more dangerous than a bureaucratic coward. Only Ariari was in that suit down on the deck, well cooked by now inside his armor bubbling with fumes and heat. Here, curse her, was Becky Thanarat still alive and on her feet, tearfully glad to see that Havot himself had survived uninjured this almost hand-to-gripper fight with a berserker.

Terse exchanges of conversation assured Havot that the other two were blaming the man's death on the berserker. And now things had calmed down a little; it would be necessary to wait before he tried to use another grenade on Becky.

Aroused by fear and the proximity of death, Havot was now gripped by an almost physical yearning for a knife. Almost certainly there would be a good selection of edged weapons from which to choose, available among Prinsep's elaborate table cutlery.

Checking the charge on his shoulder weapon, Havot left the room and started down the corridor. Someone called after him on scrambler radio, and he tersely put them off, saying he was only scouting.

Down one deck, he went prowling through the deserted galley, excited by a profusion of knives arrayed in high racks, left lying carelessly on wooden cutting boards among the meat and fruit. Choosing hastily, he picked the biggest weapon that would fit into one of his suit pouches and stowed it there for later use.

Of course the knife was not going to be of much use as long as Agent Thanarat continued to wear armor, and she wasn't likely to take her armor off until the combat concluded—if she was still living then. Havot considered other ways, such as possibly pushing Agent Thanarat into some berserker's grasp. And even her death would not completely set Havot's mind at ease. He still suspected that some of the incriminating message might be around, perhaps still waiting to be decoded. He'd have to search Becky's dead body, if at all possible, and then her quarters.

* * *

The latest estimate from what still survived of Damage Control was that two or three or four small berserker boarding machines had actually entered the flagship. It was now thought that all but one of these had been destroyed, but only after bitter fighting that had left much of the vessel's interior in a shambles.

No one knew at the moment where the single surviving berserker boarder was.

Meanwhile, heavy-weapons fire was still being exchanged with large berserker units. By now the *Symmetry*'s drive had been somewhat weakened, and the outer and inner hulls both damaged.

Havot, after picking up his knife, made his way back to the control room. On the way the only humans he saw were dead, and he encountered no more berserkers. When he arrived he discovered that Fourth Adventurer had finally emerged from his cabin to join the other passengers, wearing his own Carmpan version of space armor.

Havot, in what he imagined was something like proper military style, reported to Prinsep that he had disposed of one berserker—said nothing about the objectionable human—and that he was present and available for duty.

Prinsep, his hands totally full with other matters, only looked at him and nodded.

That was all right. Havot again went out and down the corridor a little distance, to look for at least one more metal killer. This was fun, more fun than he had expected.

Meanwhile Prinsep, still in the fleet commander's chair, his human staff badly decimated around him, was attempting on intercom to raise crew members in other parts of the ship. The results were discouraging. It sounded like only a few wounded survived anywhere in the ship.

Then something made him look up, to discover where the last berserker boarder was. Much more nimble than its predecessor, it had just come popping out of God knew where to appear at the very entrance of the control room. One of its grippers, blurring sideways at machine-speed, knocked Havot's armored body smashing into a bulkhead before the man could get his carbine into firing position. In the next eyeblink the berserker had selected a target and fired its own weapon, killing Becky Thanarat, who had her carbine almost raised.

The next shot, fully capable of piercing Solarian body armor, was snapped off a fraction of a second later at Prinsep, a conspicuous target in his central chair. It missed the commodore only by centimeters, and no doubt would have killed him had not Fourth Adventurer, unequipped with formal weapons, propelled his suited body at that moment right into the berserker's legs. Gripper arms beat at the Carmpan like the blades of a propeller, snagged and tore his suit, mangled his flesh.

Havot was not dead. Firing while still flat on his back, slashing away coolly with his alphatrigger weapon, he cut the berserker's legs from under it, and a moment later detonated something vital deep inside its torso.

A stunned, ear-ringing silence fell.

Slowly, his back against the bulkhead, weapon ready, Havot centimetered his way back to his feet. His armor had saved him. He had been momentarily stunned, but was not really hurt.

Dead people were lying everywhere. Becky was among them, Havot saw; at the moment he hardly cared. He picked his way around and over fallen bodies, smashed machinery, back into the control room, where Prinsep still presided, though one support of his acceleration couch, that nearest his left ear, had been neatly shot away. He and the surviving human pilot, and even the surviving HO superintendent were now all looking at Havot with something like awe.

Minutes passed, while outside the flagship's battered, straining metal, heavy weapons thundered, the tides of battle still ebbed and flowed.

The embattled commodore, still presiding over his half-ruined control room from his chair near the flagship's center of mass, grimly continued to receive damage reports, news of disaster from almost every deck.

Commodore Prinsep, the once-bright armor encasing his pudgy body now battle-stained and scorched, the outer surface splashed with Carmpan as well as Solarian blood, seemed to be gradually slumping lower in the webs of his acceleration chair.

At the moment his face bore an expression of wistful calm that might almost have been despair. Yet minute after minute he continued to make decisions, to answer questions softly, logically, purposefully. Something in his very attitude of inertness, his immobility, inspired confidence.

More minutes passed, and casualty reports kept coming in, while inside the fleet's few surviving hulls, machines and people fought desperately to control battle damage, to determine the positions of surviving friends and foes, to recharge weapons and maintain shields at the highest strength attainable.

Communication among the ships in the task force had now become intermittent at best. Contact was cut off altogether for many seconds at a stretch, with nearby space a howling hell of every kind of radiation. But the coders and transmitters had been designed to cope with hell, and there were moments when cohesive packets of information did come through. Some of the human vessels were being vaporized while others were claiming kills against the enemy.

The flagship's brain, delivering with unshakable calm its best evaluation of the fight, concluded that the enemy must have sent half or more of his force dropping back to spring this ambush.

Although to some of those who lived through it, the battle seemed to go on forever, actually, by the usual standards of combat between forces of this size, it was mercifully short. In a very brief time, no more than a quarter of a standard hour, several berserkers had been destroyed. On the debit side, every vessel in the ambushed fleet was badly shot up, and half of them were gone.

Now there were suggestions that berserker reinforcements were arriving.

In any case the signals from other friendly vessels were fading, one by one, and they did not come back. Their images disappeared from the tactical stage.

Prinsep expressed a hope that some at least of the other Solarian ships were getting away; with all the noise in space, it was impossible to distinguish intact departures from obliteration.

Havot, almost at ease, one arm round a stanchion in case the artificial gravity should stutter again, was cheerful, in his element at last.

"What do we do now, chief?" he inquired. Again, Prinsep only looked at him.

No matter. Havot looked back serenely.

To extricate his vessel from the ambush, the fleet commander closed his eyes and ordered his surviving organic and optelectronic pilots to jump his ship ahead.

Before normal space dropped away, several of the survivors aboard the flagship caught a last glimpse of several ravening berserkers, barely detectable by the humans' instruments as they came darting with abandon after their escaping prey, only to encounter pulverizing collisions with almost insubstantial dust, vaporizing themselves or being sufficiently disabled to be thrown permanently out of the fight.

Somehow or other the *Symmetry,* though limping and with a number of its compartments hissing air, survived its desperate bid to break free, carrying to relative safety Havot and a handful of other survivors, half of them wounded, along with a number of dead.

With a last effort, straining the damaged drive very nearly to its limit, the computers guiding the damaged ship sought out the most open channel and maneuvered the scarred hull into it.

Not only did the flagship survive, but it temporarily retained enough speed, power, and mobility to break away from the several surviving ambushers.

The dead Carmpan, and a number of Solarian dead, still lay in the corners of the control room and the adjoining chamber.

The human pilot, Lieutenant Tongres, said: "I took what

I could get, Commodore—and now astrogation's got us back on the same old trail again."

The commodore for once looked haggard, but his voice was still steady. "Any more bandits ahead?"

"Don't see any yet. But I can't see much of anything for all the dust, so there might well be. I don't believe that was their whole force we just engaged."

"Thank all the gods of space we avoided a few of them at least."

Someone in a remote area of the ship was still on intercom, with repeated desperate pleas for help.

And so Ivan Prinsep bestirred himself—heaved himself out of his acceleration couch for the first time since the battle had started—and went to check on the wounded elsewhere in his ship. The organic pilot was busy. A couple of other people lay in their couches free of serious physical injury but totally exhausted.

Havot, so far virtually unscratched, almost jauntily volunteered to come with the commodore as bodyguard, in case any enemy boarding devices were still lurking in the corners.

Prinsep nodded his acceptance.

TWENTY-ONE

The flagship's surviving human pilot, Lieutenant Tongres, was discussing the situation with Ensign Dinant, the only other person still functional in the control room, even as they worked on the flagship's damaged instrumentation.

Soon a startling fact was confirmed: beginning approximately at the present location of the flagship, an open channel cut through the enclosing nebular material, offering relatively smooth passage. This crude tunnel of comparatively clear space led on in the general direction the enemy had originally been following.

The lieutenant marveled. "Look at it. Almost like it was dredged clear somehow."

"Almost." Dinant's admission was reluctant; the actual accomplishment of such a feat on the scale now visible would have been far beyond any known technology, and similar natural features were not unheard of. "Wouldn't be surprised if Dirac's berserker once came right down this channel, with the old man himself driving his yacht right after it."

"Wouldn't be surprised." Tongres went on intercom.

"Commodore, you there? We're really hurting. Drive, shields, everything."

Around the still-breathing pair of officers the control room's surviving holostages were sizzling, erupting like white holes in strange and improbable virtual images. The display system, like all the flagship's systems now, was obviously damaged. Power was being conserved wherever possible.

Presently Prinsep's voice came back, redundantly transmitted on audio intercom and scrambled suit radio: "Do what you can. I'll be back with you in a minute. We're going to have a problem with the wounded. We don't seem to have an intact medirobot left aboard."

Prinsep, escorted by a serene Havot, soon reappeared in the control room. They had not tried to move the seriously wounded yet.

Turning to the commodore, the pilot asked: "I think she's got about one more jump left in her legs, sir. Do we try it, or do we just hang here?"

With a sigh the commodore let himself down in his blasted chair. "We try it. We look around first, and catch our breath, and see if anything else is left of our task force. And if after that we find ourselves still alone, we jump again. Because there's nothing here."

Havot had seated himself nearby—there were a number of empty couches now available—and was attending with interest.

Ensign Dinant asked: "Which way do we aim? And how far?"

"We aim dead ahead, straight down that channel you're showing me." Prinsep's helmet nodded awkwardly to indicate direction. "Let the autopilot decide the range. Because we know what we have behind us here—berserkers—and we can see what we have on all sides. There's nothing for us in the deep dust."

It was true that at the moment cleared ports showed the flagship hanging, seemingly motionless, in a wilderness of dust and plasma. In several directions rolled disturbances that a fanciful observer might have been taken for Earthly thunderstorms magnified to planetary sizes but condemned to eerie silence, dark clouds sparkling and flashing with electrical discharges.

In every direction, except straight forward and astern, spread the subtle tentacles of the Mavronari, deep dust leaving ominously few stars in view, black arms outstretched as if about to bestow the last embrace that any of the intruding humans were ever going to feel. From this point even the Core could barely be distinguished with the naked eye, and that only if you knew where to look. Only straight astern, in the direction of Imatra, could anything like a normal Galactic complement of stars be seen. Straight ahead lay the night.

"Where's the rest of our fleet?"

"With any luck, we'll be able to rendezvous with them, somewhere up ahead."

Gradually Havot, not forgetting to watch the doorways while he listened to the crew talk jargon, got a better grasp on what was happening. The commodore hadn't just cut and run out of the space fight; in ordering that last escape jump, he'd had some reason to hope that his other ships or several of them—or at least one—might also have managed to escape the ambush by jumping on ahead. It appeared to be certain that at least a couple of other vessels had made the attempt to do so. Now the flagship was coming into a position from which he might expect to contact those ships again.

Now Prinsep and what was left of his crew were repeatedly trying to do so, but so far with no success.

After a conference with Dinant, his surviving astrogator, the commodore decided that his only remaining hope of reassembling his fleet, or what might be left of it, was to rendezvous with any other vessels somewhere ahead.

"The rest of our people are up there, ahead, if they are anywhere. If they are not there, they are almost certainly all dead."

"So we jump again."

"We do."

"Yes sir."

Once more flightspace closed in, then fell away. All those who still lived and breathed—except the badly wounded who had not been moved—were still gathered in the control room of the *Symmetry,* and they sent up a tentative collective sigh of relief.

They had just survived the last c-plus jump that the battered warship was likely ever to achieve. The drive had taken them out of normal space and brought them back again more or less intact.

But where had reentry dropped them? Into what looked like a murky tunnel, a half-clogged remnant, extension, of the intra-nebular channel from which they had just jumped.

The ship's computers were quick to offer the calculation that the last jump had covered millions of kilometers. More important, the flagship was no longer alone. In the control room, even an inexperienced reader of displays and instruments like Havot could tell that.

An approximately ship-sized object—in fact several of them—lay nearly dead ahead, within much less than interplanetary distances.

The flagship's remaining weapons had already locked themselves automatically upon the largest target, which, Havot now realized, was vastly larger than the *Symmetry.* Again, he felt peculiar, conflicting feelings as he studied that monstrous shape.

But for the moment Solarian hardware and systems were holding their peace. And so far no enemy fire sprouted.

Under tighter optical focusing this target was quickly resolved into a double object. The larger component, amply big enough in itself to qualify as a large berserker, dwarfed the smaller one, and was only very slightly more distant than the smaller. And behind the smaller object of the pair, no more than a couple of kilometers from it and also in line with the approaching flagship, hung a third image, target or vessel, by a slight margin the smallest of the three.

Within moments, this last blip had been tentatively identified from the old records as Premier Dirac's armed yacht. The *Eidolon* was now holding its position relative to what gave every appearance of being Dirac's berserker, actually still linked to the space station it had kidnapped three centuries ago.

None of the handful of survivors gathered in the control room had time or energy to spend on great excitement. What resources they had left were now concentrated in an effort to assure their own continued survival.

To which the appearance of yet another berserker was decidedly relevant. Someone asked in a dead calm voice: "Are those vessels dead?"

"We'll soon see. At the moment none of them, including the berserker, are radiating anything more than you'd expect from so much scrap metal. But stay locked on with whatever arms we still have."

"Acknowledge." Pause. "We're still closing on them, sir."

"Well, keep closing. Prepare to match velocities." The commodore felt no need to spell out the reasons for this decision—if it could be ranked as a decision. They hardly had any choice. A quick inventory, balancing damage already sustained against resources available, had already disclosed to the ship's surviving officers and their computer aides such a degree of irreparable ruin that much calculation would have to be undertaken, much energy expended, just to preserve from moment to moment the lives of those aboard.

"The last thing we need right now is another fight." That, from Superintendent Gazin, was too obvious to need saying, or to deserve comment after it was said.

But Prinsep made the effort anyway. "I'm no longer looking for a fight. I'm looking for a way to stay alive. I'm assuming that's Dirac's berserker we're locked onto, and if it's not already shooting at us, I think we may risk the assumption that it's dead.

"If that object just this side of the berserker is really the missing bioresearch station, we might just possibly be able to board it and find some of the help we need. I don't see any other course of action that offers us even a ghost of a chance."

Within an hour the battered flagship had closed to no more than a few hundred kilometers from the small parade of objects dominated by the huge, dark, silent, but very ominous mass occupying the lead position.

Everyone kept watching that leading unit, expecting weapon flashes or some sharp maneuver, alert for a display of violence that, for whatever reason, did not come. All that happened was that the images of the three objects became ever more clearly visible.

"It *is* a berserker," Prinsep announced laconically at last. "A damned big one."

"Yes sir. It sure is—or was," Lieutenant Tongres added hopefully. "I suppose we can safely assume, given the presence of the other objects nearby, that it's Dirac's."

"Yes."

Havot, watching and listening with the others, had a hard time making any connection between the enigmatic, half-ruined mass ahead and the murderous machine that had once cornered him back on the Imatran surface.

"Hold battle stations," the commodore ordered. But still, despite urgings from his crew to get in the first blow, he refused to pull the trigger and order aggressive action.

Commodore Prinsep allowed the closure with the three tandem units to continue, while his two crew members still fit for duty, along with such shipboard robots as were still functioning, took turns applying themselves to damage control, caring for the wounded, and attempting emergency repairs of life support and weapons systems.

An ongoing monitoring of the situation confirmed that repairs to the drive and power systems were impossible, and the other palliative measures taken to keep equipment functioning were going to prove futile in a matter of hours at the most.

"Fleet Commander Prinsep." It was his dying ship itself which thus so formally addressed him.

"That is my name," he replied softly. "But I no longer have a fleet."

"Strongly suggest that you issue orders to abandon ship."

"I acknowledge the suggestion."

Still, the commodore delayed giving that command. Now a mechanical voice from the deck where the wounded lay began calling urgently for help, until one of the people in the control room, who had no more help to give, overrode the system's programming and shut it up.

At this point the commodore tried to obtain from his

instruments a better optical image of the station. In his quietly controlled near desperation, Prinsep continued to pursue the chance—at first mentally rejected by Havot and others as fantastically improbable—that he might be able to find some functional help for his wounded aboard the captive biostation—if the giant berserker was really as dead as it appeared.

"A facility like that, for biological research, certainly ought to have medirobots on board, oughtn't it?" He sounded almost wistful.

Tongres said: "Sir, I suppose it would have mounted some such devices, three hundred years ago. What it must have on board right now is berserkers, if anything."

Prinsep shrugged fatalistically. "If things turn out like that, maybe we can at least take a few more of them with us. One thing I can assure you—all of you—if we simply sit here on this ship, we're all going to die in a few hours. A day or two at best."

"Are we to abandon ship, sir?"

"Let's not rush it. But I want to get the wounded into a lifeboat. And I'd rather not be seen abandoning ship if the enemy is indeed observing us."

A pair of undamaged lifeboats remained aboard the flagship, offering survival perhaps for many days, but hopelessly inadequate to the task of getting home.

There was now every reason to expect the warship to self-destruct uncontrollably within a matter of hours, perhaps a standard day at the most. With this in mind the commodore, having got his wounded packed into one of the lifeboats, did not bother trying to program the *Symmetry* to blow itself up. The near hulk would be of no value to the berserker enemy if they should take it over. Prinsep contented himself with making sure that key encryption systems and a few other other secrets were destroyed.

As the minutes passed, with closure continuing at a steadily slowing rate, the nature of the most distant object became more and more unmistakably, ominously clear. The nearer vessels were far too small to obscure much of it. That most distant shape of the three was defining itself with deadly finality—if any confirmation were still needed—as a berserker of truly awesome size. One huge enough to have given Prinsep's original fleet all it could handle in the way of battle—if its murderous brain and its arsenal of weaponry still worked. For this berserker too had been through hellish combat.

What appeared to be functional weapons were to be seen projecting from its hull—and indeed, the giant, half-ruined enemy had been for some time in range, and was certainly in position, though not absolutely the best position, to fire on the new arrival approaching from astern. But, for whatever reason, the berserker's weapons still remained silent as minute after minute of the battered flagship's approach wore on.

Dinant had an announcement. "Sir, I can detect some kind of heavy forcefield, connecting the berserker and the station."

"A field like that could be a relic. Am I not correct? I mean it might persist locally, surrounding the objects to which it had been attached, for an indefinite time after the machine that created it was effectively dead?"

"Possibly, sir. The berserker's drive is obviously still functioning also. Putting out very steady, low power. At the moment only course-correcting, not accelerating. The towing field could be driven from the drive, or it could be on some low-intelligence automatic function. We can still hope that its real brain is dead."

Both the trailing yacht at the end of the small parade, and the berserker in the lead, showed signs of substantial damage, while the station, at least at this distance, did not. Some of the damage to the supposed berserker could now be observed to be fresh, judging by the heat radiation from the scars, and some definite outgassing of various elements and compounds.

Was there a thin cloud of fine, very recent debris drifting in nearby space, dispersing at a rate that proved it could not be very old? Yes, something of the kind could be confirmed.

"Where the hell did that come from?"

It created some excitement. The commodore, on observing this evidence of recent combat, said: "We must assume that our ships, or some of them, did get through this far after all, and did engage the enemy."

"Then where are our other ships now?"

"If they're not here, they evidently didn't survive the fight."

"Unless they simply gave it up as too tough a job, pulled out and headed for home?"

In either case the missing Solarian vessels were not going to be of any help to Havot and his shipmates.

The people on board the slowly approaching warship were now also getting a clearer look at the kidnapped bioresearch station. The identification could now be absolutely confirmed by matching the appearance of this object against images on the duplicate old recording the approaching humans had brought out here with them from Imatra. After three hundred years the outer hull of this structure at least appeared essentially undamaged, though there was some scarring such as might have been caused by heavy explosions in nearby space.

Presently the approaching Solarians, whose autopilot had now reduced their rate of closure to only a few kilometers per minute, were able to get a better look at the antique forcefield bonds that held the berserker and the bioresearch station together. The opinion that this was a relic field received some support from further observations.

Meanwhile the continued gentle deceleration—almost at the limit of what the flagship's failing drive could have managed in any case—steadily slowed the rate of closure. The *Symmetry* was going to come to rest relative to the yacht when the two were no more than a few kilometers apart—perhaps less than one kilometer.

The little triad of antique objects, and now the warship that had joined them, were moving quite slowly relative to the surrounding nebula.

Dirac's yacht, now the nearest to the new arrivals, had been identified beyond any possibility of doubt. The *Eidolon* drifted steadily at the outer limit of the field uniting its two companions and maintained the same inert silence. Perhaps, someone mused, it was only by accident that the yacht had become attached to them and was being gently towed along.

"Evidently Premier Dirac did succeed in catching up," someone commented.

"Much good it did him, from the way things look."

Under the careful supervision of her surviving human pilot, the flagship had now succeeded in smoothly matching velocities with Dirac's once-proud vessel.

And Ensign Dinant, the remaining astrogator, now came up with a plausible explanation for the flagship's emergence from flightspace so close to the three antique machines. The explanation had to do with the channel in the nebula, which locally provided minimum resistance and maximum speed. The distribution of matter and force in nearby space and flightspace was such that any vessel traveling nearby would tend to drift into this channel; it was a path, a condition, that would not have changed substantially over the last three hundred years.

So far, as they had done ever since the flagship had come into observational range, yacht, berserker, and research station continued to maintain virtual radio silence, none of them emitting anything like a deliberate signal at any frequency.

At last Commodore Prinsep let out a sigh of something approximating relief. "You can see as well as I can, my people, that this berserker appears to be dead. But as we know, some very active bandits were close on our heels when we risked that last jump. If it's so damned easy for everything that comes this way to wind up on the same path, we might find them joining us at any moment. I fear we must assume they're going to try."

"I wouldn't be at all surprised, sir, if the berserkers we got away from do show up. If we did in fact leave any of them still functional." Ensign Dinant, a combat veteran when this voyage began, paused. "God, Commodore, but that was a fight."

"Yes, young man, indeed it was. But as we all know, those of our opponents who survived were not in the least discouraged by it. They will be doing their best to grope and crawl their way in our direction. So we must continue to bear in readiness whatever loaded arms we have."

"Sir?" This was Tongres. "Our ships aren't the only ones missing. We can't forget that there was another component to their force too. I don't think they used their full strength to ambush us."

"No, I don't suppose they did. Given the fanaticism of their pursuit of these three objects, some of them must have stayed with that. But that component of their force must somehow have overshot, or else have been thrown off the trail. Because they're not here now, which is one small piece of luck for us."

It was Superintendent Gazin who amended: "At least they're not here yet." He had not spoken for a long time, and everyone turned to look at him.

Havot had a contribution too. "We keep coming back to the same question. We can't avoid it. If only we knew what the big damned attraction is out this way, the berserkers' object in starting this whole rat race . . ."

The commodore shook his head. "We can only guess at that. But the immediate goal of *our* berserkers seems pretty well confirmed now. I think they must have been simply trying to catch up with this parade, the antique component of this rat race, as you put it." He nodded in the direction of the three enigmatic spacecraft so neatly miniaturized upon the one holostage now functioning, their short file graded in size from front to rear.

"And when they do catch up?"

"Then possibly, if we are still on the scene, we will learn something. Perhaps at least the mystery of their behavior will be solved."

Returning to the familiar argument served at least to give the surviving Solarians something to talk about, a minimal relief from contemplating their own desperate situation.

Ensign Dinant argued, "I still say that whatever the goal of the berserkers we've been chasing, it couldn't have been simply to catch up with the Premier and his yacht. Berserkers absolutely would not have abandoned a successful attack, in a heavily populated system, just to come to grips with this man who for three hundred years has been effectively if not actually dead—a man who no longer has any fleets, no power of any kind."

Tongres was ready to debate. "All right. Then tell me what they are hunting, if not Dirac and his yacht?"

"I admit that the alternatives seem little if any more reasonable. Possibility Two seems to be that our modern berserkers are trying to overtake a bioresearch station full of prenatal specimens of Solarian humanity—specimens which have been effectively frozen as long as or longer than Dirac's been gone.

"And Possibility Three—ah, that's the real winner. It says that a whole berserker fleet is fanatically chasing one of their own machines—don't ask me why. And there you have all the apparent choices. I don't like any of them. But, damn it, there just isn't anything else out here."

Anxiously the small group of human survivors, aided by such of their faithful slave-machines as were still in operation, scanned observable space in every direction, at every moment fearing and expecting to discover fresh berserker hosts. But no enemy materialized.

The sensors and the analyzing systems on the warship were, like everything else, degraded by battle damage; but there definitely was fresh hot debris in nearby space in clouds already very thin and still rapidly dispersing, indications of recent fighting. And some of the damage on the huge berserker, whose details became plainer the longer they were studied, could now be confirmed as intriguingly recent, inflicted perhaps within the past few hours: still flaring, still glowing, traces of the great machine's inner chemistry still outgassing.

Commodore Prinsep, his face a study in despair, nevertheless continued to be relentlessly decisive in his low-key way. "We're going to check out the yacht first. I intend to lead a live boarding party over there. If we survive that excursion, but fail to obtain the help we need, we'll try pulling up right behind the bioresearch station and checking it out."

"Boarding!"

"Yes, Lieutenant, boarding. Do you have a better suggestion?"

There was none.

With a gesture Prinsep indicated displays showing the most recent damage control reports. "I'm afraid we really have no choice, given the condition of our drive and our life support. If we can find functioning medirobots on either the yacht or the station, and put them to work, our wounded may have some chance. Not to mention the fact that if the yacht's drive is still working—and for all we know that's possible—it might be capable of taking us all home."

Those words brought a general murmur of enthusiasm.

The commodore went on: "If we can't obtain help from one of these vessels, none of us are going to keep on breathing very much longer."

Prinsep had no indecision as to who should go with him to the yacht—he wanted Havot at his side. Havot nodded agreeably at the prospect.

Prinsep added: "Our task may be easier in one respect. I think we must assume that the biostation is, or has been at some time, occupied by berserkers. I do not believe the same assumption need necessarily be made about the yacht."

There followed a technical discussion, which Havot did not really understand and largely ignored, of the nature of the forcefield connections obviously binding all three of the antique objects together—how strong those fields might be at various locations, and whether they represented any danger to small craft or suited humans entering them.

The consensus of opinion now was that the yacht had probably been accidentally enmeshed; it appeared to be much more weakly connected than the other two bodies.

The commodore calmly began such simple personal preparations as were necessary to go aboard the yacht. Havot watched him for a moment and then began to get ready too.

They were to attempt the boarding in one of the small and unarmed lifeboats.

Two possible sources of hope, faint but real, lay before them. The yacht and the biolab. Two out of the three antique objects. As for the third . . .

Commodore Prinsep thought to himself that no one was going to board a berserker willingly, not even a berserker as dead-looking as this one. Not while there was any other way to go.

Then he thought of an exception. Maybe Havot would.

TWENTY-TWO

Havot was on a high, far removed from any care about what might be going to happen two hours from now, or three.

It was going to be damned interesting to see what happened next. On top of everything else, it gave him a kick to realize that by shooting down two berserkers he had now achieved heroic status in the eyes of his shipmates. Even Superintendent Gazin seemed to be impressed. Doubtless there were any number of planets where he'd be nominated for great honors—provided all the identities he'd had before that of Christopher Havot could be wiped away, and provided he and any of his shipmates did manage to survive.

At least any charge of goodlife activity would now look utterly ridiculous. And as for Havot's inner demons—whatever mesmerized pledge he might once have been coerced into making to the bad machines, he didn't belong in that category now.

The commodore, though, was not entirely taken in. Havot thought he could tell by the way the man sometimes looked at him.

To hell with it. He, Havot, was not going to hurt Commodore Prinsep; being around him was too much fun.

And Havot understood, too, whenever he stopped to really think about it, that if he should survive and return to what people called civilization, someone might propose him for a medal, but they'd bring it to him in a cell. He could not actually expect any kind of pardon. No human society tolerated the kind of things he'd done. But what the hell. He hadn't lost anything by getting free back at the spaceport, and at the moment he was content to ride the wave, to see what the universe put up to amuse him in the next hour or so.

Meanwhile, Christopher Havot was enjoying the way his shipmates looked at him. Sheer survival had now become the sole concern of all the flagship's remaining survivors, and under these conditions he was a good man to have around.

For the time being, at least. He understood quite well how swiftly attitudes could change.

After a short pause for rest and reorganization, he followed Prinsep to the flight deck—which was badly shot up, like every other part of the flagship—and into one of the two still-functional lifeboats.

The two men in the lifeboat, and the people they'd left on the flagship, all kept casting nervous looks in the direction of the huge berserker—or the seeming hulk that had once been a berserker. That mountainous, half-mangled mass of metal still gave no sign of life. If it was tracking the little lifeboat now beginning to move toward the yacht, they could not tell.

The name of the vessel they were approaching, *Eidolon,* was clearly visible as Prinsep and Havot in their tiny craft drew near. Dirac's antique yacht was not all that much smaller than the battered flagship, but both were dwarfed by the berserker.

In the middle of their passage in the lifeboat there came a strange silent moment in which the two men exchanged glances in a way that seemed to indicate some mutual understanding. Havot could see fear in Prinsep's eyes, but since the battle had begun he himself had experienced no fear at all. It was usually this way for Havot when he got into something genuinely exciting. He was eager to do this thing for its own sake, to go forward, to go and see whatever there was to see aboard the seemingly lifeless yacht. Active danger lured him on, as always. And there was also the reluctance to die passively. If there was any way out of this situation, it would be found only by going forward.

On impulse he said: "I'm glad you picked me to come along, Commodore."

Prinsep nodded slowly. "I rather thought you might enjoy it. And you're good with weapons. Better than any of the rest of us."

Havot tried to look modest.

"Sorry about Becky. I know the two of you were close."

Havot felt uncomfortable.

The commodore checked to make sure that for the moment they were securely alone, maintaining radio silence with regard to the outside world. Then he added quietly: "No, I'm not worried that you're going to murder me, Havot."

"What?"

"Not yet, at least. First, I can see you've decided to sign on with me, as it were, and second, the chances are that both of us are soon going to be dead anyway. But right now we make a great team, you and I. And I don't care what you did before you got on my ship, and I don't want to know."

"Murder, Commodore?" But even as he said the words, he knew they sounded false; he wasn't capable just now of uttering them with the proper shocked surprise. He supposed his heart just wasn't in the effort of trying to fool Commodore Prinsep, who kept looking at him steadily.

Getting the little lifeboat next to the yacht and selecting one of the yacht's airlocks presented no particular problem. The yacht routinely accepted docking.

Moments later, Havot and Prinsep, both with weapons ready, were standing inside the yacht's airlock, and its outer door had closed behind them, shutting them in, and now the inner door was opening. *Here ought to be the trap, or the first trap. When the door opens, a berserker will be crouched there, ready to kill—*

But the inner door slid out of their way routinely, very quietly, and there was nothing. Only the prosaic corridor extending to right and left, adequately lighted, properly atmosphered according to the visitors' suit gauges, oriented by normal shipboard gravity.

A few minutes later, having made a good start on exploring the yacht, Prinsep and Havot had found nothing to indicate that it was not really deserted, peacefully abandoned, as forsaken as might be expected in the case of a ship last heard from three hundred years ago.

At least the vessel on first inspection gave evidence of having been completely lifeless for a long time, though the *Eidolon*'s life-support systems were still functional.

That was puzzling, in a way, as Prinsep murmured to his companion. The yacht's own brain might have been expected to shut down life support when it became apparent after some substantial length of time that nobody was using it. But that evidently hadn't happened. Which suggested that someone—or something—might have told the yacht's brain not to do that.

Ship's Systems responded promptly to routine checkout commands when Prinsep tried them. It told the newcomers: "Drive inoperable," but could give no explanation.

Prinsep sighed.

The ship responded promptly to his next questions, about the location and availability of medirobots, showing how to reach them from the explorers' present location.

As they moved about the yacht, both Havot and Prinsep noticed certain old signs of combat damage.

The hangar deck was as deserted as the rest of the ship, empty of all small vessels.

Soon the two explorers found their way to the yacht's control room, without provoking any berserker counterattack, or, indeed, discovering any signs of berserkers' presence. At this point Prinsep, risking the division of his modest search party, dispatched Havot to seek out the medirobots, to confirm by direct inspection that such units were available on board.

Meanwhile the commodore himself stayed in the control room, and started checking out its systems. He totally ignored the possibility of booby traps—things were too desperate to worry about that—and concentrated on trying to start up the drive and weapons systems.

Havot gave brief consideration to the idea of quietly disobeying the commodore's order, lurking around the control room instead, protecting Prinsep, waiting to see if a berserker indeed appeared as soon as the two of them had separated. It would be fun to ambush another of the deadly machines. But just waiting for a berserker seemed too passive a course. Still, he took his time about making his way through the large, unfamiliar vessel. He moved alertly but not hesitantly, feeling intensely alive. He would play this game at his own pace, in his own way.

As if his indifference were paying off, the directions given by the ship's brain proved correct. Be ready for tricks and you didn't get them. Havot easily found his way to a narrow corridor housing the medirobot berths. There were five of the devices, like fancy coffins, each clearly marked with the Galactic emergency symbols.

Havot observed with mild surprise that one medirobot was currently occupied. Stepping close, he saw that it was doing duty as an SA device. He gazed briefly at the indistinct image of a frozen face, Solarian and male, directly visible behind statglass. Then he called up and read the legend, a plethora of detail regarding one Fowler Aristov, a youthful man who three hundred years ago had evidently volunteered to spend his life nurturing innocent young colonists as part of some grandiose pioneering scheme hatched by the Sardou Foundation. Whatever that had been.

"Knock, knock, Fowler Aristov. Time to get up. You haven't paid your rent," said Havot, taking care not to transmit his words anywhere. Even as he spoke, his gauntleted fingers were locating, arming, and activating the EMERGENCY REVIVAL control. Muted lights within and around the occupied coffin immediately indicated that things were happening. Time for Fowler Aristov to rise and shine; the commodore wanted to put someone else in this nice comfortable bed; and Havot, for the time being at least, was backing the commodore all the way.

It occurred to him to wonder whether after three hundred years these medirobots were still fully functional.

He'd warm them up, get them ready for the commodore's people. Hitching his weapon into a different—but still handy—position, Havot went down the row, calling upon each unit for a checkout. Indicators showed that the special berths were all in good shape, the currently vacant ones ready to receive patients. Presumably the one currently occupied would be available in a matter of minutes. It was common practice to make such units interchangeably useable for suspended animation—in therapeutic use, hopeless cases were generally shunted by the robot into the SA mode, pending the availability of superior medical help or at least an organic decision maker.

Warily trying out the yacht's intercom, Havot communicated with Prinsep in the control room. The commodore sounded faintly surprised to hear from him—and very tired. He wasn't having any luck in getting the yacht's drive up and running.

Havot soon made his way uneventfully back to the control room, where the commodore, a study in exhaustion slumped in a command chair, looked up at him.

"Damn. Whatever's wrong with this drive, it's going to take some work, if there's any chance at all to get it going—but you say at least the medirobots are operational?"

"Yes."

"How many of them?"

"Five."

"Too bad there's not eight. But at least we can get our five worst cases into care as quickly as possible. Let's call up Tongres and Dinant, and get them started ferrying people over here."

Sandy Kensing was slowly coming up out of deep SA sleep. It was different from the arousal from ordinary sleep, vaguely like recovering from a long illness—only faster—and vaguely like being drugged. Over the last four or five subjective years of Kensing's life the sensation had come to be familiar to him, and he recognized it at once.

The gossamer threads of some glorious dream had just begun to weave themselves together, as part of the sensation of being drugged, when they were brutally torn apart. The dream had had to do with Annie and him. In it they were, for once, both out of the deep freeze at the same time, and Dirac was going to let them go, somehow send them home . . .

But already the dream was gone. Kensing was on the biostation, where he had been for too many years, for what seemed like eternity. Where he was always going to be.

Still on the biostation, in his usual SA unit. And a big man, graying, powerfully built, was bending over Kensing's coffin. "Time to get up, kid," he urged in his rasping voice.

"What?" Kensing still lay there in his glassy box, half dazed. "Give me a few minutes."

"No. Wake up now." The big man was relentless. "You're the defense-systems expert, and I want to talk to you before I go waking the boss. He's very touchy about being got up. But we've got information that someone's moving around on the yacht."

The temporary disorientation attendant upon revival from SA sleep was passing quickly. Sandy Kensing was sitting up in his glassy coffin, remembering.

"How many years this time?" he demanded of Dirac's bodyguard, Brabant. At the moment, with mind and eyes a little foggy still, asking was still easier than looking at the indicators for himself.

The graying man didn't look any older than Kensing remembered him. But Brabant himself had doubtless spent most of the interval asleep. He answered: "How many years have you been out? Shade under five. Not very long."

Kensing nodded. That would make the total length of this damned voyage—if this ordeal could be called a voyage—still only a little over three centuries. He himself had not spent more than four or five years out of those three centuries awake and active, metabolizing and aging. But subjectively he thought that he could feel every second of them, and more.

"What's up?" His coffin lid had now retracted itself all the way, and Sandy Kensing moved his legs and started to get up. "I want a shower."

"Shower later." Brabant moved back a couple of steps to give him room. "Right now I need a consultation. Someone's visiting the yacht. Someone, or something."

Naked, Kensing climbed out of his coffin, reaching to accept the clothing offered by an attendant service robot. Automatically his eyes sought the other medirobots nearby, in which several of his shipmates lay temporarily entombed. Not Dirac, of course. The Premier, damn him, took his rest imperiously apart.

In *that* one, there, lay Annie. The readouts on that unit all looked normal—and that was as close as he was going to be allowed to get to Annie now.

On the way to the flight deck, where they would board a shuttle for the short trip to the yacht, Kensing asked: "Who's on the yacht?"

Brabant looked at him morosely. "That's what we're going to find out. If anyone's really there. Nick got me up, with some half-assed story about intruders, and the first thing I did was come to get you. I'm having a little trouble communicating with Nick."

"Oh?"

"He's probably over there on the yacht now. But I want to see for myself what's going on, and I want you to back me up."

Meanwhile, Commodore Prinsep was temporarily abandoning the yacht's control room, shifting his efforts to other areas of the ship. He was determined to wake up its drive and weapons systems, if at all possible.

It would be a hideous disappointment after discovering this ship, seemingly miraculously intact, to be denied its use as a means of escape.

As for the yacht's weapons, the indications were that firepower still remained; but Prinsep was not about to risk arousing the berserker with a live test.

Superintendent Gazin of the Humanity Office had slipped without protest into the role of ordinary spaceman, at least for the time being. He and the two active survivors of Prinsep's crew, Lieutenant Tongres and Ensign Dinant were taking turns watching the berserker, making as sure as possible that the enigmatic mass at the head of the small procession was still completely quiet.

Seen from this close—berserker and yacht were less than

a kilometer apart—that mass was big enough to stop a Solarian's thought processes altogether, if he allowed himself to think of it as a berserker. Its hull, rugose with damage, bulged out on all sides past the considerable bulk of the captive bioresearch station.

The lifeboat carrying the badly wounded people from the *Symmetry* had now docked successfully with the yacht, and Prinsep led his troops in their effort to stretcher the five worst cases in through airlock and corridors and lodge them in the yacht's five medirobots. He was pleased to find that Havot had the quintet of devices all checked out, warmed up, and ready.

Havot acknowledged the commodore's commendation with a dreamy smile. "What next, sir?"

"Next, you and I go to check out the research station. Dinant, you and the superintendent hang around here and keep an eye on our people. Tongres, go to the control room and take a look at the drive on this bird. Possibly I missed something."

No one questioned the implicit decision to abandon the flagship. The risks of returning to that vessel were steadily mounting, as the *Symmetry* telemetered indications that a killing explosion threatened at any moment.

Despite their growing weariness, Havot and the commodore soon reembarked in their lifeboat and headed for the research station. As they approached within a few meters of the station's outer hull, their instruments allowed them to observe closely the binding web of forcefields connecting the station with the giant berserker. But the towing field was discontinuous, leaving large areas of the station's hull readily accessible. The two explorers had no trouble in locating a suitable airlock and docking their lifeboat.

Brabant and Sandy Kensing, approaching the yacht, observed the flagship—obviously Solarian military, and looking very seriously damaged—just beyond it. And there was some movement of lifeboats between the two large ships.

"Not a false alarm, then. We've really got visitors." Kensing paused, knowing a feeling of mingled awe and hope.

He looked at the bodyguard. "You didn't wake the Premier yet?"

"No." Brabant hesitated marginally. "I don't know if Nick has or not. Or if Loki would let him. Anyway, I got my orders not to wake him unless it's something I can't deal with—but in this case I better."

Kensing said nothing. It would be fine with him if Dirac was allowed to sleep on through all eternity.

Brabant, opening a tight communication beam to the station, roused Loki, and debated briefly with his optelectronic counterpart. Brabant's temper had been aroused before he felt satisfied that the guardian program was really going to initiate the hour-long process of waking Premier Dirac from his self-scheduled slumber.

"Now," said Brabant to Kensing, "you and I are going to see what's really going on. So we can let the boss know as soon as possible." He eased forward on the little shuttle's drive.

As far as they could tell, none of the small handful of people plying between the mysterious, damaged warship and the yacht had yet sighted Brabant and Kensing's small craft. "Must be intent on their work, whatever it is they're doing."

Soon Kensing and Brabant had docked against the *Eidolon,* on the far side from the hatches where the boats from the strange ship had attached themselves.

Once inside the yacht, Brabant paused near the airlock to open one of the ship's lockers and take out a holstered side arm that he attached to his belt. "You'd better wait here, Kensing. I want to take a look at these people, see what they're up to." The bodyguard hesitated marginally, then gestured at the arms locker. "Maybe you'd better put on a gun too, just in case."

So, Sandy thought, *you're going to trust me with a weapon?* But of course the answer was yes. Brabant, and Scurlock, and Dirac himself, would know that Kensing could be trusted—as long as Annie lay in suspended animation, effectively the Premier's hostage.

Kensing helped himself to one of the handguns in the locker, and then with a silent wave saw Brabant off on his reconnoitering mission.

A few seconds later, Kensing followed. Entranced by the prospect of seeing new Solarian faces for the first time in three hundred years, he was not going to wait.

He hadn't gone far before he tensed and stopped. Someone in space armor—not Brabant, he hadn't been wearing armor—was walking down a side passage toward him.

Then Kensing relaxed, recognizing the insignia, twin antique towers of masonry painted on the armored torso. It was only Nicholas Hawksmoor, in suit-form.

Even after all these years, looking in through the blank faceplate, seeing only the empty helmet, gave Kensing an unsettled feeling. He said: "Nick, I hear there are strange people on this ship."

"Yes," said the airspeakers of Nick's suit. His voice, as always, sounded very human. The suit came to a stop near Kensing. Its speakers said nothing more.

"You've changed, Nick," Kensing remarked impulsively.

"Yes, I have, haven't I? But people always change, don't they?"

"Yes, of course."

"But you meant something more. How have I changed, specifically?"

"Oh. I suppose all I meant was—well, thinking back to before you were reprogrammed—then you were—different."

"That seems a tautology, Sandy."

"Yes." Kensing considered that it probably wouldn't be wise to encourage Nick to ponder his own history. At least it could be dangerous.

But now the subject had been raised, Nick was not disposed to let it drop. "How have I changed? I'm really interested."

"Oh . . . I think you were more independent several years ago."

"Was that why I was reprogrammed? I was too independent? You know, I'm certain large chunks of my memory were taken out."

"You'll have to ask our master about that. No one's ever

told me the details. But obviously you were reprogrammed about four years ago—in my subjective time, that is. Just about the time the Premier announced that Lady Genevieve had been found and was rejoining us."

"I wonder if there was a connection?" Hawksmoor sounded innocently puzzled.

Kensing said nothing.

"I'll ask the Premier sometime," Nick decided. "He's not awake right now."

"He soon will be. I think Brabant has argued Loki into getting the old man out of his box."

Nick seemed to have mixed feelings about that, because his suit turned this way, turned that way, shook its empty helmet. "He doesn't want to be awakened, ever, unless something we can't handle should come up."

"That's what Brabant said . . . so, who are these people coming aboard the yacht? Their own ship looks all shot up."

"I noticed that, of course. But I don't know who they are. All the organic humans I know are in their assigned places—except one."

"Oh? Who's that?"

Hawksmoor sounded uncharacteristically uncertain. "I had thought his name was Fowler Aristov, but now I'm not sure of his identity. I'm not sure of what to do."

"Where is he now?"

Nick's suit raised an arm and pointed down the corridor.

Kensing started that way, turned back. "Coming?"

"Not now. You go and look. See what you think. I'll join you later."

Moments after that, Kensing was near the place where the medirobots were installed, when he heard someone call his name.

"Sandy?" The word was spoken in a soft, incredulous whisper. The voice, coming from somewhere behind Kensing's left shoulder, startled him so that he spun round.

A white-faced figure, wearing common shipboard-issue shirt and trousers and sandals like Kensing's own, was advancing toward him out of a softly lit side passage. The form was that of a young man, backlit by ambient illumination so that Kensing could not at first get a good look at the face. But the more he did see of the young man's face as he approached, the crazier it seemed. Because this looked like—like—

But it couldn't be—

"Sandy?" And now the voice, a sound from the dim past, was thoroughly recognizable. "Sandy, is Dad here? What's going on?—I know this is his yacht. I woke up here an hour ago, lying in a medirobot—"

Kensing took a step closer to the tottering figure. Softly, incredulously, he whispered: *"Mike?* Michael Sardou?"

Going aboard the bioresearch station with Commodore Prinsep, prowling and exploring, Havot happened to be the one to make the first historic contact with one of the long-term residents.

Advancing cautiously through one of the biostation's corridors, a passage astonishingly almost choked by a mass of semicultivated greenery, he encountered a woman who was proceeding cautiously toward him. The look on her face suggested that she was expecting to encounter something out of the ordinary.

Her small body was glad in casual shipboard garb. She was youthful in appearance, with coppery-brown curls framing pretty, vaguely Indonesian features.

On catching sight of Havot, an armored figure pushing his way through vines and stalks, the young woman stopped, staring at him in pure, open wonder. "Who are you?" she demanded. "And bearing weapons? Why? What—?"

"Only a poor shipwrecked mariner, ma'am." He gave a little helmet nod by way of bow. "And who are you?" Although Havot, who in his spare time on the voyage had studied the history of Dirac and his times, felt fairly certain that he had already identified this woman from her pictures.

She confirmed his recognition in a kind of automatic whisper, as if she were still shocked by his very presence. "I am the Lady Genevieve, wife of the Supreme Premier, Dirac Sardou."

It was only a few seconds later when Commodore Prinsep, advancing cautiously in stable artificial gravity, through air as good—if somewhat oddly scented due to the prolific greenery—as that he'd ever breathed on any other ship, rounded a corner and, to his considerable surprise, encountered Havot speaking with Lady Genevieve.

Shortly thereafter the threesome were joined by Dirac, a living, reasonably healthy, and unmistakably recognizable Premier.

Clad in a self-designed uniform of sparkling elegance, but blinking and rubbing his eyes as if he'd just been wakened, the Premier spoke imperiously to the newcomers, in his eloquent actor's bass. "You won't need your weapons, gentlemen, I assure you."

Prinsep allowed the muzzle of his carbine, which was already low, to droop still farther; but Havot still held his in a position from which it could be leveled in a fraction of a second.

And Havot, now finding himself confronted by creatures of flesh and blood rather than metal, moved one hand casually on his weapon's stock, unobtrusively detuning the OUTPUT control to razor-beam setting, for greater effectiveness against a softer target.

The imperious man, having verbally dismissed the weapons, now ignored them. As if the newcomers' silence offensive, he snapped at them: "Probably you can recognize me as Dirac Sardou? Or am I overestimating my historical durability after this length of time? In any case, you have the advantage of me."

The commodore, in a voice dominated by fatigue, introduced himself. "And this is Mr. Havot."

Conversation proceeded slowly. Dirac explained that he had been asleep when the newcomers unexpectedly arrived. "Rather a deep sleep, gentlemen. One needs perhaps an hour for full recovery, before one can function as one would like. But come, I am forgetting my hospitality. It's been rather a long time since we've had visitors."

Other denizens of the station now began to appear. As Prinsep and Havot later realized, these were only people Dirac now wanted awake, including Varvara Engadin and a man called Scurlock. Scurlock mentioned his companion Carol, who evidently slept on, as did Drs. Hoveler and Zador. Men named Brabant and Kensing were absent somewhere at the moment.

None of the long-term inhabitants who appeared looked anywhere near three hundred years old, and Prinsep commented on the fact.

The Premier explained tersely. "We have a great many SA units available, and we've been taking advantage of them, relying a great deal on our nonorganic people to stand watch."

Prinsep was not interested in nonorganics at the moment. He said: "I hope you have at least three ready to be used."

"Sir?"

"The SA units you mentioned. I have wounded who need them badly. We went aboard the yacht first—found five medirobots there and filled them up. But three more of my crew still need help as soon as we can get it for them."

Dirac's countenance had suddenly assumed a strange expression. "One of those units on the yacht was occupied," he pronounced in a changed voice.

Frowning at the solemnity of this objection, seeing that it must be taken seriously, Prinsep turned to his companion. "Havot?"

The young man nodded casually. "True, one of the machines had a tenant. A would-be colonist, as his label described him. I turned him out to make room for our wounded."

Dirac stared at Havot for several seconds, as if he were deeply interested; perhaps almost as much in Havot as in what these intruders might have done on the yacht. Then he asked: "Where is he now? The one you turned out?"

Havot shrugged.

For a moment, Havot thought, something quietly murderous looked out at him from the cave of Dirac's eyes—as if perhaps it had been three centuries since anyone had treated any of the Premier's demanding questions quite so casually. Well, well.

Prinsep hastily stepped in, offering to communicate with the people he had left on the yacht. He would ask them to look out for "—what's his name?"

The Premier looked at him thoughtfully. "Fowler

Aristov. Thank you for your concern, but I believe some of my own people are on that vessel now. You may summon yours to join us here." It sounded like a command. "Now, if you will excuse me, I think I had better go over to the *Eidolon* myself."

"Certainly, Premier Dirac. But before you go, let me repeat that three more of my people coming from the yacht will need intensive care."

Dirac, already stalking away, snapped over his shoulder orders for his associates to take care of whatever number of blasted wounded might arrive, and to see that Dr. Zador was awakened. Then he was gone.

The tall, disheveled man named Scurlock, under the beaming supervision of the Lady Genevieve, hastened to assure the new arrivals that the station offered more than enough medirobots to care for all of Prinsep's wounded.

The commodore rejoiced to hear it. But he suggested rather firmly that the injured he had already installed in units on the yacht be allowed to remain there. "Moving them again would certainly be traumatic. Unless there is some compelling reason—?"

Lady Genevieve was soothing. "I expect Premier Dirac will have no objection."

Scurlock also assured the newcomers that live medical help in the person of Dr. Zador would be available in about an hour. The process of her awakening, he said, had already been begun.

The necessity of dealing with recently wounded people naturally led to the discussion of berserkers, and this to description of the brisk fight the newcomers had just been through.

With sudden apprehension, Scurlock asked: "I take it, Commodore, you have not engaged in any hostilities with the machine? I mean the one we're attached to?"

Prinsep blinked. "No. You sound concerned. So this giant berserker may still be active?"

"I should think we have very little to worry about in that regard. But with berserkers one can never be sure, can one?"

"I suppose not. No, a few hours ago we found ourselves pitted against a different enemy. A more modern force." And

Prinsep briefly outlined recent events, beginning with the latest raid on Imatra.

Dinant and Tongres, and the three severely wounded crew people still in their care, soon joined the group on the station. They had lost track of Superintendent Gazin, they said, somewhere on the yacht, and hadn't wanted to delay their passage to search for him.

Havot, though now weighed down by a leaden weariness, retained the curiosity to ask: "Lady Genevieve, we'll all be interested in hearing how you personally managed to survive."

"Survive, young man?"

"Your first encounter with the berserker, back in the Imatran system. Historians are almost unanimously agreed that you died then." And he favored the lady with his most winning and seductive smile.

Seated in one of the spare cabins on the yacht, Mike Sardou was telling his old friend Sandy Kensing how he had very recently awakened, to his own intense astonishment, in the glassy coffin of an operational SA device here on his father's yacht. He didn't know how he'd come to be there or who had given the order to revive him. He didn't know how long he'd been there, until Sandy broke the news.

Michael related now how, as his mind had cleared fully, he'd prudently kept out of sight of Prinsep's people, while watching them bring their seriously wounded aboard and start putting them into the medirobots.

Here was evidence that some kind of battle was going on, or had recently been concluded. Mike couldn't recognize any of the people, or even the space armor they were wearing.

Nor could he guess what connection they had with his own predicament. But Mike strongly suspected that his father—or some faction among his father's supporters—had put him in the coffin, under a false identity, in an effort to get rid of him. Alternatively, he might for all he knew have been kidnapped by some of the Premier's enemies.

Kensing asked: "Does the name 'Fowler Aristov' mean anything to you?"

"That's the name that was on my SA unit. Beyond that, no, I never—" Mike broke off. Someone was coming down the corridor.

In a moment Nicholas Hawksmoor, still in suit-form, had appeared in the half-open doorway.

Kensing quickly performed the necessary introduction. Hawksmoor with his encyclopedic memory had already recognized the Premier's son, the image of whose face showed up in a thousand records of one kind or another.

But all the records to which Nick had access also agreed that young Mike had gone off on some kind of a long trip, only vaguely specified, three hundred years ago. His confirmed presence aboard the *Eidolon* was contradictory and astounding.

At first Nick was suspicious of the contradiction in his records. "You're Mike Sardou?"

"Yes." Warily.

The wariness existed on both sides. "What're you doing here? Your father told me, told everyone, that you had gone off traveling."

"If my father really said that, then obviously my father lied."

Nick didn't answer.

Mike went on: "Damned if I know what I'm doing here; I mean, I'm not surprised to find myself here on the yacht, because the last thing I can recall is going to bed in my stateroom . . . where are we, by the way? Where in space?"

It took the others a couple of minutes to bring him up to date on events, after which there was a pause while Mike tried to digest the information. Then Nick demanded: "Can you think of any reason why you should have been put to sleep, under the name of Fowler Aristov, three hundred years ago?"

Mike looked at them, his first stunned incomprehension swiftly turning into rage. "Yes, I can think of a reason—of a man who thought he had reasons, and who would have stopped at nothing—my father. Oh, damn him. Damn him!"

Nick's helmet nodded. "I can believe that, yes. You've

been . . . reprogrammed, in a way. As I have. By the same man. Our father. I acknowledge him as my creator too, you see . . ."

Nick paused, lifting, turning his empty helmet to reposition the airmikes, in an eerie semblance of a human tilting his head to listen. In a moment the others heard the footsteps too.

Brabant arrived, to stand in the doorway looking at them all in indecisive anger.

Mike recognized him immediately. "Brabant, what is this?"

"Kid, I think you just got a little too big for your britches, is what it is. The old man doesn't put up with any back talk. You should've known that."

"So he did this to me." There was a seething, quiet rage behind the words, reminding all the others of the Old Man himself.

Brabant looked around at the others, then back at Mike. "If you hadn't been his son, he would've wiped you out, instead of saving you here. But he doesn't put up with any crap, from you or anyone else."

Nick said: "Our father puts up with nothing from anyone. He always gets what he wants."

Brabant's expression altered profoundly. "So, you've figured it out."

There was silence for a moment.

The bodyguard, sensing a crisis but uncertain of its exact nature, went on: "What the hell, kid? It could be worse. Part of you's had fun for three hundred years, being an architect and a pilot on the old man's staff. And the other part's had a nice long peaceful nap. Maybe the old man will let you reintegrate sometime."

Brabant's voice trailed off as it came home to him the way the other three were looking at him.

"We hadn't figured it out," said Kensing slowly. "Not quite. But we have now. Dirac recorded him. Recorded his own son, and then reprogrammed him, to make him what he wanted—a useful, obedient architect and pilot."

"All of you," said a new, unfamiliar voice. "Stay where you are."

All four turned to see a stranger in an armored suit, aiming at them a weapon usually effective only against hard surfaces. Superintendent Gazin, suspicious, as always, of goodlife.

On the station variegated greenery, grown from odd stocks of potential colonial materials, much of it deliberately mutated, had over the centuries overgrown rooms and corridors, almost a whole deck, not originally intended as gardens. Vines twisted around doors, groped blindly for controls, tested the seals of hatches. Already, as a result of neglect, the growth was hiding some things, keeping others from working properly.

Dirac's lady and his aide Scurlock were smoothly cooperative in the effort to care for Prinsep's wounded, and quite properly concerned. Soon the Lady Genevieve, with the air of a gracious monarch, assigned the commodore and his surviving shipmates a corridor of cabins on the station.

There were a good many cabins and staterooms waiting to be used. Overcrowding had not been a problem, even if, as some remarks by the old inhabitants suggested, the Lady Genevieve had not been the only person born—or reborn—here in the last three hundred years.

As soon as the commodore's bleary eyes had seen to it that all of his wounded were receiving the best treatment available, and that the handful of his people who were suffering from nothing worse than exhaustion were as well off as seemed possible under the circumstances, he considered giving in to his own need for rest. But for the time being he still struggled to stay awake.

Privately Prinsep now at least half suspected all of these long-term survivors, or at least Dirac, of having become some exotic kind of goodlife. But he didn't want to voice his suspicions until he could talk them over with his own trusted people—the remnant he had left.

With this in mind the commodore, struggling yet a little longer to keep awake, warned Dirac's contemporaries that there was a good possibility of continued danger from the pack of bandits he and his people had just been fighting.

The commodore worriedly renewed his inquiry: "I take it your berserker here hasn't made any aggressive moves toward you lately?"

"It has not," Scurlock reassured him. "I think we may assume our ancient foe poses no immediate threat. We've had no trouble with it for a long time. But if you were planning—some aggressive move toward it—I'd advise caution."

"Aggressive moves on our part were a possibility as long as we had our flagship. But now . . . unfortunately, as you can see, we are here in the character of refugees rather than rescuers. At the moment we find ourselves needing help rather than offering protection. Of course, we do bring certain weapons and equipment that you may have been lacking. If there is anything that we can do . . ."

"There's no hurry, after three centuries—can it really have been that long? We must begin by offering what we can in the way of hospitality."

Sounding urbane and eminently reasonable, Scurlock, after checking with Lady Genevieve, commanded the still-working service robots to bring refreshment for everyone.

Gradually the story of the past three centuries aboard began to be told by the long-term residents—or enough interesting fragments to make it possible to start trying to guess the pattern of the whole.

And now Prinsep, though almost asleep on his feet and about to retire to his room, inquired with anxious delicacy about food; he was visibly relieved to hear that that area of life support was still in excellent condition.

Prinsep, divesting himself of armor in his newly assigned cabin, on the verge of letting himself give way to exhaustion, in turn warned the best available approximation of a trusted aide—Havot had to play the role—that they would have to watch out for Dirac.

They were talking through the coded communication still available in their helmets.

"You want me to watch out for him?" Havot nodded. "I was about to suggest the same thing myself."

"I see signs that he's a dangerous man, Havot—is that really your name, by the way?" Then the commodore shook his head. He shed the last bit of his armor and in his underwear reeled toward his bed, speaking uncoded words in air. "Sorry, I'm getting punchy. No matter. Yes, I want you to do the watching-out."

"You still trust me, then."

"Oh yes. Actually there are some matters, Christopher—is *that* really your name?—in which I trust you profoundly."

Havot thought it over. "You know, Commodore . . . ?" But the commodore was sound asleep.

TWENTY-THREE

Kensing watched, poised for action, as the stranger advanced one hesitant step and then another. The weapon in the newcomer's armored hands swung unsteadily to aim at first one and then another of the four men who confronted him. Blink-trigger carbine, alpha, or simply manual firing? It could make a very important difference.

"I am Superintendent Gazin of the Humanity Office," he proclaimed, in a voice that seemed to be struggling to establish authority. "Investigating goodlife activity."

Brabant's voice was infinitely more confident, though his own weapon still rested in its holster. "I'd take it kindly if you didn't point that thing at me."

Immediately the barrel of the superintendent's weapon swung back to aim at him. "Drop your own gun first!" he commanded. Then Gazin glanced at Nick, who was standing in suit-form near Barbant. In the next instant the superintendent seemed to freeze, as he became aware of the empty helmet and, presumably, of some of its implications.

Exactly what triggered the eruption of violence Kensing

could not have said. He threw himself down, rolling on the deck, trying to get his own unarmored body out of the way as Gazin's weapon flared, beam searing ineffectually at Nick's armor. Beside Kensing, Mike Sardou was also trying to save himself.

The man from the Humanity Office—whatever that might be—had fired at Nick, and Brabant had shot back. Brabant's heavy sidearm proved the most effective weapon, force packets puncturing Gazin's suit and driving the man staggering against the bulkhead behind him. Gazin's weapon fell from his arms and he crumpled to the deck on top of it.

Nick, his armor scorched and glowing but still intact, had already decided on his next move, and now performed it with nerveless optelectronic speed. He spun toward Brabant, both metal gauntlets of the hollow suit lashing out.

The bodyguard went down at once and soundlessly. Brabant, his head smashed, twitched on the deck and died without another word.

Kensing, climbing slowly to his feet, found his own side arm in his hand. Slowly he reholstered it.

Mike—the two examples of him—stood beside Kensing, his organic form close to Sandy Kensing's right side. The hollow suit, inhabited only by patterns of information, was just at his left.

"Two men dead," said Kensing, gazing with gradually developing shock at the still forms on the deck, Brabant and the stranger. "What do we do now?"

"Easy," said Mike, raising his eyes to look past Kensing into the empty helmet of the other version of himself.

The airspeakers on Nick's armor had the answer ready: "We go after the old man."

Mike nodded. "He'll be coming over here, all right. To see what's happened."

"And I know just where we can take him," the speakers said. "I know just how."

"Nick?"

No answer.

Dirac was standing now in the cavernous space of the

Eidolon's flight deck, right beside the open hatch of the little shuttle from which he had just disembarked.

He tried again, raising his voice—only modestly, he didn't want to advertise his presence on the yacht to any of Prinsep's people who might still be around.

"Nick?"

Still no reply. The sheltering spaces of the *Eidolon* around him were all silent. A certain quality in the ship's silence, he thought, momentarily letting himself be fanciful, suggested that his once-proud yacht had been waiting for him. Well, he would investigate, and by the time Loki had transmitted himself over from the station, he, the Premier, might have uncovered some answers. Loki had orders to remain on the station until Scurlock felt sure of being able to manage these well-armed intruders.

As for himself, fully armored and armed as he was, the Premier felt confident of being able to deal with any emergency that was at all likely to come up, at least until Loki should arrive.

Proceeding cautiously to the deck where the medirobots were located, Dirac found all five units occupied, just as the ineffective-looking commodore had announced. None of the devices were in SA mode, and each of them contained a semiconscious stranger, man or woman.

There was no one else around. The members of Prinsep's crew who were still active had by now probably joined their commanding officer on the station. But where were Nick and Kensing and Brabant?

And—on a deep level the most disturbing question—what had happened to Mike?

When Dirac tried asking the ship directly, its bland, imperturbable voice informed him that the people he was trying to locate could be found in the ten-cube.

"Why in the devil—" But there was no use trying to debate these matters with the ship. He would go and see for himself.

At the threshold of the VR chamber, the Premier discovered that the facility was indeed in use. Most of the interior was glowing with a huge and elaborate presentation.

Letting the entrance door close behind him, Dirac frowned at what he saw. Nick—or someone else?—had called up and was displaying a certain design project the Premier had meant to keep secret for some time yet. The display was not truly interactive, a simple holograph that required no special helmet for viewing. It was the model of a projected colony, the heart of a new plan he had been perfecting in secret. It showed how the colony he now intended to found would very likely look when construction was well along.

The solar system and the world on which this plan would eventually take form were yet to be determined, of course, still unknown even to Dirac himself. The site would depend to a great extent upon where his—partner—wanted to take them.

At the center of the model as it was now being presented arose a palatial residence . . .

And voices were discussing it. He couldn't see the speakers—he supposed they were behind some portion of the glowing image—but he could hear them plainly.

"—and whose house is that going to be?"

"Can't you guess?"

Two voices, those of Nick and Mike. They were quite different. Both sounds were intensely, equally familiar to Dirac, though he had not heard one of them for centuries.

Mike was saying: "The great mansion must belong to the man who even now—in his own warped mind—is becoming less and less a man, and more and more a god. The one who's going to rule it all."

And Nick: "Except that he isn't going to have the chance."

"To sit in this house and rule this colony."

"Oh yes, definitely, this is a colonial plan. The outer defenses. Right here in the middle, the palace for god to occupy. And a lot of other housing round it."

"But—I wonder what this is over here? Some kind of temple? Church? Monument?"

Dirac judged that it was time for him to break in. "That is another kind of house," he proclaimed in a loud voice. "For the machine. I think it will be pleased to have that kind of a facility."

"Hear that? he calls it a machine," Mike's voice

commented, its owner still invisible to the Premier. "What he means is the berserker."

Dirac saw no reason to put up with any argument. "The machine with which we have been co-existing for three hundred years. Whatever we call it, it's basically only another machine. As such, it can be managed, used, if the problem is approached with sufficient intelligence, and the proper attitude."

Even before he had finished speaking, a vast rippling, a sea change, passed over the holographic representation before him.

The glowing images re-formed themselves, dimmed and cooled their colors, became old stone washed in the mellow illumination of stained glass transmitting sunlight.

Dirac found himself standing in the Abbey near the foot of the few steps leading up to the sanctuary, looking east, in the direction of the high altar just beyond.

What he was seeing was a true VR display, and it ought not to have been so clearly visible, accessible, through a helmet faceplate built to withstand harsh reality and not for playing games and dealing symbols. The fact that he could see the imaged Abbey with such clarity must mean that someone—it had to be Nick, of course—was directly manipulating the light of the image as it approached the Premier's eyes.

Was this an attempt to induce him to take his helmet off, thus exposing himself to physical attack?

The image frayed and flickered at one side. Now Dirac could see Brabant, walking in his armored suit, coming toward him through layers of illusion, raising one arm in an urgent gesture, beckoning the Premier to come closer.

Dirac, suspecting something was wrong, did not move. Fighting down a momentary impulse to panic, the Premier realized that he had at least temporarily no control over what was happening around him.

Urgently he attempted to summon Loki by means of his suit radio. But he feared that the signal was not getting through; Loki had been temporarily baffled, cut off from contact with his master.

Now another human figure loomed, this one towering above the Premier as it confronted him. It was the magnified image of his son. Dirac could not be sure if this was real at all, but he brought up his weapon. Mike's clothing kept varying, in some quirk of the disturbed Abbey programming, from medieval robes to imaged armor to modern shipboard dress and back again. His hands looked empty, but Dirac knew better than to assume they really were.

The huge mouth of Mike's image moved, and a voice came forth. "Do you recognize me?" it demanded.

"I—" For some reason the Premier found it difficult to speak.

The young man, his expression distorted and unreadable, was staring directly at him. "I'm here, in the flesh, just as you are. Father. *Do you recognize me?*"

"All right. I know you. Mike."

"You don't know me."

"How about me?" This voice came from a different direction, and Dirac spun around. An armored suit, its helmet empty, was standing in the south transept, down near Poets' Corner. Nick's voice pressed at him. "Who am I? *Father,* can you tell me who I am?"

"Nick, someone's been fooling with your programming." He wanted to sound calm and eminently reasonable. "You shouldn't be acting like this." *(Loki, where are you? Come to my help at once!)*

The empty suit advanced a step. "Fooling with my programming? My programming! Someone's been doing worse than that."

Now letting his anger show, the Premier demanded: "Is this your poor idea of a joke, Nick? What does this mean?"

And now Brabant's image loomed once more, shambling toward him from the north transept, beckoning and clad in armor.

"Brabant—?"

Then the bodyguard's armor became modern, and the Premier realized with a hideous shock that Brabant's face inside the walking suit was dead.

With his gun he shot down the walking corpse.

Return fire blasted at Dirac. His armor, the best made anywhere, pounded at his body, burned him, but it saved his life. He caught brief glimpses of Kensing and of Mike, both armed with heavy pistols though unarmored. They were shooting from positions concealed in the VR's room distorting displays.

Dirac cut loose with more rounds of his own, setting his weapon on full automatic. Meanwhile he went groping his way backward through the virtual reality of the Abbey, around stone columns, past stone skeletons on tombs, trying to find the exit. No wonder they had lured him in here to be assassinated; here in the ten-cube Nick had some hope of being able to control the flow of events. Or thought he did.

Nick's voice came at him, inexorably. "This is my territory, Father. Only my dreams can be real in here, not yours. And Loki will not be able to get in here to help you."

Dirac fired again. And again. Plenty of force packets left. He couldn't tell what he had hit. But get off enough rounds, and the machinery maintaining the VR world was bound to be damaged into failure.

The complex battle circuits in his helmet had now wakened, tuning in to alpha waves and feeding back. As lower levels of his consciousness inevitably became engaged, symbolic images emerged to confuse and trouble him.

And then a fragmentary message came through on Dirac's suit radio, just a few words and it broke off again, but it was enough to provide a surge of hope. Loki was aware of his peril, was coming to his aid, was raging just outside the barriers put up by Nick, an immaterial juggernaut, a tidal wave of information assaulting an optelectronic drawbridge, battering and roaring to get in.

Here inside the VR pit, the fight was very material and real. Dirac, still heavily protected by his armor in spite of everything, still only battered and bruised, not seriously hurt, battled for his life. At moments of great fear or horror he closed his eyes to avoid the images, but that was little or no help. The terrible images still offered information, if he could interpret them coolly.

Before him he saw dueling knights, and one of them was himself—thoughts of conflict, of weapons, evoked images of medieval swords and armor.

Now the combatants were dueling gargoyles, as the stone creatures crawled down from their waterspout niches, marking the edges and the channels of the Abbey's leaded roof.

A hideous throng of demonic enemies swarmed about him.

Knight against monster, bright sword against white fangs, then points and edges all blood red. But he no longer knew which combatant he was, or which he chose to be.

And then at some point the portcullis failed, the gates gave way, and Loki came roaring in—inevitably, because Dirac had taken great care in his creation to make sure that Loki should be stronger than Hawksmoor.

From that point on, the tide turned swiftly, and cold reality was winning. Solid flesh and blood, and metal, would inevitably have their way with dreams and images.

Swathes of deceptive image were peeling and falling away now, exposing to Dirac's eager, realistic gaze the dull black walls of the ten-cube chamber.

Moments later, most of the images were gone, and Dirac could see out of his helmet clearly and realistically again. At this point, when a last burst from his weapon seemed to slice open the imaged stone of one of the Abbey's royal tombs—Henry Seventh, master of his own transcendent chapel—he discovered the body of Superintendent Gazin lying there in state.

The fight was over now. Mike had fallen, and so had Kensing. Only the latter was still alive. Loki, bursting in physically at last, animating his own team of armored suits, had simply been too strong.

In the ringing silence after the battle, looking down coldly at the fleshly body of his dead son, Dirac thought: what a terrible mistake. I should have—I should have—

But he didn't know, he couldn't tell himself, just what his mistake had been. Having a son in the first place? He didn't know. He couldn't say just what it was he should have done.

Nick had held out longer than the organic men against Loki's overwhelming power, but Loki after all had been designed and built to be able to manage Nick. Now Hawksmoor, still in his suit, was being confined, bottled up like a genie, like so much hydrogen power plasma.

The suit Nick inhabited was now effectively paralyzed, able to maintain its balance only by leaning against one of the VR chamber's polyphase matter walls. Meanwhile Nick was being granted an experience very few humans ever had, that of looking on his own dead body.

Nick, the loser, had a few last words to say before he was turned off. Perhaps it was involuntary, because Loki was already rifling his programming—Dirac did not particularly want to listen, but he could tell that Hawksmoor's voice seemed to be reciting, almost singing, ancient poetry. Something about a kiss, and a chair.

Dirac shook his head sadly. "Well, here we go again. Goodbye, Nick—only until you can be reprogrammed, mind. We've been through this before, but I'm not ready to give up on you. Not by a long shot."

Loki invisibly clamped down.

Nick's suit, now truly empty, crumpled softly to the padded deck.

Dirac and his guard Loki were left standing as victors upon the field of half-shattered images.

Slowly, wearily, Dirac loosened his helmet and pulled it off. The sight of the distorted, gun-riddled chamber round him was no help. Ten meters, three stories high, the same distance wide and deep. Now he could confirm the dull black reality of the ten-cube room, dusty and littered with the mixed debris of battle damage.

For a few moments all was silence. Then a small force of prosaic robots, summoned by Loki, were coming in to clean things up.

The dead bodies of Mike Sardou and Superintendent Gazin and Brabant the bodyguard were left to be disposed of by the service robots.

Wearily Dirac gave the machines their orders. "Yes, just get rid of all three of them somehow. I don't care how."

Kensing was the only survivor on the losing side. Loki, still in solid suit-form, with tatters of medieval armor-image clinging to his shape as long as he remained inside the ten-cube, and Dirac himself, dragged the half-conscious

Sandy Kensing away. Loki had methodically, neatly, bound the captive's hands and feet.

"Don't kill him. Don't hurt him seriously. He'll have value, as an intact life unit, being given away."

Commodore Prinsep, on waking with a start from the sleep he had so desperately needed, found himself sprawled in his underwear on the bunk in his comfortable new quarters aboard the station. Havot, still in his armor and with his carbine at his side, was sleeping on the floor directly in front of the room's only entrance.

Sitting up, the commodore made it his first duty to cast a wary, jaundiced eye at Havot's carbine, reassuring himself about the relative safety of the setting. Then he began to dress.

The slight sound of movement aroused Havot. The two men talked briefly.

Then Prinsep set about communicating with Tongres and Dinant, who were lodging in the rooms on either side of his. He made sure that his remaining crew members were safe for the moment, and that their most urgent needs had been met.

Where was Superintendent Gazin? None of Prinsep's people had yet seen him aboard the station. Not that any of them felt vitally concerned.

In a few minutes Dr. Zador, alerted by the station's brain to the fact that the newcomers were now awake, came calling with news. Premier Dirac had returned from the yacht only a couple of hours ago, in a glum, uncommunicative mood. Now the Premier was sleeping in his quarters—ordinary sleep, not suspended animation—having left orders not to be disturbed except for the most serious emergency.

Deciding there was no use fretting over Gazin for the time being, Prinsep sat down to enjoy a vitally needed breakfast with Annie Zador and with Havot, who had at last shed his armor. Both men had showered and ordered up new clothing.

Poached eggs and ship-grown asparagus came to Prinsep's order, with commendable speed. He was relieved to find that robot service was as good here as on most ships. Nothing to complain about, though of course not up to the commodore's preferred gourmet standards.

* * *

In the course of their morning meal Prinsep resumed his historical probing in conversation with Dr. Zador. One of the commodore's main objectives was to find out all he could about Dirac's berserker. But he was also concerned about the obvious peculiarities marking this society. It gave a first impression of having evolved into a kind of benevolent-seeming dictatorship.

"The kind of thing that historically is often not really benevolent at all."

Dr. Zador several times expressed concern over what might have happened to Kensing. She feared that the Premier might have ordered him put back to sleep, this time before she had even had a chance to talk to him. She said that Scurlock and the optelectronic Loki obeyed Dirac slavishly and would have seen to it.

Havot was eating pancakes with a good appetite, and listening with interest. But he offered no comment.

Prinsep made no bones about his objections. "A bit high-handed, isn't it? Ordering people to spend years in unconsciousness, without regard for what they might want?"

Annie Zador said with quiet bitterness: "The Premier keeps reminding us that he is in command of this ship, and that we are all subject to discipline. No one disputed that at first. What we have now is a situation that's—crept up on us somehow."

The commodore let that pass for the moment. He told Dr. Zador that he would like her, as soon as possible, to check on his seriously wounded people occupying medirobots both here on the station and on the yacht.

Zador agreed. She was eager to go over to the yacht, because she was beginning to be worried about Sandy. Dirac on his return had refused to say anything about Kensing at all.

Before Prinsep and his two companions had quite finished their meal, a woman the commodore had not seen before appeared, to stand in the doorway of his room looking at him balefully. Zador informed him tersely that this was Carol, Scurlock's consort.

To Prinsep, this latest caller at first glance appeared

mentally unstable. Her behavior during her visit did nothing to counteract this impression.

"So," she began, having subjected Prinsep and Havot to a prolonged scrutiny. "Does the machine know that new people, you people, have come aboard here? But of course it does."

"The machine?" the commodore inquired politely.

"Don't play innocent with me!" she flared at him. "I mean what the badlife call the big berserker. Very big. Do you know, I have seen the shadows of a hundred berserkers, crossing the face of the full moon?"

Havot chuckled artlessly; he found this entertaining. Prinsep frowned at him, then turned to ask the glaring woman: "The full moon? What planet's moon is that?"

"Don't play innocent with me. I have seen them. I have watched! I know!" Havot's louder laughter bothered Carol and she snarled something and moved on, stopping several times in her passage down the corridor to look back.

Dr. Zador, who was now casting uncertain looks at Havot, informed the men that Carol was periodically tranquilized. But she was still demented, a crabbed and crazy elder, still youthful in appearance because she was usually brought out of deep sleep only when Scurlock wanted her.

Prinsep asked: "Have I met everyone now? All of your contemporaries?"

"You haven't met Dr. Hoveler. A good man, you must talk to him. But he will still be in the freezer, I expect."

"Then we must see about getting him out. Nor have I seen much of the Lady Genevieve. Now hers must be a curious story."

Annie Zador told them as much of it as she knew. Not much about how the lady had been recorded, something of how she had been restored to flesh. And other people, other bodies at least, had been born on the station during the past three hundred years. When the advanced machinery was properly employed, a human body could be grown to physical maturity in only three or four years.

Prinsep listened carefully. "I shouldn't think this—this voyage, this exile, whatever it is, was precisely the situation where one would expect reproduction to be high on the list of desirable activities."

Havot yawned and stretched—deep moralistic talk was boring. Presently he rose, murmured some polite excuse, and drifted away. The young man was wearing fresh garments ordered from the robots this morning, a fashionable outfit topped by a flowing robe. It suddenly occurred to the commodore to wonder whether the flowing robe concealed weapons. Considering the nature of the authority that now ruled here, he didn't know whether to hope that it did, or that it did not.

Today he meant to bear his own weapon as if it were just part of a uniform.

TWENTY-FOUR

Kensing regained consciousness slowly, with the feeling that the universe was roaring and collapsing around him, a titanic VR display being suddenly reprogrammed by some indifferent god.

He was lying on his back in an acceleration couch, and his immediate surroundings made it plain that he was now aboard some very small space vessel. In fact it had to be one of the little shuttles commonly used to travel from station to yacht and back again. From where Kensing was lying he couldn't really see out, but he could tell from subtle hints of sound that the small craft was in motion.

When he tried to move, he realized with a chill that his ankles were tied together, his wrists firmly bound behind him.

His last clear memory was of the fight in the yacht's ten-cube. But he could not recall just what had knocked him out. His body felt battered and bruised, but he seemed to have suffered no very serious injury, apart from having been stunned.

The shuttle seemed to be making one of its usual brief unhurried passages. Turning his head, Kensing could see that

Scurlock, not wearing armor, was at the controls. No one else appeared to be on board.

Whoever had bound Kensing's arms and legs—probably Loki, he supposed—had done a well-nigh perfect job, doing no injury but leaving not the least room for trying to work free.

"We're going back to the station," he murmured aloud, with the fog of unconsciousness still not quite cleared from his mind.

Scurlock turned his head to give his passenger—his captive—a look that was hard to read. "Not exactly."

Kensing made an effort to consider that, but was forced to abandon it. "Where are the others?" he asked at last.

"The Premier is seeing to the cleanup. Brabant is dead, as I'm sure you must remember."

"Mike?"

"I don't know of anyone by that name. You also killed a volunteer mentor called Fowler Aristov."

Kensing took a few deep breaths. "Scurlock," he said. "You don't really believe that, do you? That that was his name, or that I killed him?"

Scurlock turned his gaze forward again. "The Premier and Loki have explained to me what happened on the yacht."

The shuttle suddenly dipped and sighed in flight, then grated on something hard. It didn't sound like any ordinary docking. Kensing was suddenly shocked into full consciousness.

"It doesn't matter what you think," said Scurlock, getting out of his own couch and coming to undo the fastenings on Kensing's. He sounded as if he were talking to himself.

"Wait a minute. What're you doing now? What's going on?"

Scurlock chose not to answer Kensing directly. "You're getting off here," he remarked.

Still it took Kensing another moment or two to realize that they must actually have docked with some other object than the station. The berserker? If so, then at some time during the last three centuries an actual airlock must have been put into its hull, matching the specifications of Solarian hardware.

The shuttle's little airlock was opening now, into a larger, alien chamber—and in that somewhat greater space stood a machine, a typical berserker boarding device, waiting for what was evidently a prearranged meeting of some kind.

Scurlock was strong; he lifted Kensing's helpless body from the couch quite easily against the shuttle's standard gravity.

Only now did Kensing understand how Dirac must be bargaining, arranging to stay on good terms with his unliving partner. Only now did he finally let out a yell. As Scurlock dragged him into the airlock, the berserker machine stepped forward and reached out, ready to take Kensing in its grippers and carry him down into the black lightless guts of the great metal killer.

An hour or so after that, Havot and his companion of the moment were jarred out of dozing sleep, rocked by some remote shock that set the whole massive station quivering around them.

"What was that?" the Lady Genevieve demanded in a hoarse whisper. Here in this remote cabin the two of them had felt quite safe from observation; Nick was still in the shop, so to speak, being reprogrammed, and Loki as a rule concerned himself only with people who approached Dirac.

Havot said what he thought the noise had been: the blast of the commodore's flagship finally exploding, the impact of wavefronts of radiation and fine material debris slamming, in indistinguishably rapid succession, against the station's protective outer hull.

"That must be it!" And Genevieve, relieved, sank back in bed beside him.

He hadn't needed a great deal of time, nor much exertion of his seductive powers, to maneuver himself into this position with the Lady Genevieve. He was soon going to try to get Varvara Engadin off in some remote stateroom or secluded leafy bower, and see what fun it was possible to have with her.

Havot's current companion, like so many women, found his handsome youth quite fascinating. He knew he could project an image of almost childish innocence. Somewhat irreverent, but basically a decent fellow—a dealer in educational materials.

He'd told the Lady Genevieve: "Your husband is a very fortunate man indeed—of course I'm sure he deserves his good fortune."

The lady didn't know quite how to take such a compliment. Probably, living with Dirac, she had not heard much flattery of any kind over the last century or two.

Now she snuggled up to him as if seeking protection, reassurance. Apropos of nothing, seemingly, she inquired: "Christopher? What is it that frightens you?"

"Not very many things, I suppose." He paused, thinking. "There was a time when berserkers really did."

"But they don't now?"

He lay with hands clasped behind his head, studying her. Then he responded to her last question with one of his own. "What really frightens you? The Premier?"

Jenny began now to tell Havot, in a rush, of her experiences with Nick, of the horrors of discarnate life as she remembered them. The body Havot was now gazing at, stroking, with such obvious appreciation, was actually the fourth she'd had since her return to flesh. Dirac was interested in keeping her freshly young, and also in the experiments themselves.

The truth was that Jenny, ever since Nick had plucked her from the courier's wreckage, whether in a body or not, had become obsessed with her own image. She felt compelled to refine her appearance to match some dazzling ideal of her own, but at the same time she wanted to remain unchanged, recognizable to anyone who had known her in her first incarnation.

Several times she had discussed with Havot her difficulties in finding the exactly perfect body. She craved reassurance from him regarding her appearance.

Havot was intrigued by the idea of people being able to replace their bodies practically at will. But it was not something he wanted to try personally. He felt well satisfied with the way he looked, the way his natural body functioned.

Havot was always interested in finding out what truly frightened people. Sometimes it was something really surprising. Now he probed at Genevieve, trying, gently at first, to discover the best way to provoke her. He said: "Sooner or later you won't be able to turn up such close genetic matches for your original appearance—even if you do have a billion samples to search through for a match."

"I'll worry about that when it happens. We won't come close to running out of close matches for a long time yet."

Immediately after breakfast, Prinsep had convened a planning session with Lieutenant Tongres and Ensign Dinant.

The commodore said: "The questions of overriding importance are, as I see them, first: Has this damned berserker really been finished off, or hasn't it? Second, if it's not really dead, can it be killed? And—this is a rather more breathtaking question, if possible—can its drive be taken over, in one way or another, to help a group of stranded Solarians get home?"

The more Prinsep looked at the situation, the more certain he became of one thing: for whatever reason, Premier Dirac had evidently placed himself squarely in the path of any such enterprise, as if determined to prevent it.

Over the next few hours, while Dirac's aides were still maintaining that the great man was resting and not to be disturbed, Prinsep found that the station's other long-term residents either would not or could not help him much. Carol uttered vaguely disturbing nonsense, when she said anything at all. Scurlock was openly antagonistic to the newcomers' intrusion, and neither the Lady Genevieve nor Varvara Engadin was inclined to be useful.

Compounding Prinsep's other worries, Superintendent Gazin was still missing, as were Sandy Kensing and the man called Brabant, the latter evidently Dirac's bodyguard.

Scurlock, who came to keep Prinsep company for a time, dropped a few hints that all three absent people might have fallen foul of the berserker in some way.

"Then it *is* still active? There might be berserker devices on the yacht?"

Scurlock replied mildly: "When you've had a chance to accustom yourselves to our situation—which has now become your situation as well—you'll understand that we are neither goodlife, nor exactly prisoners."

"Perhaps you will explain to us, then, just what our situation is?"

Scurlock looked up past Prinsep's shoulder, and his face changed with relief. "Here comes the Premier. He can explain these things better than I can."

Dirac, elegantly dressed and looking somber, was approaching from the direction of his private quarters. He appeared to be ready to carry on with the explanations. "Your people in the medirobots, Commodore, are healing peacefully, or at least resting undisturbed."

"Where's Sandy?" Annie Zador, just arriving on the scene, urgently wanted to know. She appeared to have been waiting for Dirac so as to question him.

The Premier turned his gloomy gaze upon her. "I don't know any good way to break the bad news to you, Dr. Zador."

Annie stared at him a moment, then brought both hands up to her cheeks and screamed.

Dirac, grim and unbending, went on: "There was a fight on the yacht. Your Superintendent Gazin"—he shot a glance at Prinsep—"evidently killed the unfortunate Fowler Aristov and then shot it out with Brabant and Kensing. All four men are dead. And the events left Nicholas Hawksmoor in a state of shock that necessitates his being reprogrammed." He looked back at Annie, his gaze at last softening into a kind of sympathy.

Meanwhile Tongres and Dinant had opened a conversation with Varvara Engadin and were hearing a larger version of the truth from her. Four years ago, rebellious Nick had done something that enraged Dirac tremendously. His offense had had something to do with the Lady Genevieve.

On that occasion, Nick had been caught by Loki and Dirac, overpowered and reprogrammed, forcibly regressed to his state before the berserker had attacked the station. Something vaguely similar seemed to have happened again.

An hour after Dirac's announcement of the deaths, Dr. Daniel Hoveler was awakened, partly at Prinsep's request and partly in response to the pleas of the violently grieving Annie.

Both Zador and Hoveler, when Prinsep talked to them alone, were inclined to doubt Dirac's version of the deaths of Kensing and the others.

Commodore Prinsep wanted to learn for himself what other resources and assets, concealed by Dirac or perhaps unknown to him, might be available. And he was concerned about the poisonous, mysterious mental atmosphere of the place as it had evolved under Dirac's dictatorship. Therefore he requested a general meeting of everyone on board the station and currently awake.

Dirac agreed, with seeming willingness.

When everyone had gathered, the commodore demanded: "What really keeps us from making a concerted effort to take over the berserker's drive and using it to get home?"

In response the Premier argued that between the forcefield obstacles, and other passive defenses the berserker was sure to have in place, reaching either its brain or its drive was quite impossible, and any effort along that line must be suicidal.

Another argument, this one put forward by Scurlock, was that the dead grip of the berserker's forcefields on the station was just too powerful to be overcome by the technology available to the station's inhabitants. It would be physically impossible for them to get to the berserker and to penetrate its hull, if they tried.

"How can you know until you do try?"

None of the long-termers had an answer satisfactory to Prinsep and his aggressive crew members.

Prinsep said: "Well, we've brought with us a few items, at least, in the way of technological reinforcement. And in the absence of any convincing arguments to the contrary, we intend to try them. If the yacht can't move, our only way out of this situation may be to board the berserker and turn it around—or at least turn it off!"

Prinsep turned back to Dirac. "In your opinion, Premier, is the berserker towing this vessel dead or not? Or how would you describe its condition?"

The other was, as usual, icily ready for a confrontation.

"This berserker has been for some centuries basically inert."

"For some centuries, you say. Could you be a little more specific about the time?"

Dirac said: "It has been inert almost from the start."

"You're telling me that this berserker's condition, its behavior, hasn't changed substantially in three hundred years? And still you haven't been able to do anything against it?"

"It may be easy for you, Commodore, to accuse—"

"You haven't even *tried?"*

"I say, it may be easy, for one who has not shared our struggle for survival over the last three centuries, to criticize the path which we have followed. I'm sure that technically the berserker is not entirely defunct."

"Because its drive is active."

"Partly that, yes."

"And because some kind of astrogation system is evidently functional. An autopilot, enough instrumentation to keep the machine on a steady course. And the towing forcefields, obviously. Anything else?"

"Beyond that we enter the realm of speculation. We wouldn't want to trust a berserker, though, would we?"

"Let me put it this way. It long ago stopped trying to kill people, as far as you know?"

Dirac, a model of tolerant restraint, shook his head. "I fear it may be only—exercising a great deal of patience."

"I don't understand. What about the three men who seem to have perished on the yacht? Did they really all die simply as a result of a fight among themselves?"

"None of them were members of your crew. I don't consider that what they were doing is necessarily any of your business."

"Members of my crew are in medirobots aboard that vessel. And I—"

"Your crew members are as safe as any of the rest of us. Commodore, you are an impetuous man. We have reached a point where I think I had better state bluntly a fact I had planned to withhold until you had a better appreciation of our situation here. The fact is that we have been in communication with this berserker from time to time."

"Ah. What kind of communication?"

"It has been necessary for us to reach a truce with it. An accommodation." The Premier announced the fact calmly, with no hesitation or indication of guilt. Guilt and Dirac Sardou were strangers; they had never met.

"What sort of accommodation?"

"An implied one." The Premier gave the impression of being still very much in control. "You do not begin to understand our situation, sir."

Lieutenant Tongres burst out: "It is now our situation too!"

Dirac looked at her imperturbably. "Agreed. But you still do not seem to understand it."

The commodore raised a hand, putting a stop to the accusations, at least for the time being. He asked, reasonably: "I very much want to understand our situation, as you call it. In fact I'd damn well better know what's going on. We all had. I insist on knowing: Just what do you mean by having reached a truce?"

"It will take time for you to understand. Do not attempt to bully me, Commodore Prinsep. I am not subject to your authority on this vessel. Actually you are subject to mine." And Dirac turned his back, majestically, and walked away.

Scurlock intervened, almost apologetically, when some of Prinsep's people would have gone after the Premier: "All he's trying to say is that it comes down to this. We don't try to kill it; it doesn't try to kill us."

Commodore Prinsep, putting aside his dark suspicions concerning Dirac's sanity and intentions, also tried to avert or at least postpone a showdown. He feared an all-out fight among the humans now present on the station.

Still, the more Prinsep considered the situation, the worse it seemed. The appearance of the long-term survivors at their first meeting had been deceptive. Everyone on board when the people from the *Symmetry* arrived had appeared at least tolerably well fed and clothed. The station life-support systems were still functioning smoothly and unobtrusively, at least as well as those aboard the yacht; here too the hydrogen power lamps still put out power—as they could be expected to do for many generations. Maintenance machines still worked.

Medirobots obviously had retained the ability to care effectively for even serious illnesses and injuries.

The fields created by the station's own artificial gravity system still held their proper configuration inside the hull. Recycling machines could be programmed to regularly produce new fabrics—if anyone cared—and were quite capable of coming up with new designs—if anyone was interested. Some machines aboard might have been originally installed for testing with a view to eventual use by future colonists.

Prinsep also continued to be concerned about his wounded, trying to keep an eye out for their welfare even after they were all safely lodged in medirobots. He saw to it that these units were inspected regularly by one of his own people, or by Dr. Zador.

Hoveler and Zador questioned Prinsep closely about what might have happened to the remainder of his fleet. The medical workers now longed for—even as others aboard feared—the arrival at any hour of more people, real victorious Solarian rescuers in a powerful ship. The Premier was at the same time wary of this happening. For Dirac saw his own new dreams of power endangered by the arrival of possible intruders. Centuries ago he had written off any real possibility of rescue. In his planning he had ceased to allow for any such turn of events.

Prinsep decided it would be wise to give the impression that he believed the arrival of a fresh ship was a real possibility, even though his belief was quite different. Simply considering the possibility would tend to undermine Dirac's control.

The latest version of Nicholas Hawksmoor, just restored to duty after his reprogramming, pondered the situation of great complexity in which he found himself.

Other people on board, the ones who had evidently known two earlier versions of himself, were now calling him Nick^3. To Nick himself those earlier versions usually seemed utterly remote, even though he shared certain memories with them.

One of the few things he could be sure of, in this

entrancing and perilous world he was now being allowed to reenter, was that the Lady Genevieve was very beautiful. Another thing, which Nick discovered almost immediately upon returning to his duties, was that this intriguing and appealing woman was now having an affair with Christopher Havot—whom Nick immediately began to hate.

One more discovery was that the Lady Genevieve was very wary around Nick, as if she were afraid of him. He had no idea why this should be so. He could not believe that any earlier version of himself could ever have caused her any harm.

Tentatively he approached her, establishing his presence on holostage, in her room, at a time when she was alone and he could feel reasonably certain they were not going to be interrupted.

He said: "Mistress, I think you know me."

She looked sharply at the unexpected intruder. "I know you are called Nick. Nicholas Hawksmoor. What do you want?"

"Only to reassure you. I have the impression that you fear me, and I don't know why. I want to promise you in the strongest terms that you have nothing to fear from me. Doing you any harm, even alarming you, would be the last thing in the world—"

"Thank you, Nick, thank you. Was there anything else? If not, please let me alone."

"Yes, my lady. But if you would answer one question for me first?"

"What is it?" Reluctantly.

"I do not sleep, as I suppose you know. Yet there have been times—I suppose it has something to do with being reprogrammed—times when it has seemed to me that I have dreamed. Dreamed that I was in a body, and you were in a body too, and with me. I don't know if you can tell me anything about these dreams of mine—if that is what they are—but I felt I had to say something to you about them."

The lady was staring at him in an entirely new way. "How very strange," she breathed.

"My lady?"

"No, Nick, we have never been in bodies together. You have never had a body at all."

"I know that."

"But you do appear in certain of my dreams. Just as you say I have appeared in yours. Gods of all space, how I wish I could be rid of them!"

Moments later, Hawksmoor withdrew, relieved that the lady did not seem to hate him, but otherwise no wiser than before.

He found the thought of being subject to endless cycles of reprogramming somehow depressing, though it did seem to confer a kind of immortality.

Nick, as far as he could remember, had never made a backup copy of himself, nor did he want to do so.

But he was afraid that Dirac might well have copies of him.

Havot told Prinsep and others the story of Nick[1]'s rescue and recording of Dirac's bride, and her subsequent restoration to the flesh, as he, Havot, had heard it from the lady herself.

For Dirac, the confirmation of his bride's death, like any other obstacle he had ever encountered, had evidently been only a temporary setback. In fact it was not really Genevieve herself he needed—though he had chosen his bride from several candidates because of her valuable qualities—but rather the power, the alliance, she represented. He refused to allow himself to be deprived of those advantages.

Actually, before the Premier learned that a recording of the Lady Genevieve's personality existed, he had already begun to calculate how closely an organically grown approximation would have to resemble his original bride to be acceptable politically.

One thing was certain: by the time the battered flagship had arrived with its small band of refugee survivors, Dirac had been operating the artificial wombs intermittently for centuries. His first determined effort had been to duplicate his beloved—or to recover their child, as a first step in bringing back its mother. And fairly soon he had discovered that Nick[1], with the help of Freya[2], was conducting a very similar operation.

After the treachery of Nick[1] had come to light, and that unfortunate version of Hawksmoor had been reprogrammed into Nick², Dirac had continued his own experiments, but now with different aims in mind.

Zador and Hoveler agreed with Prinsep and his people in their doubts about Dirac's version of what had happened to Sandy Kensing and the other men who had disappeared on the yacht.

"Why such a delayed announcement of their deaths? Why the cleanup before anyone was notified?"

Dirac on being confronted with these questions responded that he was not required to account to anyone for his decisions. But he denied that there was any real mystery.

In general the Premier seemed rather surprisingly indifferent to reports of what had been happening back in civilization, even on the worlds he had once ruled. He seemed to choose to disbelieve whatever news he didn't like. When he talked at all about the people he had formerly governed, he spoke as one assuming those folk—or their descendants—would still be eager to have him back, if they were given the choice.

Dirac spoke calmly of how much he missed his homeworld and his people. But he did not seem to have any real wish to rejoin them.

Prinsep thought he was gradually coming to understand the situation. Ever since the station had been isolated, centuries ago, Dirac had become increasingly the prisoner of his own mania for power. The tricks with the artificial wombs were a significant part of the story, but no more than a part. He had also read the labels on thousands of tiles, hatching one zygote after another, in an effort to recover, reconstitute, his lost beloved. Putting himself away in a guarded vault for years, sometimes decades, between hatchings of his latest experiments, thus preserving his relative youth, and avoiding long subjective waits to see how the latest specimen had turned out.

Dirac would trust no human, and only one artifact, to stand guard over him while he slept his long sleeps.

Only Loki, the specialist.

And Prinsep felt sure there must be times when the Premier worried about Loki.

TWENTY-FIVE

Nick[3] had been summoned to see the boss, and now he was waiting for Loki to let him in.

Hawksmoor had not come to the Premier's private quarters in suit-form—in fact he had been ordered not to do so. Rather he tarried in electronic suspension, poised in certain delay circuits, anticipating the command that would allow him to appear upon the Premier's holostage. Meanwhile he tried, with no success, to hold some conversation with Loki. Nick now perceived Loki as he usually did, only an ominous presence, rather like a heavy static charge on the verge of outbreak. Loki communicated orders or questions and listened to the replies, but that was all.

Word from the boss came at last, and Nick, admitted to the inner sanctum, hovered optelectronically on a holostage close beside the master's ordinary bed.

Not far from the ordinary bed there was another. The Premier'd had his own private medirobot installed in this stateroom fairly early on in the voyage. The device sat there like an elaborate food freezer or a glassy coffin, overlooking the much more ordinary bed. Digits of information glowed in muted light from several panels on its sides. A bier surrounded, in Nick's enhanced perception, by a ring of fire—a visual manifestation of the electronic being called Loki.

Nick^3, in the long moment before Dirac spoke to him, found himself wondering exactly what Dirac's face must look like during those long stretches of time when it was frozen hard and solid. In a way Hawksmoor thought that his master's countenance might look quite natural that way.

Loki had already informed Nick that a woman was with Dirac, and Nick had speculated—uselessly, as far as provoking any reaction from Loki—as to who today's visitor might be. Hawksmoor doubted very much that the Premier's private caller was Dr. Zador, who loathed Dirac more with every passing year. And the Premier had as yet made no effort to get the female newcomer, Lieutenant Tongres, into his room and bed—he was intrigued by her, though. Nick felt sure of that.

Today's visitor turned out to be the Lady Genevieve, her attitude and her expression quite unhappy. And Hawksmoor felt sure, as soon as he got a look at the couple, that they had been arguing. It did not seem that the lady was here today for any purpose of romantic dalliance; both of the organic people were on their feet and fully dressed.

The Lady Genevieve barely nodded in response to Hawksmoor's formal greeting. The Premier too was ready to go straight to business. "Nick, I have a question for you. An important question."

"I'll do my best, sir."

"I'm counting on that. I believe I can still safely count on that, although your predecessors both lied to me egregiously. You—Nick^3, I mean—you haven't been in existence long enough to be corrupted yet. Have you, Hawksmoor? D'you still want to keep that name, by the way?"

"Yes sir, I'll keep it. Unless there's another name that you'd prefer I use."

"Let the name stand for now. Well, Nick? Here's my question: Has my lovely wife here been granting her favors to any other man?"

Nick was fully, terribly, aware of the lady's pleading eyes, though he took care that the eyes of his own image should not be observed to turn toward her at this moment. He answered with restrained shock. "Sir, I have never seen a molecule of evidence to support any such—such—"

"Oh, spare us, Hawksmoor, your imitation of a righteous pillar of the community. I swear, you're blushing. I don't know how you manage to acquire these routines. In fact there is much I don't know how you manage to acquire."

"Sir, to the best of my knowledge the Lady Genevieve is completely innocent."

"Have you ever seen my wife alone with the man called Christopher Havot?"

There had been a few totally innocent encounters, in corridors or other public places, as there would have been between any two organic folk aboard the station. Briskly and precisely Nick recounted the ones he had happened to witness, omitting any meetings that were not completely innocent.

Dirac questioned him on details. It was futile, of course, for a man relying on a merely, purely organic brain to try to catch out an optelectronic intelligence in omissions or contradictions concerning details. Nick, when he chose to do so, could weave a seamless cloak of deception regarding such matters, and do it all in a moment.

Presently Dirac seemed to realize this fact. He charged Nick with the responsibility of spying on Havot in the future, and soon after that dismissed him.

Nick's immediate reward from the lady, the last thing he saw as he vanished from the holostage, was a look of desperate gratitude.

As he resumed his regular chores, Nick pondered his new assignment. He was quite willing to create trouble for Havot, but not at the price of causing the lady any embarrassment.

Perhaps, he thought, his wisest course would be to warn Havot to stay away from her. Hoping to accomplish this indirectly, Nick sought out Commodore Prinsep.

Prinsep appeared to take little notice of Nick's indirect attempts to pass along a warning. The commodore had other things in mind. He tried to question Nick about the yacht's defective drive and other matters.

Nick thought he could be somewhat helpful in the matter

of the drive. He remembered perfectly that three hundred years ago the yacht's drive had been damaged in the fighting when Dirac's little squadron of ships had caught up with the berserker and its captured station.

"Are you sure, Nick?"

"I have an excellent memory, Commodore," Hawksmoor ironically reminded the organic man. But then Nick paused, vaguely wondering. The memory of how that damage had occurred was quite cool and unemotional, like something learned from a history tape.

"What's wrong, Nick?"

Nick tried to explain.

"Like something you learned from a tape, hey? Or, maybe, like something that never really happened, that was only programmed in?"

"What do you mean?"

"I don't know much about your programming, Nick. But I do know that the yacht's drive shows no physical evidence of damage. Take a look for yourself next time you're over there."

Nick went over to the *Eidolon,* and looked at the undamaged hardware, wondering. He no longer knew which fleshly people deserved his loyalty—if any of them did. But he was determined to do everything he could for Jenny.

Brooding about the yacht's drive, and about why he had been programmed with erroneous information, led Hawksmoor into fantasizing about finding a quick and easy way of restoring the machinery to full function, and then taking off in that vessel—with only himself and the Lady Genevieve aboard.

Nick^3 in general disapproved of fantasies. He supposed he was subject to them only as a result of some stubborn defect in his programming. Experimenting with your will only in the privacy of your own mind was like fanning the air, shadowboxing. It accomplished nothing and proved nothing.

Nick had already spent—wasted, as he saw the matter now—a great deal of time wondering how he had been able to manage the seemingly profound betrayals that, as the facts and his memory assured him, he had already accomplished.

By now Nick^{3} had deduced that the long process of his betrayal of the Premier must have started when he—or rather his predecessor Nick^{1}—had flown to the damaged courier to try to help the Lady Genevieve. Up to that point he had still been running firmly, or so he seemed to remember now, on the tracks of his programmed loyalty. His only objective in boarding the doomed vessel had been to save his employer's lady any way he could.

But no, any betrayal that had really happened must have started later. Because in fact his saving the lady, and his recording her mind and personality, had in the end been a benefit to Dirac. Suppose he had not interfered. Now Jenny would be really dead, just as her husband had long believed she was. How would the Premier have gained by that? He'd have lost her permanently. And the stretch of time she'd spent in optelectronic mode hadn't caused Dirac any suffering—at least not until he had found out about it.

Prinsep, following his talk with Nick, picked up Lieutenant Tongres and Ensign Dinant and went with Dr. Hoveler into a region of the laboratory they had not seen before, to inspect the site of the experiments and bioengineering projects Dirac had been and evidently still was conducting.

Hoveler had been involved only intermittently in that work, and only reluctantly admitted his participation, because he had serious reservations about the morality of using the zygotes to grow new bodies in which to house old personalities. He served as a good if sometimes reluctant guide.

Dirac, as Hoveler explained, had always felt himself perfectly justified in trying to recover his lost bride by whatever means were necessary. And other experiments had grown out of that.

Hoveler introduced the new arrivals to Freya^{2}, and explained to them how and why she had been created by Nick^{1}.

Freya appeared to her visitors on a holostage in the lab, using an image Nick had once suggested to her, that of the head of a handsome woman, her age indeterminate, long silvery-blond hair in motion as if some breeze were blowing through the optelectronic world in which Freya dwelt.

After a brief exchange of pleasantries, Prinsep got down to business. "Freya, can you tell me what is commonly done with dead organic bodies, here on the station or on the yacht?"

The imaged woman seemed serenely immune to surprise. "Ordinarily, Commodore, there are no dead bodies of any organic species. Such food products as meat and eggs are synthesized directly by the life-support machinery."

"I am thinking of the Solarian human species in particular. There must be experimental failures here in the laboratory. And lately there have also been dead adult human males."

"I store all such material for future use in genetic work. So far, the storage space available is more than adequate."

"Ah. And may we see what specimens you now have in storage? I am thinking particularly of adult humans."

"You may." It was Freya's business to answer questions.

She directed the visitors to another alcove of the laboratory complex, where presently they stood gazing through glass at three human corpses. Freya said the service robots, instructed only to get rid of them, had brought them to her as organic debris. Hoveler instantly recognized Brabant's body, and Prinsep and his shipmates identified Superintendent Gazin's, which was marked with obvious gunshot wounds.

The commodore stared blankly at the third body. "But who's this fellow?"

"It's certainly not Sandy Kensing," replied Hoveler, scowling. "I was expecting to see Kensing. But this definitely is someone else."

Freya told them: "Nick has identified this body as that of Fowler Aristov."

"Ah." Prinsep nodded. "The would-be colonial mentor Havot evicted from the medirobot on the yacht."

The body of Sandy Kensing remained notably missing. Freya knew nothing of what might have happened to him, alive or dead.

Nick, having noticed what the newcomers were doing,

and growing curious, presently joined the group. His image, standing beside Freya's on the 'stage, confirmed the identity of Aristov. Before Nick's latest reprogramming, he'd seen that face in one of the yacht's medirobots—a memory, as clear and calm as that of the yacht's damaged drive, assured him of the fact.

Nick dropped out again at that point, but the tour proceeded. Soon Prinsep and his two aides, in the company of Nick^3 as well as Freya^2, were observing a developing female Solarian fetus, through the glass sides of an artificial womb.

"Another body for Lady Genevieve?"

Hoveler unhappily admitted that he didn't know the purpose of this particular project, or even how many bioengineering projects might currently be running.

Freya said firmly that she had been constrained not to discuss such matters in any depth, unless the Premier was present.

A few minutes later, when the tour was over, Prinsep sought out Dirac, who seemed willing and even anxious to talk to him. The commodore discussed what he had seen in the lab. But he left out all mention of the three adult corpses.

Dirac appeared eager to know what the commodore thought about the growth, the manipulation, of new human bodies.

Actually the Premier felt a great urge to explain, to someone whose opinion he respected, the advantages of his gradually developed plan to cooperate with the berserker. Prinsep was undoubtedly the best candidate currently available.

Dirac began by asking: "You disapprove of my efforts in bioengineering?"

"I have some doubts about what I've seen so far."

"Commodore Prinsep, I would like to satisfy your doubts. The fact is, that since our isolation here, I have become intensely interested in truly fundamental questions."

"Such as?"

"Such as: What is humanity? For a long time there has been no simple answer to that question. But now there are fresh ideas."

"And you look forward to exploring them."

"Shouldn't we all? *Think,* my friend, of what kind of society could be built with the variety of human components now available! The word *society* seems inadequate to describe the transcendent possibilities. And we here, on this vessel, as an isolated offshoot of humanity, we are free to remake ourselves anew."

"And what part does the berserker play in this brave new world you plan to forge?"

"Death, Commodore Prinsep, is an inevitable part of any world. Death and life are perpetually bound in co-existence. Either would be quite meaningless without the other, don't you agree?"

"Perhaps." Prinsep frowned. He had never been much for the abstract pleasures of philosophy. "Do you mean that when it becomes necessary for some of the human components of your new world to die—"

"I mean that their deaths will not be random, or entirely meaningless. In the form of the machine, death becomes quantified, organized, manageable and meaningful at last."

The commodore stared at the Premier. Dirac's face wore an expression of achievement, of satisfaction, as if what he was saying did indeed make sense to him.

"And who," the commodore demanded, "is to quantify and organize, as you put it? To decide which human life units are to die so meaningfully, and when, and for what purpose?"

"Who decides? The minds with the clearest, deepest vision!"

Prinsep did not try to hide his anger. "Reaching a truce with a crippled berserker, more or less by default, is perhaps forgivable. But this—no, what you seem to be suggesting is intolerable!"

Dirac drew himself up. He reminded his accuser that for the great mass of a billion protopeople aboard, the only possible future lay on some new world where some kind of independent colony might eventually be established. They were not wanted elsewhere; that was why they were here now.

He challenged Prinsep to name any Solarian world, whatever its type or degree of civilization, that would extend a cheerful welcome to a billion strangers, that would take in that number of people who, no matter how much they might eventually contribute, would first have to be nurtured through all the difficulties of immaturity.

Prinsep shook his head, condemning. "You would give them life only to serve you. To be coins in some damned bargain you think that you can make with death."

"I say it is only my bargaining with death, as you put it, Commodore, that has kept us all from being exterminated."

Prinsep demanded: "Then you have definite evidence that the berserker retains a capability for aggressive action?"

Dirac nodded slowly. "It is possible that it does. More than possible."

"You seem to know a lot about it."

Slowly the Premier was becoming enraged. "At least you should admit that I know more on this subject than you. You've been here in our little world a matter of days, my friend. I have been dealing with this problem, keeping my people alive, for three centuries."

Prinsep, on leaving Dirac, went wandering the decks and corridors of the station alone, trying gloomily to decide whether his only course was bloody conflict to overthrow the Premier's rule. Such a conflict might well kill every Solarian on board, and only succeed in doing the berserker's work.

The commodore's feet carried him into Freya's territory, and presently he once more stood looking down at the three dead men she was preserving.

He mused aloud: "Too bad their minds could not have been recorded. I suppose there was no hope of that by the time they reached you."

"None," agreed Freya^2. Her image had sprouted in welcome on a nearby 'stage. "The mind, the personality, ceases to be detectable with organic death. It is still possible for some hours afterward—longer with good preservation—to obtain a distinctive individual pattern from the brain cells, a pattern which would appear also in the recorded personality. But as yet we can do no more than that."

"Interesting," was Prinsep's comment. "So, for example, if the Lady Genevieve's original body were still available—"

"Yes, it could be shown to be hers. Even as this body here

is readily identifiable as the organic basis for Nicholas Hawksmoor's matrix." And she indicated the still, dead form of Fowler Aristov.

Prinsep's head turned slowly, wonderingly. He stared at the calm image of Freya, her long hair tossed gently by an invisible wind. "Tell me that again?" he asked slowly.

Nick^3 soon heard the story of his own origins, from Prinsep. The story as Freya told it included the fact of Dirac's parenthood, which she had been able to deduce from the Premier's genetic pattern kept on file.

When Nick knew the truth, his thoughts churned with murderous rage—as had those of his immediate predecessor on hearing the same revelation. He wanted to strike for revenge, this time beginning directly against Loki. But Loki's physical storage was inaccessible to him, almost certainly in Dirac's private stateroom.

It would only be possible to get in there when Dirac was elsewhere, and Loki with him, concentrating his attention as always on protecting Dirac.

Meanwhile, the Premier wanted to consult once more with the berserker, before making a final choice on what his own next move should be. Now, less worried than before about the secret contacts being discovered, he had taken steps to establish a video link—he wanted to present the graphic of his proposed colonial design.

He had wondered, with deep curiosity, what image if any a berserker would present upon a holostage to represent itself in a dialogue with Solarians. The answer turned out to be that there was only noisy emptiness. No real video signal at all was coming through.

Dirac was ready to concede that his plan for a new colony, a new mode of human life, might well require additional centuries to perfect. Probably it had been a mistake to talk about the plan to Prinsep. He had known from the day the commodore and his people arrived that there would be virtually no hope of getting them to cooperate in the scheme. No. They would have to be dealt with in some other way.

He paced now in the narrow cleared space of his private quarters, occasionally turning his head to glance at the image of noisy fog, as if he half expected the noise to coalesce into something more meaningful. The little communicator Scurlock had brought the Premier so long ago now lay forgotten on a table. Scurlock and Varvara Engadin stood by listening anxiously.

Dirac was saying to the berserker's chaotic image: "It has been obvious from the beginning of our—I might say partnership—that you are being forced to operate under severe physical limitations. That massive damage of one kind or another prevents you from fulfilling the basic commands of your programming directly."

Only a droning near silence came through the audio channel.

Dirac paced some more. "For three hundred years now you have been in possession of a billion potential Solarian lives—and you are still unable to put them to your original purpose. To an organic intelligence, this would be very frustrating indeed. You must experience some analogous . . . feeling."

At last the voice of the machine responded. It was clear enough, but it seemed to come from a great distance, and it spoke as always in unpleasantly ugly tones, as if even the minimal amount of stress thus created might be of value in wearing away the endless resistance of Solarian humanity.

It said: "I assume these statements indicate that you have some further accommodation to propose?"

Dirac nodded. "I have. A long-term plan indeed. A great bargain between life and death, the organic and the inorganic. A number of details will have to be worked out. But I have a holographic display to show you—and I will soon send you another Solarian life unit. Perhaps several of them."

The holostage in Havot's cabin lit up, showing the signal which meant that someone was trying to call in. He had been lying in his bunk—alone—and thinking, and now he rolled halfway over, raising himself on one elbow. "Display," he said.

The head and shoulders of the Lady Genevieve appeared.

Breathlessly Jenny's image demanded: "Chris? I must see you at once."

He was surprised. "Won't that be rather dangerous for you, given your husband's suddenly suspicious attitude? I don't know . . ."

"He's out of the way for the moment. Come as soon as you can. To the place you called our leafy bower. Will you come?"

Havot sighed. He smiled. "All right, within the hour."

"Please hurry!" The stage went dark.

Frowning thoughtfully, Havot was halfway through the process of getting dressed when his 'stage lit up again. "Display!" he ordered the device.

This time the imaged head was that of Nicholas Hawksmoor, who wasted no time in preliminaries. "Havot, I know you've just been summoned to a meeting. But you'd best not go. I don't care much what happens to you, but I want to save the Lady Genevieve from any further trouble."

The movements of Havot's arms, pulling on his clothing, slowed to a stop. "Ah. Aha. What sort of trouble exactly?"

"That wasn't really her, you know. The image on your holostage just now."

"What?" Though now that the suggestion had been made, Havot realized that something about the image had been just a little—*odd.*

Hawksmoor nodded. "It was Loki. He can do tricks with recorded images and voices. Not quite as well as I can do them, but still well enough to serve the purpose."

"And I suppose if I respond to the summons, I'll die?"

Nick seemed to hesitate momentarily. "Perhaps you won't die instantly. But something will happen that you won't like. Loki is already waiting in suit-form near the rendezvous. And a small shuttle is standing by, with Scurlock at the controls."

Havot sighed. "Thanks for the warning."

"I don't give it for your sake."

"I see. Thanks anyway." He paused. "Nick? One good turn deserves another. We ought to be able to work out something where I do one for you."

The image of Nick[3] looked at Havot steadily for what seemed to Havot a long time. Then Hawksmoor said: "At the moment I am inclined to give an alliance favorable consideration."

TWENTY-SIX

Nick needed only moments to locate the Lady Genevieve. He knew that currently she was nowhere near the leafy bower, nor was she in her quarters, where, unknown to her, her enemies and Nick's were ready to monitor any incoming calls. Instead, Jenny had gone wandering through the laboratory deck, and now at Freya's recommendation she was visiting the station's ten-cube.

Jenny was suddenly aware of a need to come to grips with, attain an understanding of, her own past life.

Three centuries ago, as Dirac's bride, she had come aboard this station intending a brief visit for a special purpose. Having handed over her offspring, boy or girl—actually she could not remember ever asking the sex—to the blandly tender organic doctors and machines, the Premier's young bride had then fled the station and proceeded to get herself killed—or so almost everyone had been convinced.

Her donation of three hundred years ago, the zygote sought so assiduously by the Premier when he first came aboard, had never been located. Evidently that tile had been truly lost among the enormous mass of other genetic material, as a result of Hoveler's successful scrambling of the records.

Certainly, she thought now, as she watched the development of the elaborate display that she had ordered up at Freya's suggestion, her husband was right about one thing: for the billion protopeople aboard the biostation the future existed, if it existed anywhere at all, only on some new world, where a Solarian colony could eventually be established.

Jenny's fanatical determination to cling to her restored flesh had never wavered. But she had come to feel only hate and fear for her husband. And he was jealous of her, not because he cared for her particularly as a woman, but as he would have resented any other encroachment upon his exclusive rights to anything.

Recently Dirac, gripped by jealousy, had threatened his wife with something worse than an extended deep freeze: a re-recording, followed by a reprogramming such as he had more than once inflicted upon Nick.

Centuries ago, when this Solarian bioresearch station had functioned normally, its VR chamber, like similar devices in many other scientific establishments throughout the Solarian portion of the Galaxy, had been one of the most favored research tools aboard.

Inside such a facility, researchers could easily blow up a microscopic zygote—or even a single cell or a single molecule—to room size or to the imaged size of Westminster Abbey, accommodated within a comparatively modest thousand cubic meters of real room, and could go climbing around among the imaged components sculpted by the chamber's software out of polyphase matter. Working through such modeling, researchers could obtain exactly the view they wanted of their subject; and then, with the proper tools connected, they could alter individual molecules, or even atoms, as desired.

Under normal conditions, one of the most important uses of the chamber on the biostation had been the imaging of individual specimens, in preparation for various efforts at genetic engineering.

Freya of course did not need this kind of help in grasping

physical relationships and patterns. Nor did Nick. But for organic humans such graphics could be a great aid to visualization.

Today, somewhat to Nick's surprise, he found the lady standing among gigantic representations of complex molecules, getting what was evidently her first serious look at the image of human origins, the architecture of genetics.

She looked at Nick through the eyes of the VR helmet and greeted him abstractedly. He delayed delivering the warning that had brought him here, long enough to conduct a very brief tutorial session, explaining what some of the exotic shapes in the graphic represented.

Lady Genevieve appeared to be impressed with all the looping, spiraling intricacies. "So, this is what we are."

"This is how we start, my lady. Or, rather, what we look like only a very little way out of the starting gate. Or while we're still in the gate, if you prefer to look at the matter that way."

"Nick, you say 'we.' But none of this really applies to you."

"Jenny, there is something I have just learned about myself. Something I want you to know."

And even as Nick explained to the lady his recent discoveries about himself, he was simultaneously carrying out two other operations, jobs that would not, could not wait.

First, acting in discrete microsecond intervals, slices of time abstracted from his talk with Jenny, he was skillfully deceiving Loki as to Havot's whereabouts.

Actually Havot, clad now in full armor and carrying his carbine, was stalking Loki near the leafy bower, approaching from a direction in which Loki was not expecting to see him. As the young man advanced, he remained in almost continuous communication with Nick. And Nick, by employing various service machines he had at his disposal, was able to provide slight noises, carefully timed distractions meant to conceal the slight sound of Havot's quiet movements from Loki's perception.

Presently Havot came to a stop, standing very quietly in

front of a door that impeded further progress. Silently he lifted his carbine in both arms.

Nick silently and partially slid open the door in front of Havot.

Not ten meters down the corridor which was now revealed, Havot could now see Loki. Dirac's optelectronic bodyguard was waiting in suit-form, his inorganic attention focused away from Havot. Somewhat farther in the same direction, just round the next corner, Nick was using a service robot to fabricate the sound of cautious human footsteps, thus creating a phantom Havot, a pseudovictim, who was walking steadily if somewhat suspiciously straight into the planned ambush.

And where was Dirac himself? For a moment Nick was frightened, thinking he had lost track of the Premier. But no, there he was, in a small room just out of sight of the spot where Loki waited. The old man, in accordance with his usual behavior nowadays, was curious and jealous and worried about what his wife was doing. But for the moment at least the Premier was ignoring her. Intent on getting word from Loki and Scurlock, he was standing by to make sure that the intended abduction of Havot went off without a hitch.

And Nick, even while talking with Jenny and guiding Havot, was concurrently conducting yet a third enterprise. At this moment he came bursting, in suit-form, into Dirac's private quarters, his violent entry triggering alarms that for the moment rang unheeded. There was also the detonation at knee level of some kind of booby trap. The explosion was only partially successful against Nick's armored suit, which lost one leg just at the knee.

But that was not enough to stop him. Even damaged, Nick's armored shape crawled on to discover Loki's physical storage, three skulls' volume of metal concealed behind a bulkhead panel. In a moment Nick was rooting out his enemy with fire.

And on another deck, at the last possible moment, the avatar of Loki waiting to ambush Havot became aware of the threat behind him. Loki's suit-form blurred into evasive action at superhuman speed. But the bodyguard program had been waiting to take Havot alive, not to kill him. Therefore Loki had to draw a weapon before he could shoot back, and the fraction of a second's delay proved fatal.

For once the optelectronic reactions could not be fast enough. Havot's alphatriggered carbine stuttered and flared, spitting armor-piercing packets of force. Enough of the missiles hit home to blast another set of Loki's hardware into ruin.

And now events outside of the ten-cube abruptly demanded Hawksmoor's undivided attention. When he suddenly abandoned the Lady Genevieve, just as the distant sound of alarms and fighting reached her ears, the lady was terrified.

The unexpected sounds of fighting also interrupted a conference Prinsep had been having with Lieutenant Tongres, Ensign Dinant, and Drs. Zador and Hoveler.

Before the fighting started, the commodore had been telling his allies that there seemed no way to avoid launching a direct assault on the berserker, but how soon they could mount any such operation depended to a great extent on Dirac.

Some of those present thought that before undertaking such a desperate course of action it would first be necessary to depose Dirac as de facto ruler.

When Dirac to his horror saw the pieces of Loki's armored suit scattered along a corridor seared and pocked with fragments of debris, and when the Premier's bodyguard ominously failed to respond to an emergency call for help, he quickly realized that he had been deprived at least temporarily of his most powerful and loyal defender.

Catching a brief glimpse of Havot in the distance, he fired a few shots in his direction, with no effect. Then the Premier, his mind almost paralyzed in terror and rage, hurried to the waiting shuttle which Scurlock was holding ready at an airlock near the site of the failed ambush.

* * *

Prinsep and his allies were astounded to learn facts that were soon confirmed by Nick. First, Loki had effectively been destroyed in a two-pronged attack. Second, Dirac, accompanied by Scurlock and Varvara Engadin, had fled the station in a small shuttle. The shuttle had not gone to the yacht, where Nick would soon have had the fugitives at his mercy. Instead it had gone to the berserker.

Evidently the Premier had been ready to risk the danger of seeking sanctuary with a berserker, confident that he could talk it into helping him, still holding out his offer of collaboration in the disposal of a billion protolives.

Christopher Havot, having survived without a scratch the shots taken at him by Dirac, as well as the firefight with Loki, was smiling and enjoying himself, quite ready to go along with whatever plan the commodore might think up next.

When he looked at the situation objectively, however, Havot had to admit that the Premier still seemed more likely than Prinsep to come out on top in this complicated struggle. Utter ruthlessness counted for a lot, as Havot understood full well. And the last thing Havot really wanted was to be returned to mainstream of Solarian civilization, where he would sooner or later inevitably face punishment for his crimes.

But Havot did not want to be part of any group controlled by Dirac. And anyway, what did such future considerations matter against the joys of the moment? This was fun!

Hawksmoor, still retaining his built-in but rather vague compulsion to protect Solarian humanity in general, felt a great wariness regarding the likelihood of continued bloody conflict among the Solarian factions. Definitely inappropriate, especially with a berserker waiting to pick up the pieces.

Nick thought about all that. But mostly he thought about his father, and what Dirac might be doing now and planning to do next.

Nick said to the commodore: “If he’s gone to the berserker—well, we’re going to have to go after him.”

TWENTY-SEVEN

Prinsep, having convened a meeting of his little force of friends and allies, looked earnestly round the circle of their faces. There were Havot, Drs. Hoveler and Zador, Lieutenant Tongres, and Ensign Dinant. Lady Genevieve and Carol, the only two other organic people on the station, had declined to attend the meeting and were in their respective quarters at the moment. Nick Hawksmoor had said that he would be on call when he was wanted.

The group had completed as best they could an inventory of both problems and resources. It was now time to discuss their chances of somehow surviving their present predicament and eventually getting home.

Prinsep began by admitting that he did not claim military authority over most of those present, adding that in a matter as grave as the decision they now faced, all had a right to be heard from.

Seeing encouragement on the faces around him, he went on. He maintained that, with Dirac now absent, there was no longer any reason to delay an armed invasion of the dead or dying berserker. Unless they confronted the monster directly, there appeared to be no hope of ever escaping from its grip.

It was true, the commodore admitted, that pushing the plan of direct confrontation to its ultimate conclusion appeared almost suicidally dangerous. Eventually it would involve cannibalizing drive units, or components, from the berserker, modifying them, sometimes drastically, with the help of service robots, and installing them in the yacht as a means of restoring that vessel's drive. Such a technical feat would present heroic difficulties, but it was not necessarily utterly impossible.

An alternate plan, which all agreed would be of equal or even greater difficulty, would be to completely (or adequately) pacify the berserker itself, take over control of it and establish habitable living quarters there, then drive it into the vicinity of some trade route. There they would abandon it for fear of being blasted by human warships, commit themselves to the deep in one of the existing small craft, improvise a beacon, and hope to be picked up.

Taking his turn to speak, Ensign Dinant protested that, while he was still ready to obey orders, an invasion of the berserker would be disastrous. "For a handful of us, armed as we are, to attack a berserker of this size directly won't be *almost* suicidal. It'll be the real thing. I say the damned monster must have some powers in reserve. Even if it lacks mobility, it will have booby-trapped everything. There'll be traps and tricks everywhere inside its own machinery."

Lieutenant Tongres held a different opinion. "Of course the berserker would do that if it could. But really, the thing must be dead, or very nearly so. And we can send a robot ahead. If Nick's willing to try transmitting himself, he can try getting in through the berserker's antenna systems. It must have a great variety of those. If that doesn't work he can do his tricks inhabiting the suit."

A number of armored suits in a variety of designs were still available, including those worn aboard by the newcomers, as well as suits that had been standard equipment on the station. And there was no lack of hand and shoulder weapons powerful enough to be effective against berserkers—against the enemy's man-sized units, anyway.

When Prinsep summoned him, Nick appeared promptly on holostage, ready to present technical information. The current physical separation between the captive station and its enigmatic captor was only about a hundred meters; this distance had varied over the range of a few hundred meters during the course of the long voyage.

The forcefields with which the alien marauder had attached itself to its prey three hundred years ago were still as strong as ever, as far as Hawksmoor or anyone else on the station could tell.

Tongres and Dinant, who both had engineering training, agreed that those fields must require continuous and substantial power to maintain the great machine's firm grip on its prize catch—to that extent at least the berserker could not be dead.

The balloting on the question of direct attack was tied after six folk had voted, with Prinsep, Havot, and Tongres in favor, Dinant and the two medical workers opposed.

Prinsep looked to the holostage. "Nick?"

The optelectronic man had been silent during the voting, as if unsure whether the others wanted to include him. Now he answered instantly: "I still say we must go."

When it came to a discussion of tactics, Hawksmoor decided against testing the hospitality of the berserker's antenna farm. Rather he would traverse the gap between vessels in suit-form, carrying a duplicate of his physical storage in his own belly as he moved.

He informed the Lady Genevieve that he was leaving his own prime physical storage units on the station, in a place where she would be able to activate them if she needed help.

After a final hour spent in preparations, the party of armed investigators—Ensign Dinant, true to his word, made no further protest—assembled on the flight deck, boarded a shuttle, and in moments had departed from the station through one of its hatches on the side away from the berserker. This route was chosen in the hope that the enemy might not notice, for a time at least, what they were up to.

The party was equipped with several small relay communication units, through which they hoped to be able to maintain contact with the people remaining on the station. Drs. Zador and Hoveler had promised to do what they could from the station to support the effort.

Both bioengineer Hoveler and physician Zador still regarded their billion helpless wards as a myriad of still-sleeping brothers and sisters. Hoveler regretted his work with Dirac in a series of ever more radical experiments. Both bioworkers retained a strong feeling of kinship with the vast horde of protolives, and some of their shipmates more or less shared these feelings.

On departing the station, Lieutenant Tongres took the shuttle out in a wide slow loop, then approached the berserker's hull from a different direction.

Through the shuttle's cleared ports, surrounding space pressed in on every side, the tendrils of the Mavronari engaged in their slow inevitable drift to close in berserker and Solarian ships alike. The peril was probably not immediate, but was inexorably increasing. The last hope of any swift escape would probably be destroyed within a few years. Such a change might be brought on more quickly by the disturbances resulting from their own and the berserkers' intrusion into the nebula. Here the bow wave of a ship or a large berserker machine could produce something analogous to projected sonic shocks against steep mountainsides piled with snow.

And now the planetoid-sized mass of the berserker grew ahead of them, a lifeless landscape of sprouting weapons and old destruction, some surrealist artist's curse of war. Clutching at the faintest hope of concealment from the dreadful machine which held them captive, Tongres took the little shuttle close along one bowed strand of the towing forcefields. Even inside the shuttle, inside their armor, the invaders felt themselves being pulled or pressed, first one way then another, as if something analogous to tidal force was trying to turn them around inside their suits.

But worse was the fear, now grown much more intense. Was the berserker only allowing them to crawl into a trap before it exerted its last reserves of weakened power and finished them off?

* * *

Actually the passage, even conducted at a drifting slowness, was very short. Soon they were free of the towing fields and Tongres was bringing their little craft with feathery gentleness into contact with the enemy's scarred hull.

As silently and stealthily as possible the Solarians disembarked. Naturally there was no welcoming airlock to be found, no artificial gravity. According to plan, with Prinsep in the lead, Havot and suited Hawksmoor close behind him, they began to make their way in an irregular file along the scarred and blackened outer surface, suits clinging with light magnetism to the metal beneath them, seeking the best place to try an entry.

Ensign Dinant had the feeling that a great cold was soaking into him from the ancient fabric, even through the insulation of his suit. He was keenly aware that he and his companions were climbing over, making their way around and through, metalwork that might be almost as old as *Homo sapiens*.

Prinsep moved steadily ahead, as if he knew what he was looking for, even where he was going. No use expecting a berserker to mark its hatches plainly for the convenience of live visitors, and indeed none were marked. But certainly any vessel, any machine of this size would need hatches of some kind. And there were obviously other, unplanned openings in the ravaged outer hull, the damage of a dozen or perhaps a hundred battles down through the millennia.

Then the commodore, maintaining radio silence, was gesturing for a halt, and pointing. They had reached the rim of a deep crater, where the berserker's outer hull had once been holed by some weapon of infernal violence, metal thick as a house left slagged and torn and folded back upon itself. Far down within the underlying cavity, the intruders' suit lights picked out the damaged complexities that had to represent a second layer of defense.

Nick, alone, went down a little way to look. Then he paused, shook his empty helmet at his companions, and came back. He could see no viable passage leading on in that direction.

Exercising relentless patience, Prinsep next led his band of adventurers climbing, drifting, and crawling, maneuvering among minor craters and patches of slagged metal, following a zigzag course fully a quarter of the distance around the berserker's bulk. Twice they stopped to position small communication relay units. Periodically their armor pinged and rang, buffeted almost palpably by shrieking gusts of nebular dust particles.

Dinant had begun to think they were not going to be able to get in, and he was beginning to experience a strange feeling, half let down, half elation, at the prospect.

But within a few minutes the commodore had located a more promising path. Here, where one damage crater had impinged upon an earlier one, overlapping, disrupting what appeared to have been an earlier effort at repair, destruction had left an opening of adequate size for human passage, through a crack that appeared to penetrate the full thickness of the ancient, ravaged hull.

With the commodore still in the lead, the party moved in.

Moments later they found themselves in another surrealist region, airless and lightless of course, surrounded by shapes and constructions of no immediately discoverable purpose. Now Prinsep decided to allow limited, coded, radio communication.

Proceeding with suit lights extinguished, faceplates tuned for broad-spectrum vision, including the infrared, they soon determined that they were now standing on an inner hull, which was connected to the outer by gigantic pillars and struts.

The inner hull stretched away to right and left, forward and rear, so big that standing on it was almost like standing on the surface of a planetoid. Here too signs of damage were everywhere, though not as ruinous as on the outer hull above. Still, whole segments of this inner shield were missing, some gaps looking as if material had been cut out neatly, perhaps cannibalized for repairs elsewhere. This machine badly needed a repair dock, or a complete rebuilding while it rested in secure orbit somewhere.

The intrusive Solarians steadily made their way inward,

though experiencing some setbacks, encountering some blind alleys in these uncharted passageways.

"Look here."

A sizable hatchway had appeared in the inner hull, evidently giving on some passage meant to be used by maintenance machines. The door was standing open, and Prinsep used a weapon to weld it in that position before once more leading the way inward.

Now the intruders had truly reached their enemy's interior. Real hope began to dawn that they would be able to force a passage all the way to the berserker's unliving heart.

But it soon became obvious that the great machine around them was not truly dead. There were occasional vibrations, distant heavy movement, once even a dim flare of light revealing twisted alien shapes of unknown purpose.

The brief flash startled them all. "What in all the hells was that?" asked Havot.

The commodore grunted. "I don't know. Maybe it's welding something somewhere, trying to do repairs."

They moved on.

Some of the intruders knew moments when they were near to panic. Now once more their goal began to seem discouragingly remote, perhaps impossible to reach.

But Prinsep methodically persisted. He drew encouragement from, and called the attention of his followers to, the absence so far of active opposition.

Progress continued, though with painful slowness. Twice, then three times, it was necessary to enlarge tiny openings to human size to allow passage. Nick took the lead during these operations, cutting and then even blasting their way through bulkheads and too-small hatches, creating a crude tunnel.

Then suddenly Prinsep called a halt. Reading his suit gauges carefully, he called the attention of his companions to something very strange.

"There's been a recent minor outgassing of oxygen somewhere in this vicinity. I'm picking up traces of helium and nitrogen too, as if from a breathable atmosphere."

"Dirac?—Dirac and his people, maybe. The damned thing might have made some space to keep its goodlife in."

"That's reasonable. It probably once had Carol and Scurlock aboard."

"See if we can follow the traces."

The scent was picked up again, lost, then found, somewhat stronger. The evidence now seemed solid that some kind of life-support system was, or very recently had been, in operation here.

"This is Builders' metal," Dinant muttered presently, after scraping off a minute sample of an exposed structural member, and analyzing it on the spot with an engineer's gadget he took from his belt.

Lieutenant Tongres was ready to argue. "Were you still in doubt of what this thing is? It's a berserker, all right. But it's a very old berserker, much, much older than our station. Older than *Homo sapiens* would be a safe estimate. And in fact, though there's still some hardware movement, it's now practically dead."

"All right, old, I grant you. Worn out—it could well be. Unable to be properly aggressive—quite possible. But how can you be so confident it's dead?"

"Look where we are! Look at what it's allowing us to do! How long has the whole station been riding tied to its tail? Its drive is still at least partly functional, but nothing else can be. Certainly its brain has to be moribund. If it wasn't dead, it would have long ago accelerated until it destroyed itself and the station with it."

There came a new flare of light, much brighter than before, from somewhere above, in the direction of the outer surface.

Pressing on, the explorers soon reached a passage where the traces of atmospheric oxygen were very strong on sensitive detectors, and another meter sensed the field of artificial gravity nearby. Then, without warning, came another scare. Machines that looked like service and maintenance robots could be seen moving at a distance of less than fifty meters. Obviously the great berserker was not totally dead.

At this point the first message came through, from Dr. Zador back on the station. An ominous sign, because the people there had agreed not to initiate communication except in an emergency. This message was a string of mostly garbled sounds indicating that at least the chain of little relay devices were functioning, but barely. In content, this signal was not reassuring.

". . . there's fighting going on, in space . . ."

A few more words came through intermittently. The burden of Zador's message seemed to be that the explosions of combat were brightening the darkness of the Mavronari. Judging by what she and Hoveler could see, looking out of their cleared ports, some kind of onrushing attack force had englobed the three closely positioned objects, station, yacht, and the scarred berserker hull. But the attackers were facing fierce opposition from some source.

At one point Annie's words suggested that small units of some kind might be landing directly on the station.

Prinsep's frame was locked in rigid concentration. "Say again? Can't read you, Zador. Say again?"

". . . fighting . . . one more . . ."

And, for the moment, that was all.

When contact with the station was so ominously broken off, Nick hastily informed Prinsep that he was abandoning the expedition to rush back to the station, to defend his beloved Jenny at all costs.

The commodore was suddenly a powerful leader. "But you are there already. You left a version of yourself aboard the station, didn't you? For just this contingency? So you stay here. Going back would only create confusion. Dirac is here, and the berserker. We're going to have to beat them here, if we're going to do your Jenny any good at all."

TWENTY-EIGHT

Dan Hoveler, feeling as he usually did hopelessly awkward in an armored suit, had grabbed up a weapon and left the laboratory deck, waving Annie Zador what he thought was going to be his last goodbye. Hoveler was hurrying as fast as he could to defend the precious cargo bays. Only moments ago the station's brain, working on full alert, had reported the intrusive presence aboard of what appeared to be a pair of berserker boarding devices, entering the station separately on opposite sides.

Annie Zador, also armed and armored, was sticking to her regular battle station near the middle of the laboratory deck.

As Hoveler passed between decks, the station rocked and sang around him. Fighting still flared, even more viciously than before, in nearby space, apparently surrounding the station on every side. The people aboard had been unable to tell, so far, what forces were arrayed against each other there—certainly none of the contenders had made any effort to communicate with them.

Hoveler, even while running in his clumsy armor, continued to receive regular reports from the ship's brain which helped him keep track of the intruders. He was faintly surprised to find that neither boarding device appeared to be intent on destroying a billion Solarian zygotes, as he had somehow presumed they would be. Perhaps such an assumption was irrational, given the berserker's long peculiar history. But for whatever reason, both invaders were now converging on the deck where the great majority of the station's artificial wombs were housed.

A number of the helpless unborn—exactly how many, only Freya knew, and presumably Dirac—were there too, in Freya's semi-secret laboratory.

Dan Hoveler ran as hard as he could, doing his best to head off the mechanical killers, though he hardly expected to survive the encounter.

Moments later he dashed around a corner, only to be abruptly engulfed by a murderous crossfire from weapons much heavier than the one he carried. One of Hoveler's armored feet slid on a patch of newly molten metal, and he went down, skidding across the passageway flat on his back, the accidental fall undoubtedly saving his life. The whole corridor around him was erupting in flame and detonation.

Force-packets reflecting from the bulkheads beat like great hammers at his body. He needed a timeless moment to realize that the crisscrossing gunfire passing centimeters above his helmet was not aimed at him.

There to his right, no more than about ten meters away, the well-known and long-dreaded shape of a berserker boarder crouched on its cluster of metallic legs, twin weapons flashing from ports built into its shoulders. Hoveler had the dreamlike feeling that he could count the flashes in slow motion.

And there, back at his left, coming into view as his own body completed a sliding roll, stood what looked like the very twin of the first machine, the two of them shooting it out *against* each other.

The intensity of destruction could not endure. The machine on Hoveler's left started to go down, legs shot from under it. The metal torso was caught by three more blasts in the second before it hit the deck, transformed into a great spewing, driven splash of molten wreckage.

* * *

The roar of battle filling the enclosed space broke off abruptly. Near silence reigned, a quiet warped by the groaning of the corridor's tortured metal.

Hoveler, dazed by the battering he had received despite his suit, regained his knees and then his feet. As if he were observing the scene from a great distance, he noted that the passageway around him was ruined, shattered, wavering with heat from the bombardment. Without his armor he would have been roasted, cindered, in a second. Overhead, the long pipes of Damage Control, somehow surviving, began projecting damping fields; later there would be cooling sprays of liquid.

But one of the berserkers had survived the duel.

Unsteady on his feet, aware of his fatal organic clumsiness, knowing himself completely outclassed as a warrior, Hoveler began to raise his weapon.

His gunbarrel quivered with the unsteadiness of his grip. Just down the corridor, the victorious piece of hardware was not aiming at him, but waving metallic tentacles. And now speech came from it—its speakers were producing very unberserkerlike words, in the tones of a very human voice indeed.

It said: "Don't shoot, don't shoot! Colonel Frank Marcus here."

The Lady Genevieve, tremulous when she heard that her husband had fled the station, terror-stricken when the fighting started, had sought counsel and protection by hastily evoking the station's version of Nick^3.

Immediately after Nick joined her, she had retreated with him, at his urging, to the sheltering cool stonework of Westminster Abbey.

Standing in the ten-cube—unlike the yacht's, the station's facility was still intact—the lady pulled on the VR helmet and started walking down the long nave. This was the scene of her recurring nightmares of being bodiless again, and yet at Nick's urging she found the strength to face it.

"Will I be safe here from the machines?" She could hardly recognize the tones of her own voice.

Nick, now appearing to her in his familiar minstrel garb, was walking at her side. "I don't know about being safe. But when your husband—my father—comes looking for you, we will both of us be as ready as we can be to meet him."

Nick guided her steadily onward, as if he had some well-defined goal in mind, through the cavernous spaces of imaged stone. Oddly, Genevieve's first terror at finding herself again in these long-dreaded surroundings soon abated. This was the first time she'd seen the Abbey through organic eyes; and the differences, though subtle, gave her an important feeling of being in control.

Premier Dirac was congratulating himself on having neatly outflanked his enemies.

When, to his surprise, they had dared to follow him to the berserker, he had been able to observe their approach. Then he had dared to double back and return alone to the station, the base his persecutors had abandoned. That was where his only real chances lay for his future, for his power—if the battle flaring now in space around them, evidently some new Solarian attack, was going to leave him any chance at all.

Landing his shuttle again on the station's flight deck, oblivious for the moment to any other conflict taking place on board, Dirac was welcomed by Varvara Engadin and Carol, the latter looking even more than ordinarily demented and distraught.

"Where's Scurlock?" Carol demanded, looking with wild eyes past the Premier into the little empty shuttle.

"He decided to stay back there on the berserker. I don't need him. Where's my wife?"

"She's gone into the ten-cube," Varvara informed him, and paused. Then she added bitterly: "I thought perhaps you had come back for me."

Dirac at the moment had no interest in what Varvara thought, or said. He snapped: "I'm going after her. You'd better wait here." And he stalked on in his armor, toward the ten-cube.

Scurlock had indeed elected to remain with his old protector, the berserker. He was in his heart glad to be rid of the Premier, and he had no wish at all to go back out into those other, dangerous places. The machine had fitted out a snug little anteroom, just inboard from a small private airlock, a room as big as he needed, and comfortable with properly humidified air, easy gravity, and a few items of furniture. There was even a little holostage, offering a means of looking out into space. But Scurlock wasn't really interested in those.

The little anteroom had another door, in the inboard bulkhead, obviously leading to regions deeper inside the machine. But that door hadn't opened yet. Maybe it never would.

When the shuttle docked again at the airlock, Carol got out of it alone and came into the little room.

Scurlock smiled a twisted smile to see her, and that she was alone. She smiled back, and even seemed to relax a little. It was almost like the old days, the two of them all alone with the great berserker. He had the feeling that the machine was once more going to take care of them.

He had come to realize that it was only when other people came around that trouble started.

Dirac found, as he had expected, that the ten-cube was firmly in Nick's control. This time the Premier did not have Loki at his side, but he refused to let that lack deter him. He pushed on.

He had gone quite a distance inside the Abbey, as far as St. Michael's chapel in the north transept, when he was brought to a halt by a startling sight. This was the tomb of Lady Elizabeth Nightingale, mounting on its top eighteenth-century statues that despite their nature had somehow escaped Dirac's notice until now, here among a thousand other antique images. Skeletal Death had been carved bursting out of a tomb, drawing back a spear with which to skewer the cringing Lady Elizabeth. Meanwhile a stone man, presumably her husband, stretched out an arm to try to block the blow.

"Father," said a soft voice behind him, and Dirac spun around to discover that Nick^3, the optelectronic thing that had once been his son, was there, clutching a weapon that the VR circuits molded visually into a barbed lance very like the stone one wielded by Death.

"So, you'll never learn!" the Premier snarled, and raised his own weapon and fired point-blank.

Commodore Prinsep did not want to admit the fact, even to himself, but he feared that the tenuous link of communication between his party and their friends back in the station might now have been broken. No more messages were coming through.

Quite likely the break had not been accidental. The Solarian expeditionary force had just caught a glimpse, at a range of forty meters or so, of a mobile machine very much resembling a berserker boarding device. Havot had snapped off a shot at it, but with no visible effect.

If the enemy's plan had been to trap the small band of human challengers, it seemed that the trap might well be closing now.

However that might be, the commodore had no intention of trying to turn back. Instead he continued to concentrate to the best of his ability upon the original objective: to go after the berserker's central brain and at all costs to neutralize it.

That was the only way to win. But Prinsep could admit in the privacy of his own thoughts that it was really a bleak and almost hopeless prospect; anyone who knew anything about berserkers understood that it would be difficult if not impossible to disable or destroy the brain without setting off some final monstrous destructor charge.

At that point, as Dinant now bitterly remarked, all their seeming success so far would mean very little.

The version of Nick^3 who was still accompanying Prinsep's people in suit-mode pressed forward in a fierce search for his hated father.

Now that he was here on the berserker, one unanswered question that had lain for centuries in the back of Nick's mind was once more nagging him insistently: exactly what had happened to Frank Marcus all those many years ago?

Almost three hundred years had passed since the arrival of Frank Marcus's intriguing and enigmatic last message, in the brief interval when he, optelectronic Nick, had been the only conscious entity aboard the yacht. But the memory of

Nick³ still preserved without detectable degradation every word, every tone and shading in that voice. It had been an odd but very human voice, produced by mechanical speakers that were driven ultimately by the neurons of an organic Solarian brain.

Of course, as Nick was well aware, eventually an epoch must arrive, thousands or tens of thousands of years in the future, when even his memory would fade.

And he reflected that such a span of life would be part of what he would give up if—when—he finally succeeded in his renewed ambition of equipping himself with a fleshly body.

But the last message from Frank Marcus had never ceased to puzzle him. Thousands of times he had played back those words and their tones, out of one bank or another of his own memory, doing his best to calculate the right interpretation.

It had sounded like a very important message, coming from a man who, everyone agreed, would much rather have died than work out any accommodation with a berserker. From a man who worshiped life as much as the berserkers hated it. From one who cherished and guarded—some would say beyond all reason—the last few handfuls of the living flesh with which he had been born, and who moved his fleshly remnant around in armored boxes. From Colonel Marcus himself.

Nick had never doubted that the important-sounding communication had really come from Frank. Berserkers, without exception, were as notoriously poor at imitating the voices of human beings as they were at mimicking human appearance. Whatever the real reasons for this deficiency, it conveyed the impression that the killers detested life so violently that they refused even to assume its likeness. Or else they were too contemptuous of human resistance to make such an effort at deception. The voices used by the bad machines, whenever they deemed it necessary or convenient to employ human language, were no better than a parody of speech. In some cases this parody was said to have been molded clumsily from real voices, the recorded syllables of tortured prisoners.

* * *

Though his acquaintance with the colonel had been brief, Nick, if asked, would have described Frank Marcus as probably the least suicidal person he had ever met. Frank's move directly against the foe hadn't been simply a gallant sacrifice. If the odds were hopelessly against Colonel Marcus—a situation he had encountered often enough—well, that was what they were. Whatever the odds, he went on sincerely trying to defeat his enemy, to keep himself alive and win.

Nick had enormous respect for Frank, despite the emanations of contempt he had sensed radiating in the other direction. No, contempt wasn't quite the right word for the colonel's attitude. Frank had been constitutionally incapable of feeling contempt for a computer program, any more than he would have wasted energy disdaining a map or a pair of pliers. All these items were useful tools, deserving of respect and proper use.

The explorers continued to advance, sometimes in a group, sometimes strung out along a corridor or two parallel corridors, but being careful not to lose contact with one another.

To everyone's intense surprise, they once caught a glimpse of what looked for all the world like green plants, vegetation actually growing behind glass somewhere inside this—this *thing*.

That seemed an extremely unlikely amenity for any goodlife quarters, no matter how willing Death might be in some cases to pamper its fleshly worshipers.

Havot, greatly intrigued by the incredible sight, wanted to turn aside and check on it.

But Prinsep insisted they stick to the goal for which they had begun this perilous exploration. He sharply warned the more easily distracted that anything alluring, enigmatic, or interesting visible down a side passage might be part of an elaborate and deliberate trap.

Dinant seconded that. "It's had plenty of time to get ready for us. To make its plans and charge whatever weapons it has left."

Lieutenant Tongres said: "And I say it is dead, or as near

as makes no difference. We're right here in its guts, and it hasn't been able to kill us yet."

They moved on.

After a time, the voice of one of their number, murmuring on suit radio, could be heard uttering a prayerful hope for help.

The embattled survivors could feel reasonably sure that the reinforcements the commodore had called for, before leaving Imatra, would sooner or later be probing space in this general direction, looking for them. But "sooner or later" and "general direction" were cold comfort. There was no guarantee, far from it, that the search would succeed, even it it was pushed hard—and every reason to fear that it would not even be pushed. Realistically, the chance of any relief expedition, from Imatra or elsewhere, actually reaching them in the near future, was vanishingly small.

Back on the station, the alien boarding machine that claimed to be Colonel Marcus had insisted on accompanying Hoveler, peacefully and companionably, back to the lab deck. It had been a long time, the colonel's voice said from the alien hardware as they walked, a long time since he had been able to talk to anyone. Actually he didn't sound all that much dismayed about the fact.

Annie Zador came to meet them at the door to the main lab. Her skin, despite its strong component of African heritage, paled at the sight of Hoveler's companion.

Hoveler could only stutter ineffectually in an effort to explain. But the machine at his side seemed eager to converse. Its male Solarian voice rasped out: "This is not a berserker you're looking at, people. This is me, Frank Marcus, badlife in a box. I can explain—more or less. I got put in this new box because it gives me a definite advantage in my current job."

The machine proceeded to explain. It seemed that in any battle against the common unliving foe, one important component of the value of Colonel Frank Marcus (ret.) or any other comparably equipped Solarian human, lay in the fact that this person in his box or boxes, into which no normal human adult body could fit, was able to imitate a small berserker machine in such a way that he might fool a real berserker—especially one not being particularly attentive.

Annie Zador said dazedly: "Of course the presumption among us has always been that Marcus was killed."

Hoveler nodded agreement. "I didn't suppose there was ever any question about his being killed, even if at first the berserker didn't recognize his little pile of hardware as human. It would certainly recognize it as something dangerous."

The machine scoffed. It laughed a human laugh. *"I'd* be recognized, all right. Knowing me, I'd probably find some way to advertise the fact. 'Here I am, what're you going to do about it?' "

Then the colonel's voice, issuing from what still looked like berserker hardware, told both bioworkers that his current job had brought him aboard the station to stand guard over the valuable cargo.

Zador and Hoveler, their minds reeling, agreed that the cargo of a billion protolives was very valuable.

The colonel—neither of his hearers any longer disputed his identity—said: "Right. No argument. But that's not exactly the cargo my present employer is worried about."

The station rocked with a nearby explosion. Hoveler demanded: "What's all this fighting in space around us? Who's attacking?"

"Berserkers, who else?" And with that the colonel left them, to take up his guard duties where he could best protect the deck of artificial wombs.

But just as he went out the door, he turned back a kind of metallic eyestalk and added: "If one of you, or both of you, want to come along, I'll tell you where I've been for the past three hundred years."

For some time after his recent awakening by the great machine, Frank, despite the startling things he'd glimpsed just before his capture, had clung fiercely to his first belief that he was the captive of a berserker; any other suggestion was nothing but sheer berserker trickery.

The machine, ignoring this attitude for the time being, told Frank in good Solarian speech that it had recalled him to duty because he was the finest tool available with which to fight real berserkers. No one else could do that quite as well.

And very quickly he had been forced to abandon his belief, because the machine could show him too much evidence, evidence that he must at last accept. Puzzling objects, of which Frank had caught only tantalizing glimpses before he had been overcome and captured and put to sleep, were now offered for his free inspection.

At last he had admitted: "All right then, you're not a berserker—or at least you're the damndest berserker I've ever . . . you know, the standard behavior pattern is very simple. Berserker see life, berserker kill. Just like that."

At that point Frank had stopped, and sighed, and capitulated; the sigh was a realistic sound, a good imitation of real organic lungs, an effect practiced for so long that Frank now used it unconsciously. "But you don't operate that way. You never have. You've killed, but you don't live for killing. All right, I give up. You look exactly like a berserker, but you're not a berserker. You can't be. But then just what in all the hells *are* you?"

It told him, and then it showed him. It had the evidence to prove these statements too.

Frank thought about it. "The artificial wombs," he said. "That's it, isn't it? They're what you've wanted all along."

TWENTY-NINE

Dirac, heavily armed and armored, was stalking the latest optelectronic version of his son through the ten-cube's virtual version of Westminster Abbey.

And vice versa.

Devoutly the Premier wished that he could turn off at least some of these damned images. But at the moment the full complement of illusions was still firmly in Nick's control, and Nick had the interactive quotient high.

He, Dirac, would have to prevail once more by managing reality.

Dirac told himself, not for the first time, that virtual people, programs, had their drawbacks just like those of flesh and blood. One of the problems with the former, from his point of view, was that beings like Nick could not really be made to suffer.

Light falling through graphic images of stained glass painted the virtual stones of the original, antique Hawksmoor's towers in muted pastels, and left deep shadows around and behind the roots of tombs and monuments and columns. Dirac as he advanced became aware, by means of subtle clues of sight and sound, of another presence in the Abbey besides his own and Nick's. But one glimpse of this additional form in passing, wreathed in the virtual image of an angelic statue, indicated that it was only Jenny. The Premier decided that she, definitely a nonviolent woman, could be safely disregarded for the moment.

His stalking had carried him a considerable way in the virtual dimensions of the ten-cube, some distance east of the high altar and well into the royal chapels, before a more suspicious movement caught his eye, an unwonted stirring in the detailed mirage. The Premier pounced quickly, moving to grapple with his armored hands the lid of a great stone sarcophagus. The polyphase matter of the ten-cube's deck and walls instantly reshaped itself to accommodate the signals from his own visual cortex, feedback forming a firm stone ledge for him to grab.

With a surge of violence Premier Dirac wrenched open the last resting place of the half sisters Elizabeth the First and Mary. But in this time and place it was neither of the ancient queens who lay inside. The form of a much more modern woman leaped up screaming.

Dirac shouted retribution at his wife, and drove her off, a screaming wraith among the monuments and tombs.

He prowled on, himself a solid ghost among the thousand imaged graves and statues.

Without warning gunfire chattered near him, missiles glancing from the Premier's superb armor. The salvo bruised him, spun him round and sent him staggering, but that was all. It'd need a better angle, at shorter range, to bring him down.

Dirac gritted his teeth, delaying his return fire till he should have a clear target. He was wary of shooting this facility to pieces as he had the ten-cube on the yacht. He meant to do a lot of planning yet in this one, designing his new colony.

Once more Nick^3, still successfully keeping himself concealed, was shouting threats and imprecations.

His father shouted condemnation back and then moved promptly in pursuit.

"I am damned," Dirac was muttering now to himself,

"damned if I am going to be killed, or beaten, by any recorded person—or, to state the thing conservatively, with legalistic prudence—by any computer program that behaves as if it believes itself to be a recorded person."

And Dirac stalked on, gloriously aware of his own fleshly mortality. He was now entering the huge, magnificent chapel of Henry the Seventh, fan vaulting as delicate as forest leaves above his head. He had always disdained having any backup recording of himself. The Premier enjoyed being flesh, and intended to retain his body.

More than once over the years Dirac had considered having himself recorded, as insurance against accidents or assassinations. There had been moments when the idea seemed tempting, but he had always rejected it. Because such a procedure could not fail to create a real potential rival.

The Premier had even imagined how it would be to undergo the experience, the splitting of his very self in half: he would put on the helmet and then later take it off, and nothing would have changed. At the same time, and just as validly, he would put the same helmet on, and then gradually become aware that he had said goodbye to his flesh forever. No. A deeply unsatisfactory invasion of the center of his being.

He had come out of Henry's great chapel now, letting his instincts move him back toward the center, spiritual if not quite geometrical, of the whole Abbey. Just ahead of him Edward the Confessor's chapel waited, cavernous and complex, a temple within a temple, centered on the shrine of green porphyry. There in the real Abbey's early centuries, or so the stories said, miracles abounded.

The Premier entered.

Abruptly the empty helmet of Nick's suit, transformed by illusion into a medieval casque, loomed up before his father. In the same instant Dirac's carbine, alphatriggered, shot it clean off the armored suit, which crashed and fell into a corner of illusion.

Dirac kicked at it jubilantly. "Reprogramming again for you, young man! What is it about you that you can never learn? What is it—"

Dirac was never able to complete the thought. For that was the moment when Varvara Engadin, who had followed her former lover broodingly into the Abbey, came up close behind Dirac and shot him in the back.

And now the Premier was down, and knew that he was dying. This time his superb armor had saved him from instantaneous death, but that was all.

Dimly he was aware that Freya had come from somewhere and was bending over him, long hair blowing in an invisible wind. Dirac couldn't grasp the details of what she was saying, but it seemed that, after all, he was going to be recorded.

Commodore Prinsep's mind was whirling as he and his small band of followers advanced. It was maddening, it was impossible, that there should be such an altogether inordinate amount of breathing space on board any berserker. They had now been moving for long minutes inside that space, having entered it by means of the most startling discovery yet, an actual working airlock. The controls and markings of that lock were formed according to no Solarian system that the explorers had ever heard of, yet the functioning had been smooth and accurate.

"This thing is a bloody *ship.* It's got to be." The words were delivered in a harsh, fierce whisper by Nick, who understood that they bore incalculable implications.

The other intruders, being careful to keep their suits and helmets sealed, stared at the empty helmet that had just spoken.

One of them objected: "But it can't be a ship!"

"Well, what *is* it then?"

"The damned machines didn't build a whole ship just to accommodate goodlife! They couldn't, they wouldn't."

"Maybe . . ."

"Never! Not a battlewagon like this one."

Still the intruders had encountered no real opposition. Weapons ready, they continued to advance cautiously through one of the incredible, incongruous air-filled corridors that wound its way through the belly of the beast.

Here and there on the bulkheads, which in certain corridors had been worn smooth by the agelong passage of serving machines, were engraved signs obviously intended to be read by living eyes. These notices, mostly located near apertures or controls, were in the recognizable script or printing of the Builders. A few of the signs still glowed, while time and wear at last had entirely sapped the energy from others.

Following certain lines and conduits that appeared to be concerned with information input and control, making their way through twisted corridors and voluminous ducts, avoiding any moving machinery they saw, the survivors advanced, still seeking the berserker's brain in order to destroy it.

But what the armed intruders came upon instead was something very different.

"Come look at this."

"Damn it, keep radio silence—"

"No. No more radio silence. I tell you that doesn't matter anymore. Come look."

Those who had been summoned went to look. And found themselves entering a steel-vaulted chamber whose deck space was well nigh filled with screens and chairs and stages.

The stages and the screens were acrawl with information in alien and unreadable symbols.

At the center of the vaulted space, a dais supported three chairs or couches of peculiar shape, somewhat bigger and more elaborate than those in the lower levels of the room. The three central chairs were all closely surrounded by the most intricate machinery, and two of them had been swiveled to face away from the people who were now entering.

This chamber could be nothing but a bridge, a control room, whatever you might call it. The suggestion was overwhelming that this was an insulated, defended place from which the huge machine could be commanded.

The invaders gazed at one another in wonder. No Solarian had ever seen or heard of a berserker mounting any facility at all like this.

Besides the peculiar chairs or acceleration couches—a dozen of them in all, including those in the farther reaches of the room—there were visual displays, some utterly unearthly, some tantalizingly almost familiar.

Was it still within the range of possibility that this, all

this, was only some virtual reality, berserker subterfuge, illusion? The hardware in the room felt every bit as solid as it looked. No virtual reality, no polyphase matter, here.

The Solarians, advancing slowly, were momentarily lost, distracted, in sheer wonder. Such substantial, comprehensive controls could never have been built for goodlife.

From somewhere outside the vast machine, dimly apprehended here, came the whine and scream and smash and vibration of heavy combat.

The controls and furniture in this chamber had been designed to accommodate creatures about the size and strength and dexterity of ED humans, but whose bodies must have differed from the Solarian standard in several important ways. The lighting, for one thing, designed for different vision. For another, the intended occupants of this room had obviously been somewhat taller and a great deal thinner than Solarians. The shape and positioning of the controls also implied considerable differences.

"No." Dinant was denying, rejecting, what he saw.

Havot muttered, "A mockup, then. The damned thing has constructed a real-world simulation of some human ship."

"Not a Solarian ship," said Prinsep. "And I think not a simulation."

"This room is full of air, good breathable air." Lieutenant Tongres at least seemed on the verge of opening her helmet, declaring her acceptance of the miracle.

Havot was bewildered. "Some Carmpan vessel, then?"

That suggestion moved the commodore to something like amusement. "When did the Carmpan ever build a ship like this, or want one? No, not Carmpan either."

And then all of the intruders fell silent.

Because the central chair on the dais, which had presented its high back to the intruders, was swiveling around. And that high seat was occupied.

Filled by a figure instantly recognizable, because it came out of ancient video recordings with which all the visitors were familiar. But this was not video. The intruders were standing in the presence of a live Builder, perhaps clothed—it was hard to tell—though not visibly armored in any way. He (or just as likely, she) was sitting there regarding the intruders with a single eye centered just below the forehead, an eye whose bright pupil slid back and forth with a quivering speed that somehow suggested an insect. The being on the dais appeared, by Solarian standards, inhumanly thin.

Skin and flesh moved in the lower portion of the face, the face of a living body whose ancestors had never known the light of Sol. From between folds of loose saffron skin, a voice emerged, a muted torrent of clicks and whines. The sound was being amplified, translated for the visitors' airmikes by an artificial speaker somewhere.

It was a Builder who confronted them. Beyond all argument, a living Builder. A fabled relic, incredibly alive, rising from his (or her) control chair, staring at the intruders with his/her liquidly mobile central eye of gray or blue.

"I am the acting captain of this vessel," the being on the dais told them, "and I welcome you aboard my ship."

THIRTY

The Builder who now stood towering over the gaping little audience of intruders was a slender, fine-boned being, taller than all but a very few Solarian men but topologically like a Solarian except for the single eye that stretched across the upper face, with a bright bulging pupil that slid to and fro with the rapidity of thought.

After a stunned pause, Commodore Prinsep responded to the short speech of welcome, but the commodore was never able afterward to remember exactly what he had said. The thin orange-and-yellow figure looming above him on the dais listened as a machine swiftly translated Prinsep's words into bursts of whistles and clicks.

From the first moment, the ship's captain was a convincing presence. Neither Prinsep nor any of his companions had any doubt of the nature of the being now confronting them. All of them had seen, times beyond counting, images of the Builder race, pictures extracted from a precious handful of alien video records that were older than Solarian humanity. Copies of those videos reposed in every general encyclopedia, in every comprehensive data storage bank. Images of Builders were as widely recognizable as those of Solarians from the first century of photography.

In most of the ancient Builder graphics, no matter how elegantly enhanced, the berserkers' creators showed as hardly more than stick drawings of orange glowing substance. Now for the first time in history it was plain to Solarian eyes that that orange color and brightness were the result of some kind of clothing, the exposed skin being a dullish yellow where it showed on the face, the four-fingered hands, and across part of the chest.

Before the commodore and his boarding party had fully absorbed one shock, another fell. A new flurry of excitement passed among them when one of their own species suddenly appeared on the dais within arm's length of the captain. A biologically youthful man with sandy hair, dressed in modern ship's issue clothing, arose from another of the central chairs, the tall back of which had concealed him.

Among the people who had come in with Prinsep, only Nick immediately recognized Sandy Kensing. Nick quickly informed the others of his identity.

Kensing distractedly greeted the new arrivals. From the moment he rose from his chair, he had been looking anxiously among them for Annie Zador. Now he was relieved to hear that Dr. Zador had been well when last reported. It came as no surprise to Kensing to learn that she and Dr. Hoveler had elected to remain back on the station.

"But we had given you up for dead," Prinsep reminded Kensing sharply.

The youth looked haggard. "I know that—I was about ready to give up myself, until Colonel Marcus welcomed me aboard here. Now he's gone back to the station to try to help out."

"What? Who's gone where?"

"I'll explain as best I can about the colonel's survival and my own. But first I'd better tell you we've got immediate problems—real berserkers are attacking, and this vessel—the one we're on—is their prime target. And it always has been. To berserkers, this particular ship has a higher priority for destruction than any Solarian ship. Much higher than a mere billion Solarian protolives."

Then Kensing, taking pity on the hopeless silence of bewilderment before him, drew a deep breath and slowed down a little. "I can quite appreciate your confusion, shipmates. I've been in the deep freeze, and I'm only a few hours ahead of you in the process of learning about—this."

His expansive gesture included the self-proclaimed captain beside him, as well as the ship around them all. "But you're better off than I was. When I came on board, Dirac and Scurlock thought they were giving me to a berserker. And I believed them, until . . .

The speaker drew another breath. "Let me start over, by introducing the captain more thoroughly. Her name—his name—I'm not yet sure which—will translate at least approximately as 'Carpenter.' "

The captain, still listening to simultaneous machine translation, bowed, a strange, stiff gesture.

Tersely Kensing went on to inform his compatriots that Captain Carpenter was very likely the last mature Builder surviving in the universe. Originally part of the ship's reserve crew, he/she had also been thawed out, at the orders of this ship's optelectronic brain, only a few hours ago—but in the captain's case, after a longsleep of some fifty thousand standard years.

Acting Captain Carpenter was one of an elite corps of individuals, fanatically dedicated to the preservation of the Builders' race, who had boarded this ship when it set out on its desperate voyage—part of a last effort to escape the destruction being visited on the Builders' civilization by their own creation, the berserkers.

Prinsep, who had been attending carefully, supposed that under the circumstances he could accept that. Actually he supposed that he had very little choice. "All right," the commodore demanded, "then what is this damned thing, anyway? Where are we?"

Kensing gazed at the older man uncertainly. "The best translation I can give you, Commodore, for the function of this vessel seems to be 'seedship.' "

Captain Carpenter, following the conversation with the

aid of his own machines, quickly confirmed the fact. The vessel they were on was only one—almost certainly, the last surviving—of a great many similar craft that had been launched by Carpenter's desperate race in its last days, and represented their last-ditch attempt to establish a beachhead in the future for their posterity. It was a frenzied gamble they had undertaken only when they realized that their war against their own creations, the berserkers, was certain to be lost.

The great majority of seedships had been destroyed by the implacable berserkers soon after they were built. Also obliterated at that time had been all of the Builders' other ships and other spacegoing installations.

Every one of the Builders' planets, fruit of a long, aggressive campaign to expand their empire, had been sterilized.

But this one seedship, and most likely this one alone—its individual name seemed to translate as something like *Phoenix*—had escaped destruction. Though it had been heavily damaged, its original live crew wiped out, it was still carrying deep in its metal guts more than a billion encapsulated zygotes—almost certainly the only examples of Builder genetics still extant anywhere in the universe.

But all of the artificial wombs it had originally carried, as well as the capacity to construct more, had been destroyed by berserker boarding devices and other weapons.

Relentlessly pursued almost from the moment of its launching, this vessel fifty thousand years ago had narrowly escaped destruction by plunging into a deep nebula—that which Solarians now called the Mavronari—a cloud of gas and dust hanging broad and high and dense enough in Galactic space to baffle any effective pursuit. Inside this nebula, travel at c-plus velocities was impossible.

Ensign Dinant was still inclined to be skeptical. "It looks just like a berserker. All our experts have identified it as one."

Kensing nodded soberly. "Of course it does, of course they have. Not only did it come out of one of the same original Builder shipyards, but it was deliberately designed and built to look like a berserker—enough to fool, if possible, the killing machines themselves."

Except for the basically benign programming of this

vessel's computers, the match had been very close indeed. Certainly close enough to fool Solarians. But of course the objective of fooling the unliving enemy had ultimately failed of attainment.

Evidently sensing that some doubts still lingered, Captain Carpenter was willing to offer proof. A simultaneous translation of his speech came through: "We must be quick. But I will show you all this vessel's cargo. Please follow me."

Even a freight consisting of some billions of encapsulated zygotes, a cargo having the same magnitude of volume as that of the Solarian research station, did not occupy a high proportion of the space available. Not on a battlewagon the size of this one.

And now, as Kensing, accompanied by Captain Carpenter conducted Prinsep and his companions on a tour of this vessel's cargo holds, their last lingering doubts were satisfied.

Prinsep picked up a sample to inspect it closely. Each Builder zygote was protected inside a small circular plate, not much different in size, though subtantially dissimilar in texture and composition, from the Solarian tiles with which all the Earth-descended people present were well familiar.

Tongres even did some half-abstracted calculations: A billion tiles or disks would seem to need a volume of about 90 meters × 90 meters × 50 meters.

Prinsep wondered, keeping the question to himself for now, whether Builders knew sexual attraction and love in the Solarian sense. And decided in his own mind that probably they did.

Even this vessel, immense enough to tuck away such a bulk of cargo, was still only in the middle range of size for a berserker mothership. In this vast interior, the secret cargo might remain indefinitely unexamined and unremarked by a handful of tired, frightened boarders who were necessarily intent on other matters, in particular their own survival.

And still, around them, the fight against the latest attacking waves of real berserkers was going on. From time to time, Captain Carpenter in a few terse phrases reminded his visitors of the fact. The full combat resources of the *Phoenix,* hoarded for millennia against the need for this final stand, an arsenal including extra defensive shields, and weapons that could have annihilated the planetoid Imatra a hundred times over, were being mobilized and thrown into action now.

"What can we do to help?" asked Prinsep.

An immediate expression of gratitude came from Captain Carpenter together with the answer: not much at the moment. But if and when the berserkers could again be beaten off, perhaps a great deal.

Not only were their own human lives at stake, Carpenter explained, but also the survival of a viable drive aboard the seedship. And, aboard the bioresearch station, the survival of a fleet of artificial wombs which would be usable by either species.

That statement momentarily staggered the commodore and those with him. "Usable by either species?"

"Right!" said Kensing, adding: "And that, you see, is the key to the whole mystery of this ship's behavior."

For one race's artificial wombs to be used on the other's zygotes would certainly require heavy modification in both hardware and software. But both races shared the same fundamental chemistry of life. Tools and energy and comprehensive libraries of information were available. It had been determined centuries ago that with time and effort and ingenuity, the Solarian wombs could be modified to handle satisfactorily the protoindividuals of the other race.

Briefly interrupting Kensing's explanation, Captain Carpenter clicked and whistled for his new allies a kind of apology for the way his ship had treated certain Solarians over the course of the past three hundred years.

When the live crew of the *Phoenix* had been wiped out early in the agelong voyage, leaving the seedship's computers to do their best absent the conscious control of any living Builder, the elaborate software entities inhabiting those machines labored under the certainty that ultimate success or failure rode on the decisions they were now forced to make. At times the strain had proven too much for the command computers, leading to decisions that were contradictory and counterproductive.

Approximately fifty thousand standard ED years (as confirmed rather precisely by the seedship's master clocks) after plunging into the sheltering nebula, this particular ship had at last emerged again. In the course of its tortuous passage through that protective but also dangerous darkness, it had found one or two sites where a colony might be established. But without the hardware to grow organic beings, or the necessary software to construct and operate it, the sites were useless.

Therefore, a very little more than three hundred years ago, on emerging from the dark nebula into more or less clear, normal space, the bright, wary, dangerous shipboard computers, charged with the preservation of their cargo, and the eventual establishment of colonies at any and all costs, had begun to cast about for the means of making a colony once more possible.

And the computers commanding the *Phoenix* encountered something new. The signals of Solarian civilization, sent into space both deliberately and accidentally for centuries in this part of the Galaxy, were detectable at several points along the radiation spectrum commonly used for communications.

For a Solarian standard year or two after its emergence from the most heavily constricting clouds, the ship had hung back in the fringes of the Mavronari. For all its computers knew, the Galaxy into which it had reemerged, some fifty thousand years older than the one it had escaped, might well be completely dominated by berserkers; indeed the shipboard computers felt compelled to assign a pessimistically high probability to that situation.

During the dark millennia of steady groping through obscurity the onboard computers had done such research as they could manage on the problem of surviving the berserkers and ultimately defeating them. The odds were not good. Further delay in the establishment of a colony was undesirable.

But reckless haste, their basic programming impressed upon them, might produce results that were disastrously worse.

With mechanical patience, using such tools as remained

after the long-accumulated damage of battle, time, and travel, the seedship's computers investigated the new world before them. They again evaluated the option of reviving one of the precious few organic Builders of the reserve crew, but continued to judge that the optimum time for that step had not yet arrived.

The computers representing the last hope of the Builders began, cautiously, an active search along the Coreward fringe of the Mavronari, still seeking favorable places for the establishment of a live colony, but concentrating upon the lack of nurturing hardware and software.

The course followed by the seedship in its seeking, along the ever-more-attenuated outer fringe of the Mavronari brought a fortuitous discovery that altered and delayed all of the computers' other plans.

Traces of very fresh activity on the part of the newly dominant intelligent race suddenly appeared in the electromagnetic spectrum. These were rapidly decaying signals, undoubtedly artificial, echoing in multiple reflections from one interstellar cloud to another, no more than a few years old but already faint almost beyond the most sophisticated detection.

The seedship computers expanded their field antennas as best they could. They watched and listened, recording all artificial signals with an omnivorous greed for information.

Presently scout machines were programmed and dispatched, clever, heavily armed devices superficially indistinguishable from berserker scouts. These moved swiftly, in wary silence, homing on the signals just discovered and listening with particular attention for more.

Presently more such transmissions were detected, recorded and analyzed, and bearings taken. One of the seedship's scouts returned with new information.

Presently the small scouting machines drifted forward again, as warily as possible, in the direction of the signals' source. They listened again, and then advanced and listened once more, to younger and ever younger samples of the alien communications spectrum. Thus cautious exploration proceeded in small increments.

Eventually direct contact was effected. Abruptly a small

Solarian ship—an utterly new phenomenon to the seedship computers—was detected within visual range.

The electronic strategists were wary about approaching the Solarians openly, because they knew that, to humans of any race who knew anything about berserkers, their vessel was virtually certain to be identified as an old, battered berserker.

Surreptitious observation had not continued long before certain evidence came to the attention of the seedship computers, evidence tending to confirm that the small vessel was under the control of living beings, not berserkers. Warily, and experiencing something analogous to gratitude and joy, the computers accepted this fact as evidence that even now, some fifty thousand years after their victory over their creators, the berserkers had been unable to expunge intelligent life completely from the Galaxy.

But caution was still essential. For one thing, the seedship knew that it looked like a berserker. Perhaps its controlling software entities were capable of appreciating irony. To be attacked and destroyed as a berserker, after fifty thousand years of strained survival . . .

Provoking either attack or panicked flight on the part of the alien was undesirable.

There was another goal: whatever effort might be necessary, it was very important to learn at least one Solarian language, or preferably several. In the absence of any wealth of recorded information, there seemed no alternative to either taking an unacceptably long time about the job, or else learning from live beings.

To somehow establish contact with such beings without alerting their whole race to the presence of a formidable stranger seemed essential—on the other hand, to be caught taking prisoners was predictably almost certain to create hostility among the very beings the ship hoped ultimately to enlist as allies.

Therefore the ship planned very carefully the acquisition of its language tutors—though in the end it had little real choice as to who they were going to be.

It appeared feasible to capture the small ship, and that was easily accomplished.

Upon investigation it became clear that the little craft had been part of a small, private operation in space, with only a couple of people on board. Fortunately for the seedship's purposes, it was small enough to be taken undamaged and without a fight.

Unfortunately the universe held other deadly dangers besides the killing machines. The Builders' own history demonstrated amply that one intelligent race could be perfectly capable of waging war upon another. Were this not a fact, the berserkers would never have been created. Therefore great diplomacy was called for; the seedship's brain would have to predict (and much depended upon the accuracy of the prediction) just what the attitude of these unknown beings was going to be toward a billion Builder zygotes.

Ensign Dinant was the last to doubt. "But—when it attacked Imatra—it killed defenders, it seized the station violently and carried it off."

The commodore responded soberly. "Of course, the Builders and their machinery would have been willing to wipe out all Solarian life—if such a thing were possible—if they saw that as the only way to capture our biostation or its equivalent. The only way to save their own race. Hell, we'd do the same to them, right?"

The Builder who had ordered the first Imatran raid, Carpenter's predecessor as captain, might have planned to tell his pair of kidnapped Solarians the truth. But he, having gone out in a small combat scout to oversee the operation, had unluckily been killed in the first fighting. And after his sudden death his machines, once more forced to grapple with unwelcome responsibility, had failed to carry out that plan.

At the conclusion of the violent combat that had accompanied the seedship's seizing and carrying off the station, the stored body of only one adult Builder remained in viable condition—and the computers soon decided that before they risked playing that final card, rousing their sole remaining master, they had better gather as much information as possible about the newly discovered Solarian race.

Early in their occupation of the station, the machines

examined several of the Solarian artificial wombs, the priceless replacements for Builder devices destroyed beyond recovery. The captured machinery appeared to be adaptable—and so, as far as could be determined, were Freya and her counterparts. But no real trial had been attempted. The tricky complexities of alien biology were difficult even for big computers; and their situation would have to be even more desperate than it was before they would have dared experiment on Builder zygotes without prolonged and intensive computer modeling.

And the computers had been willing to accept almost any risk rather than allow the Solarians to realize just what the real prize was—these invaluable artificial wombs, and the expert systems that made them functional.

The one disaster the computers had never dared to risk was the destruction of these priceless nurturing devices, so miraculously obtained. At the threat of open fighting aboard the Solarian biostation, the seedship it had withdrawn its combat machines, leaving the belligerent Solarians to their own devices while keeping open some channels of communication and observation.

The seedship had installed sensors, recorders, on the Solarian station's womb-deck, and some of these devices had survived the Solarians' suspicious search. The Builders' master computers wanted constant reassurance that the Solarians left in control of the station were doing nothing that would put the artificial wombs and associated systems at risk.

Hundreds of years had passed since the seedship computers had seized and made off with their Solarian treasure. In that interval they had succeeded in getting it almost out of sight of berserkers and Solarians alike. The planners could afford to be patient. It was necessary only to outlast the few Solarians still on the station—those violent, weapon-carrying beings living in such perilously close proximity to the artificial wombs. For a time the all-important goal grew more and more likely of attainment.

Then suddenly, without warning, upsetting all calculations, more Solarians had come threading their way out of the nebula in a badly damaged warship, bringing with them confirmation of an approaching berserker presence in nearby space. Now mobilization was necessary, preparations must be made to fight off these potential attackers.

The whole situation, long fraught with possibilities for disaster beyond calculation, suddenly became vastly more complicated and dangerous.

The damaged seedship computers, working sometimes on the verge of breakdown, continued to do the best they could.

In its first contact with Solarians, the seedship had deliberately passed itself off as a berserker. First, because it would have been difficult to convince suspicious humans that it was anything else. Later, it preferred not to reveal to the handful of organic aliens what an advantage they had in controlling all the artificial wombs.

If the Solarian aliens were willing to accept their captor as a berserker and still to maintain communication with it, then the seedship would humor them. To try to argue them into the truth seemed to carry the risk of unguessable complications. And it was possible to make the hopeful computation that in a few years, a few decades, a few centuries at the most, they would all be conveniently dead.

And thus, more or less gradually, the deal between Dirac Sardou and the alien machine had evolved.

Through discussions between Dirac and his unliving counterpart, their plan for establishing a cooperative colony had evolved—each partner in the scheme planning to double-cross the other as soon as possible.

Up to the time when the commodore's band of refugees arrived at the bioresearch station, the seedship brain had been uncertain about the value of the treacherous, brutal Premier as any kind of long-term ally. Of course the Builders' machine had had little choice; the man had firmly established himself as leader of the small surviving group of humans. And alliance was at least a possibility, with any known entity other than a berserker.

In fact the seedship's archives held records of certain Builder individuals who had equaled or surpassed Dirac in the capacity for violence and personal ambition. There was no reason to assume that Dirac was more closely typical of human leaders than those Builders had been of their own race.

In any case, the ship had trouble coming up with a better plan for using these aliens, or learning more about them.

But now other and perhaps more satisfactory human partners had become available, in the form of the fleet commander and his associates. The Builder ended by telling them that he would bring out the reserve fighting machines the ship had been hiding, and depose Dirac.

Hawksmoor had listened to the story with a sympathy for those beleaguered Builder programs.

In Nick's opinion, any advanced computer or advanced program ordinarily felt intrinsically more comfortable dealing with another computer or another program than with a fleshly person. The Builders' creation was surely no exception to this rule.

Nick could sympathize with his program counterparts aboard the seedship, though now from the vantage point of what he considered to be his own dual nature, he judged them rather colorless.

Another question that occurred to Nick was this: Had the Builders ever experienced any ethical, moral, or social problems with the idea of making electronic recordings of themselves? Well, he wasn't going to raise the point just now; there seemed to be plenty of other problems that would have to be considered first.

Captain Carpenter resumed the story. The seedship's plans for retreating to some hidden sanctuary, and building its colony with the help of Solarian equipment, had to be put on hold as soon as it received convincing evidence—from listening to Solarian communications, or from its own observations—that the bad machines might be about to appear.

At that point, feeling some computer analogue of desperation, the seedship computers had awakened Frank Marcus.

An array of other Solarian people were also being kept frozen in the seedship's archives—those who had been sent to it by Dirac in the belief that he was placating a great berserker.

At the moment Frank was taken prisoner, he had already been half convinced that the machine he was fighting was no berserker.

The seedship's brain continually reconsidered the possibility of reviving the sole remaining qualified Builder, and when (s)he was checked out healthy, relieving itself of command.

But the last time the seedship controller had revived a Builder, shortly before the first raid on Imatra, he/she promptly got himself killed by the Solarian humans; and now it had only one mature Builder left. No margin remained to accommodate another error.

If the seedship was ever to make an open and serious partnership with Solarians, it would not want to be perceived as guilty of slaughtering the young that they were making at least some effort to preserve.

For centuries now the seedship had been trying to protect its own most vital secrets from the Solarians, even while struggling to learn theirs. But ultimately it would rather reveal its true nature to these intruders than kill them off. They were not necessarily its mortal enemies, but berserkers were.

The seedship had now spent three hundred years studying the alien species who called themselves Solarians. But for any machines to study any of the Galactic varieties of humanity was extremely difficult, and the seedship was extremely reluctant to reach any firm conclusions without still more study, now that additional subjects were at last available.

The seedship knew it must to make a deal with the quarrelsome Solarians—or with one faction among them, if they were divided in deadly earnest.

But now, with real berserkers coming to the attack, time for hesitation had run out.

As had the time for explanations.

"Battle stations, everyone. We must at all costs defend the bridge," said Captain Carpenter.

One of the seedship's service machines was already

bringing Kensing battle armor, tailored to his Solarian shape and size. Prinsep and Havot, Nick and Tongres and Dinant, readied their arms.

Reports from the Builders' auxiliary machines were now coming in rapidly, and Carpenter ordered immediate translation of all messages. The news was grim: more berserker machines had landed on the *Phoenix* and were even now fighting their way inboard.

Carpenter remained in command on the bridge, while on the captain's orders Prinsep swiftly deployed his people to guard the passageway through which they'd entered. Their armored forms took shelter as best they could in niches and corners, and behind hastily mobilized service robots.

In moments the enemy was upon them, in the form of bizarre shapes darting forward at inhuman speed. In a hail of fire and force, fighting side by side with the Builders' defensive robots, they tried to protect the bridge and other vital installations against the boarding machines.

Kensing, his senses ringing with the violence of battle, saw Nick in suit-form on his right fighting until a swiftly advancing berserker caught him and crushed the suit to scrap. On Kensing's left, Havot and at least one other Solarian went down, to be dragged off by friendly service machines, whether bound for medirobots, or simply for disposal as dead flesh, Kensing could not tell.

And then, quite suddenly, the shooting stopped again. Prinsep was saying in his helmet radio that an all clear had been sounded, and Sandy Kensing realized that he himself was still alive.

Still, for long moments, he had trouble breathing. Until word came that contact with the station had been restored . . . and yes, Annie was still there. She was still alive, and for the moment safe.

THIRTY-ONE

Something like twenty-four standard hours had gone by since the last shot quelling the failed berserker boarding attempt. The enemy had not been heard from again during that time, but it was entirely possible that more of the killing machines would materialize out of the nebular dust at any moment, coming on in another kamikaze charge.

Certainly the Galaxy still harbored vast numbers of berserkers, and they would still be making every effort to locate the *Phoenix.* From the point of view of the enemies of life, an alliance between warlike Builders, with their intimate knowledge of how berserkers were originally built and programmed, and the bellicose Solarians, who had already taught themselves to fight berserkers to a standstill, would be about the worst possible scenario.

Sandy Kensing and Annie Zador, both of them still in armored suits and ready to grab up weapons at a moment's notice, were walking together through the Builders' gigantic vessel, exploring some of its more interesting byways. They and their shipmates visiting aboard moved in artificial gravity that Captain Carpenter had ordered especially tailored for Solarian comfort.

At the moment, Zador and Kensing were watching some of Captain Carpenter's service robots bringing out from the engine room of the *Phoenix* the small physical storage units containing an expert engineering system.

Fortunately the Builders' ship was able to spare an analytical expert system, which in theory ought to be capable of bypassing if not undoing Nick's old scrambling of the drive controls upon the *Eidolon.* In return, Carpenter had been granted a working share of the biostation's hardware and expertise, including several versions of Freya and forty Solarian artificial wombs, which would soon be on their way over from the station to the Builders' craft.

Annie, breaking a short silence, asked her companion bluntly: "Are you coming with us?"

Sandy Kensing did not answer impulsively. Instead he gave himself another long moment to think about it. This was literally a once-in-a-lifetime decision.

If all went well, the yacht, with its stardrive restored to marginal function (better than marginal was possible, but not to be counted on) would be ready in another day for the attempt by some of the surviving Solarians to return to their own worlds.

"If our jury-rigging doesn't blow up on us halfway there," Prinsep had warned them. "And if we don't run into more berserkers."

The trip home would be a dangerous gamble, but some people were ready to risk it.

Declining to take that risk would mean accepting another at least as great.

Drs. Zador and Hoveler, still dedicated to the welfare of the entities they thought of as their billion children, had elected not to try to have the biostation towed back to civilization by the yacht, a clumsy arrangement certain to increase greatly the perils of that voyage for all concerned. Nor did they want to overload the yacht by somehow packing aboard it a billion zygotes—miniature life units, in the berserker term—thus returning the protopeople to a place where they weren't wanted anyway.

Instead, Drs. Zador and Hoveler had elected to go on, joining the fortunes of their children with those of Captain Carpenter and his. If a real future existed for these Solarians anywhere, it was not at home.

Annie did not want to leave Sandy Kensing, far from it. But it seemed that her conception of duty left her no choice.

The seedship, its own mission rendered viable by Solarian technology, would of course continue towing the station on into the Mavronari, still seeking a good site for a Builder colony.

Prinsep was determined to bring Scurlock and Carol back to civilization with him, under forcible confinement, though it was doubtful whether any indictment for goodlife activity could be made to stand against them. Havot, currently in a medirobot with critical injuries, was also going back.

The Premier, too, was returning to the worlds he had once ruled, though he—or at least his optelectronic version, which was all that now survived—had not been consulted in the matter. Prinsep had left it up to the Lady Genevieve, as next of kin, to decide what ought to be done with her husband's recorded personality; none of the Solarians currently in a position to make decisions were in the mood to give Dirac Sardou, or any program by that name, the right to decide anything.

Anyway the Premier in his newly discarnate mode could simply be left turned off for the time being. There were still more immediate problems to worry about.

One version of Nicholas Hawksmoor, kept in reserve on the station by Premier Dirac, had survived all the shooting. By common consent this version, an equivalent of Nick², had been turned on, brought up to date on the situation, and allowed to make his own decision.

This avatar of Hawksmoor had needed only a fraction of a second to renounce all future possibility of contact with the Lady Genevieve, and to go on, accompanying the seedship in its effort to find a new world deep in the Mavronari.

And Sandy Kensing was going to have to decide his own future quickly, before the *Eidolon*'s drive was fixed. The yacht's departure could not be postponed, for with every passing hour the nebula around grew thicker, the journey home more difficult. Captain Carpenter was refusing to consider any course adjustments that would delay his vessel and keep it in this region, where at any moment more berserkers might arrive to finish its destruction.

Kensing turned to stare into the Builder analogue of a holostage nearby. At the moment the device displayed a graphic of the three small vessels moving in deep space, ahead of them the blankness of the Mavronari, like an unknowable future.

"I don't know what I'll do if you're not with us, Sandy," Annie said suddenly, as if his prolonged silence was suddenly too much for her.

"Hey, Annie. Relax, relax!" Kensing reached for his woman, took her armored hands in his. "A future with you in it, and a billion screaming kids—"

"More like two billion," she said, "counting Builders."

"Two billion, then. Hey, I wouldn't miss that for anything."